ALSO BY PATRICE NGANANG

FICTION

Mount Pleasant

Dog Days

POETRY

elobi

WHEN
THE PLUMS
ARE RIPE

WHEN THE PLUMS ARE RIPE

PATRICE NGANANG

TRANSLATED FROM THE FRENCH

BY AMY B. REID

FARRAR, STRAUS AND GIROUX

NEW YORK

Farrar, Straus and Giroux
120 Broadway, New York 10271

Printed in the United States of America
Originally published in French in 2013 by Éditions Philippe Rey, France,
as *La saison des prunes*
English translation published in the United States by Farrar, Straus and Giroux
First American edition, 2019

Library of Congress Cataloging-in-Publication Data
Names: Nganang, Alain Patrice, author. | Reid, Amy Baram,
1964– translator.
Title: When the plums are ripe / Patrice Nganang ; translated from the
French by Amy B. Reid.
Other titles: Saison des prunes. English
Description: First American edition. | New York : Farrar, Straus and Giroux,
2019.
Identifiers: LCCN 2018060813 | ISBN 9780374288990 (hardcover)
Classification: LCC PQ3989.2.N4623 S3513 2019 | DDC 843/.92—dc23
LC record available at https://lccn.loc.gov/2018060813

Designed by Jonathan D. Lippincott

Our books may be purchased in bulk for promotional, educational, or business
use. Please contact your local bookseller or the Macmillan Corporate and
Premium Sales Department at 1-800-221-7945, extension 5442,
or by e-mail at MacmillanSpecialMarkets@macmillan.com.

www.fsgbooks.com
www.twitter.com/fsgbooks • www.facebook.com/fsgbooks

1   3   5   7   9   10   8   6   4   2

This work received the French Voices Award for excellence in publication and
translation. French Voices is a program created and funded by the French
Embassy in the United States and FACE (French American Cultural Exchange).

This story about men and women is, like a handful of red earth from the village, dedicated to my mother, Kemi Rebecca.

One clarification: The whole world is my country, Cameroon my subject, and Yaoundé my field of definition.

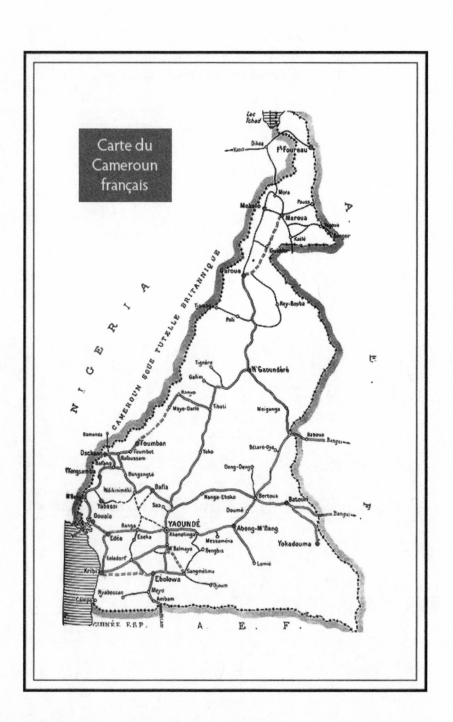

Carte du
Cameroun
français

When there are many laws, the people cannot be wise.
—Sultan Ibrahim Njoya, *Saan'gam*, 1921

WHEN
THE PLUMS
ARE RIPE

This Story Does Not Begin in 1939

In Yaoundé, the heart of the country is revealed when the plums are ripe. *Dacryodes edulis*, the African plum or bush pear, peeks out, a burst of red in the tree's greenery. Then, in groups of five or ten, they make their way along the streets, filling up bags at the market, spreading out across grills set up on street corners, where they delicately take their place alongside the plantains or grilled ears of corn: a perfect combination of flavors. The plums are sold wrapped in sheets of shiny paper or newsprint, three for a hundred francs, a price no one could grumble about without sounding ridiculous. Sometimes, at the end of the day, they are dumped into piles on the pavement, just like that, a pile of garbage attracting flies. Left to be crushed under the wheels of passing cars or smashed into a slippery goo that sticks to the soles of your shoes. Because their season is quite short, and all it takes is a little bit of sun for the plums to ripen, the market women or *bayamsallams* sell them off cheap every evening, unwilling to let the price fall in the morning, before the plums have even made their way onto the coal-fired grills. They know even more will be flooding into the city the next day.

So when they're in season, plums are everywhere. Even Ongola, as the center of Yaoundé is called, is imbued with their heady scent. The plums are usually eaten at nightfall. Plums are nothing like mangoes, oh no, they don't have that intense flavor that the storm spirit uses to justify jacking up the price, a trick the city is all too ready to go along with. No, plums are more honest in their dealings with men, with the city's poor neighborhoods. Plums scatter their bursts of red across the trees' shaded boughs before slowly turning to a deep bluish black, thanks to the sun. All it takes is a gentle shake of a branch for piles of plums to fall all around. For children it's a real celebration: to cook the plums, they just put them in a paper bag and cover them with a handful of ashes. The plums need only a little bit of heat for their skin to release a coating of oil, then their rich tender flesh takes on that singular flavor that makes them the favorite dessert of the street—no, of the city itself. Because the plums are offered up to the city's stomach at stands in front of every little bar, people eat them quickly, right there in the street. Once the season is over, the plums' color—blood-red at first and then black—and their sweetness live on in everyone's mind. No one can escape their succulence.

As I write this story I think about the men standing on street corners, who suck on a plum and then toss the pit on the sidewalk, and I know that one image says it all: the sensory feast offered up for the lowest price; the nonchalance of a city that eats its plums swathed in shiny paper, as if it were trying to construct in its stomach the shelters it refuses to provide on the streets; the violence of the gesture, so useless, really, of wrapping the plums up in shreds of newspaper, newspapers that are like portals open to the world, echoes of all the stories that will be trampled underfoot; the negligence of those who take the plum or life itself as a given, undeserving of notice; and yes, yes, also the trace of the plum's exquisite, tender blackness that is accessible to all, for such a small price. I think of Makénéné, of Tonga, of Edéa, of all the little plum towns spread along the endless road—but most of all I think of Yaoundé. Why, tell me why, at the start of plum season do I think of all the waste in the capital—a city that really doesn't give a shit whether there are plums or not, but that adores them just the same? Ah, the very short season always reminds me of the time when our country discovered, if not the crux of its own violence, then that of the world; when it sent off along the road through the desert its many sons—young soldiers who were then known as *tirailleurs sénégalais*—just like the fruit sellers toss away each evening the plums they haven't been able to grill. For us, the people of Cameroon, 1939 isn't the start of the Second World War, it's the date inscribed on the façade of our Central Post Office. This novel is as much our story as it is that of our city, but most of all, it's the story of the poet Pouka. That's why it gets a bit of a late start, relative to the rest of the world. But after all, the home front has its own schedule, and its own stories.

THE PUTSCH
IN ONGOLA, 1940

𖤍 𖥓

1

June Vacation Back in the Village

"To make a long story short," M'bangue concluded, crossing his hands on his knees, "that's how Hitler committed suicide."

Then he began to describe the deceased dictator, his blue jacket, his black tie, the barricaded toilets whose doors had to be broken down to get him out. Everyone was staring, their mouths agape, especially Pouka, who no longer recognized his father, whose hands were now tracing outrageous symbols, expansive symbols. The seer's face was lit up for an instant, then his eyes quickly disappeared into the fractals that his fingers had traced on the ground, into the geomantic mystery of the signs that gave shape to his pronouncements. No one called his word into doubt, for who could challenge his dream? Until that moment it had been nothing more than monologues, whispers, and murmurs: a spitting of distant sounds that evolved into words in the hollow of his belly.

"In the toilets," he continued, "mark my word."

No, Pouka no longer recognized his father. For everyone there, and him most of all, it was impossible to take this tale seriously. Besides, the month of June was strange enough already. Why would Hitler have committed suicide after occupying half of Europe? The Old Man didn't say—but that was the real question. Oh, his son didn't push for an answer: he just wanted to rest. The village held out that hazy promise to anyone returning from the city. Yaoundé could turn a man into a dog, as some would say. It sounded like a taunt, and this time they were right. And yet, with plum trees laden with fruit, where rows of pine and flame trees and bushes full of daisies meant it always smelled of Christmas, the village held out a promise of happiness that he could not turn down.

"He ate a good sausage," M'bangue concluded, "and then he killed himself . . ."

There were some who chortled. But not Pouka. No, he didn't laugh.

To think it was already 1940! Three years had gone by since he'd last set foot in Edéa; yes, three years when he hadn't come home. Maybe that's why he was staring at the Old Man's gestures with more surprise than anyone else; why he jumped at the end of the prediction. Clearly, Pouka was no longer the adolescent he'd been, torn from the shirttails of his cousin, the boxer, and sent to the mission school. It wasn't just that he'd converted to Catholicism in the meantime; no, he'd been promoted to the position of writer (really more of a secretary), *écrivain-interprète*! And that meant something! If reading shifting signs in the dirt was his father's business, juggling with words and filing folders was his. He, too, lived in the place where the future was created; or at least that's what he believed.

Or rather, no, that's what he hoped. How else to explain the meticulous care he took getting dressed each morning? Pouka could very well have given up on wearing his polished shoes, his tergal pants, his formal shirt, his multicolored cap, and . . . what else? But then he would have reverted into the barefoot little boy he'd left behind long ago. A kid. A native. Since then he had set his eyes on a goal, even if it was a little blurry. But now he'd come back. During the trip, he had come up with a reason for his visit: he told his father that he wanted a wife. Obviously that was a diversion, a way of avoiding the confrontation to come.

"I didn't send you to the white men to have you become a . . ."

What had he become? What? Wait a moment, dear reader, for this is a scene he had played out for himself several times. Never had he managed to say just what it was he had become. Yet it was obvious. A tall man, a head taller than anyone else. And on that head, Edéa would soon grow accustomed to seeing, come rain, come shine, a puffy cap that he never seemed to take off. Looking around, he saw respect inscribed on the faces of all the villagers. Envy, too. Jealousy, sometimes. Or maybe curiosity? Just what had he become? And they wondered: Why didn't he ever lift his cap to greet people? Did he screw with it still on his head? As for girls, no, no need to talk about girls. Still, there were a lot of stories told about him, racy stories. Stories, he knew, that worried his Old Man.

"When are you going to get married?"

Pouka hadn't yet found a good answer for that question, which he'd read long ago in his father's inquisitive gaze, on the day he left the village. He was the eldest son, the first of some fifty children, many of whom already had passels of children to show the Old Man. And then there were his friends—especially Fritz. We'll come back to him later, but really, his name says it all. Yet right then, as he stared at his father, whose eyes still glowed with distant visions, Pouka suddenly realized that the war had become an ugly distraction in this peaceful forest.

"Hitler . . ." M'bangue continued.

This time, however, he didn't finish his sentence.

2

The Collapse

Pouka's return to the village had been abrupt, but necessary. After June 14, a sudden change in the winds made the capital's offices aware of their own superfluity. The news had come just a week after school had let out, unleashing crowds of children. It seemed like the whole territory was on vacation. And yet! Ongola, the city center, had fallen under the sway of a particular type of fever: one instant stretched out infinitely, a point turned into a zigzagging line. It wasn't just that there was no more paperwork to file or notices to circulate. Since the start of the war officials had been spending their days glued to the radio, and the rest of their time trading improbable stories from Paris—from France. What was new that day was the dramatic expression on their faces.

"I always said," one voice began, "that Lebrun is an idiot."

If failure can take on several forms, powerlessness has only one.

"A traitor, you mean!"

Useless words, superfluous mouths, transparent hands gesturing endlessly, caught up in a chattering, toothless conspiracy.

"The Reds have taken Paris!"

"The Communists?"

"Hitler, you mean."

"That would be the worst!"

"You said it!"

"My dear friend, better the Brown Shirts than the Reds."

The face of the man who had just spoken looked around and, suddenly noticing Pouka, his native assistant, shooed him away angrily.

"The government is on the run," someone repeated.

A government only falls if it has already been crushed; otherwise, there is always hope it will rise again. And yet, "on the run"?

There was very little credible news. Rumors were inflaming the spirits of those starving for updates from the metropole, and hope buoyed up imaginations.

"In exile," said someone over here.

"Relieved from duty," corrected another over there.

"In Bordeaux," a third added, "but not defeated."

"But not defeated."

"Never defeated!"

Hope is the drug of the tortured.

"In Africa!" the prison warden announced the next day. "My brother told me that the government is now based in Africa."

"In Africa?"

All the colonists stared at each other, mouths agape.

"Where in Africa?"

Days of doubt; days of suspicion. In all truth, the atmosphere had grown unbearable. His boss's irritability made it imperative that Pouka leave on vacation. No one challenged his request for leave. The offices were empty, decisions superfluous. The rhythm of war flooded over the city, imposing a sense of emptiness none could ignore. One day Pouka asked for a month's leave, since the future really didn't mean anything anymore. Days of uncertainty. What excuse had he given? No, he hadn't said he was going home to take a wife, since that would have been ridiculous . . . who gets married in times like these?

What times!

The truth itself would have been judged, if not ridiculous, then at least stupid, and would have resulted in a resounding no. Can you imagine if he had simply said what he intended to do: "I want to start a poetry circle in my village"?

First off, who would have believed him? Although he had written many manuscripts that had failed to find an editor—"not yet, not yet," he told his friends—he was still the most celebrated poet of his generation, having published pieces in *La Gazette du Cameroun* and in *L'Éveil camerounais*. So he was fed up that no one in his village had heard of him—even though he'd received the Palmes académiques d'outre mer, as well as colonial medals for poetic distinction—while his cousin Hebga, the boxer, remained the area's favorite son, just for the strength of his muscles. No, Pouka hadn't won the Goncourt Prize, but still. He had finally realized that these French institutions that awarded him prizes didn't give a damn that none of his compatriots had ever seen any of his books, that the natives were unaware of the definition of a rondeau, and so he had decided to take matters into his own hands.

Rebellion? No, he considered himself a French subject. The need for recognition can sometimes lead to folly, but the mere thought of rebellion scared him. In truth, he despised his brothers, yes, he despised them. Yet, the idea that they couldn't even read made him angry. In short, what he really wanted was to create a reader for his poems in his village, and to his mind that made him no different from Hugo, or Mallarmé, or even Gautier, whom he saw as his model. He couldn't confide the goal of his trip to his boss, of course. But he was too honest to say it was because of a death in the family, although that would have been the most believable excuse. No, you never know what consequences will come from claiming that your father has died, or of killing off your grandfather again, although he'd been buried years before.

On the bus that took him to Edéa, he thought of just how he would explain his unexpected arrival—or rather the three years since his last visit—to his father. Our dear Pouka wouldn't be the first one to invent some story: in those days, people were afraid of truth more than anything else. For who on earth would admit that what was going on—whether it was a Swiss watch losing time, gusts of wind coming through new zinc roofs, or the whimpering of an infant in a closed room—was actually happening? And so our hero, a rather haughty, but timid, young man, prone to avoidance, and who had built a temple to the scents of women, had suddenly realized that being alone in a bus filled with passengers meant sharing all of their silent illusions. Vacation! The old village!

At the very moment when his father kissed him in the courtyard of the family compound, the clamor that had followed him since the bus station fell silent. A woman selling grilled plantains had recognized him and shared the news of his arrival with the Bassa hills. Then she followed along behind him, accompanied by the kids from the missionary school who had just been let out into the playground for four months of vacation.

3

The Old Man's Four Eyes

In Edéa, the world kept turning, which at that point meant following the rhythm of the Old Man's deliberate gestures. M'bangue had a power that made everyone who could be considered a figure of authority in the region bow down at his feet—everyone, that is, except the French, who had never forgotten that once he had spoken German. Maybe there were other reasons, too—dubious ones, to be sure, for why on earth would anyone have doubted the accuracy of his visions? Once he had crossed the forest in the middle of the night to wake up his brother, arriving just in time to save him before the roof of his house could come crashing down on his head. Those who didn't believe his words had always paid dearly for their skepticism. Take, for example, his brother-in-law, a woodcutter who had gone to cut down trees one day despite his warnings, only to have one tree, which he hadn't even touched, twist around strangely and fall right on top of him. Where the Old Man was really unbeatable was in predicting rain. Though many others shared this gift, his was beyond question. M'bangue could tell you the hour the storm would start, how long the rain would fall, and even where it would come down hardest, along with the number and even the names of its victims— if there were any men stubborn enough to ignore his warning not to make love to their wives the night before the storm.

"Did he screw?" M'bangue asked about a man he'd warned and who had been struck dead by lightning.

Embarrassed, the dead man's wife opted not to answer; maybe she even went into hiding to avoid retribution. No one ever cast doubt on the Old Man's dreams, except for his Hitlerian predictions, which were, you had to admit, rather preposterous. This wasn't the first time M'bangue had done something out of the ordinary, however. That his son had gone, like only a handful of other village boys, from the Catholic school to the French administration, without ever asking for his approval—well, people said that was enough to explain why he hadn't come back to the village for so long. Was it because of a bad dream? Or just a sulking father? What? Looking back on this now, it would be easy to write that M'bangue had foreseen what his son would become! But don't read too much into the squabbles of a father and son! There were stories about voices raised in the house one night, or maybe it was one afternoon, or why not even a morning . . . A mother's tears shed in a darkened room, curses offered up right in the living room. But then again, what didn't people say?

Flourishes of a Far-Off Conversation

These sessions of divination were for M'bangue what the writing of a poem was for his son, poetry's newly converted disciple. The Old Man had traced a circle in the dirt in front of his feet. He counted once, twice, three times, calculated the odds, and then checked his equation. He wiped his face with both hands, as if trying to come to grips with the truth of his own prediction, before describing what he had seen. His words had made Pouka shudder, then stand up and leave. Pouka was well aware that, had he repeated this paternal declaration to his bosses, who were so caught up in their own whispering back in the capital, they would have burst out laughing. Clearly, not much would have changed if the colonists had a good laugh from time to time, if Yaoundé had been shaken up by a resounding peal of laughter, especially in these uncomfortable days, but still, yes . . . still! And besides, many of his father's visions hadn't come true, after all, his son could bear witness to that. But Pouka would never forget that dream about Hitler. Much later, when his mocking compatriots began to call him Trissotin, he remembered the words his father had spoken with such confidence to the crowd gathered there in Edéa as he emerged from a trance, and Pouka thought, deep in his heart: That time I was right.

Being right means nothing, except in history's long view, as we all know. And the history in question here was improbable, unbelievable, the most obvious of tricks. The young man just shrugged his shoulders, as anyone would have done upon hearing a story too far-fetched to be true, then stood up and dusted off his behind. A moment later, as he arrived in the courtyard of his cousin the boxer, he was already thinking of something else. He had no choice, really, his father's words were chasing him away.

"Hey, cuz," the boxer shouted as soon as he opened the door, "you've turned into a white man!"

He pulled Pouka in and hugged him tight, then grabbed him by the shoulders and stared: first at his face, then peeling away his clothes with his eyes and stripping him bare to the bone. His booming voice roused everyone around who hadn't already heard who'd just come back from the city, and by that I mean, just his friends.

"Take a look at this! Hebga!" they exclaimed.

It's true he had really changed. Pouka was no longer the little boy who trailed in the boxer's shadow, who wrapped Hebga's fists with cloth before each match, massaging his muscles, slapping his stomach, saying just the right words to build up his courage so he could smash his opponents' faces. Pouka was no longer the *ambianceur* who livened up Hebga's matches, but did that mean he'd become a white man? The thought amused the writer, just as he was amused by the famished eyes eating up his clothes and shoes, seeing on his shoulders an aura of success—something quite unimaginable to the overworked drudge he'd become. This called for a celebration, for exuberant toasts in the bar. Never would the newly returned prodigal son have deprived the village of its deserved bacchanal.

What luck—there in Mininga's Bar he met up with Um Nyobè, an *écrivain-interprète* like himself, another kid from the village who'd been educated in the missionary school and then joined the French administration, but whose boyish looks and sartorial simplicity were in stark contrast to his own exuberant style. "The seminarian, that's Um," Pouka would say. Um Nyobè had arrived in the village before him, called back by a sudden death in his family—"an uncle on my father's side"—and his need to attend the funeral. He was only going to stay for a few more days, but still, still . . .

"You never come to visit me, either," Pouka shot at him. "You'd think I was some kind of a criminal!"

"Oh, Yaoundé," Um Nyobè replied. "You know how it is."

"Pouka lives in Madagascar, did you forget?"

Um Nyobè stifled a laugh. No, Pouka hadn't changed at all. After all this time . . . his vanity hadn't waned one bit. He still always talked about himself in the third person. Ah, Pouka! In fact, Pouka's neighborhood, Madagascar, was right next to Messa, where Um Nyobè and other civil servants like him lived, just one or two kilometers away, really.

"Are you forgetting that I'm your elder?" Pouka added.

Although surprised that these two guys from Yaoundé only ran into each other in this village courtyard, the villagers were all of one mind: it was up to Um Nyobè to make the first step.

"Oh well, then my apologies," he conceded, adding, "big brother."

As expected, Pouka recognized many other childhood friends. Fritz, for example, already the head of a family, whose business interests were in Douala rather than the capital, and who seemed to want to list all the benefits of his lifestyle: "when you don't work for the white men," when you are "your own boss," as he said. Before he could, Hebga cut him off.

"Ah, my brothers," the boxer jumped in, "tell me all about Yaoundé!"

Today you'd be more likely to hear, "Tell me about Paris!" And in fact, there in the middle of June 1940, that's what Hebga would have asked if he hadn't been, like all the rest of the local population, cut off from history's twists and turns. He should have asked what had happened in France, why she had surrendered so quickly, how the City of Light could have fallen so easily and allowed herself to be occupied by Germans; and then, most important, what would this mean for Cameroon? Yes, was Cameroon going to remain under the control of a defeated country? The guys who were so busy giving each other hugs, drinking beer, and eating grilled plantains and plums, they would start asking these questions soon enough, believe me. All you had to do was see the cold look in Um Nyobè's eyes to realize that—even if Hebga's endless questions dominated this comical welcome-home party until the night gave way to snores.

Like Mythical Cousins

Hebga was a young man, about twenty years old; his bulging pecs, adorned with a few scattered tufts of hair, stood out as a challenge. His braids hung down on both sides from a middle part, a reminder of the German haircut he once had, an elegant look that was accentuated by the billowing pagne wrapped between his legs, like an ample diaper, and tied at his hips. For Pouka, he was a godfather. He always had been. What joined these two together was stronger than the blood that linked the writer to his father's fifty other children: a mysterious bond born in the bush, the work of a tenacious woman, if truth be told. For Pouka had really been raised by our Sita, Hebga's mother, his father's eldest sister and, for all the residents of Edéa, the Mother of the Market. She had never come to terms with having only one living child and so had accepted her brother's firstborn as if he were her second. This wasn't a problem in the eyes of the young Pouka, who readily accepted his adopted older brother, since he had none of his own.

In the depths of the forest, the bond between the two boys had strengthened. After his father's death, Hebga had become the village's woodcutter. He was only sixteen at the time. That it was an iroko, an African teak tree, that had made him an orphan seemed to have instilled in him an endless need for vengeance. The forest was filled with too many enemies to count. He faced off against the tree trunks alone, when usually it took a whole legion of men to cut one down. Pouka always went with him into the bush, balancing on his head the food and water that fueled his cousin's strength. Once Hebga began his struggle with the chosen tree, Pouka would shout out words of encouragement, sometimes intoning hymns to spur him on. Their bond grew quite quickly through this routine of song and grunts, of words and effort, and soon was so strong that it would have been difficult to say which one of them needed the other more.

It was only a question of time before everyone would learn of the bonds of sweat and words that made them brothers. One morning Edéa awoke to a chorus of voices announcing the arrival of the boxing champions. This was nothing surprising. Several times each dry season, the railroad company crisscrossed the bush, putting on its show and raking in money. They were as much actors as wizened athletes, trained by a wily manager—a Frenchman, to top it off— who understood how much money he could make by putting on spectacular, if rigged, fights. For the villagers, this was an opportunity to break the dull monotony of their day-to-day. Two hulks smashed each other's face to the pack's applause, while women covered their children's eyes and grumbled about men's stupidity. The men preferred these boxing matches to the itinerant movie showings organized by the Catholic church, because after a while the films chosen by Father Jean made only the children laugh. Boxing, that was what they clamored for, and the company took advantage of the breaks between each round to keep raising the stakes.

But one day this happened: someone in the crowd, a kid, burst out laughing when the referee lifted the arm of the declared winner. What kind of fly had bitten Pouka? That disrespectful little kid couldn't contain himself when the man named the Champion of Cameroon stared at him with his red bloodshot eyes. No way! As if galvanized by the attention of the crowd now fixed on him, the boy shouted in his loudest voice:

"My cousin is the real Champion of Cameroon!"

The boxers burst out laughing. But they were the only ones there who didn't know Hebga. Sometimes, as they toured the country, they had met villagers, lacking in modesty, whose long struggles in the fields had led to fantasies of incredible victories: weak men blind to their own delusions of grandeur. Thinking perhaps that this would be a chance to make a bit more money by adding an unplanned battle to their routine, the manager asked the crowd: So who is this champion? No one stepped forward.

"Where is your cousin?" he asked the kid.

Pouka pointed him out. The spectators' eyes were drawn to the calm and powerful man who, like everyone else, had been watching the boring fight. People in Edéa still talk about the match that took place the next day, or maybe the next week. Not just because the man crowned champion the day before fled into the forest in the middle of the battle, but rather because the impresario hadn't been able to convince our Sita to give him her son as a replacement, despite the suitcase full of money he held open before her market-woman's eyes.

Sita seemed to have seen it all before. As the Mother of the Market, she was the one who rented stands to the women. She was also the one responsible for collecting the monthly contributions that served as a sort of health insurance fund. She was used to handling money, that was clear. But this time they were talking about a "suitcase full of money" opened right in front of her eyes—even if that was a bit of an exaggeration. They were in our Sita's home when the white man first brought up taking her son to Yaoundé. Hebga's mother was so disinterested that he suggested Douala instead. When our Sita showed no more enthusiasm for that, he moved on to taking her son to Paris. Nothing doing. That's when he mentioned the suitcase full of money. But even that didn't sway the most stubborn *bayamsallam* in the equatorial forest. The versions told of this story are as malleable as the books in which they've been written, but they all agree on the words Hebga's mother used to shut him down, for they have become legendary in Bassa land:

"Over my dead body."

The man was dumbstruck. Our Sita repeated herself: "Only over my dead body will my son go to Paris."

An incredible stubbornness, really, for who among us didn't dream of going to Paris? What ill could come of using your talent to make money? But this woman had buried her husband and didn't want to lose the only son she had left of the ten children she had given birth to.

This story is also about the birth of Pouka's poetic talents, for after his public intervention, he had had to convince his cousin that within him lay a pugilist capable of making a professional boxer flee right in the middle of a fight. He had to find the right words to convince Hebga, who as yet had only measured his strength against tree trunks, when the crack of his ax was the only sound in the deep silence of the bush, that he could fell a human giant in just the same way. From the start of the first fight Pouka's words flew with gymnastic speed, rising up to mythic heights. The boy crouched down, the better to whisper in his cousin's ears, to massage his soul and his pride, to firm up his fist and his body, to set his eyes aflame.

He invented all the adjectives he could to persuade his cousin of his own grandeur, to prove that his opponent was nothing but a rank amateur: a "nuthin'," "a worthless piece of crap," a "*sansanboy*." The true poet creates greatness in the very heart of doubt.

"Son of a cat!" Pouka said.

He was talking about Hebga, but that wasn't all he said.

"Lion of the bush!"

"Born of a genie's fart!"

If these words turned Hebga's fists to steel, when Pouka intoned the champion's hymn the feet of that boxer for a day started in on a rhythmic dance that left his opponent totally unnerved. On Pouka sang, and as the crowd clapped its hands and stomped its feet, the village's boxer landed blows to his opponent's eyes, nose, and temple.

"Eagle, eagle of the bush!"

And Pouka continued, "The Ax!" And everyone repeated, stressing both syllables, "The Ax!"

"The Ax!"

"The Ax!"

"The Ax!"

One punch can carry the weight of a whole city. Hebga's were those of a forest. "The Ax!" He was fighting for all of Bassa land— "The Ax!"—and Pouka's songs let him tap into its strength. "The Ax!" Soon the shouts of the crowd slowed down: "The Ax!" "The Ax!" "The Ax!" Hebga had knocked out his opponent. He marched around him, chanting spells, trumpeting out insults, cursing. The boxer tried to stand up. "The Ax!" "The Ax!" "The Ax!" He was struggling for all he was worth. But his knees, no, his feet, no, his spine, his whole body, suddenly went on strike. He was shaky, but managed to get up on his feet.

"Break his nose!"

Crowds can spin out of control. Right then a voice rose up and shattered the silence around the man who was fighting as much against himself as against the village's favorite son.

"Poke his eye out!" Pouka said.

Hebga paused, suddenly disoriented by a kid's crazy words, but also by his opponent's strange wobbling.

"Smash his gut!"

Then Pouka quickly shifted gears.

"Kill him!"

Everyone was shocked to hear such words coming from a kid's mouth. A moment of hesitation. His opponent took advantage of it to pick himself up and rush headlong through the crowd, which, caught by surprise, opened a path for him. The man bolted through like lightning and disappeared into the bush, which closed up tightly to hide his shame. There were those who wanted to give chase, voices that sent amused exclamations along after him, bursts of laughter that compounded his humiliation. The tale of his crushing defeat became legend that night in Mininga's Bar; as the drinkers laughed and laughed, everybody took a turn acting out the scoundrel's flight. Hebga's opponent had opted for shame over death. As for the myth of the boxer that was born that day, well, Hebga was still powerless in the face of the determination—the intransigence, I'd even say—of our Sita, his mother. That was the day Pouka began to write songs, first to temper the violence of which he'd never before thought himself capable, and then to provide a rhythm for the story of his hero's grandeur. Every athlete has his poet. We were in the 1930s. Well before the child grew into the man familiar to us all, the man who took himself for an aristocrat.

6

Battling a Hypothetical Opponent

Then came 1940. What had changed in the meantime? Pouka would learn soon enough: Hebga had become fixated on probabilities, obsessed with the lottery, always studying the patterns in the winning numbers that appeared in *La Gazette du Cameroun*. He couldn't read, of course, but the winning numbers didn't get by him. Had he ever won the big prize? All you had to do was look at him to know he was still holding on to his dreams. Yet he hadn't stopped going into the forest. Pouka quickly realized that, too. But now the goal was more to strengthen his muscles than to cut down trees. Despite his mother's efforts to wear it down, his Parisian dream lived on, kindled by the music of Josephine Baker and others that Mininga played from morning to night in her bar. Making his dream come true overshadowed everything else—it was crazy, really. It seemed as though Hebga had been dragged into the forest by his opponent and forced to go at it for round after round, just in hopes of seeing the doors to Paris's paradise open for him. The day of his first fight he hadn't chased after his fleeing opponent. Now, come rain, come shine, he got up in the morning and headed off into the forest. He walked alongside the first planters heading to the fields, rising like them at cock's-crow. It's just that his mission wasn't to dig yams and *macabo* from the ground. No, he knew well that his victory over the boxer was more a bit of luck, a gift from the fight manager, than the result of any serious training on his part.

He had used wrestling moves when his opponent was expecting uppercuts. He didn't yet know the rules of boxing, but he knew how to use his body. Swinging an ax, smashing it into tree trunks, had shown him what his body could do. He knew he needed to manage his strength if he wanted to survive a long fight. Let's go back to the fight where it all began, and I'll explain why he landed only a few blows on his opponent. Hebga was aware of his double advantage. First, he was the crowd's favorite and Pouka was its mouthpiece; his cousin shouted words of praise and all bets were on him. Then, there was the fight he had watched the night before. He had observed the tactics of his future opponent and knew how he used his body. The body, after all, is like a tree trunk, Hebga was sure of that: it is shaped by the blows it has received.

Hebga had learned from his father how to train his body, and the importance of always keeping his muscles on alert. He had planted the roots of Hebga's future. Hebga remembered his father's words: "The woodcutter's enemy isn't the tree, it's his own body." And that enemy appeared in the form of horrible cramps. Getting rid of them required consistent training of the arms, feet, spinal column, neck, and hands. You had to take care of your muscles continually, coax them on, tone them up. You had to exercise each part of your body every day, because cutting down a baobab tree required that the whole organism work together in a gigantic symphony of effort. I can say, yes, that if Hebga's father had treated his body like a perpetual opponent, for his son it was the tree—the tree that had crashed down on his father one day—that was the real enemy. Each of Hebga's gestures was dictated by his focus on that goal, but that first victorious fight against a clown of a boxer had released adrenaline he didn't even know he had.

The woodcutter, who thought he had found his enemy in the silent trees, suddenly realized that in a true battle, your opponent gives it back to you blow for blow. Fair play is the rule of a good fight, but only training reveals your moral fiber. That's why Hebga began training against hypothetical enemies. At first he imagined them using only their fists, like the boxer he had knocked down. Then he imagined that, out of treachery, his opponent used his feet, too. He trained to take on anyone who would use both their hands and their feet. The list of weapons kept on growing, since, if they could use their feet, why not their head? Yes, why not their head? Soon Hebga grew accustomed to using a knife, and then a cutlass. By the time he switched from a cutlass to a straight blade, and then to a curved one, Pouka no longer accompanied him into the bush. Nor was Pouka there when he began developing attacks with first a small and then a long lance. The missionary school had swallowed up the boy.

In the end, Hebga had closed the circle, coming back to the place his father had shown him. Of all weapons, the one he preferred was the ax. He held it delicately with both hands and kept his movements slow, to avoid stressing his joints. He splayed his feet and set his legs in a solid triangle. He raised his arms, now holding the ax firmly and lifting it up to the boundless and evanescent sky above. A ray of sunlight peeked through the trees, sliding along the dew-covered leaves and glinting on the blade of his weapon. It was as if the spirits gave him their blessing, letting their silent strength flow through him. He'd let his hands fall and strike: bam! He'd repeat the move several times: bam! In the end, he'd be covered in sweat. Or maybe it was the morning breeze that covered him with its cottony shroud. Then he'd sit down in the shade of a tree, breathing deeply, attentive to all the pulsing of his body. He knew that little by little he had transformed his lungs into a prayer. He looked at his hands, which had grown tough as rocks. His pectoral muscles, as hard as wood, rose and fell. His biceps, covered with circular tattoos, trembled. It was as if the trees that stretched out above him toward the heavens knelt down to offer him the whispered praise he no longer got from his cousin, now that the missionary school had torn him from the forest and led him off to Yaoundé. As if, with their rhythmic murmur, they intoned the hymn of the champion that Pouka hadn't yet composed, and that he never again tried to write.

The Ax!

The Ax!

That's the big strong man who, surrounded by his friends, there in the clamor of drinks and words, now asked his cousin to tell him about Yaoundé.

"Tell me about Yaoundé," Hebga begged.

More than a thirst, it had become an obsession.

7

The Reversal

Still in 1940: one day Um Nyobè announced to his friends who had gathered at Mininga's that General de Gaulle had become a dissident and had called on all French forces, wherever they might be, to continue to fight. "In short, to join the Resistance." Doing so, Um Nyobè showed one of the traits that would never cease to amaze Pouka, and which Pouka would later invoke when he wrote the long, never-published poem "Rubenism: The Hymn of Cameroon," which he dedicated to his childhood friend. How had Um Nyobè gotten hold of that news? For the moment, the question on everyone's lips was simple.

"De Gaulle?"

Hebga put it more clearly.

"Who is this de Gaulle?"

Even Um Nyobè couldn't provide a simple answer, and he was the most political of the bunch. He tried to recall the members of the Lebrun government, his eyes flickering this way and that, but the image that kept coming to mind was the impassive face of Pétain, which he'd seen in various administrative brochures.

"And where is he, this general of yours . . . ?" Hebga asked, snapping his fingers as he tried to remember the name. ". . . De Gaulle?"

"In England."

No one burst out laughing, but they came close.

"In short . . ." Fritz began. He slunk down in his chair, crossed

his legs, carefully weighing each of his words to lend them heft, holding his bottle in midair. "If I understand well, he has *fled*?"

He stressed the word "fled," with a knowing nod. Hebga and
Pouka looked at each other warily. Fritz wasn't done yet.

"Fled," Hebga echoed.

"And," Fritz continued in the silence that followed his words,
gesturing dramatically with his hands like an orator, "he's asking
others to fight."

The silence that had fallen over the bar was broken only by Mininga's heady perfume; she brought another round of beers and set
them down in front of the talkative friends.

"If he has fled," she tossed out in the arena, "then let him come
to Edéa. We'll hide him in the forest, right?"

Her smile lit up the fellows' faces, although her suggestion raised
an interesting question. They hadn't really thought about it, but why
not? Of course, they would have hidden de Gaulle in the *maquis*—
in the bush around Edéa—or maybe in the bar. Mininga's question
caught them off guard and made everyone laugh. So the woman who
had added her coda to their story stood there for a moment, hands
on her hips.

"We'll feed him ourselves," she went on, "with grilled plantains
and plums, am I right?" She glanced at the woman selling grilled
plantains.

She was amused by the idea.

"*Na so-o*," said the vendor, "bean fritters *a day for ya*."

"Or else," Mininga wondered, "we'd be guilty of . . . oh . . . what
is that called . . . ?"

Her questioning eyes scanned the drinkers' faces. None of
them could guess the word she was looking for. She didn't wait for
them to reply. No, standing behind her bar, next to the barmaid
who was helping her, she just continued with her thought as blithely
as she'd begun.

"Failure to assist a person in danger."

A loud burst of laughter.

"Hey, war isn't some sort of lottery . . . !"

"Of course he wants the fight to go on," Fritz added, looking at
each of his friends closely before hammering home his point. "He'll
be safe in London."

Everyone laughed, but Fritz pretty well summed up the idea that had almost been derailed, first by Mininga's exuberant suggestions, and then by someone else who chimed in, "And speaking of plantains, can you bring me . . ."

His eyes met Um Noybè's.

"The whites are tearing into each other," he concluded. A wave of emotion flowed through his veins. Only a German word could express it: *Schadenfreude*. He didn't say it, but just rubbed his hands.

"Okay, so de Gaulle is in England," Hebga summarized, as he stood up, "with the Allied forces."

"You mean he's deserted, right?"

"Which means he's done for." Hebga stood there chuckling. "So where are the toilets in this place, my *mamy nyanga?*"

"Who knows?"

That was Fritz.

"The way to the toilets hasn't changed since yesterday, uncle."

"The French are unbelievable, am I right?"

The woodcutter's laughter faded away in the back of the bar, drowned out by the splash of piss hitting a stone. That's how things stood in that middle of June, when friends back in the village on vacation gathered at the bar, childhood friends happy to see each other after several years apart. They needed something new to talk about, for surely there were more interesting things than the fate of a general from faraway France who was on the run. After all, nothing had changed on the home front. But what could they say? Whenever these friends got together, the talk always turned to Paris. Not long before, Pétain's portrait had appeared in all the government buildings in Yaoundé, as well as in Douala. Even after the defeat, French colonists still wrote the laws in Cameroon. Um Nyobè was just making that point when Fritz called him out: "But for how long?"

Those two had a long history of arguments. Since elementary school, people said, they never missed a chance to debate each other, even as their lives kept drawing them closer together. It was as if they'd come into this world just so they could always disagree, although they followed similar paths in life. It was obvious to all that they were really athletes playing the same game, each strengthened by their ongoing struggle: verbal boxers, if you will! In his house, for example, the young patriarch Fritz reigned over his living room from his bamboo chair at the head of the table, the place reserved for the father. He sat like a king on a throne, with a sailor's hat on his head, a shirt on his back, a pagne wrapped around his waist: you'd think he'd inherited it all, just like that. Um Nyobè, on the other hand, who would take his seat at the far end of the table, his head held high and no less proud, had opted to pursue the meaning of life in the hallways of the colonial administration. Neither one had really chosen his path, though they shared a number of experiences: the mission school, then the normal school in Foulassi, teaching as a *moniteur indigène*. In that living room, the dining table became the arena where they jousted.

Fritz, who had inherited his place as head of the family too soon, had needed to grow up fast because he had to take care of all of his father's kids, as well as his wives: so he had quit teaching. Um Nyobè, on the other hand, had followed a path marked out by the sharp edges of his temperament. Rebellious by nature, he had been kicked out of the normal school on disciplinary grounds: it seems he had organized a strike among the students to protest the bad quality of the food served in the canteen. Everybody had been surprised, except his father, who recognized in his son his own boiling blood; in his day he had protested against forced labor. Back then, the Nyobès lived in Makon, the center of German colonial power, since it was the hub for the railway. One word too many had earned Um Nyobè's father a sort of exile, if that's what you can call being expelled from the German enclave. Now he had gone to live in his second wife's village—his first wife, Um Nyobè's mother, had died in childbirth. As for Um Nyobè, he preferred Edéa over the new village, even though that meant he had to live with friends instead of family. For now, it seemed, he was staying with Fritz.

"I always told you that France wasn't worth it," Um Nyobè hammered home. "Look at what's happened to her."

"And yet you work for her," Fritz shot back.

Then he poured himself a glass of beer. Among his friends, Um Nyobè was known for his obstinacy. In short, once he took a position, it was hard to convince him otherwise. He'd cling to his ideas, even to the point of absurdity. Fritz seemed to have come into this world just to help him see how murky his thoughts were; a bit older than his friend, he used that to his advantage.

"No one can ever talk with you two," Pouka often said, and he was certainly right.

In Um Nyobè's eyes, Pouka lacked conviction.

Hebga would just have said, "He's a little brother."

As for me, I'd say they were old friends, back together and reliving old stories.

8

Creating a Poetry Circle in the Forest

Pouka was correct, history is a difficult thing to write. Which is why he wanted to take a break from it. I'd say, and maybe you'd agree, that Pouka had chosen a bad time. To his mind, however, there was no better time. He had already waited three years, with his belly full of alexandrine verses, his mouth full of impatient rhymes. Talking with his friends, he was distracted. Not just because of the intense memories the place had awoken. His eyes scanned around Mininga's Bar, looking at the few illegible signs posted, and pausing when he saw the bar's display of drinks. He tried to reinvent the place as a reading room, and to imagine Nerval—yes, Nerval!—and Gautier, too—no joke!—there with their friends, sitting on overturned crates and discussing art. Of course, it was no longer 1830, no, and we were certainly not in Paris, but in a disreputable corner of Edéa. Yet it was precisely that difference that made him wonder. A poetry circle in the forest, yes, that was his idea. His goal.

When he came back to the bar the next day, other people were sitting there. He recognized two or three regulars who stood up as he came in and greeted him with respect and also with surprise—surprise at seeing the colonial civil servant, the *ngovina*, as he was called behind his back, there two days in a row. He went straight to the bar, trying to gauge Mininga's mood.

"Just say that you missed me, *mon chéri*," she teased.

She had said *mon chéri* in French. That woman's playing to the crowd, he thought. But Mininga wasn't through. She was the mistress of the place—"madam" would be a word too light to describe her. She had the easygoing attitude of someone not from around there; the brazenness of someone who doesn't know what the taboos are and so transgresses them innocently or because she doesn't give a darn; and the comfortable ease of someone who speaks the local language extraordinarily well, without any accent, even if her choice of adjectives, just like the colors she wore, always surprised the locals. When she spoke, she touched her clients as if each were her lover. She was Ewondo.

Mininga placed a bottle of beer in front of Pouka.

"I haven't forgotten what you drink," she added as she opened the bottle, "isn't that right, *mon chéri?*"

She shimmied a bit, showing off her generous breasts. Pouka began to think he'd made a mistake coming back to this place where a reputation could be ruined in a minute. Feeling a slight pang of despair, he took hold of the woman's hand and, happily, she fell silent.

"A *tontine?*" she asked, after listening to the details of his plan.

"Pretty much," he said, "pretty much."

It wasn't easy for this businesswoman to accept that her stools would be filled for several hours by people who wouldn't be buying drinks, but she consoled herself with the thought that they'd be coming in the morning.

"When you don't have any customers yet."

"I always have customers," she protested, looking at the three regulars sitting in a corner; even at that early hour their eyes were already bleary.

It was just a formality, really, Pouka knew it. Yet he didn't want to offer more than the compensation he had already decided upon. Just as important as what Mininga thought was what the priest thought. Not that the man had any ideas about poetry—it was all canticles to him. But Father Jean was the one who had convinced Pouka's father to send him to the mission school way back when, and the priest remained, in a sense, his benefactor. The priest's protection would allow him to organize something in the village without attracting the attention of the colonial administration. For the moment, he would have to convince the man that the little poetry circle wasn't just some sort of midnight mass.

"Sadly the schoolkids and students are on vacation," he began, "or else I would have gone to the headmaster. This is just something to fill up the vacation, after all."

Too feeble an excuse to be taken seriously. Pouka realized that even before he saw Father Jean's skeptical face.

"I would have held it in the church, if it weren't for catechism," he continued, "obviously."

That was the best he'd come up with. Father Jean smiled. Even though he was a priest, he knew when someone was giving him a line. The only thing that had ever tripped Pouka up was his own vanity. Neither Catholicism nor his job as a writer were responsible for turning the boy he used to know into the man he saw before him. Regardless, the priest's opinion of Pouka was too clouded by paternalism to be taken seriously.

"Precisely," the priest began, "you should come say hello to the catechumens. They'll be happy to see you."

He spoke of the zeal of the new generation and the promising futures he saw for them.

"You could organize a course of Bible study."

Pouka had been part of the first class the priest had taught. Evidently, the priest had expected his efforts to be paying off already. He had been pleased when Pouka first chose to study for the priesthood. That he later decided to become a writer hadn't surprised the prelate—the colonial administration was particularly tempting for the local youth—but he couldn't think of it without feeling sad. The village, on the other hand, had rubbed its hands in anticipation when Pouka, who had been a *moniteur-indigène* at the *petit séminaire*, the church-run school at Akono, had abandoned the robe. Father Jean said that if it hadn't been for all those poetry prizes, maybe he wouldn't have lost his young colt, who had been dubbed by his teachers the "Luther of Africa."

"Why not at your father's home?" the priest asked.

"You know my father," Pouka replied; he and the priest both sighed.

The cleric recognized that if it was difficult to organize poetry gatherings in a church, it was out of the question that they take place in a pagan temple. So Pouka and the priest found common ground in opposition to the Old Man, and for the defense and promotion of poetry in Edéa.

"So what are you going to read?"

That was the priest's way of signaling his tacit accord.

"I'm not sure yet," Pouka replied, realizing at once that he'd made another mistake. The best way to bring the priest around to his side was to show no hesitation.

"Claudel, of course," he began, counting off on his fingers the names from the pantheon of French poetry that he most admired.

"That's good," Father Jean interjected, "he's not a Communist."

Pouka smiled, as if keeping Communist poets out of his anthology was a given that didn't need to be stipulated.

"Of course, no Reds."

"Especially during wartime," the priest continued, "when what we all need is faith. And prayers."

That same day, a notice posted on the church door invited all who wanted to learn how to write poetry to come to Mininga's Bar Wednesday morning at 9:00 a.m. The announcement was signed, "Pouka, Writer."

9

The First Meeting

When Pouka saw the line that had formed in front of Mininga's Bar on Wednesday morning, he first thought he had gone to the wrong place. Never would he have imagined that poetry would attract so many people. Talking with each of them, however, he quickly realized that many, in fact, hadn't understood what the meeting was about. Despite the misunderstanding, he didn't tell everyone to head back home, because he hoped that among these men and women—who were expecting to be hired by the French administration or to take part in a new campaign against sleeping sickness, or who thought Pouka was the manager in charge of a white boss's household—he'd find some aspiring poets. Some had walked for miles to take their place in line, there in front of Mininga's Bar.

It goes without saying that most were illiterate.

"It's my fault," Pouka told himself, slapping his forehead.

Mininga wasn't complaining. Her girls had been able to sell a few drinks, and it looked like this would turn into a busy day. As far as the proprietor was concerned, Pouka could have kept the poor devils waiting in the courtyard a little longer—they'd surely soon be falling over from thirst or hunger or whatever.

"They'll eat and drink," she said. "First lunch . . . and then beer."

The Anglophone vendor who set up her stand in front of the bar each morning was thrilled. Never, never had she ever sold so much! After just two trips around, her trays were empty. Pouka, for his part, realized that he should have written his notice in French. That would have drawn a different clientele, more selective, less colorful. He just couldn't imagine that in these peasants who had torn themselves from grimy bamboo beds that morning slept the poetic craftsmen he wanted to invent. He might as well teach poetry to Pygmies, he thought. Had anyone told him he ought to be a bit more generous, that the missionary school, which had made him who he was today, had begun its work with the same stock, he would have smiled. Ah! Let's not forget that his time in the city had already planted in him the seeds of an elitism shared, it seems, by all who write verses. Let's just put down to a bit of early morning frustration how he snapped when faced with the blank gaze of a peasant who really had no idea why he was even there. Then he had to send away a man with runny eyes (he hadn't dared to ask the man if he had any idea what a poem was), and a woman with a case of chiggers so bad he didn't even ask her the usual questions. He also needed to explain to all those he sent back to their daily prose why they needed to give up on writing metaphors.

"Metaphors?" one man asked.

His eyes expressed a wordless prayer: never had being deprived of metaphors made a man so unhappy.

The man explained that he knew how to use a screwdriver, to put together an electric circuit, to take apart a car engine and put it back together again.

"I'm an electrician, a mechanic."

He meant "day laborer."

"Anything you want, I can do it, boss."

He showed his tools: a screwdriver, a hammer, a few electrical components. He dug out of his pocket a letter of recommendation, red with dust and folded in quarters, and unfolded it carefully. It was signed by a white man.

"By the commander," he said. "By the commander."

Ah yes. If Pouka had better explained in his announcement just what he intended, there certainly would have been fewer people interested, but at least the poet would have had less of a headache. And yet, wasn't this really what he wanted? Wasn't this why he had come here and riled people up? Wasn't he looking for . . . how should I put it . . . naïveté?

When he ran into the priest again the next day, he couldn't bring himself to say how things had gone.

"What?"

"The recruiting."

"Oh, you mean the auditions!"

"I saw quite a lot of people gathered at your place yesterday," Father Jean remarked, with a touch of jealousy.

"Yes," Pouka replied, "there were a lot of people."

He didn't say that, of the hundred or so, only six seemed worth his trouble. Nor did he say that he had begun the first meeting under a shower of curses from those turned away. Did anyone ever take rejection well? The war had let loose along the ragged bush tracks all the manual laborers that the administration's public work projects usually kept busy. The region was shrouded in a heavy cloak of want, with unemployment the new status quo. The people he sent back home after the audition predicted that the sky would fall on his head. And with good reason! Some stayed in the courtyard of the bar, staring like starving dogs waiting for him to make a move, and shying away as soon as he met their eyes. They probably understood that becoming a poet was an existential question, and didn't want to see their chance slip away. Or maybe they were on the verge of suicide, chased from their own courtyards by howling children. Neither Mininga nor her girls were able to shoo them away from the bar, despite all the sarcastic comments and snickers such women could come up with.

"Get out of here!" they said, then added an insult borrowed from German: "*Schouain!*"

In the end, Pouka had to give in. He accepted one man, a bearded guy with the face of a priest, who had whispered to him that he was a Hilun, a seer, a man of the word, and had made him laugh with a ridiculous proverb: "*Macabo* is eaten cooked." Pouka swore on his father's name that he'd never seen the man before. And he was sure that the name the guy had given him was fake. For who in Edéa or anywhere in the region didn't know the local family of Hilun? To win Pouka over, the man had intoned the hymn all Cameroonians know. Because he was worn out after a long day, that song was evocative enough to make Pouka's heart forget the three years he had spent far away in the city. The song awoke in him happy memories of his childhood. Happy but for that phrase, "Kill him!" He was so swayed by the fraudulent singer's performance that he realized that sometimes even a badly turned verse can comfort one's soul. Yet he didn't tell the singer with the limping but effective tongue that he'd accept him into the poetry circle right away, for there was still something about the man that turned his stomach, making it impossible to take him seriously. What was it?

When he asked him to recite the epic tale of the Bassa people, a classic of the spoken word, the man couldn't go beyond the introduction. And he recited even that with hesitation, searching for words, misplacing the stresses, and starting over when he saw people smirking. Still, these gaffes didn't disqualify him. This was a meaningless test, really, for what Pouka wanted to teach in the village was French poetry, not the thousand verses of the Bassa masterpiece. The man was older than the five others Pouka had already accepted, but his face was still childlike. An unbelievable joy filled his eyes as he struggled with the words, and it soared up and shook the treetops when Pouka told him he could stay. The man jumped from side to side, thanking the heavens and dancing through the courtyard. From what Pouka could gather, he was a school dropout who had abandoned his wife and kids back home. The others Pouka had accepted were all former students who missed being in a classroom. Some of them were older, yes, and more muscular than your average high schooler, but they were still hankering for rhymes.

"That guy is crazy," Mininga said. "So you're taking the mentally ill in that *tontine* of yours?"

She always called the little poetry circle a *tontine*. When everyone had gathered around for the first meeting, Pouka understood why schoolteachers in the city always asked their students to wear a uniform. Because there was no more extraordinary group than this one: a pandemonium of defrocked peasants, yes, a real conspiracy of thugs.

"I guess I'm the crazy one," he said out loud.

Surprisingly, that thought gave him some comfort. That's what he'd really been looking for when he came back to the village, wasn't it? Just when the whole world was going crazy. At least, that's what it seemed.

10

Let's Talk About Poetry!

For the world really had gone crazy. But not Edéa. Obviously not Edéa. Here those recruited by the word showed up at eight o'clock, setting down at the bar door the tools they would use out in the field or in the bush: a machete, an ax, a hoe, what else . . . ? They wiped their hands on their pants, or their pagne, and sat down quietly. It was still dark, the sun wasn't really up yet. For these country folk, this was not a punishment. Not for Pouka, either, who had been transformed by the missionary school but was still as punctual as a villager. At first they all sat there silently, their uncertainty palpable. In silence, each wondered just why he was there. Even if none of them had written a line, they were already caught up in the age-old tradition whereby each poet is the slave of the other, or else his mortal enemy.

"Welcome to our little poetry circle," Pouka said.

He smiled, as if he had said *"petit séminaire,"* as the Catholic high school was called. He looked over his shoulder at Mininga's girls where they stood planted, all so curious, especially the woman who sold grilled plantains, who was clearly hoping for another day full of sales. He wasted no time explaining to the chosen what a circle was, nor what this one, which he termed "little," would do. Those are obvious things that poets only talk about among themselves. If one day a poet suddenly tells you that he doesn't share Lautréamont's opinion on rhyme, don't ask who Lautréamont is, or what his opinion on rhyme was, or in what context or in what book he formulated his thoughts, or, even, why the person who spoke doesn't have his own opinion about rhyme. Pouka took all of this for granted and forged ahead, relying on the givens shamelessly and without making any excuses. It was up to his interlocutors to get used to it. He was there because of his conviction—one acquired during his stint teaching Latin and music—that he needed to lift these people up. Wasn't not explaining his references the best way to lift up his students? Ah, there he was lucky: in those days education was so esteemed in the region that you could cover up the biggest bluff imaginable in pedantic phraseology.

Yet Pouka soon realized that for all the members of his poetry circle, however small it was, their meetings were just another version of the open-air school under the village tree. What had he expected? He was reliving the horrible experience of the art critic who spends his days correcting spelling and grammar mistakes. Yet this was what had to be done to bring about the birth of Cameroonian poetry! To contribute to the evolution of his village, as colonial wisdom would have it. When he asked everyone to introduce themselves, a deathly pall fell over the bar. It wasn't like he had asked anyone to stand and recite a poem! Much less to read a poem of their own. He called on his first disciple, who spoke not in French, but in Bassa. That's when Pouka realized what had escaped him the day before, when everyone had lined up with his best French on his lips, so eager at the thought of being chosen, in the same way that we put on our Sunday best to go to mass. Yes, the truth finally dawned on Pouka: the group was comprised of illiterates. Before he could teach them to write alexandrines, he'd have to teach them the alphabet!

This would be no small task. The next day one member of the group didn't show up. Pouka had only a vague recollection of his face, but could clearly recall his buckteeth, which made his smile something to remember. Five others were there. What made Pouka smile was that the young guy who looked like a pickpocket had come back. He had just hit puberty; his name was Bilong. The day before, he hesitated to introduce himself, but after being asked several times, he had finally taken the floor with a cocky swagger. He really enjoyed talking about himself, emphasizing his heroic deeds and the legendary story of his birth, stories that were news to everyone there. He looked intently at each face around him, inscribing his words on their silence. He seemed quite taken with himself, or rather lost in the ether of his own praise, which made everyone laugh. Obviously, he was the opposite of what Pouka expected from a villager, but he didn't try to bring him down a notch, as he would have before, when he was teaching at the Catholic school. During the break Pouka listened to the Narcissus telling the rest of his tale to Mininga's girls, who burst out laughing, too. They scurried away as soon as they saw the teacher-poet approaching, whispering among themselves as the young devil rejoined the group of future poets. He made no apologies.

But you, at least, Pouka thought about Bilong, you'll stick with it, right?

Things moved quite quickly from there. On the morning of the third day, when Pouka arrived to set up, there at the bar was Bilong, ready to greet him. The young man did nothing to hide the fact that he'd spent the night there—he practically zipped up his pants in front of him. No doubt that's when Pouka realized that with this little poetry circle he'd created in Edéa, the alphabet and grammar mistakes would be the least of his worries. But it was already too late to turn back.

His three friends said he was crazy, Um Nyobè first of all. When Pouka told them about the ups and downs of his poetry class, he focused on the comic side of things—it was the only way to save face. Caught up by a laugh he just couldn't stifle, he described for them the blank face—"I mean, really, really blank"—of that peasant who didn't even know how to write his own name, but whom he hoped to teach the rules of prosopopoeia. He wasn't talking about Bilong, of course, but the guy with the beard. His friends didn't even let him finish his story.

They were all at Fritz's house again—a repeat that spoiled the routine that had them meeting up at a different place each time since they'd come back to the village. Pouka wasn't a good storyteller—that's for sure. It wasn't just that he'd drowned his own tale in his own burst of laughter; he had taken all the zing out of the story of his poetic adventure in Bassa land. It was Fritz—who else?—who called him out.

"*Prosopopoeia?*" he exclaimed, unable to cover up his own ignorance as he tripped over that dirty French word. "What is *that?*"

He leaned back in his seat, waiting for the explanation. The friends all stared at each other. "What does it matter?" the offended poet asked them. "What does it matter if I teach the peasants to drink Calvados or the basics of poetry?"

He didn't need to say anything else.

"Calvados?"

That's when Um Nyobè delivered his diagnosis: Pouka was certifiably insane.

As for Hebga, he just muttered, "You're joking." He was really stunned. And each of the friends, especially those who had never left Edéa, imagined the life of decadence . . . no, sheer depravity . . . that their childhood friend led in the city.

"What do you think?"

Hebga left the question hanging, but his eyes spelled out the remainder of his painful interrogation. He slunk back in the sofa and shook his head. He saw Pouka avoiding his gaze, and for the first time he felt clearly that his cousin was ashamed of him. Of all the guys in the group, he was the one who'd had nothing to do with the white men. He was the woodcutter. Never had he imagined that that word could be an insult. And yet, it was Pouka—Pouka!—who had made him feel its sting . . . To reclaim the attention he had lost, and erase the many misunderstandings caused by his tale, Pouka had to recount the enthusiastic response his announcement had received, the hundred people who had shown up the day before.

"Pouka never would have believed it, either," he added, puffing out his chest and looking left and right. "Ah yes, dear friends, Pouka would never have believed that the folks around here were so hungry for poetry."

"Poetry?"

"Work, you mean work."

That was Fritz, chiming in as he opened a beer.

"My dear friend," Um Nyobè began, shaking his head, "don't

you think this country has already worked too hard since the white men arrived? You've heard of forced labor? Slavery?"

His rough voice underscored the horror of each of the terms: "white men," "forced labor," "slavery."

"Unless you want to start colonization all over again . . ."

And with that, they were back at it.

"You know very well what I'm trying to do, Um," Pouka began.

Um Nyobè smiled. Pouka only called him that when he was irritated by him. He wanted to make clear how aggravated he was.

"No, my brother," Um Nyobè replied without losing his smile, "don't tell me that you, too, are talking about the *war effort*."

He said "war effort" in French. He had the habit of smiling when he unleashed his harshest criticisms. Happily, his sarcasm was broken by the children who came running and shouting through the living room, bumping into chairs, almost knocking over the bottles. Immediately Fritz became the father he was, giving orders here, cajoling over there, scolding.

"You shouldn't play in the living room," he shouted, and then, "Bikaï!"

His wife didn't respond immediately. He got up and went looking for her in the back of the house.

"Bikaï!" his voice echoed again.

Um Nyobè was amused to see his friend caught in the tentacles of family; his face burst into a broad, toothy grin. He knew something about all that. He thought of his own wife, Martha, and then suddenly, again, of the war. Once back in Yaoundé, he'd be caught up again in that strange war. His time in the village had been a peaceful break, but he couldn't keep on burying his uncle forever. His bags were already packed and standing there in a corner of the room. This gathering was a farewell, even if it didn't really feel like one. Except, perhaps, in the eyes of Ngo Bikaï, Fritz's wife, who quickly popped in and out. Out of habit, they all called her by her maiden name, although she was now over twenty years old and looked like a true matron: rounded features and a calm authority that quickly brought the children to order. It was only when her back was turned that the children had invaded the living room, bringing their loud voices and games with them, and her husband pointed that out, of course.

"But what were you saying?" Fritz asked, turning back to his friends.

Um Nyobè was still a bit thunderstruck, as if the noisiest of family scenes couldn't have kept him from doing something stupid. But it was almost time for him to leave.

"I have to go."

It was true. The news from Yaoundé was rather alarming. The city was preparing for its most unpredictable Fourteenth of July celebration since the French had occupied Cameroon, that is to say, since 1915. It was the sort of event that could make your head spin. And how! History is our one true mistress.

11

The Problematic Little Poetry Circle

Let's get back to the problematic little poetry circle. Pouka couldn't stop a certain familiarity from developing among the members of his group and Mininga's girls. Despite the years he'd spent at the missionary school, he knew that whole chapters of French poetry—and not the least among them—had been written in bordellos. Proximity with vice is the gateway to transcendence, that much he knew. And besides, the little poetry circle, what was it if not a gathering of bohemians? Of course, he had promised Father Jean he wouldn't read any Communist poets, but what about the depraved ones? Baudelaire, Rimbaud, and even that rascal Verlaine, known as the "prince of poets"—was there any way to do without them? And what about that devil Villon, whose poems were really enticing ballads about fornication? Now, dear reader, you must be thinking, My God, Pouka, why are you burying your head in that weighty tome, the history of French poetry by Lagarde and Michard (the fourth edition, published in 1936) that you use as a prop, when you could be losing your head in the little burning bush of the mistress of the house!

I know, that's not quite how you would put it: "burning bush"—what kind of metaphor is that? Besides, Pouka hadn't yet started calling Mininga "La Seigneuriale"—"Her Ladyship"—but would that have bothered her? He showed up that morning and the words that the women of the place exchanged didn't help open his eyes!

"Oh, shush, you stupid fool, you *imbouc*," someone said. "Your lake is so full in the morning that whales are swimming in it."

"Whales?"

"You mean sharks!"

He had no idea that these exchanges were volleys of bullets flying through the morning air. Had Pouka forgotten that duels, the real ones, were held in the morning, when the mist was still rising from the grassy paths? We know that when it comes to this sort of thing, it's just a question of time—the truth will out. The time was approaching, coming over the green mountains, rousing everything that slept, hurrying people along, knocking on doors still shut: knock, knock, knock! Mininga went to open the door, surprised since people usually didn't knock at the bar, but just let themselves in. Pouka heard women's voices outside, some whispers, some shouts, but he didn't pay much attention. Knock, knock, knock! He paused, but still . . . Then Mininga came back in the bar, tiptoeing toward him. What she whispered in his ear lit up his face and left his mouth agape; then he asked the question that everyone in the little circle heard.

"My mother?"

What on earth is she coming to do here in this bar? That is certainly the question that flashed through his mind as he rushed out into the courtyard where our Sita was waiting for him. Pouka should have slowed down a little, taken a moment to think, strategize, come up with a plan. For when he opened the door, there were four women waiting for him. Hebga's mother was standing in front, wearing her fighting pagne, her head swathed in her angry scarf, apparently in no hurry to head off to the market as she usually did. Behind her were three women who looked worried, somber even, you could say. He recognized Ngo Bikaï, Fritz's wife. But it was our Sita who spoke first.

"Is Bilong here?"

You can tease history as much as you want, sooner or later it'll come knocking at your door. Pouka was surprised, but he ought not to have been.

"Is Bilong here?"

"Bilong?"

"He hasn't come home for three weeks."

And Bilong's mother added her laments to this scene, which was growing more startling by the minute, as the women behind her glared reproachfully.

"Just what are you doing with my son?" demanded one woman, her head wrapped in an orange floral scarf.

"Three weeks?"

Back in the bar, Pouka's eyes met Bilong's calm face, surrounded by the knowing smiles of everyone else there. He also saw the face of one of Mininga's girls peering out from the shadows and realized he was the last to know.

"Three weeks?"

"Yes . . . longer, even."

"Let me explain, maestro."

Everyone there called him "maestro." That was the first rule he had set, following Mallarmé's lead. He was the one giving the orders, strutting around like a giant surrounded by all his little colts. But that morning, faced with those four women, his usually imperious tone cracked. Bilong looked crushed, although it wasn't clear he thought he was at fault.

"You owe your mother an explanation."

Pouka should have demanded that he do more than that, for who else in Bassa land ever would have had a boy explain himself as punishment? Either he was the maestro, or he wasn't.

"Mama, I'm living with a woman." That's what Bilong said to his mother. It left her speechless.

What could Pouka have said after such an admission? The little devil didn't even have the decency to keep quiet while his mother and everyone else erupted in surprise.

"You don't need to worry about me," he went on, showing the muscles of his arms, his body. "Look, I'm well fed. She makes me breakfast every morning. She makes the most delicious meals for me. I'm eating three times a day—morning, noon, and night. And then at night she—"

"Shut up right there," our Sita cut in, "you little shit!"

Our Sita was so scandalized that she said "little shit" in French. But the boy's insolent speech couldn't be derailed that easily; he had clearly run through it several times in his head so he could deliver it with confidence now, knowing it would set off a bomb.

"Okay," Bilong went on, trying to ignore the reactions of the women, including his mother, to his speech. "We are living together *like man and wife*, and of course we'll soon be married, if that's what you're worried about. Nguet is *the woman of my life*."

Nguet, the barmaid.

"'The woman of my life'?" screamed Ngo Bikaï, clapping her hands. "'The woman of my life'!"

"Do you hear this?" Our Sita called on all the women as witnesses. "*Like husband and wife*. Just what has gotten into this boy?"

"'Like husband and wife,'" another woman repeated.

"The gentleman is rolling out his best French!" his mother added. "The gentleman is speaking like a white man!" She imitated her son's voice: "*The woman of my life!*"

"He says that to his mother!"

"A real piece of work, hmm," underscored Ngo Bikaï.

The boy started to say something, perhaps to take back that phrase "the woman of my life." But mostly because Ngo Bikaï was his older sister and her words covered him in shame.

"Just shut up, Bilong," Pouka cut in. "Don't you see you're making your mama suffer?"

"You want to kill our mother, is that it?" Ngo Bikaï added.

His sister's suffering came out cloaked in sarcasm.

"Just tell me, you little know-it-all, do you know what she does for a living, that *nyama nyama* of yours?" his mother asked.

Here Ngo Bikaï backed up her mother's words with her own accusations.

"Your *mamy nyanga*?"

Bilong didn't say another word, for he hadn't imagined he'd have to face up to the tyrannical power of a group of women, to his sister's wide mouth, or answer for his girlfriend's profession, for that matter. Or rather, yes, he had, but deep down he just really didn't give a shit about Nguet's profession.

"She's a whore," Ngo Bikaï declared, and then, as if her brother didn't understand, she clarified, "a prostitute," adding "a *wolowolos*."

"I am not a *wolowolos*." The words came from the back of the crowd.

"So what are you, then?" Ngo Bikaï spat back.

Nguet wanted to answer. Nguet wanted to make her stand. Nguet wanted to defend her honor before those four women from

the village. Nguet wanted to do just what all those women were waiting for: start the fight.

"Just shut your trap, Nguet!"

That's when Mininga stepped in, speaking in French. It was the
best advice she could give. Fortunately, Nguet stayed out of sight.
But Bilong's mother would have liked to know which girl, yes, which
girl it was who had stolen her boy, as she put it. She would have liked
to see her, but most of all, she really wanted to do lots of little violent things to her, to that girl, things she didn't have the words to
name.

"*Mouf,* aren't you ashamed?" she asked, speaking to Nguet, although she still couldn't see her. "He's just a child, only sixteen!"

"I'm not a child!"

Bilong took offense at that. But what he hadn't yet understood,
the women were ready to explain to him.

"You louse!"

"*Chiendent!*" someone exclaimed in French.

"Individual!"

"Runt!"

No one was asking Bilong what he was, they just told him. Yet,
believe me, what he wanted most was to tell everyone what he was—
not just a grown young man, but a poet. He would have said it with
a cocky tilt of his nose, a gesture he had picked up from Pouka, for
a poet's arrogance is a lesson quickly learned. Ah, but not even his
maestro Pouka would have laughed had he said such nonsense (and
I'm saying "nonsense" euphemistically). No, he'd have given him a
slap that would have made the women cheer: "Finally!" "You teach
him!" "Show him!" "Thank you!" But here's what really happened:
the peasant woman no longer recognized her child.

"*You* are the one who's come here to ruin our children," she spat
out, pointing at Pouka. "I am going to the *police!*"

Pouka raised his hands in a show of innocence. Standing behind
his teacher, Bilong shrugged: he knew his father wouldn't complain;
he'd be happy that his youngest was going through that masculine
rite of passage. But his comrades had another idea. The members of
the little poetry circle had all snuck out during this scene. Each in
his own way was trying to put out this early morning fire that was

threatening to spread through the bush. Because no one wanted to see the tirailleurs make an appearance. Did anyone not know how violent they were? The Hilun in particular made a real show of diplomacy, trying to quell the women's rage with flattery, reciting a whole litany of words of gratitude.

"Ah, kids these days," he said.

Pouka realized that in a colony poetry cannot be innocent, but did they need all this brouhaha to make the point? He would have preferred to read about the morning's surprising twists and turns in the alexandrine verses of a poem—let's say "Prelude to the Afternoon of a Runt"—but as it happened, he'd been confronted by a mother's teary face, a furious Sita, and two agitated women. On top of that, there were the faces of the other scandalized women in the back of the bar—because it seemed Mininga was the only one to keep her calm amid the chaos. The poet recalled the words of Um Nyobè: "You are crazy, my dear friend!" What Mininga couldn't swallow—and Pouka understood this well—was that anyone would call her establishment a . . . a whorehouse. A cathouse. A den of iniquity. A *baisodrome.* That, no, she'd never tolerate that, because if it was a *baisodrome*, then poets wouldn't come here, would they? Let's set that aside, shall we, for clearly she didn't know anything about those French renegades, the *poètes maudits.*

12

A Black Man's Roll of the Dice
Can Abolish History's Chances

Let's move on, for obviously there are more important things to this bit of history than a runt losing his virginity. Pouka was very touched by his group's esprit de corps. As a result, he gave each of them a nickname drawn from the Parisian poetry circle that had inspired him. Since he really enjoyed being the eccentric of the group, he kept the name of Nerval for himself. As for his fake bard Aloga, who had defended him against the Furies, he dubbed him his Théophile Gautier. The boy with the cat-like head who never spoke and who seemed to have been torn straight from the depths of the jungle was the group's Philothée O'Neddy, and two others, who still hadn't done anything to distinguish themselves even after two full months of intensive sessions, became Augustus MacKeat and Xavier Forneret. Bilong was called Charles Lassailly. These names meant nothing to the boy—no more than his mother's words. He didn't even ask just who Charles Lassailly was. Pouka didn't make the members of the circle take any oath, but it was almost as if he had: their new names were proof they belonged to a brotherhood of eccentrics. As for Mininga, who was truly amused by the proceedings, she became La Seigneuriale, a name that certainly did not displease her. Far from it, far from it. There was nothing better than flattery to revive the spirits of this woman who, only minutes before, had been fuming about the uttering of the word "prostitute."

But there was another whose name change led to unexpected

consequences in Cameroon: Philippe François Marie, comte de Hautecloque, that noble who one day decided he'd henceforth be called François Leclerc, a name so common it could have been found in any phone book in Picardy, his native region. He had already biked across occupied France disguised as a monk, then swum the English Channel, and, once in London, shaken the hand of General de Gaulle, who made him his right-hand man. This time the limping officer and his friends had arrived in Douala in a pirogue, but his cane was not just a joke, and much less so his broken foot. Still, luck was with him; he arrived on the shores of the Wouri River and on the streets of Douala just when the troops led by Captain Louis Dio—let's inscribe that name, lest he be forgotten—found themselves on a forced vacation; they'd crossed the whole length of Cameroon only to realize that France was done for. Some traces of the celebration of the Fourteenth of July, 1940, were still hanging in the trees, sad symbols of the republic's collapse: colored light bulbs left dangling on the walls, even if no one remembered that there had been a ball.

Ah yes, the war was full of uncertainties, including the one that had forced Captain Dio's tirailleurs to hunker down for winter in Douala, where they'd been for the past month without getting any clear orders from Faya-Largeau, their command post in Chad. Life in the territory had grown elastic—such a strange war!—but Captain Dio was used to the flexibility of the colonies; he had twelve years in Africa under his belt. Still, when a telegram asked him to put himself and his men at the service of a squadron leader named Leclerc, he jumped.

Just who is this Leclerc? he wondered.

He had never met him, not in the whorehouses of Douala or in the barracks, where nobody else seemed to have heard of him, either. Dio hadn't yet realized that he had been put under the orders of a soldier of the same rank as himself. Later, when he found out, he was sitting in the trenches in Tibesti, Italian bullets whistling overhead, an old machine gun from the Great War in his hands. Then he really felt like laughing, especially since the soldier in question had a limp, to boot.

The telegram that he had received and that put him under Leclerc's orders was, first and foremost, the solution to a problem that a soldier like Captain Dio could never understand, although it was in fact quite straightforward. For Dio's boss, Félix Éboué, the governor of Chad, it was impossible to both be black and support Vichy. It was one or the other, never both. He had no choice about being black, but as for supporting Vichy . . . Éboué's crisis of conscience had immediate consequences, for it placed under General de Gaulle's orders the military base of Faya-Largeau, one of the five bases that girded French Africa, and one of the most important militarily, because it was located at its center and heart. Éboué's decision also had global consequences, for it opened up an African front against one of the Axis forces, Italy. If you want to talk about a roll of the dice abolishing history's chances, this really was one.

Éboué had written the letter announcing that he had rallied to the Resistance by hand, on the back of the racist letter he had received the day before from the Italian authorities in Libya, with which Chad shared its northern border. That letter that was addressed—no joke—"*To His Excellence É—Boué*" (a spelling that, in French, turned his name into mud). The immediate result of that racist taunt was that the first squadron of the Free French forces was comprised of black soldiers, under the direction of a black man. Yes, because the racists from Berlin, Paris, and Rome who sought to dominate the world had written one letter too many. *Your Excellency*, the perfidious letter began—and I would like to quote it in its entirety:

I cannot fathom what effect it must have had on you, a Negro—that is to say, not belonging to a dominant race—to have been named governor of the French colony of Lake Chad. I do not know if you have or have not expressed your colored jubilation with one of those beautiful dances, so popular in your homeland, performed with bare feet and exposed buttocks, or if you have celebrated the happy event with a new tattoo (another charming custom that sailors have learned on your shores) of a beautiful "equality, fraternity, and liberty" scrawled from your sternum to your belly button. But I expect you drank champagne as are wont to do . . . those you administer, even as they swath themselves in the vainglory of the battle waged at Mentana, finding succor in the broad and sagging bosom of the Third Republic between Montmartre and the Eiffel Tower. This revenge by your snub-nosed race for the

*traditional tyranny of whites must have seemed to you worthy of
an epic. And you will have certainly imagined your future life as
a military officer, wearing high boots and a top hat, your shirt
untucked. The celebrations held upon your arrival—the white
faces of your new subjects bowed in a sign of democratic respect, the
grace of their ladies, tinged by cupidity and gloom—will no doubt
appeal to your simple and primitive soul. But, please, do not allow
yourself to succumb to nostalgia for your native tom-toms . . .*

That's where I stop! I must stop! The future was still trying to
sort out its vocabulary, but no black man, whether a colonial governor or a tirailleur, a rascal or anyone else, could ever imagine a future
where they'd read such shit. For the Antillean governor of Chad, that
letter was proof that the dice had been rolled.

Meanwhile, in Edéa, the future was appearing to the Old Man in
grandiose visions that no one wanted to listen to anymore. Because,
really, you shouldn't push things. M'bangue had for the fifth time in
a row dreamed of Hitler. There are those—and they were many—
who had already closed their ears to the phrase he kept on repeating: "he committed suicide." They didn't even have the patience to
hear him describe Berlin, as he promised to do. Time, and especially
age, must have softened his head, they said. His sporadic visions of
the apocalypse were the only things that lit up his eyes, and that
really did nothing to convince the skeptical. Some interpreted his
dreams as foretelling France's defeat, because, between us, this time
France couldn't count on the Americans to save her, as the whispered
voices put it. Bassa land had much to hold against Germany, but even
more against France. In reality, the heart of this forest had never belonged to Paris. Upon hearing news of the French defeat, there were
those in Edéa who danced in the street. The tirailleurs had smashed
a few teeth, but hadn't been able to silence the crowd. Here the bel-
ligerents' worldwide conflict had the feel of a boxing match that divided living rooms, with members of the same family supporting
opposite sides. Some, mainly the older ones, remembered the first
round of the fight that had taken place in their courtyards back in
1915. A family legend: Fritz, for example, still wrote Cameroon with
a *K*, German-style: Kamerun. M'bangue's dreams had deep, historic
roots, but everyone around knew who was the loopy boxer.

13

The Man of Letters

Just to say that, when all was said and done, the group that had been meeting every morning for the past two months in Mininga's Bar stood out like a sore thumb. Take a moment to imagine the scene: France has fallen and French Equatorial Africa has rallied to the Resistance and General de Gaulle; M'bangue keeps dreaming of Hitler. Meanwhile, in the Bassa forest, six fellows are spending these dark days reading French poetry. They had to do it. Obviously, stranger things were happening: France was discovering the daily routines of collaboration, for example. Pouka smiled as he recalled his promise to Father Jean, that he wouldn't start some sort of commune. He thought about Louis Auguste Blanqui and all the other madmen of French history, and recognized that he himself lacked the courage for that sort of dream. Nor did he share Rabelais's goal of founding a utopian Abbey of Thélème. It was hard enough for him to know that the villagers made expressions of polite surprise or sarcasm behind his back; when he'd arrived, they'd seen him as a civil servant rather than a writer, and couldn't understand why every morning he headed over to a disreputable bar run by a *wolowolos*.

"You say he's a writer?"

Try explaining to those villagers that he was a visionary, and their conclusion would be simple:

"It's the French who did that to him."

In truth, Pouka's doubts only really caught up to him the day he arrived and found the bar empty. Mininga, her serving girls, and the three regulars were the only ones there. Suddenly aware of the seductive powers of those stylish women, he sat down on a crate and waited, gazing out at the thousand trees that revealed nothing more than their trunks, dappled with red and black, and at the village that gazed back at him with amusement. Women passed by. One elbowed her companion and then waved at Pouka as she whispered to the woman, who in turn stared at Pouka, greeting him with a broad smile and respectful nod. Men hurrying by returned his hello automatically, then gave a start and waved again enthusiastically, surprised to see him there. They kept asking how things were in the city, how life was for him in Yaoundé, trying, it seemed, to confirm what they already knew. Some of the ruder ones were too surprised by the sight of Pouka there in front of Mininga's Bar to do anything more than stammer out the same stupid phrase:

"Oh, I didn't recognize you, my son!"

With the slew of scandalized exclamations he'd heard from our Sita and her women still ringing in his ears, Pouka discovered the face of small-town hypocrisy.

"Yes, you did see that," he heard as well, "that's M'bangue's son."

"*Wandafoot!*"

Thinking he was seeing things, the man turned back to take another look.

"Good day, my son," he said, with a great show of respect, a broad smile plastered on his face.

Pouka responded to his greeting with a bow of his head.

"Good day, father."

What imbeciles! he thought. His former disdain for villagers came rushing back. He really thought he had tamped down the women's anger over the to-do with Bilong. That morning, his solitude showed that he'd clearly failed. Pouka watched the people passing by and realized the peasant women had gotten the better of him. He knew them all too well, oh yes, he was their son, after all. He knew the details of their treachery. He heard what those men whispered to each other: not that he had fallen, but that he'd surely been chased out of the city, and that even his father was losing his mind over it. That M'bangue, to make matters worse, had gone half blind. That he was possessed by witchcraft—that was why he kept dreaming about Hitler! "That's the Old Man's son? You're joking!"

"He's the one who wanted to *corrupt* Bilong?"

Happily, the sainted plum took it upon itself to punish these troublemakers, for the woman who'd just spoken slipped on a pit—tossed there by the grilled plantain vendor—that she'd been too distracted to notice. The woman kept on chattering, despite the impossibly heavy load she carried. Her friend was just barely able to keep her from falling, but the basin full of fruit that she'd been carrying went flying out all over the ground, much to the amusement of everyone there. Pouka rushed over to help her gather up her mangoes and oranges. Embarrassed, the woman stammered, "Pardon me, papa, pardon me, papa."

When he escaped from the confusion, the writer found Philothée sitting in his chair and trembling. The boy was out of breath. He looked like he'd been running, or that he'd just gotten out of a brawl. Pouka hadn't seen him come out of the forest.

"You are late," he began dryly, before switching quickly to the fatherly tone he'd adopted since his humiliating confrontation with our Sita. "What's wrong?"

Philothée didn't answer.

"Where is everyone?" he asked, beginning to worry.

Philothée was clearly the last person he expected to see that morning. He'd realized long before that he'd made a mistake when he'd let this guy join the little circle. Was it pure stupidity that made his eyes go blank every time he was asked a question? Pouka wouldn't have been surprised if one day he just stopped coming. And now, on this morning of surprises, he was the only one to show up! Couldn't have been more ironic. Thanks to this unexpected turn of events, he sidled over to the boy and realized that, as well as being out of breath, Philothée was struggling to control a stutter that made his eyes cloud over, made him weigh each syllable, massaging it, cajoling it, shaping ever so carefully in the trembling fullness of his mouth the word he wanted to say.

Pouka didn't recall him stuttering like that when he'd interviewed him on the first day, or in any of the sessions since, but on this day he was too happy that at least this one member of the group had shown up to press the point. Instead, he changed the topic.

Or rather, came back to it.

"Where is everyone?" he asked again.

Philothée lined up all the vowels and consonants of the word he wanted to say, stared blankly around, as if begging the recalcitrant syllables to let themselves be spoken.

"In the ff . . . ff . . ." Pause. "Fields."

It was August, plum season. How could Pouka have forgotten? That morning his father's house had emptied out, too, when everyone headed to the fields. He'd gotten up at seven o'clock—that is to say, they'd let him sleep in; they were obviously used to his city ways. Still, he was surprised none of the members of the little circle had mentioned the day before that they wouldn't be there. Yet Philothée's beaming face expressed an even greater certainty.

"And you," he asked, "aren't you going to the fields?"

Pouka immediately regretted the question, for Philothée began to stutter beseechingly.

"Read," he said. And Pouka understood he had made a choice, even if he didn't have the words in him to lay out the whole story.

He chose poetry, Pouka repeated to himself, although he wasn't quite certain this was what the boy had wanted to say. Still, he didn't forget what Philothée had shown him with just one or two words: that the alphabet can take possession of a soul. That letters are inscribed deep in a body's flesh. That words find their way out in bursts. That every sentence is a prayer. Which means that each poem is a hymn. That day he led the class with just one member, the one who had to wrestle the hardest with the letters of the alphabet that were buried in his gut. But the struggle he saw in Philothée's eyes each time he tried to say a word or a phrase helped him to devise the group's motto: "Welcome to all men of letters!"

It was a sincere invitation addressed to all who weren't there that day. Pouka hadn't yet begun to see the alphabet as the real matrix of poetry, but he would soon enough. What he knew was that he'd just discovered the first lettered man of his utopia: Philothée.

"Are you trying to chase away all my customers?" Mininga asked when he told her about his discovery that day.

She was right. Still, the idea that he was building his literate society in a bar made him smile.

"The bordello of letters," he murmured to himself, looking

silently in turn at the woman, her serving girls, and the grilled plantain vendor. "That is poetry."

"What's that, now, my dear?" Mininga asked.

"Give us two beers," he shot back.

He was happy to seal the pact that now joined him with his very first lettered man. And then he tossed a coin to the woman selling grilled plantains, who was looking at him like a hungry dog.

"Two plantains and four plums."

He stared out into the flame trees and the forest beyond.

Edéa's forest.

14

The Daydreams of a Solitary Woodcutter

Which brings us back to the forest . . . Hebga hadn't expected Pouka to turn back into the personal troubadour he'd been as a child. He'd given it some thought, smiling because his little brother had become a writer, but was then distracted by the women's voices filtering through the trees. He stopped his exercises and looked in the direction of the noises. Among the dozen or so women who were walking in a line through the bush, he recognized his mother, our Sita, at the head, followed by Ngo Bikaï. It was August, the time of the annual harvest festivals. "I'll see you later, ladies," he said apologetically. He smiled again at the thought of how close Fritz's wife was to his mother. Those two don't need me at all, he thought. Really, they were a real couple, a "husband-and-wife" pair, he told himself with a chuckle. He greeted the women politely. All of them jumped when they saw him in the bushes, but replied happily. When one woman made a face, he realized she must have thought he was taking a shit. He smiled.

So Ngo Bikaï is our Sita's right-hand woman, huh? he wondered as they disappeared in the distance, their voices no more than an echo.

He thought that type of relationship was more common among men, but still it didn't surprise him. To his mind, his mother was a man, and she always had been, even when his father was alive. He smiled again at the thought that our Sita needed a right arm, since he'd always thought what she needed was a pair of trousers. His mind turned back to Pouka, maybe because he was still impressed by the neatly pressed trousers his cousin had worn since his return. How did he manage to avoid all the dust? He could still see him as a little boy, hitting the ground with his right hand each time he, Hebga, completed a push-up, which was how the boy had learned to count. He saw him singing songs he made up, and thought of what he was now doing each morning, surrounded by his pupils in Mininga's Bar, teaching poetry to the peasants. Time passes quickly, Hebga had to admit. Yes, Pouka had been acting quite strangely lately. His return to the village had everyone scratching their head.

Ah, he was really a poet!

During his training sessions, Hebga gave free rein to his thoughts: Was there anything that didn't cross his mind? More to the point, was there anything he didn't see? The forest is truth's sanctuary. He would happen upon men crouching in the bushes, relieving themselves, and in typically Cameroonian fashion, they'd stand up to tell him off. "Hey, what are you looking at? *Imbouc!*" Sometimes he stumbled upon couples making love, and only the girl would cover her face. As for the man, ah! The other day, for example, he had seen Nguet by the river with her new red-hot lover. The two grabbed at each other hungrily, thinking they were all alone. Hebga had smiled because he wasn't at all interested in our Nguet. He hoped they'd be happy, very happy, although that didn't stop him from recalling the shape of her body, especially her heavy breasts, her hips "so round it seemed she was carrying weapons on both sides," and then her buttocks. He stopped daydreaming about Nguet, mostly because the story he'd heard about her current rhythm man amused him so— who hadn't heard that story? The guy's answer made him laugh, and he lodged his ax deep in the trunk of a tree: "Mama, I'm living with a *wolowolos.*" Hebga repeated the phrase out loud right there in the middle of the forest. For him, Nguet was just a *wolowolos.*

When the men told and retold that story, each added his own little bit. One said, "Mama, I'm living with a *mamy nyanga,*" while for another it was a *mbrakata*—each had their reasons. They all found Bilong's phrase equally entertaining, for, in the end, it came down to: "Mama, I'm living with a whore." The things kids say these days, am I right? The word "whore" had spread all over along with the story of the boy whom some called Bilong while others opted for Charles. All the men went wild over his carefully polished phrase. It took something to say a sentence like that "to his own mama," and Hebga added, in front of our very own Sita, "for God's sake."

"That little guy is something else," people said, and Hebga thought just the same thing.

"Just how old is he?"

"Ten years old," some said.

"You're lying!"

"Just ten and he's already screwing, oh, daddy."

All the men agreed he was about "thirteen, fourteen," admitting that it was pretty precocious to be using his *bangala* "already at that age for something other than peeing," even if they thought it wasn't too early for a "good Bassa man." Hebga had seen the guy. He knew he wasn't just a little kid. Mostly, he knew Nguet. Her scent, he could have picked it out in a field of flowers. Nguet, he had screwed her several times, once she'd even sucked on his thing. Just thinking about it gave him a hard-on. He stopped in the middle of his exercises—he was stretching and crossing his arms in front of him while marching in place, like a tirailleur. He watched his loincloth rising slowly, as if buoyed up by the thought of Nguet's body, which he saw bit by bit, from her bare feet to her hips, her tummy and belly button, her breasts and the tattoos on her chest, her hair gathered into three braids, thick like goat's horns, with cowrie shells at the end, and then her eyes—oh, her eyes!—her cat-like eyes that stared at him while she was doing it, doing . . . doing what? He decided he couldn't keep going with his exercises given the circumstances. He just couldn't concentrate, yes, that's what he told himself, so he decided to stop. He wanted to think about something else.

The woods can tear your soul apart. Their scent is intoxicating and the solitude leads you into the wildest, most disorienting daydreams. Right then he was dreaming of Nguet sitting in a clearing, surrounded by the other girls from the bar and his friends—Um Nyobè, Fritz, and some others he couldn't identify. It was just like that day when he had actually come upon Mininga, dressed in her Sunday best, jewels displayed on her breast, sitting there with her girls in the bush: "We're having lunch," she said with a smile, passing plates here and there. "Will you join us, my dear?"

Hebga had already completed his exercise routine for the day. So he pulled his ax out of the tree trunk. Right then he heard a piercing scream in the distance. And then women crying. He shuddered, thinking of the women who'd gone by just a bit before. He heard the scream again. No need to say that his erection disappeared as soon as he thought of his mother. When the third scream came, he was already tearing through the bush with his ax. He no longer felt his feet or his hands, not the branches that tore into his body or the tree leaves that slapped him. The women's cries had become sobs, scattered but distinct.

"Sita!" said one voice.

"Sita-o!"

Hebga's heart was beating like crazy.

"Help!"

Soon a woman came toward him, holding her breasts as she ran. He stopped her, grabbed her by the shoulders, and looked deeply into her eyes, which reflected only fear.

"H . . . h . . . help!" she stuttered.

Her whole body was trembling.

"H . . . h . . . help!" she repeated, as if possessed. "Help!"

"What's going on?" Hebga demanded. "Tell me!"

"Help!"

Hebga didn't wait to hear anything else. Holding his ax aloft, he rushed into the bushes. He jumped over farming tools that were scattered in the grass. He didn't even see the blood spilled across the path. He was wholly focused on the desperate voices of the women around him. And most of all, of that one cry:

"Sita-o!"

All the women were pointing toward the bushes. He dived in, unable to think.

"Sita-o!"

"Sita-o!" said the women with one voice.

"Sita!"

"Sita-o!"

"Sita-o!"

Hebga had lost all feeling in his body. He was an animal, a lion, an eagle . . . what else? His mother's name echoing through the bush had taken hold of his spirit, his body, his feet, his hands. He had recognized her voice, her voice calling him: "Hebga, help me!" That frantic cry for help, he would hear it for the rest of his life, the unending sob that would wrest him from sleep in the middle of the night—his childlike call, "Mama!" making his friends laugh—and leave him trembling and covered in sweat. He burst into a clearing, searching for the source of the cries, its hiding spot. He looked around, all around, but the cries had stopped. There on the ground he saw a splash of blood, and then an arm. Yes, an arm.

"Mama!" he screamed.

There was no answer.

"Mama!"

The forest fell into a conspiratorial, criminal silence. The trees were spinning overhead. The light shattered them into a thousand shards. The wind, the wind alone stirred the branches. The birds that usually filled them with their lively songs had all fallen silent.

"Mama!" cried Hebga, and he heard a voice.

A voice saying, "My son!"

He rushed toward it and found himself in front of Ngo Bikaï. She was standing there, naked, in the middle of the bush, her body lacerated and covered with blood. With her arms held like an upside-down cross over her chest, she clasped her breasts and shook her head from left to right, right to left. When she noticed him, she suddenly lost the balance that had held her upright till then. She didn't even hear the question posed by his frantic gestures. Slowly, quietly, she collapsed into his arms. Ah, how Hebga would have preferred that this was all a dream!

"Mama!" he screamed, but there was no one to answer his cry.

In the depth of the forest, he heard a groan.

15

One Dream Too Many

"Show your face!" he shouted, stepping into an empty clearing, "show your face, *schouain!*"

He ran right and left, slashing at grass, branches, and trees with huge swings of his ax.

"Son of a cockroach! Scoundrel!"

Silence was his only answer.

"Show your face!"

The invisible opponent was hidden in the infinite expanse of bushes. It drove Hebga mad.

"If you have any courage, show your face!"

He held the ax out at eye level, challenging the sky, the trees, the spirits, everything all around.

"Come show me what you're made of!"

That wasn't all.

"If you are a man!"

Ah, but that wasn't enough.

"If you have any balls!"

Silence alone responded. He swung his ax all around in big strokes. He hit and hit. He hit and cursed. He cursed and hit. Soon he had created a clearing, a gigantic clearing the size of a ring set for the match of the century. The last bush he struck down revealed the nightmare that he, in his darkest despair, had refused to imagine: a foot, which was connected to a leg, and then the splayed body of his mother. He jumped back, then quickly gained control of himself and fell down on his knees. Wracked as much by nausea as horror, he crawled toward what had been spread out there: our Sita had been cut to pieces by her invisible opponent and left there. One leg was missing, her belly slashed open, her intestines spilling out on the grass. Her arm had been torn from her shoulder. Only her face was untouched.

She almost appeared to be living, to be smiling still.

"Mama!" cried the son.

He covered her body with his own, then got up and shook her head, before realizing he was only breaking her apart even more.

"Mama!" he cried again. "Mama!"

He had thrown his ax, now so useless, down on the ground. Never had he felt so completely possessed by the cry—his cry—that shook the trees. He gathered up his mother in his arms, hugged her tight to his chest. His eyes looked all around, scanning the trees, the sky, the universe, asking if this forest had been abandoned by God. But all he saw was the empty void of the clearing he had created with his ax, the silence of the trees that watched him, and soon the cries of the women who burst through the bushes.

"Sita!"

"Sita-o!"

"The coward!" he roared.

He clasped his mother even more tightly in his arms.

"Mama!"

But his mother didn't answer him.

"The coward!"

This time Hebga had been beaten in a battle he hadn't even waged. He kissed his mother and whispered in her ear, "The coward!" Silence alone set the rhythm of his gestures. "The coward!" He repeated the word as he crossed back through the forest, bearing Sita's body. He believed she was still alive, because her face, even in its silence, remained as it had been. The women ran after him, their voices rousing the bush, the villages, the whole region, letting them know about the drama that had played out in the heart of the forest.

"The coward!" Hebga said. "The coward!"

"Sita-o!" called the women.

"*Feigling!*" he repeated, now in German.

"Sita-o!"

"Woyo-o!"

"Woyo-o!"

Holding his mother in his arms, Hebga crossed through the market leading the whole town behind him. At Mininga's Bar, he tore Philothée away from the courtyard, where he was eating plantains and drinking beer, even at that early hour of the morning, and of course Pouka, who for once was speechless. Then he went to Father Jean's church, as the catechumens filed out noisily. A hundred, no, a thousand arms reached out to help carry our Sita. The whole population of Edéa rushed headlong into its distress—woyo-o!—feeding on the son's strength—but why did he need to be strong?—and giving voice to the forest's great sob. Everyone there wanted to believe, as did her son, that our Sita was still alive. Everyone wanted to see her stamping her feet. Wanted her restored to the height of her virile grandeur, so familiar to all. No one could think of anything but "coward" to call out whoever had done this—a coward who had destroyed such a majestic woman! He had attacked from behind, whoever it was who had cut her down—there's no other way it could have happened. He had caught her off guard, the coward, because this woman—who led all the other women in the town, who was the queen of the marketplace, who had gotten a woodcutter to adapt to her rhythm, who had made her son sit down when he was told and a poet fall silent—only a snake could have cut through the spine of this woman.

"A snake?"

"It was the panther!" M'bangue declared when Hebga laid down his mother's body in his courtyard. "Nearby, but invisible!"

Everyone looked at each other.

"Woyo-o!"

"Just who is this panther?"

The question spread through the crowd. Pouka would later ask his father the same question several more times, once the cry of the forest had been transformed into tears and a funeral procession. But M'bangue would always reply that the two fighters of the century had taken their duel with them into the far-off distance.

"Just what *man* could have dared?" people wondered. "What man did this?"

Pouka realized quite suddenly how brutal Edéa actually was. He knew that this panther wasn't, could not be, an animal. No, an animal wouldn't have done this. It was a man—he stressed the word. Yet M'bangue wouldn't answer. That's because the night before, instead of dreaming of that evil *man*, of that sorcercer—instead of warning his own sister—Edéa's most respected seer had again dreamed of Hitler's suicide. He didn't need Pouka to tell him that his Hitlerian dreams had crossed a line. This was the sixth time— one time too many.

16

Big Things Happen to the Little Guys

Death is fundamentally unjust. The loss of one's mother is no trivial matter. Still, the chaos unleashed in Edéa when our Sita's cadaver was carried through the town's courtyards dissipated quite quickly as history marched on. Not long after the burial of the Mother of the Market, the village was shaken up by the noise of a British plane—a Westland Lysander—cutting across the sky. The noise and confusion brought everyone into the streets. This wasn't the first time they'd seen a plane fly by. But this time, the machine seemed to fly just overhead. The villagers started running right and left, in total chaos, bumping into each other. Some shouted orders, but no one was listening. Panicked mothers cried out for their children, like hens under a scavenger's shadow. Kids shouted and pointed at the sky. In their excitement they jumped, trampling on the clouds of leaflets that fell like rain at their feet. "We are coming to your defense," some read, while others announced, "We are coming with supplies for you!" or "Join us and liberate France!" "Cameroon declares its political and economic independence!" "Long live a Free Cameroon!" All were signed by General de Gaulle.

By September 1, 1940, news of General de Gaulle had already arrived in Edéa's forest, but not because of his military exploits. What we'd heard was that he'd been condemned to death by Pétain, the President of the French Republic, who had allied himself with the Germans. News like that traveled fast. "The whites are attacking each other," people said, adding, "They're gonna eat each other alive." Could you believe it was no longer Um Nyobè who was talking? It was impossible to silence the old folks who'd lived through the era of German colonization, and for whom the score on the French occupation was far from settled. Some, eyes opened wide in horror, cautioned against pro-German sentiment. Others, over the course of years and with the growing record of atrocities committed by the French, had transformed the pain and humiliations of the past into a measure of the grandeur of their former torturers. They had borne witness to Teutonic power, even if it had kicked them in the balls. Many of the youths sympathized with the pro-German point of view, and they really didn't want to see the French defeat as treason. They had never lived through a war, it must be said, and so had no point of comparison. They had firsthand experience only of French colonization, and they detested it. Passionate hatred bolstered their sarcastic arguments.

"Just imagine," one young boy said, "imagine giving your sister to the one who killed your brother."

"Right, your brother's assassin is balling your sister," another translated, before concluding: "You just let it happen."

Everyone burst out laughing—it was so obviously absurd.

"Who could take that?"

"Who?"

"Cowards!"

"But France gave up the fight."

"If someone is stronger than you," one voice piped up, "carry his bag."

"What bag?" another asked.

"The bag of cowardice!"

For some there, Germany was avenging those who had suffered twenty-five years of French colonization. For others, all that was old news. Their basic argument was that if you had to choose between the French and the Germans, there was no good choice.

"White men's business, my brother."

"Might as well choose between piss and poop."

That was Hebga's thought.

"But still, if you have to choose . . . ?" someone shouted.

And it was on that question of choice that lines were drawn. Emotions started to rise, buoyed up by healthy shots of *arki*. Germany for some; France for others. The Second World War was playing out in bars and in family living rooms. There was no need to hide—there was no risk in supporting Germany, especially since the colonial authority in Yaoundé, and everywhere else in the French Empire, was now under Pétain's orders. And right there in Yaoundé, July fourteenth had provided an occasion to introduce the new regime publicly, although Commissioner Brunot's parade was met by hecklers shouting "Fascist!" and "Nazi!" In short, the Bastille Day celebration in the capital had been pretty much a failure. Still, the ears of many colonists—always ready to don the mantle of paternalistic authoritarianism whatever its source—were receptive to the proclamations of a Leader who was cited as often as possible by the partisans of the new order based in Vichy. Things went differently in Douala, however. With the support of Dio's soldiers, as of August 29, Leclerc put the administration under his orders, and therefore under those of General de Gaulle. When he was in Yaoundé, Pouka had caught his bosses practicing the Nazi salute. Douala, on the other hand, was turning into Free France's first victory. In the depths of the forest, the differences between these two cities had consequences that the French perhaps did not imagine.

"Forget the French," someone said in Mininga's Bar. "Germany is colonizing us now, whether we like it or not."

With those words the big talker, his eyes red with *arki*, summarized the scale of the changes upending the French colonial world, from Dakar to Brazzaville.

"It's recolonizing us."

For Cameroon, that distinction was significant.

"Except it's also colonizing France."

That was met with laughter.

"It's *occupying* France. Slight difference."

And the debate was on. And not just at Mininga's.

"Regardless, we have never been a French colony," said a man with a bald spot a kilometer wide.

"Cameroon is occupied," someone interjected. "Let's be precise."

"What does that mean: occupied?"

"France has occupied Cameroon since 1916."

"Being occupied means being colonized."

"Even if France has always treated us as its colony, my brother, we are a protectorate, not a colony."

"An occupied territory."

"Like France."

"By France."

"Cameroon has never been a French colony."

"Never."

Those who claimed that Cameroon was nobody's colony and that, besides, it had ceased to be a colony in 1915 easily won the war of words. They had passion and youth on their side. They were the ones who wrote—and always will—Cameroon with a *K*, German-style: Kamerun. Fritz was the most loquacious of that group. And many of the discussions took place in his living room. They were lively evenings, it must be said. Yet no one, not even him, could ignore the revelations being made in Edéa's forest about Hitler.

17

The Chiasmatic Enchantments of History

Let's leave Hitler alone—that's what everyone there would have said. The one who mattered was Leclerc. Not just because of his name. History books wax eloquently about the captain's rapid promotion, their amazement certainly heightened by these brief words from General de Gaulle: "As if by enchantment," Leclerc had himself named colonel upon his arrival in Cameroon, de Gaulle writes in his *Mémoires de guerre* (on page 324). History books describe this famous ceremony of self-promotion as taking place in a pirogue off the coast near Douala. Pleven, who along with Boislambert had accompanied the captain, tore the buttons off his own shirt to fashion military stripes for him. And thus this bit of "enchantment" was woven into the great legend that is the history of the Resistance and the Free French. Ah, these books so full of words, why do they forget that the status of Cameroon—a territory under mandate—was what de Gaulle found so enchanting? Because it meant there were few French forces there, unlike Senegal, Gabon, and Côte d'Ivoire, where there were well-established military bases. What's more, the very long border between Cameroon and Nigeria—1,690 kilometers in all— left the territory open to the British Empire, and created a second, parallel transit route toward Chad.

"Cameroon is the weak link and the heart of the French Empire in Central Africa," de Gaulle declared, "its Achilles' heel and its right arm."

Why, then, do these books forget that it was Staff Captain, then Colonel, soon to become General, and then posthumously Marshal Leclerc who turned Cameroon from a territory under mandate into a French colony when, on August 29, 1940, as if by enchantment, he proclaimed himself governor, taking the place of the high commissioner, which had been until then the title of the head of the French authorities? That, as if by enchantment, Cameroon ceased right then to be a protectorate and, with the same move, was placed under a state of siege? That therefore, as if by enchantment, the country was put under lock and chain on the very day that it sent the first of its sons with Leclerc to liberate France, then on her knees? That, as if by enchantment, we Cameroonians became slaves the day we took up arms to go to the assistance of France in her moment of defeat? Ah, let's read Colonel Leclerc's own words, shall we, for they talk about us: "*I have seen natives sincerely determined to collaborate with us,*" he wrote. "*We should allow them to reap all possible benefits of French civilization. I have seen others already more aware of their rights than of their duty; they must be firmly put back in their place. We are not afraid of them.*" Words from 1940. But this, clearly, is a chiasmus of history; in time it will be dealt with by Fritz, or maybe Um Nyobè.

18

The Enchanting Colonel's Village Sojourn

In due time, yes, in due time! Yet, my dear history books, this is what you will never know—not even much later—and that I, novelist that I am, can now tell you without hesitation: It was in Edéa that Colonel Leclerc learned of Hitler's suicide, more than four years before the date that you know so well. Ah, the enchanter had met his match in the forests of Edéa. Our man knew everything about forging documents and handling weapons, but he was no more than a child when faced with Bassa witchcraft. He arrived in a military vehicle, just a day after his men had flown over the village and announced his coming. He immediately demanded that the population gather in the town center. He wanted to repeat to them in person the words written on the leaflets that had flooded their courtyards. Simple words: de Gaulle, de Gaulle, and so on.

Happily the forest had been called to attention by the singing of his soldiers who came marching along behind Captain Dio.

> *We were in the heart of Africa*
> *Jealous guardians of our colors,*
> *When, under a magnificent sun*
> *Resounded this victory cry:*
> *Forward! Forward! Forward!*

These soldiers had put themselves under Leclerc's command in Douala, and he had told them that the path back to Fort-Lamy went through Yaoundé. That meant there would be a fight, to force out those faithful to Vichy. These tirailleurs had enough songs in their arsenal to keep them marching in time all the way to the Cameroonian capital, and enough bullets in their rifles to shoot a hole through the gut of anyone who stood in their way. They marched in formation, standing straight as arrows, stomping their bare feet on the ground and swinging their arms. Their rifles pointed up behind them, over their heads. Their chechias were as red as flames. But many here thought they looked too much like the German askaris, the only ones to have come through the region before, marching in formation and singing at the top of their lungs.

Leclerc and his men stopped in front of Mininga's Bar. Their trek through the forest had turned them into zombies, but it was news of their arrival in the village that made time stand still. The hour of their arrival was badly chosen, however, since almost everyone was in the fields. Maybe that's why the first villagers they met on their way in gave them a very strange impression of the place: they were the bar's regulars, sitting in front of Mininga's door, and even at this early hour, their eyes were bleary from the *arki*. The first official act of the future governor of Cameroon was to chase them away with a quick swing of his cane. Mininga, for her part, walked toward the new arrivals, thinking they were her first real customers of the day. She offered her bar's few chairs to the white men, gave some quick orders to her serving girls, who disappeared into the back of the bar, and with a smile turned toward Colonel Leclerc, who had taken a seat.

"Welcome to Edéa," she said with a broad wave of her arms, adding, "the most hospitable town in all of Cameroon!"

Leclerc expected no less. He quietly tapped his cane on the ground—a nervous tic.

"Where is everyone?" he asked.

Without answering, Mininga gave a discreet signal to the plantain vendor—*Bring over your plantains*—and winked at her girls—*Serve some beer fast*. Then Father Jean suddenly appeared. The only white man in the area, he had been the first to hear the news and had come running. He explained to Leclerc why "no responsible adult" had come to greet him and his men; he offered his excuses on behalf of the village and then suggested the troops set up camp in the courtyard of his church. He scowled as his eyes fell on the beer crates in Mininga's Bar. When Nguet, preceded by her perfume, came over to serve some beer, he waved her away with disdain, sending her back behind the bar. Only the one civilian of the group, Pleven, agreed to spend the night at the church.

"What are you doing there?" the priest snapped at Pouka when he spied him among his fantastical troupe. And when Pouka left his motley group, Father Jean introduced him: "Here is a clerk from the French administration."

He gave him a pat on the shoulder and pushed him in front of Colonel Leclerc, who sized him up.

"Step forward, Pouka. He's an *écrivain-interprète* in Yaoundé," the priest added.

It just so happened that Leclerc was in need of an interpreter. He looked him over twice. Pouka bowed his head politely.

"Welcome, boss."

"Colonel," Father Jean corrected, having noticed his epaulets. "He came back to visit his family. Go on, speak up, Pouka."

But Pouka stood there silently, staring at the ground and holding his wide, multicolored cap in his hands, as if the white man were talking to someone else, as if he had suddenly stopped being the maestro and reverted to the native stereotype.

"He's teaching French poetry to the villagers."

The Frenchmen in the expedition exchanged glances, then turned their eyes toward Pouka. Father Jean wasn't the sort to hold his tongue. It almost seemed as if it were he who had organized the little poetry circle. Had set up its rules and regulations. And came every morning to Mininga's Bar to teach peasants the rules of French poetry. Then the priest asked one of the circle's members to step forward. By chance he called on Philothée, just by chance. Ah, if Pouka had been able to choose the one who could best represent the work he'd done these past two months, he would had chosen someone else . . . But who? Not Philothée, in any event.

"Recite a poem," Father Jean prompted. "One poem."

Colonel Leclerc, who knew nothing about poetry, except for some military songs, signaled his disapproval. But as Philothée began to recite "La Marseillaise," all his men stood at attention. The colonel, too. And then Philothée, startled by the sudden movement, started to stutter worse than ever; he lost his place, searched for it, and tried again, only to repeat the first line once more. His eyes— staring blankly, clouding over, and then staring blankly again—would have made you think he was talking to Death itself. Never had a verse taken longer, never had a song been harder to sing. Happily the boy's voice was backed up by those of the soldiers, the whites and the tirailleurs, who supplied the words Philothée could no longer find, their voices picking up where his fell, their determination filling in for his blank stare. In the war memoirs the whites would later write, "La Marseillaise" roused the forest "as the song of the Senegalese tirailleurs had failed to do, and the people of Cameroon rose up as one to defend France."

Alerted by the noise, the people understood something unprecedented was happening in the village. They came running from the fields and soon the courtyard was filled with their curious faces. The speech Leclerc gave was a summary in prose of the words they had heard sung from a distance. Pouka translated for him, having finally found his voice. But it failed him once again. Yes, our dear Pouka lost his French when he suddenly saw his father coming through the crowd, trembling from head to toe.

"M'bangue," the crowd whispered, "M'bangue."

"Now they're all coming," muttered Father Jean, "finally!"

Everyone there stared, hanging on M'bangue's smallest gesture. M'bangue looked all around, as if trying to make sure everyone in the village was there. Then he slowly opened his mouth, eyes locked on Leclerc's; the colonel had foreseen many things happening on his trek, but not that history itself would answer his call.

"Hitler committed suicide," M'bangue said.

Father Jean gave a start.

"What?"

M'bangue repeated his words with the precision of a telegraph transmitter from the First World War. Even if he didn't show it, Leclerc was unsettled by this Hitlerian story. Since he believed that the real war had begun on June 18, certain that France had lost only the first battle, how could he accept that it devolve into a bad farce just after his arrival in Cameroon? We know, yes, we know that this

Colonel Leclerc will get to have his Second World War, oh yes! Really, that's what he'd come to find here in the forest. From all around him he heard a chuckle, then another, then a cough, and a sneeze. This crowd knew the Old Man's powers. It knew that all the chiefs of the region would gather in his courtyard to hear his predictions. Now he had come to the Frenchman, and for the first time, the village realized that age was catching up to him, blurring his vision. But let's leave that aside for now.

19

Hunting Down the Invisible Opponent

Or rather, let's come back to Hebga, the now-orphaned boxer. He had missed Leclerc's entrance into Edéa, and for good reason! After his mother's burial, Hebga had returned to the forest. His battle against his opponent had been suspended. During the funeral ceremonies, he had challenged him to meet, anytime, anyplace, but the man hadn't shown his face. Hebga had proposed a wrestling match if necessary, but that proposal had been dead on arrival. He had shaved his hair, as tradition required, leaving just one beard-shaped tuft on the front of his head. He had shaved his eyebrows, the hair under his arms, and around his pubic area to inscribe his determination onto his body.

"The *schouain*!" he repeated nonstop.

And his body was covered in the sweat of his disgust. He usually sharpened his ax in the evening. He undid his pagne, folded it in quarters, and set it down beside him. He sat on the ground, with his feet around a stone on which he placed the flat head of his ax. With his right hand he moved the file across the blade, which he called its nose. He slid the file across it, gently, methodically, firmly, his ears attuned to the sound of iron on iron. Several times he held his ax up to the sky to be sure it reflected the sun's rays. With his thumb he carefully, delicately, tested its nose, then began to sharpen it some more. His ear told him when the weapon was really sharp. Sometimes he spent an hour sharpening it, sometimes two. The next day, he'd do it all over again.

"What are you doing?" passersby would ask, as if they couldn't see for themselves.

"I'm sharpening my ax," he would reply simply, without pausing.

Just how long did Hebga spend sharpening his ax?

Some women noticed that he hadn't shed any tears, but no one made an issue of it.

The forest that had opened itself up to him had also shielded the hiding place of his opponent. He couldn't spend his life waiting for the *Man who had done that*. So he walked through the forest, sleeping next to a tree root or in a patch of grass. Sometimes he perched on tree branches, the better to see off into the distance, but also so he could catch his invisible opponent unawares. He had surprised naked women bathing and frolicking in the waters of the Sanaga, their carefree laughter shaking up the universe. He had managed to avoid their wrath at being discovered. His ax never left his hand. He would occasionally sharpen it by rubbing it against stones, as he did in the courtyard of his house. His body had grown hard as his nerves stayed on edge, and each time he picked up a file, his soul became as sharp as the nose of his weapon.

Edéa's forest had never been deeper. Maybe Hebga had crossed the Man's path several times? That was the least of his worries. He was waiting. He could have sat down under a tree, held his weapon in his hands, and waited. He could have waited forever, if that was what it took. Sometimes he heard a crackling in the branches, a dry sound. He'd jump up, fast as lightning, and find himself staring into the terrified eyes of an antelope, or he'd see a monkey flying from tree to tree. Sometimes a bird roused him with its song. Besides his ax, he had all his other weapons with him, too. He'd nock an arrow in his bow and let fly; he'd send his lance soaring, and the antelope would fall, dying before it even had a chance to move. He'd send his knife spinning through the air, and pin the porcupine to the ground. He'd shut his left eye, take aim with the sling of his *ndomo ndomo*, let the pebble fly, and the bird would fall in a cloud of feathers.

He'd cut up his catch, cook and eat the meat. Sometimes he grabbed yellow bananas from the bunches that hung here and there. He'd gently peel them as he walked, eating hungrily the mouthfuls his teeth cut off. He didn't waste the sharpness of his ax nose, he was saving that for the *Man who had done that*. Sometimes in impatience he spit and swore at the emptiness around him.

"Come out," he'd say, "if you are a man!"

No response, save the echo of his own voice.

"Ah," he went on, "you know what I'm gonna do to you!"

He'd hold his ax up to the sky. Only the glint of the sun on his weapon answered his challenge. And that was all.

He begged the *Man who had done that* to free him. His beseeching, like his threat, was met only by silence. The silence of the forest whose cutting song spoke to him of something else, of something else.

"Are you still hiding?"

He spread his empty hands out before him, exposing his chest. What drove him crazy was that the *Man who had done that* had caught his mother unawares. "A mama!" He hadn't even given her a chance to defend herself. This woman who had stood up to the white man hadn't had the chance to speak on her own behalf! In Edéa, the marketplace gossip had turned into threatening words. People knew M'bangue had spoken of a panther, that he had said it was lurking right there, invisible. But who was this panther?

"A giant of a man," a marabout had said.

"No, he's rather short," another opined.

"With fat arms."

"Skinny feet."

"A muscular chest."

Hebga didn't recognize the description of the boxer he had fought long ago, the one Pouka had told him to kill and that he had let escape. That man was rather slight, more like a clown than an athlete, if truth be told, but what did it matter? When he described him to the marabout, the seer opened his eyes wide, as if struck by a revelation.

"It's him," he'd say, "it's him."

Hebga ought to have listened to Pouka when, still a child, he had stunned him by demanding he kill the bastard. After all, the child is the eye of the future.

"I should have killed him," he murmured. "Right in front of everybody."

He gripped his ax tight.

"Is it someone in Edéa?" people asked.

"Or from around here?"

"That's unclear," the first marabout had replied.

"It's blurry," answered the second.

"It's not easy to see."

"I should have killed him," Hebga said.

And he sharpened his ax.

The woodcutter knew that the *Man who had done that* was hiding in the forest. Wasn't it there that he had disappeared after the battle that still made Hebga's hands itch, wasn't it in the forest that he had taken revenge on our Sita? Hebga had first headed back to the clearing where he had found his mother's body. It was as empty as an abandoned boxing ring. He had stayed there for many days. In his head, the noise of possible fights rose up in loud, rhythmic cheers, cries from invisible mouths, applause from hands hidden in the bushes. The forest was living through a battle that wasn't taking place. Hebga waited a long time, surrounded by those who weren't there and by the echo of their silenced songs, in agony from the stone that choked his throat; then he set out along the pathways that stretched before him.

"If you don't want to come out," he had said to the emptiness, "I'll come find you myself."

No one believed in the panther, not even him, because the Old Man's powers of foresight were fading, everyone agreed. They didn't say it out loud, but people looked elsewhere. The unbelievable dreams had managed to sabotage M'bangue's image. I'd even say—and I'm sure, dear reader, that if you know Edéa, you'll agree with me—I'd say that it was superstition that was behind Hebga's decision—a decision shared by others—to transform whoever had done that into a man. Hebga had tied the amulets the sorcerers had given him to his arms and underarms. They had asked him to refrain from sexual relations, but that showed they really didn't understand the rage that possessed his body and his spirit. The need for vengeance had lodged in his flesh, in his members, all of his members.

Rage or pain. Sometimes his spirit swelled under pressure from the stabbing pain that had taken control of his gut, his heart, his mouth, and was soon transformed into a heavy ball that moved through his body, his chest, his throat, and exploded in his head like a shot of *arki*, turning his eyes red. He saw our Sita there before him, as if she were still alive. She was standing in some bushes, on the far side of a river, waving at him.

"What are you doing?" she shouted.

"I want revenge for you," he answered, "to get revenge for you, Mama."

He told her he could find no peace because she had died so violently. He told her she could help him.

"Tell me where he's hiding, the guy who did that."

Our Sita turned away. She gestured toward a thicket. Hebga stood up quickly, slipping on the clay of the shore. His mother kept signaling to him. He cut down all the vines, branches, and leaves around him and, quietly, built a bridge. He stepped onto it like he was dancing, at first with hesitant steps and then with more confidence, holding tightly to two vines to keep his balance, setting off again on his endless journey. On he walked, through the air and through the water, over land. The breeze covered his body with a cloak of water, washing his face. The tree branches cut at his muscles. He made a path for himself through the undergrowth with his ax. He swung it in front of him and continued moving ahead.

"I can't find him," he said to the emptiness, "where is he?"

"Keep looking, my son."

Following our Sita's voice, he was led back to the village's main courtyards.

20

The Ghost

When Hebga emerged from the forest, he looked like a spirit, his body covered with grass, his head shaved, and his arms bound with charms, gris-gris: strength and beauty in motion. For how long had he disappeared into the forest? Maybe a month? Maybe a year? Or a few days? Who even remembered what time was? Hours, days, history—it was all swallowed up in a unique rhythm—very unique. The whole world had been swept up in a whirlwind—a lightning bolt for some, a tortoise for others.

Imagine Paris occupied! Imagine de Gaulle in London! Still, one thing was true: Hebga was thirsty, thirsty for a good beer. Oh, he just wanted a break, for he still hadn't caught the *Man who had done that*. Anyway, he'd still be there in the forest if, much to his own surprise, his feet hadn't led him out. It was just a short truce. He had lost a battle, but the war raged on. He hadn't yet quelled his pain.

"Ah!" He was stunned by how strange the village looked.

It was a child who recognized him and alerted the crowd. The market women didn't give him a chance to dive back into the bush. Their happy cries greeted him as if they had thought he were dead. They hadn't buried an empty coffin, no, but they'd come close. In fact, when they hadn't seen him come out of the woods, many women had concluded that he'd never come back. Now they surrounded him with their songs, treated him like a hero, one who had overcome death and emerged unscathed from the battle. On he walked, the legendary boxer once more, and all around him the women danced, their bodies so graceful, while the children jumped and shouted. Every athlete has his poets.

"*Woudididi!*"

"He has come back!"

"*Woudididi!*"

"Hebga!"

"Hebga the Ax!"

"The Ax!"

"The Ax!"

As Hebga walked through the crowds of tirailleurs milling about in Mininga's courtyard, mesmerized by the joyous celebration that had overtaken the village, they all turned to stare. With one hand on their weapons, the soldiers glared angrily. Hebga didn't ask what they were doing there. He didn't have the chance. For as Hebga reached the door of the bar, Pouka threw himself into his arms, as if he were returned from the dead.

"Hebga!" he said. "Hebga!"

The poet's disciples, surprised to see such an effusive display by their maestro, stared as the two cousins hugged each other tight. Suddenly the woodcutter felt the pain that had taken hold of his spirit fading away from his heart. There in the arms of his cousin—who had once sung of his deeds, his punches, his exploits as a boxer—he came back to life, assuming again the stance of the athlete praised by the whole village. For a moment he was caught up in the excitement of this enchanting reunion. He heard the compliment Pouka whispered in his ear: "Indomitable lion." The kingdom of childhood is a tempting antidote to the many terrors of life—of history!

Then he pulled back.

"Let's go get a drink," he said. "Let's get a beer."

The two happy fellows walked past the tirailleurs, who were apparently transfixed by Pouka's warm welcome of Hebga. In the time his cousin had been gone, Pouka had become Colonel Leclerc's interpreter. Many other things had changed. Mininga's courtyard now looked like a barracks. The tirailleurs who had come in from Douala weren't the only ones camping there. Columns of soldiers from Chad had filled it up. In the back you could glimpse tanks, model H39, and even some cannons. They were parked on the marketplace as well as in the courtyards all around. Edéa had been transformed into a military camp. White soldiers walked back and forth nervously, shouting orders in all directions.

Only Mininga hadn't lost her joie de vivre, despite the village's new face. She opened her arms wide to Hebga as if greeting an old lover, and hugged him hard and long.

"This is my lucky day," she said, without clarifying just what that meant. "My lucky day!"

The night before, a certain Captain Massu had come into town with his men. He was the one who had filled the courtyard with cannons, tanks, and soldiers from Chad. He brought the reinforcements Governor Éboué had sent from Fort-Lamy. His use of the Nigerian corridor made clear all the advantages that England was offering the Free French forces. But it had only taken one day for Edéa to find out just how hard Massu's head was. He was in charge of training the tirailleurs, and his voice, shouting orders and cursing, echoed far out in the distance. The night before he had drunk three cases of beer, that was what Mininga remembered most; she barely noticed how he kept looking at the behinds of her serving girls. Still, the arrival of Massu and his men wasn't a blessing for her business, because it had taken the intervention of "the colonel himself," as she put it, to prevent the rape of her girls.

"You'd think they hadn't seen a woman's ass for three years," she'd say later. "The animals!"

And that wasn't all.

"Even Bamenda," she said, pointing at the grilled plantain vendor whose face made clear the reason she found this so outrageous. "They wanted to screw her."

What a relief for her to see a familiar face walk into her bar: a man from the village!

"We all thought you were dead, my dear," she said.

The bush, it seems, had taken hold of Hebga's spirit. He spoke, and though everyone drank down his words, only the trees could have understood what he was saying.

"What were you doing in the bush?" Pouka asked.

Ah, did Hebga even know? Did he know? He raised the bottle

of beer Mininga had opened for him, brought it to his lips, and took a long, slow drink.

"The village has changed," he said.

"As you can see."

"But they're only passing through," Pouka added. "They're leaving for Yaoundé."

He was talking about the Frenchmen and the tirailleurs.

21

The First Recruit

"Yaoundé"?

That was all it took. Just one word, Yaoundé. Leclerc saw Hebga come toward him. He couldn't believe his eyes. He quickly realized the fellow possessed skills that would have automatically made him a captain, except that he was illiterate. That wasn't his only sin. Our Sita's son hadn't even finished his beer when his eyes had fallen on the tirailleurs' weapons. Once again, he saw his mother's image and heard the distant echo of her words, forbidding him from following his destiny. Suddenly, the revelation of his freedom hit him like a burst of sunlight. His mother—yes, our Sita—had liberated him from the forest: yes, our Sita.

"To Yaoundé?"

"Yes."

"Take me to your white man there," he ordered Pouka.

He had always thought that it would be chance, through one of its infinite combinations, that would wrest him from the depths of the forest and tear him away from his morning workouts. The forest had become a trap. But now destiny had decided otherwise. That's how the two cousins came to walk back across the courtyard crowded with soldiers and to stand before the colonel. Leclerc hadn't expected such a quick reaction. He had tried several times to convince the village boys to join his forces. Offering them the chance to fight for liberty, fraternity, and equality hadn't been enough to get them to sign up, however, for everyone knew that de Gaulle had been sentenced to death. On top of that—and this, Leclerc didn't know—many of the young men had put their bets on Germany.

"I want to become a tirailleur."

When Hebga uttered these words in the approximative French he had picked up as a customer in Mininga's Bar, Leclerc didn't understand him at first. That must be why, instead of answering his request, he ordered his men to disarm Sita's son. He was certainly right to do so. Smiling, Hebga complied, overjoyed at the thought of trading his outfit for a tirailleur's pants. He had come to the bar holding his ax in his right hand, his body still damp with morning dew, his brow covered with bits of grass. Pouka needed to repeat what his cousin had said before the white man really understood.

"He wants to fight for France."

Then Leclerc looked him over from head to toe and realized that standing there before him was the best specimen of a soldier he had ever seen.

"What is your name?"

The experienced eye of this man—who had crossed the French countryside, the English Channel, the desert, and the bush looking for soldiers to build the military arm of the Free French, as de Gaulle expected him to do—allowed him to take the measure of other men. He had met hypochondriacs who said they were ready to cross the desert in three days, starving men who, without laughing, swore they would break the necks of three Germans at once, if not more. He had met veterans of the Great War who claimed they would take on whole armies with one hand tied behind their backs. If Hitler hadn't been able to occupy France, it was because of the training he, Leclerc, had imposed on his soldiers. Now his men would have to work even harder to vanquish the dictator. He was able to ferret out the weakness hidden beneath a man's vanity, but also to recognize the body of a perfect soldier.

"The colonel wants to know your name," Pouka repeated.

Then Leclerc realized that his perfect soldier didn't speak French.

"Hebga."

"Captain Massu!" Leclerc shouted over his shoulder.

A white man with a horse-like head appeared and gave a military salute.

"Colonel?"

"Here is your first recruit."

Leclerc pounded the ground several times with his cane. He was happy, even if Hebga couldn't sign his own name. What Leclerc hadn't yet realized was that in this boy he hadn't just found the perfect soldier, he had also signed up the region's most celebrated athlete: its golden boy, our Sita's son. And what a prize, yes, for Edéa immediately began to offer up its offspring to him. The colonel did know, however, that a recruit like Hebga doesn't come along every day, and what's more, that an army, a good army, isn't made up of just attackers. The second recruit was Philothée, to the great surprise of Pouka, who had thought he'd found a poet in that boy. But the maestro's disappointment sprang from a different source: he could only stand by and watch, unable to stop the hemorrhaging of his little circle of poets.

22

War Council

Things started speeding up. Okay, let's not exaggerate. The army that Colonel Leclerc reviewed in the forest of Edéa, in advance of the war council that took place on September 3, 1940, was the most unbelievable, the most ragtag the earth had ever seen. Pouka would, of course, have recognized Hebga among the tirailleurs, and the un-certain face of Philothée, as well as those of our self-proclaimed Hilun (whom Pouka had dubbed Théophile Gautier) and Bilong. That says it all.

Yet this army was also the most significant force assembled by the Free French up till then. And I say "significant" because, obvi-ously, the hypothetical "African armies" that General de Gaulle had evoked during his meetings with Churchill in June, July, and August didn't really count, since at that point the French general had not even one soldier on his side to make the Englishman take him seri-ously. Whoever saw the soldiers Leclerc had assembled to prepare for the assault on Yaoundé could only have agreed that Churchill was right to remain, shall we say, skeptical. And with good reason!

"France is far greater than just the homeland," said de Gaulle. "It is a vast empire. That's what the marshal has forgotten. Its grandeur."

Hearing such a line, Churchill tapped his cigar on his ashtray. For Great Britain was an empire, too. And the British Prime Minister hoped that the day would never come when London would depend on the Sudanese or the Bengalis for her freedom.

"Senegal," de Gaulle continued, his eyes suddenly growing brighter, "Cameroon, Africa!"

Churchill noted that the man speaking to him hadn't ever set foot in a colony.

"I know," he replied, putting his cigar back between his lips. "I know."

Unlike de Gaulle, Churchill had had a long career along the shores of Cuba, in the dust of South Africa, and wherever else he had proven himself as a young officer. He knew the ins and outs of life in the colonies. Yes, all too well.

What else could de Gaulle add? That his right-hand man had taken over Douala with just the twenty tirailleurs Captain Dio had placed at his command? The reality of the situation spilled over the table of experience that separated them: drip, drip, drop! As for Leclerc, he had quickly realized that many of the French who had chosen a career in the colonies had done so to avoid finding themselves on a battlefield in Europe. That was the reality of the tropics. Oh yes! The events of the past years, Munich especially, had filled the ministry with an avalanche of requests for transfer to the colonies. And now, to those who had come to Douala because they dreamed of palm trees and lions, Leclerc was proposing a military assault on Yaoundé. No surprise that the colonists spoke to him of duty and professional responsibility—although they weren't actually supporters of Vichy—or that they advised him against revealing the spectacle of French disunity to the natives—although they weren't really cowards.

"It's the overseas posting bonus," one man intoned—a man with a wife and child, no doubt.

"Our mission," said another.

Setting up camp in the bush around Edéa served this purpose: it allowed the army responsible for liberating France to take root; and, more important, to develop a valid strategy before launching its first attack on a capital of the French colonial empire under Vichy's control.

Between you and me, there was some good news, too. The best was that Colonel Larminat, stationed in Brazzaville, had rallied to de Gaulle's cause. But there was also de Gaulle's speech—or rather his bluff—the radio broadcast of August 29, when he announced that all of French Equatorial Africa had joined the Free French. Of course, this announcement gave him an argument that carried weight in his negotiations with Churchill—the speech really was a sort of wink in his direction. On the ground in Africa, however, it also sped up the timetable for the assault on Yaoundé. There wasn't enough time to assemble troops. Yaoundé might get reinforcements arriving at once from Chad, Congo, and, of course, Douala. But the soldiers sent by Governor Éboué had already arrived with Massu.

Looking at his army and his soldiers, Colonel Leclerc knew something was off. It wasn't just that General de Gaulle's speech had been given too soon or because of his own fraudulent promotions. No, it was really about the uniforms.

The soldiers were dressed like bandits. There were a few officers, of course, Massu, Dio, Boislambert, Parant, who, like the French soldiers who had rallied to the Free French, were dressed respectably. But the rest, the tirailleurs who'd come from Chad, as well as the few new recruits, with their wrinkled outfits and their bare feet, looked more like waiters than soldiers in a world war. Since Great Britain hadn't yet made good on its promise of supplies, the new recruits were training dressed in their own garb, with wooden rifles. For it was also a question of the need for weapons, not to mention ammunition. Leclerc imagined with horror the moment when his soldiers would have nothing to eat but what they could take from the colonial populations.

"Captain Boislambert, what's the status of the weaponry?"

It would really take a lot of generosity not to see these men as thieves. Boislambert cleared his throat and squared his shoulders before speaking.

"Three H39 tanks," he said. "One cannon."

Leclerc didn't really care what the answer was, for who among his men was unaware of the weakness of their position? Larminat hadn't yet moved his forces from Brazzaville, which, as he explained in a telegram, was under threat of assault by the Vichy forces stationed in Gabon. "It is necessary to defend what we already hold," he asserted, much to Leclerc's chagrin. Can't trust that scoundrel, Leclerc thought. What else was there, here in the bush of Edéa? The colonel mechanically tapped out a rhythm on the ground with his cane while Massu described the training of the troops of tirailleurs, punctuating his sentences with the refrain, "I know them." He spoke optimistically, and kept looking at Captain Dio, who, like him, had spent years in Africa, after graduating from Saint-Cyr. Of course, one week wouldn't suffice to turn peasants into soldiers, especially not peasants who had never held a weapon before.

"Except for one, a woodcutter."

"Who?"

"His name is Hebga."

Was the liberation of France to fall on the shoulders of a Bassa woodcutter? Not even Leclerc found this possibility amusing. For him, his soldiers' only chance was deception.

23

And Speaking of Deception . . .

Douala had fallen, that was a fact; Edéa, too, was in the hands of Leclerc's soldiers, as we know. But Yaoundé? The Yaoundé whose fall had already been proclaimed by General de Gaulle? "As long as Yaoundé is still breathing, Cameroon is alive," Leclerc murmured, there in the depths of the Bassa forest. And so it was that he entrusted the next part of the story to one Bassa man: to Pouka, whom he sent to Yaoundé. Yes, you are reading this correctly. Pouka had never before set foot in the commissioner's palace, although he had long heard about it. Pouka was blown away: that says it all. The walls adorned with carvings of flowers, the triangular pattern on the wooden floor, the many chestnut armoires. He admired the hanging lamps, the wide seats, and most of all the sofas, but oh! he couldn't turn his eyes away from the imposing windows. The classical style of the building had been described as colonial, which always bothered Pouka, since he thought this obscured the mythical roots of Ongola, the city center. Besides, Yaoundé wasn't called the "City of Seven Hills" for nothing. The connection to Rome was undeniable. The city's current plan was clearly modeled on that of its Roman ancestor. Which made Paris a close relative. Pouka's eyes darted around and then stopped on the back wall, where a photo of Marshal Pétain dominated the room. He bowed his head.

The writer could do nothing but stare and keep silent. He stood behind his boss, who held in his hand the "alarming letter from an officer who had met Leclerc's forces in Douala." Pouka had delivered it to its Vichyist addressee in Yaoundé. The letter had in fact been dictated by the colonel; in it he detailed the fall of Douala, exaggerating the number of his own troops, that is to say, de Gaulle's, as well as the weaponry at his disposal. He mentioned twenty assault tanks that had come down from Fort-Lamy via the Nigerian corridor, a dozen cannons, hundreds of troops, and, to make it sound authentic, he referred to Félix Éboué by the epithet regularly used for the governor of Chad by the colonists: "That dirty nigger!"

"You can never trust them," he concluded.

The letter stunned Commissioner Brunot. He had always read about history in books and in dispatches. Now, when it came knocking on his office door, he was suddenly speechless. He would have liked to ask Pouka's boss, "What should I do?"

"As long as Yaoundé is still breathing," the man facing him replied, "Cameroon is alive."

Who was he trying to reassure? The commissioner had trembled as he read the letter delivered to him by his "patriotic" administrator, but quickly regained control of himself, all too aware that there was a black man in the room. No, he wasn't thinking about Brutus—"*Tu quoque?*"—when Pouka's boss told him the writer had delivered the missive.

"You were in Douala?" he simply asked.

That was the first time the territory's supreme authority had ever addressed Pouka directly.

"No . . ." Pouka began. "Yes, boss."

Ah, Pouka! One day you will crow about this; so tell me now if you ever imagined that your poetic vacation in Edéa would take such a dramatic turn! Leclerc had asked Pouka to say, if necessary, that he had been to Douala himself, although he added that he didn't have to lie. In the colonies, the truth, when spoken by a native, is really a lie. Yes, Pouka could always say that he had met Leclerc, that the colonel only had "so many soldiers," "so many tanks," "cannons," whatever; the commissioner wouldn't have believed him, for how could he have met Leclerc, that living legend? Be serious! The telephone rang. Commissioner Brunot answered. He wondered if either of the men saw his face fall.

"What?" he asked. "Where are they?"

Leclerc's forces had reached the neighborhood of Mvog-Mbi, on the outskirts of the city. What should he do, the man on the other end of the line asked, and specifically, should he call the capital's defense forces to arms? Should he sound the alarm and declare a state of war?

"No," the commissioner replied. "It's too late."

The voice on the line had mentioned three H39 tanks, one cannon, a handful of whites, and about thirty tirailleurs. Commissioner Brunot deduced that this was just a vanguard. He hadn't forgotten the details of the letter that was still in his hand. He imagined an army as soon as he heard "squadron," and in the word "attack" he saw an invasion. The announcement that Chad and Congo had already gone over to the Allies didn't help, it's true; nor had de Gaulle's speech assuring listeners that French Equatorial Africa had been won over to his cause. The incidents of July 14 had shown him that not all members of the French community were sympathetic to the Vichy authorities. It was impossible to call the citizens to arms. Feeling totally isolated, the man cracked.

Yaoundé fell like a ripe plum. Pouka was in the best position to witness the twists and turns of its fall, for he had been instrumental in its capture! Not one shot was fired. How could anyone imagine that this was because those who had just added another piece to the grand puzzle of France's liberation really didn't have any bullets to spare? If this story was about a boxing match, I would have said that the writer was right at center ring when news of Leclerc's arrival spread across the capital—when the first blow was struck! But Cameroonian literature has opted to recall, rather, that he was standing in the courtyard of the commissioner's palace when the first coup d'état in the history of our country took place—the first in all of Africa!—right there in Ongola!

24

Ongola! Ongola! Ongola!

In Ongola, the heart of the city of Yaoundé, one isolated building stands like a sly wink to history: the Central Post Office. Built for the speeches of heroes, with a platform right in front, rising above a wide boulevard adorned with a roundabout, it is the centerpiece of la Place de la Victoire—although some call it la Place de la Révolution, and others la Place de la République—in a city that up till now has known nothing but defeat. It is where the dream of this country triumphs over its past and its present oppression. It's where we celebrate the liberation of a city that still breathes the air of tyranny. Ah! The roundabout in front of the Central Post Office is where the slumbering history of Cameroon is really on display—like the beauty in the tale we all know—the history of a people still waiting for its hero to arrive. Only then will the people rise up and open the floodgates of liberty. Yes, this public square has watched the heroes of history's liberation movements pass by. To think that it has in fact written the history of the liberation of the damned! Leclerc! De Gaulle! Um Nyobè! Ouandié! Pouka! Hebga! Who can top that? Secretly this public space was renamed Ahmadou Ahidjo Square, giving it the name of a tyrant.

Yet whoever is mindful, as I am, of the history of the liberation of Paris will understand that Leclerc's entry into the newly liberated Yaoundé represents the flip side of that story. Here, too, history's chiasmus imposed its implacable rule. For the colonel didn't arrive in

Ongola leading entirely white troops, but rather at the head of proud columns of tirailleurs from Cameroon and Chad, led by a few white officers: Boislambert, Massu, and Dio. He himself stood atop his assault tank, waving at the crowds pressed into two tight rows that guided him along toward the city center. He looked at this unfamiliar city and suddenly she was his own. A woman in the distance blew him a kiss. A man tossed him his hat. The French had all come out of their homes, bonding in the jubilation with the black populations.

"Hurrah!"

People coming together in jubilation create an unending legend, a symphony of the future. Blacks and whites shared kisses in public, for a moment were brothers and sisters, lovers and spouses. Sometimes a woman broke free from the crowds on the sidewalk and threw herself into the rows of soldiers, into the arms of the tirailleurs who, thankfully, had received firm orders before entering the city: they were military men and needed to behave accordingly, that is to say, to maintain order, not destroy it. The man who'd received the woman's kiss struggled against her savage embrace, but managed to keep his place in line. Sometimes children imitated the soldiers, marching in step alongside them for a good distance down the road.

The victorious procession stopped in front of the Central Post Office. A thunderous round of applause was heard as Leclerc began to climb down from his tank.

"Hurrah!" shouted the crowd.

There were thousands of voices. The whole city was celebrating its new commander. Hundreds of hands moved as one to embrace him. It took all his soldiers' agility to hold them back. Yaoundé had met her new leader and was offering up her joy to him. She was showing him her biggest and brightest smile. That's because in the shadow of this collective celebration a sordid process of purification had already begun. Those who were known to support Vichy were pummeled, insulted, and manhandled in front of their servants. Impotent before the vindictive crowds, they didn't defend themselves. Sometimes their own servants thrashed them. Flags were thrown on the ground and trampled. The photo of Marshal Pétain was torn up, soon to be replaced in the administrative offices by a photo of de Gaulle. For the moment, however, the face of the victorious general could only be seen on the leaflets that had been distributed before the soldiers entered the city: they showed a calm man, one apparently far removed from the line of fire. This is the photo that will adorn offices and homes for quite a long time.

When the flag bearing the Cross of Lorraine was raised, the crowd cheered once again: "Hurrah!"

At the same time there came a call for "Silence!"

Colonel Leclerc wanted to speak.

"Silence!"

The crowd didn't quiet down until he climbed up onto the platform in front of the post office and lifted his cane up to the sky. Once silence had fallen, he cleared his throat. "Yaoundé! Yaoundé offended!" he said. "Yaoundé soiled!"

Those words were engraved in the city's memory. It saw in the celebration with which newly liberated Paris greeted de Gaulle in August 1944, a perfect copy of the joy that took over the belly of its own streets when it heard those words. Leclerc's flattery hit home, lighting up the city's sky from the Central Post Office in Ongola to the poor neighborhoods. Burning bright, his words shook Yaoundé to her very depths. But Leclerc didn't stop there.

"Yaoundé liberated! Yaoundé, who came out to welcome France, the one and only true France! Eternal France!"

The rounds of applause were followed by hurrahs. The colonel continued as the crowd went wild; he was caught up in the generalized excitement, in the city's jubilation.

"Courageous Yaoundé, my intention is to allow you, to allow Cameroon, to fight under the orders of General de Gaulle for the liberation of the homeland and the empire."

The name "de Gaulle" unleashed a chorus that echoed throughout the crowd: "*Vive de Gaulle!*"

"*Vive de Gaulle!*"

"Fighting doesn't mean throwing oneself headlong against an imaginary opponent," Leclerc continued, once his raised cane had again imposed silence. "Fighting means giving your all to the general struggle of the civilized universe against the barbarians. For the officers and all the mobilized soldiers, it means immediately organizing the defense of the country. This process is well on its way, and I thank all who are working tirelessly for this cause. It means building our military force as rapidly as possible. This has already begun, first with the opening of the office of European recruitment, and then with the creation of the Free French Volunteers of Cameroon."

He took the time to look over and patiently assess each one of the young men before him; they seemed ready to throw themselves into the flames of battle right then.

"Finally"—here he wiped his mouth—"I expect as soon as next week to begin recruiting natives."

From there, the excitement was spread through a series of announcements from the administrative palace. The colonel accepted the resignation of the disgraced Commissioner Brunot, as well as those of his assistants and many other civil servants. He personally oversaw the removal of the portrait of Marshal Pétain from the wall behind the desk where he, as the new governor—a title he bestowed upon himself in the exhilaration of the day—sat to sign several decrees, effective immediately. The first one designated Douala as the capital of the territory, a move that would certainly have astonished the crowd of Yaoundéans still caught up in the jubilation; the second transformed the city that he had just finished praising into a simple administrative center; the third declared a state of siege. The capital's memory has preserved this betrayal in its archives. To see a statue of Leclerc, you'd have to go to Douala. Despite the sting of the insult, Yaoundé did dedicate to him its largest high school, where the elite of Cameroon are still educated.

No, Yaoundé made no mistake. This city that was never rewarded for burnishing Paris's glory still hasn't erected a statue in front of the Central Post Office; she has built no monument there. For her history, like that of Cameroon itself, remains to be written. She knows that Cameroonian grandeur will not come by proxy. Ongola doesn't have an arc de triomphe because it is still waiting for the generation that will liberate Cameroon. The city center has no statue because it hasn't yet found the hero of our generation. Ah, citizens of Cameroon, each and every time that you pass through the city center, each and every time you cut across Ongola, ask yourself why this public square where all the main avenues of the city intersect and where millions of stories cross paths; why this square from which departed those who liberated France and remade the world; why this square—Ongola! Ongola! Ongola!—which, like other similar places in other countries, is one of the world's nerve centers, is adorned with neither monument nor statue. Well, it's because she is still awaiting her heroes; it's because Cameroon's history is waiting for you; it's because since that fourth of September, 1940, Cameroon has been lying fallow.

25

The Poor Neighborhoods
of the French Empire

For Hebga, the arrival of Leclerc's troops in Yaoundé was the fulfill-
ment of one of his wildest dreams. Yes, it's a familiar old story, really.
"Yaoundé!"—I'm sure that's what he said—"The Yaoundé of my
dreams!" He imagined many different scenarios, using his lucky
numbers he drummed up visions of rivers of gold; but never had he
imagined the city of his dreams falling down at his conqueror's feet.
How many girls kissed him? How many whites shook his hand? On
that unimaginable day, he thought of his mother, our Sita. She should
have been there to see his triumph! She should have seen him at the
Central Post Office! Then she would have discovered the capital and
experienced that sublime moment, both at the same time.

Hebga was just as amazed by the collective jubilation as by the
buildings. For the first time he saw houses with more than one story,
lampposts. And the road he walked down was paved! The city revealed its face on that very special day. A historic day, no doubt about
it! The tirailleur puffed out his chest and marched in step; he was
the master of the city of his dreams. Ah, how he would have liked
to move away from his troop, to dive into this crowd that held its
arms open to him, to kiss the crowd and tell her how deep was the
love that had always bound him to her. He thought of Pouka and
Um Nyobè.

Their separation had been abrupt, but he held on to the hope
that somewhere in this huge city he would find his cousin. He didn't

know Um Nyobè well, having only met him at the sessions at Mininga's. But the other Bassa in the regiment warmed his heart. He didn't feel alone, no. Bilong was marching behind him and he knew that Aloga was there at the other end of the squadron—beardless now, yes, but there all the same. Bringing up the rear was Philothée. In the evening, they'd be together, forming a little group in the midst of all these soldiers from Chad—these Saras whose skin was all of the same dark black, whose language they didn't understand, who used gestures to communicate with them and who, come nightfall, were almost invisible, except for their teeth. Hebga understood from their smiles and gesticulations that their first concern was getting laid. They'd hit their chest with a closed fist, then poke a finger into the fist, again and again, and then finally suck on the finger.

"Cameroon women," they said, "*gnoxe-gnoxe.*"

And they gave a big thumbs-up.

Alas, these men had no words to describe the funny twists and turns of their travels down from Fort-Lamy to Douala, or those of their whoring excursions in the port city. It was those Saras who dragged the fellows from Edéa into Yaoundé's poor neighborhoods as soon as they got their first furlough.

"Briqueterie," they said, asking everyone they met how to get there. "Briqueterie."

Not Ongola, not the Central Post Office. For them Briqueterie was paradise, the quintessence of the best that Yaoundé had to offer on that very special day. The Hausa quarter, whose fame had spread across the country and captivated tirailleurs from as far away as Chad. Hebga was struck by the two long lines of bars along the road leading up to the Great Mosque. Compared with such a display of luxury, Mininga's Bar seemed like just a little shack in the bush. On the street, girls gestured to them, big smiles on their lips. They were just as joyful as when they had greeted him upon his triumphant arrival in Ongola several days before. The spirited revelry of the liberation seemed to live on in Briqueterie. Each day was an endless celebration with soldiers from distant fields.

"Sweetie," one woman said, "sweetie, come here."

"Champ," said another, "let me give you some honey."

Hebga imagined how Edéa would react if one of these lasciviously dressed girls had walked in strutting her stuff. In a few minutes the band was swallowed up by these obliging ladies; he himself fell prey to two plump beauties, each one grabbed hold of one of his arms and wrapped her body around him. That night he wanted to burst out laughing right there in the middle of the street, he wanted to say the words that came to mind to his Bassa friends, words in Bassa. But he realized that his friends had already been spirited away by the flowers of the poor neighborhood, gone without even a wave in his direction!

"Come on, sweetie," said the girl on his right, "I live over there, just up ahead."

"Champ," said the other on his left, "this is where I live."

Ah, Hebga will never forget the Brique girl who dragged him away; in his ecstasy, he dubbed her the Marshal. Nor will he ever forget the question she asked him, "From Chad? From Chad?"

He said no and she stared at him in disbelief. Was she basing her guess on the woodcutter's muscles or maybe the shape of his head?

"From Senegal? Senegal?"

In short, there in the lady's perfumed room, the Cameroonian tirailleur realized it was best not to say he was Bassa. The woman was from the same ethnic group as Mininga, an Ewondo, and he could have kept up the conversation in her language; but he preferred to let her assume he was from Senegal, just to make her happy—in the end, what difference did it make to him?

"Grab here," she said with a smile, and she showed him the luscious flesh between her legs. "Grab here."

This woman was truly an extraordinary slut! She sent him to the heavens twice, and when, the third time, he began to show signs of fatigue, she took his penis between her polished fingers.

"De Gaulle sleepy?"

It took a minute for the soldier to understand that it wasn't him she was calling by the French general's name, but his *bangala*.

"The Marshal not so-o tired," she said.

She pointed to the place between her legs, which he thought he had already given a good workout. She took his de Gaulle in her mouth and, right then, Hebga, in surprise, uttered the name of his mother, like a prayer. That didn't bother the Marshal. She massaged his testicles, and soon our man felt a line of fire rush through his dick, igniting his belly, his whole body. He had closed his eyes. When he reopened them, his terrified eyes met those of the exultant Marshal.

"De Gaulle standing tall," she said.

He stared in disbelief at his rock-hard erection—harder than he'd ever been before.

"*Vive de Gaulle!*" said the woman, quite pleased.

"*Vive de Gaulle!*" Hebga repeated.

Those words that had shaken up the capital, those words that had echoed through the depths of the poor neighborhoods, to the far reaches of the French Empire—in that moment, staring at his furious *bangala*, the Marshal by his side, they came out as a whisper.

There are women who turn the whole world upside down. Hebga would have stood up to salute his own erection. This Marshal was one of those Mamy Wata whom men talk about in hushed voices, for never had his penis stood so tall. He didn't dare tell this story to his buddies when they met up again several hours later, back in the bars from which they had disappeared. The Saras, they never stopped talking about their exploits. Their exuberant faces beamed and they blessed the Second World War, Cameroon, Yaoundé, and Briquete-rie, all at once.

"Cameroon women, *gnoxe-gnoxe*," they said.

Bilong seemed to have found his calling once more, and Aloga the rhythm for his first authentic Hilun. Even Philothée was, for the first time, able to speak without stuttering. As they walked past buildings in the city where the French flag and banners proclaiming "*Vive de Gaulle!*" flew, Hebga thought about the Marshal. In his uniform pants there was an immediate reaction, and his eyes clouded over with shame. The day after the liberation, he walked through the city he had dreamed of for so long, his head hanging low and his hands in his pockets. He felt naked and longed for his ax, which a French officer had taken from him when he'd signed up. He thought of the forest and the surprises it held. He thought of the Marshal. The memory of that woman was beginning to haunt him.

26

Nemesis

Yaoundé does not harbor such a vivid memory of General de Gaulle. Yet he came to the city when the Central Post Office still bore his name: "*Vive de Gaulle!*" He was trying hard to prove to his English interlocutor that the French Empire was worth the bet—trying so hard that he landed in Douala only a few days after the putsch in Ongola. One of history's ironies: this visit likely had more impact on Fritz than on Churchill. Yes, on Fritz. By that I mean, it left a mark on the young man who was there watching in the crowd. Douala didn't erupt in celebration as Yaoundé had done for the colonel, but the Blenheim bomber in which he arrived was met by parades of bureaucrats who were thrilled to see and speak with him. The general shook all the hands that reached out toward him, but never bowed his head, standing bolt upright, as if he were marching, as erect and as indifferent as a priapism. A colonial cap on his head, he ran his eyes over the faces that crowded around him, people who looked so much alike and who mattered so little. His man Leclerc was waiting for him in Yaoundé.

Fritz saw him for the first time when he was addressing the traditional chiefs. Fritz was in Douala on business and he found himself, along with some others, rounded up by the order of their traditional chief. Douala's neighborhoods were then, as today, organized along tribal lines. The Bassas were, for the most part, housed in Akwa. When Fritz came to Douala, Akwa was where he ended up. He stayed with his older brother, who worked for the railroad. And it just so happened that it was in Akwa's reception hall that General de Gaulle spoke to the people. Do I need to add that several years later, in this very same hall, Um Nyobè will ask the crowds to put a stop to the Gaullist colonial enterprise and that, no joke, de Gaulle's forces will condemn him to death? Ah, history and its reversals, history and its detours!

History's chiasmus! Yet another example! For the moment Fritz couldn't know what the future held for Um Nyobè, or for de Gaulle, for that matter. He watched the general cut a path through the crowd, take a seat in front of a wall where someone had put up a white flag with the Cross of Lorraine upside down. He heard the city administrator introduce the man, speak of his exploits during the Great War, about the Resistance—a fancy, formal speech, full of adjectives—but one phrase alone echoed in Fritz's mind: "He has been condemned to death in France."

Soon, while the administrator's speech dragged on, de Gaulle stood up, cleared his throat, and, waving his arms, began to speak. His hands were very long; for a moment Fritz allowed himself to be distracted by his gestures—or was he distracted by the people, all those blacks who were following the scene, glued to the windows, but who just couldn't keep quiet?

"Continue! Perservere!" the general repeated. "Do not listen to bad rumors, to propaganda, to discouragement."

Fritz turned toward his neighbor, who wouldn't stop gushing.

"That's de Gaulle!" he said.

"So who is de Gaulle?" a voice asked.

"France has only lost a battle."

"He's the white man, the one who's speaking."

"Shut up, you idiots!" snarled a colonist.

Ah, that colonist, he would have liked to give everyone there a good whipping! But right then, the general was hammering out an important phrase:

"France has not lost the war."

"What?"

That made Fritz jump. And the menacing colonist, forgetting his anger, applauded with everyone there, while de Gaulle continued speaking of France and her empire.

"A great empire, an empire overflowing with courage, with resources, with force—the black force. Native soldiers," he continued, "our valiant tirailleurs, have taken part in all of France's battles."

That's why he wanted to meet all the city elders, Fritz thought: they'd be like amplifiers, sending their sons into battle and dragging Cameroon along with them.

"England," de Gaulle declared, when Fritz came back to the speech, "is promising to buy six thousand tons of palm and all your stocks of cocoa, at the highest price. And that's not all, that's only the beginning."

"That isn't de Gaulle," insisted suddenly the guy next to Fritz, a guy with a bald spot and red eyes. "That's Pétain."

"De Gaulle has been condemned to death," another agreed, "a condemned man wouldn't be greeted like this. Pétain's the President of France."

"You clearly don't know what's going on," another objected.

Ah, Fritz thought of his village, of the conscripts and the convicts, those forced into labor. Never had he seen a convict treated with such respect.

"The coffee harvest," de Gaulle was saying.

"That's Pétain, I'm telling you," grumbled the fellow next to Fritz.

"How much do you want to bet?"

"The war effort," de Gaulle went on, "requires the marshaling of all of the empire's resources."

"Ten francs," said the voice next to Fritz, "he's not worth any more than that."

"Cameroon will prove its usefulness by providing the neighboring colonies and our allies with certain foodstuffs, for example, meat, or certain mineral resources . . ."

"Shut up," one voice bellowed.

". . . tin and gold . . ."

It was the colonist who had screamed; now he waved his fist in front of Fritz's face and glared at him, straight in the eyes.

". . . manganese . . ."

Fritz was beginning to regret his choice of window.

". . . cobalt."

He realized that he couldn't make sense of anything being said

by the general—this man who had brought together so many patri-
archs, who were now sitting in that room, fanning themselves with
flyswatters and clapping from time to time.

"We must mobilize all possible forces for the universal struggle
of the civilized universe against the barbarians. For democracy and
peace," de Gaulle said.

The fellow with the red eyes responded with a curse in his language and his friends burst out laughing.

"Shut up," shouted the colonist inside the room, "shut up, you
sons of bitches!"

The next line of the speech was drowned out in rounds of applause, punctuated by the cry, "*Vive de Gaulle!*" Some rose to their
feet to applaud even louder. Fritz took the opportunity created by
the chaos to move away from his neighbors, for the ceremony wasn't
yet over. Now it was the traditional chiefs' turn to speak. The chiefs
rose, one after the other, dressed as if for a ball. Some spoke in their
native language, citing numerous proverbs, which were translated
slowly, each phrase stretched out, by a man with the face of a duck,
who worked for the Baptist church.

Some spoke in French, embellishing their speeches with extrav-
agant turns of phrase, moving words, caressing the French language
as if it were the only real treasure Africa had to offer General de
Gaulle, each diluting their French with the accent particular to their
native language. Fritz noticed one local chief—perhaps the head of
a section of the city—whose speech was overflowing with sentences
in the imperfect subjunctive. After mentioning his medals, he spoke
of Montparnasse and the Latin Quarter, before giving vent to his indignation: those places he had known so well when he was a student were now under occupation—people there were speaking
German! At the sixth speech, Fritz realized, like everyone else, no
doubt, that the general was bored stiff. He sat there rigidly, not moving except to wipe the sweat from his brow; he never even looked at
the administrators sitting beside him. You'd have said he was on another planet. Fritz would have liked to see de Gaulle suddenly
pound his fist on the table, as the colonists so often did, and tell the
long line of speechmakers, "Stop this monkeying around!"

Obviously then the Africans would have cried racism. Some

chiefs would have swallowed their long harangue. And just maybe then the outraged city wouldn't have sent off its contingent of tirailleurs or contributed to the war effort? De Gaulle would have gone back to England and confessed to Churchill that he knew nothing about the colonies. France, like Cameroon years before, would have become a German colony. And if the putsch in Ongola—which took place two years before the better-known one in Algiers—hadn't taken place, would Paris have been liberated in 1944? Fritz would have been the only one to applaud that scenario. Yet he suddenly felt that he could see things from General de Gaulle's point of view. He understood him, that's what he realized, and from then on he always felt that way. You see, never had any French authority visited any African country as often as de Gaulle did during those years, for he came back to Cameroon in November 1940, in May 1941, and again in September 1942. At no point did Fritz change the opinion he had formed on that first visit, on that twelfth of September, 1940: This guy is poison.

The general did not pound his fist on the table, no, he did not. But Fritz remained convinced that deep inside he was thinking: Those assholes!

Alas, I will never be able to verify that hypothesis, but so what! Um Nyobè sometimes spoke of the closed fist that de Gaulle held firmly on the table. Fritz had told him the story. The image of the French general sitting politely in Akwa's overheated reception hall, suffering through the staged ceremonies of Douala's chiefs because he realized that their sons would liberate Paris—that image stayed in his mind for quite some time. De Gaulle had the nerve to call those chiefs "members of the Resistance." He would always hold that against him.

27

History's Missed Connections

But let's get back to Yaoundé. Leclerc's entrance into the city had made Pouka's life unbearable. If the sacking of all the pro-Vichy administrators, including his boss, had suddenly deprived him of a job, his vacation in Edéa had saved him. He had had the good fortune to have already served as Leclerc's translator. And on top of that, he had carried that historic letter, the deceptive letter that had brought down the capital: he was a member of the Resistance! He would never forget it—he always considered himself "Cameroon's very first Gaullist!" He had presented himself at the governor's office the next day and been given a job in offices attached to the palace. The colonel no longer needed a Bassa translator, but there was other work for Pouka to do. The chaos of war, the confusion that reigned in the capital since the abrupt regime change, the lack of necessary food supplies, all complicated daily life and kept the colonial civil servants working overtime.

Then the arrival of de Gaulle made everyone frantic, for they had to show the general how the situation was improving—moving in the right direction. The recruitment of soldiers, the launch of the new colonial radio service, setting aside war reserves, writing up lists of European volunteers—all these tasks had the few remaining employees of the colonial administration running like mad. It was easier to dissolve an administration than to build up a new one starting from practically zero. Never had Pouka worked as much as he did in the months of September and October. Yet if anyone had asked him what he was doing, he couldn't have given a clear explanation. War, war—that was the only answer anyone could give.

Yet war is sometimes a perfidious excuse.

Three weeks went by before he could put together just how he had been separated from Hebga, before he remembered that his cousin was in Yaoundé, just like him. This shameful lapse struck him like a slap, and at the first opportunity he ran to the barracks. Inside, the tirailleurs were busy at work. In one corner, some were doing drills. In their brown uniforms, with their red chechias and bare feet, covered in dust, they all had the same look on their faces, the same demeanor. It was as if just one man were marching back and forth across the courtyard, a wooden rifle on his back, or standing guard at the gate with a bayonet on the end of his rifle. Only, that man, he wasn't Hebga.

"Hebga?" the soldier who met him at the gate asked.

He spoke in the clipped phrases of an illiterate.

"Yes, Hebga!"

"First name?"

"He doesn't have a first name."

"Tirailleur?"

The column to which his cousin was assigned had already left the city for the north. Pouka collapsed. How many times had he wished he could show Hebga the capital—the city that had been his obsession? And to think he hadn't looked for him. Worse, he hadn't even wished him farewell. For the first time he realized that an excuse deceives only the one who gives it. Hebga, well, he had stopped waiting for his cousin. The barracks hadn't given him time to think. And he had pushed aside his troubled thoughts and his regrets once Captain Massu had announced to the company that their bivouac in Yaoundé was over.

"Children," he announced, "we're going to Paris!"

Pouka realized that the war was uniquely able to tear friendships apart. Fritz in Douala, him in Yaoundé, Hebga who knew where: history scatters bits of life in a thousand places—that, for sure, is true.

THE BATTLE
OF KUFRA, 1941

1

The Ax of Witchcraft

The Tibesti desert, September 1940: Leclerc recognized his perfect soldier and gestured for him to come in. He never would have thought that this brave soldier's first exploit would be an act of insubordination. With the sun streaming in behind him, all Leclerc could make out was his muscular build. That man, endowed with a physique he wished for himself, had found a place in his heart, but he couldn't quite put his finger on when or why.

"What's the problem, Captain?"

Leclerc spoke to Massu, who'd just arrived. He was there because two of his men, two Cameroonians, disregarding the chain of command, had voiced their complaints directly to the colonel.

"These idiots don't give a damn about the hierarchy."

"They don't yet understand it, Captain."

Behind Hebga stood Philothée. What nonsense! Was the stutterer going to translate the words of the illiterate? Yet, that's what happened. With vivid gestures, Hebga described in his own language the guiding principle of his training. He explained to the colonel his metaphysics of muscles, and how he needed to keep his body in shape in order to feel good. He spoke with such passion that he didn't notice that Leclerc hadn't understood a word he'd said, and neither had Massu. The two men turned to Philothée.

Philothée's mouth gaped open. "He says," he began. He took a gulp of air. "He says . . ."

Meanwhile, several other white officers, including Captain Dio, had come in to discuss the needs of the camp and preparations for the Battle of Kufra. They took their places beside Leclerc. Hebga didn't look at them, entirely caught up in his own testimony. He stared, his eyes wide open with indignation, stressing the ugliness of the *coupe-coupe*, the machete he knew all too well and that could, at best, cut grass. He said that the rifle was no better than the musket he already had. He preferred to use an ax, for what mattered most with it wasn't strength, but technique.

"No ax," Philothée translated, with a broad swing of his arm. His glazed eyes froze everyone there in their tracks. "Him, march no pants."

I am not going to reproduce his comical stuttering. The whites stared at one another and, as if of one mind, all smiled. The two black men stood there speechless. Especially the woodcutter, who didn't understand what there was to laugh about in his explanation. Philothée fell silent, fearing he had already said too much.

Leclerc stood up and walked toward Hebga. With his characteristic paternalism, he gently patted his cheek.

"My dear man," he said, "do you even know what kinds of weapons our enemies have?"

Hebga waited guardedly.

"The Italians have rifles."

Leclerc paused, just long enough for his words to penetrate the thick skull of the man he was addressing. He knew, yes, the colonel knew that this man's insubordination would, in other circumstances, have been worthy of a court-martial, but obviously, in the Tibesti desert, the situation was more fluid. And besides, the soldier wasn't refusing to fight; on the contrary.

"Machine guns," he added, "cannons, planes."

Another pause.

"Our adversary is not a tree."

His comments were met by silence. Had the two men even understood? He glanced at Massu, who mimicked cutting grass:

"Ax *wassa wassa*."

Then Massu acted out smashing the woodcutter's head open with a quick blow to the temple. He was speaking in a clipped

French, accompanied by theatrical gestures, that he said he had learned from the tirailleurs, but Colonel Leclerc interrupted him.

"The rifle is faster than the ax," he said simply, "the rifle is stronger."

He held out a clenched fist in front of the complainants' eyes, as his own gaze moved back and forth between Hebga's face and Philothée's.

"Stronger."

Hebga commented, in Bassa, that a cannon is stronger than a rifle, and that didn't stop them from using rifles. He tried to catch the eyes of the stuttering translator, but Philothée was lost, searching in vain for the first word.

"No ax, no pants," the woodcutter repeated. And he motioned significantly at his naked flanks.

Dio, who had kept quiet till that point, now wanted to intervene. Leclerc stopped him with a wave of his hand. Captain Dio really didn't understand. It was Dio who had crafted the plan to recruit the Saras in Chad. Since they usually walked around naked, he figured they'd be drawn to the tirailleur's uniform, precisely because it was the first bit of clothing they had ever put on. Even though he had led those men from one end of Nigeria to the other, he really didn't understand what had gotten into the head of this bushman. And now Dio understood Leclerc's order even less:

"Give him back his thing."

For Captain Massu, this was the first and only time he'd ever seen anything like it: a black soldier who hadn't obeyed was being protected by his own superior. He didn't react, but also didn't forget. Colonel Leclerc wasn't sorry to move his perfect soldier out of the infantry; he was sure to find some way to make use of his talents. He ordered him to be reassigned to the trucks. What difference did it make to Hebga? Getting back his ax had lifted his spirits. He examined the sharpened length of its blade, caressing its body with the palm of his hand. It was as if he had found a lost limb.

"Ax," he exclaimed, "de Gaulle!"

His face burst into a smile. His happy eyes met Colonel Leclerc's, who turned toward Massu, then to Dio and the others. None of the French officers understood the woodcutter's joy. The name "de

Gaulle" brought the scene to a close. It gave everyone some satisfaction. One of them would later write in his memoirs of "natives whose attachment to Free France sometimes takes on surprising forms." Hebga hooked his ax over his shoulder, just as he used to when he went into the forest, except that now it had a new name: "de Gaulle." He turned around to leave when Massu's order stopped him cold.

"Attention! . . . March!"

"You have to teach them everything," murmured an officer in the shadows.

Hebga headed off, standing tall, his feet striking out a rhythm on the ground, "One, two, one, two!" Outside the tent, a stinging cloud of hot sand whipped at him. When he reopened his eyes, his gaze met those of a large group of meharists camped next to their camels. The wind was puffing out their loose uniforms. The tirailleurs were happy to have given up the wooden rifles they had used for training now that the real weapons provided by England had arrived. The firearms brought out a childlike excitement in each of them, especially the Chadians. You'd have thought they'd found a long-lost lover. None of them understood Hebga's attachment to his ax; they were content with the *coupe-coupe* provided by the French.

The same for Leclerc; he really didn't understand Hebga's stubbornness.

"The Bassas," he remarked simply. "That's just how they are. Stubborn."

2

The Birth of the Senegalese Tirailleur

Speaking of stubbornness, Bilong just wasn't the same since the new equipment had been handed out, especially the uniforms. Back in the tent he paraded in front of the Bassas in the group, showing off. Yes, he was showing off. His shirt, his brown trousers that came down mid-calf and the half chaps that made him look a bit like a charlatan—but don't say that to him. His toes peeked out at the end of his feet like little sparks, symbols of his happiness. He tried placing his chechia on his head at several different angles, but not the way Massu had shown them.

"Tipped to the left?" he asked.

Aloga tried to help.

"Like this?"

"No, a bit more to the right."

Philothée got involved.

"Look, this is how you wear it, put it on like this."

"You now, too, Charles?" Aloga asked. "You just joined up so you could play the part of the red-hot lover, is that it?"

When he said "red-hot lover"—*chaud gars* in French—it amused the other Bassas. He was also the only one who called Bilong Charles. This led to a bit of confusion, because everyone else just called him Bilong. Aloga had taken on the role of a strict father. And that's what he was. He had signed up so he could feed his kids. At first it was because of his passel of kids that he fled his house and joined the little poetry circle, only to discover that being a poet didn't get him the pay he would have earned as a day laborer, as he had hoped when he had joined the line in front of Mininga's Bar. When Colonel Leclerc had arrived, he abandoned Maestro Pouka and his rhymes to become a soldier, a tirailleur. Had he fled his passel of screaming kids only to find himself here in this far-off desert, still subject to the caprices of a child?

Bilong found this quite funny and kept chuckling about it with Philothée.

"Charles, is that your given name, yes or no?" an exasperated Captain Massu finally asked one day in the middle of exercises.

Bilong would have told him that it didn't really matter, that he was Bilong for some, while his mother called him something else, and "his Nguet" called him Charles; besides, both Charles and Bilong were really nicknames, "they're not the names my father gave me when I came out of my mother's belly." But the military code didn't allow for this sort of exchange with your superior officer. So why didn't he use the name his father had given him? And just what was it? Bilong would have reeled off a list of a dozen names, just to be able to talk about himself. That was one of his foibles, I'd say. Or, according to Aloga, it was one of the quirks that made him a center of attention.

"You're a daddy's boy, is that right?" Aloga didn't hide his disdain. "A real child."

It wasn't far from the truth. Hebga observed all the theatrics going on around Bilong and spit on the ground. The woodcutter had become a soldier to avenge his mother. After searching everywhere in the forest for her assassin, he had concluded that the *Man who had done that* was hiding on the world's endless roads. So he had headed off down those roads, had crossed forest, steppe, and desert, without realizing that by doing so, he was exposing himself to the global dimension of a very strange sort of war. He hadn't yet found the *Man who had done that*, his invisible adversary. The rage within him was the other face of his love for his mother.

Bilong, for his part, had signed up to escape from the smothering embrace of women. Even Hebga remembered that scene from the bar, the one about the *wolowolos*—really, tell me, could anyone

have forgotten that? He was fleeing our Nguet's imprisoning perfume. Or shall we say, instead, that Bilong wanted to escape from
his elder sister who had beat the drums of feminine rage in front of
Mininga's Bar? Or was it from Hebga's mother, our Sita, the leader
of that group of angry women? But maybe he was really fleeing Mininga herself? No. Had Nguet grown too possessive? One thing is
certain, Bilong had become a soldier because of an excess of love.
It was a childish reaction, just another way to try and impress the
ladies.

"You really are a child, huh?" Aloga repeated.

Hebga could only agree with that. Bilong acted as if the soldiers
in the camp at Faya-Largeau, there in the middle of the desert, were
the mirror he had always sought out, as if they were the customers
in Mininga's Bar, or rather, as if they were the members of Pouka's
little poetry circle. He held his rifle against his hip and asked once
again what people thought of his soldier's uniform.

Then Hebga got angry.

"Hey, we are not *your* Nguet!" he said.

Several times he had started to say: "And your Nguet, you know
I . . ." but he had held back. Let's give the kid time to grow up, he
told himself; boredom was filling his mouth, so he again spit into the
sand. Was he going to get into a fight with that kid in the middle of
the desert over some woman who wasn't even there? Because, truth
be told, he knew what he was talking about when it came to Nguet;
Hebga had a lot of stories he could tell, that was for sure. But he really
didn't want to humiliate "the little guy." So he just said, "Be careful
with those Bamum women," as if that meant anything there in the
middle of the Sahara. The other soldiers were listening closely now,
their attention piqued by the racy stories the Cameroonians were
telling each other in Bassa.

"Hey, Cameroon-man," said a voice from the corner, "we
tired, huh!"

"You talkin' women, women, morning, noon, and night."

"Fuck, leave us alone."

Jealousy? The evenings were pretty boring after the rather stress-
ful days. Sometimes, though only rarely, to tell the truth, the soldiers gathered in De Gaulle Hall to watch a movie. There were

newsreels from England that a French soldier translated for them, that talked only of glory and of France. The Free French had distributed pornographic magazines, which they passed around to make it easier to masturbate. They'd get together and trade stories just to keep their spirits up. The four brave soldiers from Edéa were lucky; because they had headed off as part of Leclerc's first group of recruits, they hadn't been separated. It had started as a small group, no more than a hundred or so men; but as they'd crossed Cameroon, several hundred other soldiers had joined their ranks, some Bamiléké, others Bamum or Fulani—there were a lot of Fulani, yes. As their numbers swelled, the four Bassas grew even closer. Now they were tighter than family.

"Fuck, leave us alone, too!" Bilong answered.

The tirailleur who had insulted Bilong calmed himself down; he didn't really want to take on Hebga, whose muscles made him a real threat. He was part of the so-called Senegalese contingent, although in fact there were only a few Senegalese among them. The phrase *tirailleur sénégalais* was really just a lazy turn of phrase on the part of the French that no one had bothered to correct, because Senegal, still under Vichy control, hadn't yet given de Gaulle any soldiers. What's more, Senegal had dealt de Gaulle his first military defeat, between September 23 and 25, 1940. And even worse, Leclerc's companion, Boislambert, had been taken prisoner in the Battle of Dakar. Still, the very first contingent of soldiers to arrive in Chad came from Senegal. It's said that it's because those Senegalese soldiers didn't want to shoot at the ones from Chad, as their French officers had ordered them to, and so always missed their mark, that they were given the epithet of tirailleurs—bad shooters. Who knows—but that's what people say. Still, it remains that the French soon called all the African soldiers in their army "tirailleurs" and all the Africans they recruited were deemed "Senegalese." It just made things easier, simpler. Like any other insult.

The quarrel settled down. Aloga began to sing one of those songs he sang so well. It was a comforting lullaby that allowed each man to draw out his own memories, whether of the cottony sweetness of a woman or his mother's embrace. For Hebga, the expanse of the desert that he had begun to measure for the first time when he'd arrived in camp was cut to the dimensions of his own pain. Our Sita hadn't ever left his mind, not once since his departure. He remembered the words that several had repeated on the day his mother was buried: "It's expected for a son to bury his mother." The market— what am I saying, not the market, all of Edéa had repeated that to him, for the whole town had come to Sita's courtyard to pay their final respects to her, in recognition of her grandeur. And it was into his arms, Hebga's, that the town had delivered its soothing words. Those words had been of little consolation, really, for all it took was a few couplets of Aloga's song for the pain to take hold of his body once more. The wind rushing over the sand in the distance took up his song, providing a rhythm for the couplets of the false Hilun who was still singing there behind him. To distract himself he thought of the Marshal and held his ax tightly to his heart.

3

The Mother of the Market

Meanwhile, back in Edéa, Ngo Bikaï was quietly taking on her new role. The death of our Sita had made her the new Mother of the Market, and that was no small task. The departure of the soldiers hadn't emptied out the courtyards, for Edéa had been turned into something of a military camp. All sorts of trucks and vehicles kept passing through. Once a long line of tanks moved through the courtyards and disappeared into the forest. Life had to be reorganized with this new reality in mind, and Ngo Bikaï threw herself wholeheartedly into her new role as Mother.

"A new set of responsibilities," she said.

The war had upended life on the home front. Oh, what would she have done without the support of her husband, Fritz? Even if she was at home, in her courtyard, surrounded by her children, women came knocking at her door to get their orders, to ask her advice on shared business, or to tell her of their daily struggles. She listened and gave her opinion, talking now to this woman and later to another. Sometimes she sent one of "her women," as she called them, to settle an affair far from town, but not too often. Essentially, her role, if you can call it that, was to allocate the market stalls and determine where people could sell their goods, collect fees, and ensure the place was kept clean and orderly.

Taking care of this last bit meant she had a whole troop of young men chasing after her—those who didn't have a field of their own to cultivate and who were waiting for the harvest season to sell their muscles to those who did. A number of them ended up becoming soldiers. Soon they started showing up in their new uniforms, which gave them a new air of respect that they'd never had when they were just sweepers or working in the fields for the season. They were experiencing a sort of renaissance, although the war didn't really leave them enough time to take advantage of their new status—to get married, for example. Just a few days after they had signed up, Ngo Bikaï would find them sitting in the back of a truck that would soon take them far away.

"War, it's just like *njokmassi*," Fritz said.

Forced labor? Ngo Bikaï replied that he was exaggerating a bit and teased him: "Don't you start talking to me, too, about man's exploitation of his fellow man!"

Ignoring the joke, her husband described the rows of soldiers marching in formation, their sad eyes, how they disappeared each day in the distance.

"The exploitation of the black man by the white, you mean!" he continued. "Forced labor!"

Ngo Bikaï tried to avoid discussing politics with Fritz. They were a unique sort of couple in Edéa, joined by love, even if they weren't officially married, as Mininga never hesitated to make clear by stressing maliciously the prefix "Ngo" that defined her as an unmarried girl, as if that were some sort of dirty epithet. They had gotten together in a surprising way. Among the students in Fritz's class, Ngo Bikaï was the only one who never contradicted him. That was back when he was a *moniteur indigène*. Then one day she had disagreed with him over a question of French grammar, whether a certain threadfish—commonly called a captain—was "to eat" or had it "been eaten": was it an infinitive or a past participle? In the end, they were both sort of right. And soon after that he had wooed her, gotten her pregnant. After Ngo Bikaï's father had berated the young man, his own father told him to do the responsible thing and marry her. Fritz insisted that was beside the point, for no signature on a document could mean as much as the one she was carrying in her belly. That was before Fritz inherited his father's land and set up a business transporting produce. Since then the couple had grown fairly wealthy, even if everything is relative, as Fritz would say, when he compared his way of life to that of his brother, who worked in Douala, or with his friends who "worked for the white man."

"We're not doing too badly," he concluded.

This sort of comparison had been his obsession since he had left his position working for the white man, while others were still employed by the administration. It was a sort of never-ending one-upmanship. Fritz made a show of his wealth, especially because his brother was still renting the place where he lived in Akwa. Of course, Um Nyobè had built his own house in Yaoundé, or at least that's what he'd been told. As for Pouka, Fritz preferred not to talk about him, for no one really understood what kind of life he was leading: still single although he could afford to get married, still renting although employed as an *écrivain-interprète*. Whatever . . . He said he was a poet—and Fritz really didn't know what that meant. Fritz felt quite comfortable judging others, having set himself up as the arbiter of social behavior there in the forests of Edéa. Had anyone told him that he had just taken advantage of his brother's departure for the city—which had resulted in his being disinherited—and that he owed all his wealth to that, he would have found some excuse to side-step the issue and assert his own independence.

"And what about my father," he would have snapped back, "didn't he inherit as well?"

Obviously, people were polite enough to not remind him that his father had drawn a salary as an askari during the German colonization. Hard work was the principle on which he based his life, the pedestal of his freedom, as he put it. Sons received inheritances because their parents had done backbreaking work. So what! Fritz still kept working, and just as hard. Every month he went to Douala, where he delivered produce from Edéa's fields to the Congo market—cocoyams and plantains, mostly, as well as plums, of course. Yes, his father had left him a pickup truck, but he had bought two more after that. Yes, a dozen men worked for his father, but Fritz had three times as many working for him. The war had slowed down his business. A number of his *sansanboys*, as he called them, had signed up as tirailleurs.

At the last harvest, Fritz had counted up the young men who had appeared in his courtyard; since then, one question kept haunting him: Where had all the men in the village gone?

Edéa wasn't an exception: the carnivorous war's favorite food was young men. She had also swallowed down the burly guys who loaded his trucks. She had stolen the woodcutter, Hebga, who had been his unofficial foreman. That's why he saw this war as yet another instance of forced labor gangs gathering up all the men, as they had in the past, leaving the courtyards empty. The only difference was that France wasn't forcing these men to sign up. And yet for Fritz it wasn't really any different . . . just more of the same thing.

"No one forced Bilong to go," Ngo Bikaï remarked.

That was true. After she had quarreled with her little brother—a quarrel provoked by that fuss about Nguet—Bilong announced he had signed up as a tirailleur.

"You are trying to kill Mama." That was the only thing Ngo Bikaï had found to say, but then she didn't stop there. She didn't understand how breaking up with a whore—for to her, Nguet was nothing but a whore—could push him to want to kill their mother.

"I haven't killed anyone," Bilong replied.

"Aha, and just what do you think tirailleurs do?"

That's when Ngo Bikaï said the word that hadn't stopped haunting Bilong since: "Assassin!" He had left without saying goodbye, not to his sister or his mother. Only to Nguet, who had opened her legs to him that whole night long and then tearfully said goodbye; she had wanted to teach him about love and was devastated that he had chosen war.

Without Bilong even noticing, the war had taken over Edéa and upended his life. Its violence had solidified the position of the Mother of the Market, meaning Ngo Bikaï had more power than our Sita ever had. I don't think I'm exaggerating when I say she had practically become the village chief—although no one would have said that out loud. She now took her place in front of a stand in the market, and woman after woman came to her—one asking what work still needed to be done, another to complain about some ruffian who was making her life difficult, and a third to announce the birth of a child in her family or to complain about an unbearable husband. Sitting there in the midst of the papayas, mangoes, oranges, pineapples, lemons— all the hundreds of fruits that spread out around her—she listened to all those stories, the lives these women told her, although she wasn't even yet thirty years old!

She was Christian, Ngo Bikaï, having converted from Protestantism to Catholicism, unlike her husband, who was still "pagan," as she put it. Her status as one of the first members of Father Jean's church had made it easier for her to take control of the market, even if her religious convictions, as well as her own past, often put her at odds with Mininga. An unavoidable conflict. War had also transformed Mininga's Bar, especially since the arrival of all those soldiers in Edéa. First they had brought in electric lights—one bulb hanging from the ceiling and another outside made it clear that the lady was overjoyed with the new order of things. Then came the gramophone and all that music. As a result, this war was proving very lucrative for Mininga, an impression solidified when, much to the village's surprise, the recruits—new recruits!—posted a sign over the bar's door: LA SEIGNEURIALE—a title that inscribed Mininga's noble reputation.

Soon we'd see her serving girls walking by on the arms of white soldiers, as well as black ones, and then the rumor circulated that one of them had been spotted driving a French soldier's motorcycle. She'd been naked and laughing; the soldier was taking pictures. The gossiping woman added, "Since when do Mininga's women know how to drive motorcycles?" All the gossip produced a cacophony of contradictions: whereas before women whispered that Mininga was prostituting her serving girls, now everyone was surprised to see them wearing new outfits.

"A uniform for whores," Ngo Bikaï declared.

Mininga, ever malicious, spread the word around Edéa that Ngo Bikaï was "just living with Fritz, pretending they were married." And added, "She thinks she's better than me, but she's really just a whore."

Mininga even found words to mock Ngo Bikaï's new Catholic faith.

"Instead of asking her sweetie when they're lying in bed to put a ring on her finger, the *imbecile* just goes to church and prays!"

Before long Ngo Bikaï caught wind of the slander—her women reported it to her faithfully. "A real hyena, that Mininga," the Mother of the Market cursed, nervously tightening the scarf around her head. "The worst of all the animals."

Sometimes Ngo Bikaï tried to tell herself that it was good for a woman to show some initiative, that her squabbles with Mininga were just a minor distraction. But then the next day the Christian within her would reappear and she'd be back on the warpath, planning ways to raise an army of Furies to charge at the door of Mininga's Bar. What held her back was all the soldiers—white ones, even—who hung out in the bar. They were the ones who kept the party going night and day, as if the war everyone kept talking about were just something cooked up by the black recruits Ngo Bikaï would see sitting in the courtyard, their heads shaved, wearing the tirailleur's uniform, with bare feet.

"What else did you think it was?" Fritz would say to her. "The recolonization of Cameroon started with that de Gaulle."

The Mother of the Market let her husband talk—her mind was on her little brother.

4

Beyond the Privilege of Age

As for Yaoundé, things had changed there, too. There, the war was diluted by the chattering, the debates, the verbal jousting, the shifting of personnel. At least, that is, for those who hadn't signed up. It was the stuff of living room conversations, you might say; and speaking of living rooms, it was Martha, Um Noybè's wife, who finally opened the door after Pouka had knocked twice. She started with surprise, but then kissed him roundly on the cheeks.

"Um Noybè is going to be shocked," she said. "Come in."

She apologized as he tripped over the bags and baskets of fruit piled up against the wall. "My merchandise," she noted. Bulging watermelons and baskets of oranges. She headed to the living room, where her husband was holding a meeting.

"Look who's here."

"Pouka!" Um Nyobè shouted as he rose to his feet.

He was the only one who called out Pouka's name like that—it made him happy. Um Nyobè came across the living room to greet his friend, his arms held wide open and a smile lighting up his face, giving him a hug and then shaking his hand.

"You're not interrupting at all, quite the contrary," he reassured Pouka, who was embarrassed at intruding on the gathering.

He introduced him to the group in the living room. Although Pouka recognized one or two writers, most faces were unfamiliar.

"This is my brother," Um Noybè said. "He works for Deroudhille."

The men began to sneer, as if that were proof of an undeniable betrayal.

"In the palace," Pouka corrected, "since the *events*."

The sneers were replaced by looks of astonishment.

"It's a long story," the poet continued, although he opted not to tell it.

"The events," that was how he referred to Leclerc's arrival in the capital, the onset of the Second World War. Then Um Nyobè's wife asked for news of "Bikaï"—whom she called just that, instead of "my sister Ngo Bikaï."

"I heard she's become the Mother of the Market."

"Yes, that was after the events," Pouka explained. "I was already in Yaoundé."

Um Noybè was agitated, his eyelids flickering rapidly. He didn't make his usual jokes about birthrights. He was no longer the same man that the poet had seen back in Edéa, but who among them hadn't changed? Yes, was there anyone who hadn't changed? The war had given Pouka a new job. And he wasn't the only one. Four men were gathered there in the living room—Um Nyobè introduced them one after the other. They were all caught up in a lively debate, whereas before the events they'd only gotten together to talk of this and that. First there was Jérémie, a man so black he was almost blue, like someone from Sudan; Etoundi, who had a rather elegant Ewondo profile and who smoked cigarettes nonstop; Ouandié, with a broad forehead, a generous face, happy eyes, and an easy smile; and finally a heavyset man with a mustache—he looked like a well-fed child who'd gotten caught up body and soul in an unending argument.

"Go on, Marc," Um Nyobè told him.

Marc didn't even wait till Pouka had finished shaking everyone's hand and taken a seat.

"It's simple, really," he continued, holding up his hand to count as he spoke. "There are four important things."

It was plain to see, the mention of the number four irritated everyone there: Was it some sort of formula Marc used to keep the floor when everyone else wanted a chance to speak? Or was it because it sounded like Marc was launching into a lecture? Pouka had the impression no one there had the patience to listen to the "four important things."

"Only four?" Ouandié asked with a smile.

"First," Marc began, with a serious voice, "we need to define who we are talking about."

"That's done," Etoundi cut in. "We're not talking about single women here."

That made everyone laugh, and lightened the mood.

Marc continued unperturbed. "We're talking about the soldiers France is recruiting *under false pretenses.*"

He said the words with great emphasis, weighing carefully how each man reacted to them. Apparently this was the continuation of a discussion that Pouka hadn't been part of, and of which he was only catching bits and pieces. Someone, wanting to make a joke, added, "Well, *that* still needs to be proven."

It was Jérémie who'd spoken. His Bamiléké accent enlivened his words with surprising rhythms and intonations. Clearly, he was the adversary Marc was looking for.

"Let's not forget that during the Great War," he continued, staring Jérémie straight in the eyes, "Germany recruited crowds of soldiers who were then just left to their fate."

"Well, France certainly didn't owe them anything!"

That was Jérémie again.

"Precisely, that's the point," Etoundi interjected, self-assured and looking all around as if he were in a classroom. "France was given a mandate over Cameroon, one that clearly stipulated that she was responsible for the administration of the defeated colony, which means—"

They didn't let him finish.

"Have you read that mandate?"

"No," Etoundi conceded, "but—"

"I haven't finished," Marc said, cutting through the boisterous voices that had risen in response to Etoundi.

He turned left and right, striking the theatrical pose of reclaimed authority. He looked like a general signing an armistice. But you could see the impatience written on Um Nyobè's brow as he sat next to Marc, and in the frustrated gestures of his hands; it looked like he was trying to moderate a debate that was spiraling out of control or to find a phrase that had just escaped him. He waved at Pouka.

In the midst of this verbal chaos was he looking for a foothold, a point of departure—an ally?

"I forgot to ask," Um Nyobè said, "what are you drinking?"

Um Nyobè called to his wife in the back of the house: "Martha!" He whispered in her ear the drink his friend had requested. Soon Martha reappeared with bottles that replaced the first round, now empty, standing here and there among the plates that were still full.

"Eat," she said to the talkative men. "You're not even eating."

It was true, the rapid exchange of words had kept the men from emptying their plates. Ouandié asked for another beer.

"Don't you like my cooking?"

"Of course we do!" the men protested.

And how! It was bush meat, smoked and served with cocoyam. Some offered compliments, all had second helpings. Pouka took a mouthful. He complimented Martha and licked his fingers clean, one after the other.

"Your wife is spoiling you," he said to Um Nyobè.

"Let Marc finish what he was saying," their host declared, taking advantage of the pause left by the eating. "The four things?"

Like a hummingbird caught mid-flight, Marc's entire body had been hanging there suspended, ready to dive back into the unending argument.

"One, the group," he said, hurrying this time to get the better part of his argument, at least, off his lips. "Two, their interests. Three, our goal. Four, our plan of action. That's it."

The full mouths around him didn't reply. It was a victory without a battle, like a boxer who still had uppercuts left in his fists, or the landing of a flexible gymnast in the sand. Yet Marc looked pleased, the victor of a challenge that had yet to be formulated. Pouka wanted to take the floor, but held back. It wasn't yet clear to him just what had Um Nyobè's friends so riled up. He still needed to figure out the sides and, more important, how to tell one camp from the other.

Clearly, these men spoke to each other like old friends. Pouka saw them as verbal athletes reduced to making useless gestures with their hands in a living room. Keep talking, just keep talking, he thought, while others are putting their lives on the line. He almost told them the story of the letter he had given his boss, and how that had changed the course of history, but he was stopped when Marc again took the floor.

Marc thought that the interests of the Cameroonian soldiers who signed up to serve France should be clearly laid out before they left for the front. The errors of the past must not be repeated, specifically, how colonial Germany had never compensated those who had fought on her behalf. France and England, he explained, shouldn't be able to take advantage of the defenseless Cameroonian soldiers, as they clearly wanted to do, or else "they'll just be used as *cannon fodder*." He stared at each one in turn to assess the indignation provoked by these words. Clearly defining their interests in advance was the only way to ensure that these Cameroonian soldiers would be treated like *human beings*. Once again, he paused to assess the impact of his words.

The French soldiers, Marc continued, are protected by the laws of their country and by international conventions that remain in force, regardless of the outcome of the conflict, regardless of the situation in which they find themselves, whereas the fate of the tirailleurs is contingent on the goodwill of France alone. That's how, after the Great War, France had been able to treat the askaris—the Cameroonian soldiers, like his father, recruited by Germany—as if they were enemies. The question was simple, really. He paused before articulating it.

"Who will defend the interests of the Cameroonian soldiers?"

He smiled, crossed his arms, uncrossed them, then put his left hand to his chin pensively. A silence fell. After a moment Um Nyobè said tersely: "That is the real question."

Now Marc was the center of attention, which was what he always wanted, Pouka said to himself. He was a speechifier. He smiled as he realized that when Martha had come into the room, she'd allowed Marc to take the floor, something he hadn't quite managed on his own. He was a politician, Pouka declared silently to himself. The allusion to his father had given Marc an unassailable position: the fortress of emotion. Someone mentioned the League of Nations, and everyone burst out laughing, except for the one who had spoken—Jérémie. He still had his mouth full and couldn't defend himself well. But what really could he have said?

"Only Cameroonians themselves can defend the interests of the Cameroonian people," Ouandié cut in, in a tone that was above contradiction.

A deep silence followed his phrase.

"Only black men can defend the interests of black men," Marc added.

A phrase came to Pouka's mind: "Black, that's the color of my clothes." But he didn't say anything, he didn't want to become the enemy this group had just invented of common accord, and which they defined as "the French."

5

The Idea of Perfection

And so, Pouka refrained from speaking that night in Um Nyobè's living room. He was the first to leave his friend's house.

"He lives in Madagascar," Um Nyobè said, in response to the surprised reaction of all the others.

A reasonable explanation: Madagascar was on the outskirts of Yaoundé. Pouka needed to make his way back there on foot and it was already quite late. As he left, he was able to take Um Nyobè aside and ask the question that had led him there in the first place.

"Hebga?" Um Nyobè began. "He left a long time ago."

"Left?"

"They were the first ones mobilized."

Um Nyobè had gone to see him in the camp before he left, and once he'd even taken Martha, who had insisted she needed to say goodbye in person. He was holding up well, but who knows what the future holds for any of us? He had always asked about his "little cousin."

"I went to where you work to let you know," Um Nyobè added, "but no one knew where you were."

"I was transferred," Pouka said, "since the events."

"Yes, but I didn't know that then."

Martha handed him a huge watermelon, as well as a few *mintumbas*, those tasty steamed manioc cakes: "Since you don't have a woman at home to cook for you." Each time he visited after that, she would give him other dishes, meals for the single man. Pouka left his friend's home, embarrassed because he had realized just how shallow he was. The master of vainglory hadn't gone to see his cousin when he should have. History was his alibi, but it was the only one he could find. Could he have told his friend that he was working too much? That his new responsibilities were taking up all of his time?

As he walked on down Messa Road, which leads from Mokolo back to his home, he tried unsuccessfully to calm the turmoil in his heart. A long stretch of road spread out before him—one with no electric lights—and Um Nyobè had left him with only his own guilty conscience for a companion. He thought of his cousin Hebga spending days in this capital; he had always hoped to show his cousin around but, when push came to shove, he hadn't done anything to fulfill that promise. He thought about Um Nyobè, who had also been caught up in the events, but who still found the time to make several visits to the camp, "taking Martha along, too," so he could see how his brother—or "our brother," as he said—was holding up.

Suddenly Pouka understood just what he found so disconcerting about his friend. He was always ahead of his time, ahead of everyone else, yes, but precisely because he got down to the root of things. He recalled watching Um Nyobè in his living room debating all those people that Pouka didn't know, and he was ashamed—yes, ashamed that he had dismissed them as speechifiers. He had thought, yes, that they were "politicians"—especially given the ease with which Marc massaged arguments, finding his own way of presenting them such that there was no room for disagreement: "My father," he'd said. Just who could attack his father? And, Pouka admitted, Um Nyobè, who organized gatherings like that, always found the time to do what was necessary, what he himself had let slide: visiting the soldiers before they were sent off to war, treating them with simple human compassion.

"He's a politician, and he always wins."

There in the darkness, with his hand caressing the round watermelon, he went through all the arguments Marc had made. Yes, it was their duty to defend the interests of the Cameroonian soldiers, especially since the soldiers in question were our cousins, brothers, and fathers—in short, our compatriots. That argument couldn't be parried: even if they had fought on the German side, whether they had been askaris or tirailleurs, they were still our fathers, brothers, and cousins. Pouka saw once again the face of his friend Fritz's father: he had been an askari, a position that helped him to build his fortune, which he had invested in land that he planted, and later left to his son. He also saw Hebga's face: he saw his cousin, the boxer, the woodcutter, now wearing a tirailleur's uniform. He saw him in Yaoundé, setting off for a distant war, waiting for his cousin to make the gesture of kindness that he never got, the visit he never received. His shame grew thick, then his mind responded with a burst of protestations and excuses.

But, he said to himself, comparing the good fortune of Fritz's father to his cousin's present deprivations, there is no way to think about what was in Cameroon's best interest outside of the question of history's vicissitudes, for history is really what politics leaves behind. "And the ideal in politics is compromise," he concluded out loud. Since history is then nothing more than the sum of many compromises, perfection is only possible in poetry. That idea stirred him up so much that he exclaimed, "Perfection is a poetic idea." His voice roused the homeless, the beggars and lepers who were dozing off under the stands in the Mokolo market. He hurried on. But he still wasn't done, for his thoughts kept circling back. "Only Cameroonians themselves can defend the interests of the Cameroonian people." That phrase echoed on in his mind.

But then what about France? he wondered. How to get rid of France? His thoughts were racing. Suddenly he realized that although that sentence had a rhetorical weight and could be used to drive home the final nail in a lively debate among friends who were riled up, as a political program it had only flaws. In fact, in political terms the idea was outrageous.

Just how will they be able to defend their interests?

If the defense of Cameroonian interests needed to be made on a political field, who—yes, who—could put it forward? You'd have to rely on a French lawyer, give him the case.

So it'd be back to France.

And really, just what did "standing up to France" mean?

Well, in the end, it meant placing France again at the center of things!

And besides, what language would be used to formulate this statement of opposition, or this defense of the interests of the Cameroonian people, if—according to the arguments made there in Um Nyobè's living room—it needed to include "*all* Cameroonians."

Should it be in French?

On what text should it be modeled?

On "The Declaration of the Rights of Man and of the Citizen"!

So, on a fundamentally French text, is that it?

On the text that founded the French Republic.

And that wasn't all. We want respect for our rights? Well, those are best protected by a republic!

It follows, then, that it is clearly in our interest to establish a republic. And it was France that founded the first republic in Europe!

It was as if his clotted thoughts had finally begun to flow freely: To defend our interests, what would be ideal is the formation of a republic based on the respect of our rights, in short, a Cameroonian version of the French Revolution!

He paused.

And the formation of our own republic, on the French model.

And with that, Pouka concluded, we are back where we started: France. As he opened the door of his house, he realized that he held in his hands—finally!—an idea, the one he could have shared back there in Um Nyobè's living room, where he had sat in silence. He should have said that it is naïve to want to cut yourself off entirely from the West once you have been colonized; because the identity of the colonized is a product of politics, the idea of perfection is inherently inapplicable to it, even if it is anchored in the fortress of sentiments that a son feels for his father, or a man for his compatriots. The heavens above the colonized have already been filled. The paradox of our relationship with France is that she is at once our oppressor and our ideal. How can we get out of this trap?

"We must take responsibility for France if we want to free ourselves. We must take responsibility for France," he should have said, "that's why we must defend her."

He should have said, yes, that the tirailleurs to whom France had given rifles with bayonets held in their hands the advocate—*arma maxima!*—that their grandparents, unarmed at the start of colonization, hadn't had; that their parents, who'd been disarmed and defeated alongside Germany, hadn't had.

This weapon, it's a symbol of the republic!

A symbol of the constitution!

A symbol of liberty!

He could have said a lot of things, yes, for example: "We must instead sing of the glory of our soldiers."

Yes, he would have said all that and even repeated himself: "Pouka's not going to be caught out twice." That very night he began his poem "Sincere Tears," in which he hopes that France, having been brought to her knees, will rise up again, and where he writes that to take up arms on her behalf is to defend the interests of the Cameroonian people. If Germany's past defeat had been Cameroon's as well, Cameroon's ultimate victory would come with France's. This poem expresses everything he didn't say that evening at Um Nyobè's:

In the desert night you sleep 'neath the eternal moon
None will know your names, poor men of Cameroon
In the shifting tomb where your manes lie in repose
Never will bloom willow or rose
Nothing will recall for us your sweet memory
Except, perhaps, these verses that sing your glory.

And these words, he wrote them, of course, in alexandrine verse.

6

A New Cane for Leclerc

Meanwhile, on the front lines, Lieutenant Colonel Jean Colonna d'Ornano received an order to attack Italian positions in Libya. He had lively eyes and quick reflexes. He was as imposing physically as verbally, but right then he was speechless. Colonel Leclerc had come to his tent, saluted him, and given him de Gaulle's order, straight from London. D'Ornano read it in silence and grew angry. He had expected it, so it wasn't the order itself that angered him. Let's put ourselves in his place: when a colonel is under the orders of a lieutenant colonel, you're in a really strange situation, there's no way around it. No doubt d'Ornano would have reacted differently had he known that Leclerc had promoted himself to colonel "by enchantment" the moment he set foot in Cameroon. For the moment, he focused on "this confused line of command," as he called it, because the situation was dire.

To be taken seriously, de Gaulle needed to put a military victory on Churchill's table, even if the troops were lost somewhere in the middle of the desert near Faya-Largeau. What he didn't need was a quarrel between French officers. The troops from Cameroon had been placed under d'Ornano's command, a considerable reinforcement that gave his troops a numerical advantage over the Italian forces positioned at Kufra. The lieutenant colonel went over in his mind each of the problems posed by such an attack, the most unexpected of which was dealing with Colonel Leclerc's impatience: he was ready to throw his men into the desert that very evening in order to finish off the "fascists." Used to acting on his own, keeping his exchanges with de Gaulle private, and making the most of the credit he'd gotten for having rallied a good part of central Africa to the cause without firing a shot—Leclerc was a bit full of himself. Or maybe he was a bit immature? It was hard to get him to listen to anyone else's opinion.

Why hadn't the general given Leclerc command of the troops in Chad? d'Ornano wondered. Who there could have explained that the general had only promoted Leclerc to the grade of squadron leader?

Counting the troops that Colonel Leclerc had brought from Cameroon, d'Ornano had at his disposal an army of some five thousand tirailleurs, twenty companies in total, and three units of meharists. He was happy to have found among them two officers who knew Chad well: Captain Dio, whom he hadn't seen for several months, and especially Massu, an expert in navigating the *fesh-fesh*, the desert's treacherous sands. He needed to reorganize his forces, reassign the officers, and do it all without running afoul of Leclerc's pride—Leclerc's only experience in the desert was a short training period in Morocco in his youth. If only he knew how to listen! Late in the night the two men talked, finalizing the battle plan, and mostly trying to clear up the lines of communication so nothing would muddle their exchanges in the war council.

"War in Africa cannot be fought by conventional means," that was Leclerc's opinion, and d'Ornano just couldn't convince him otherwise.

"The Italians have their askaris, too," he noted.

"Of course."

Impatient, Leclerc repeatedly struck the ground with his cane.

"They are Libyans who know their country," d'Ornano continued. "*Their* country."

"This is about defending our country," Leclerc retorted. "*Our* country."

The irritation came through in his voice. And the lieutenant colonel thought about the thousand Chadian soldiers who had already made it through the most difficult of terrains, only a few of whom were used to dunes and sandstorms. The hundreds of Cameroonians Leclerc himself had brought from the forest, armed for the most part with no more than a machete, and who were certainly exhausted: Did he intend to use them as cannon fodder? The few trucks he had, a couple dozen, were useless in the sand, and they were running low on all the essentials. The troops don't even have adequate uniforms, he thought, shaking his head. To defend our country!

"That's why," Leclerc continued, his eyes running over the map spread out between them, on which only a few scattered spots marked oases, "we have to take them by surprise."

D'Ornano noted that this idea enchanted Massu. Massu, the officer in charge of the meharists.

"By surprise," said Dio. "That changes everything."

"We need to cut their communication lines," Captain Massu began, "that means starting in Murzuk."

"Murzuk."

D'Ornano's face lit up as he repeated that name. It was as if he had found the talisman he'd been missing till then. Or maybe it was the wind-driven sand whipping through the desert outside that rekindled his hopes?

"The Italian air base," Dio continued.

And the officers looked at one another, stunned as much by the announcement of this unavoidable battle as by how ill-suited their troops were for the task. For d'Ornano, it was obvious, only perfect soldiers could pull off this operation. Leclerc, for his part, saw that as just another excuse: war is fought "with the army you have." Yet the prospect of this unequal battle enchanted d'Ornano. In the morning he appeared at the colonel's tent with the plan that they had hammered out late the previous night in his hand and, on his lips, words that made Leclerc smile: "The English." Outside, the tirailleurs were doing their exercises, despite the chill of the desert's morning air, their songs and shouts ricocheting off into the unending silence that surrounded them, their movements casting indistinct shadows in the mist.

"Clayton," d'Ornano began.

With that name, Leclerc suddenly found a new cane to lean on.

"Clayton's battalion is specialized in navigating across the sand."

"We have to contact him," said Leclerc tersely.

And that made Lieutenant Colonel d'Ornano smile.

7

Bilong's Moment

Had Lieutenant Colonel d'Ornano asked Hebga or Aloga what they thought, they surely would have advised him to choose someone else for the Murzuk mission. One can easily imagine that the officer's nerves had already been frayed by the shakiness of his authority, which was continually undercut by the colonel looming in the shadows behind him. He knew he was being watched and, that being the case, the astute politician planned on making a few moves that would mollify Leclerc. When reviewing the troops that morning, he selected the tirailleurs for the operation in Murzuk. Dio and Massu, whom he trusted, had given him good recommendations for some of the Cameroonian soldiers; Leclerc concurred and, as a result, he stopped in front of Tirailleur First-Class Bilong and ordered him to step forward.

The boy had put his whole heart into his training, you have to admit. His uniform was always impeccable, his comportment exemplary—he had become the soldier all officers dream of. His youth gave him an easy demeanor that others no longer had. It was as if the role of tirailleur had revealed in him military talents that no one in Edéa had ever suspected—or had ever wanted to see. Maybe he wanted to be done once and for all with the false judgments of men who treated him like a child, or those of his mother and older sister, who saw him as a kid. Confirming his revenge, he spied out of the corner of his eye the face of true disappointment. It was Philothée.

Philothée was the person Bilong was closest to in the camp. His friend's stuttering meant that they had moved beyond words; more than talking, what they each needed, really, was to see the other's look of encouragement. They were about the same age, and the same ironic glint lit up their eyes when they saw something funny. A smile served as their secret code. That was all. They shared with Aloga the memory of Edéa's little poetry circle, but they had never found a way to cross the bridge that separated them from the Hilun, to embrace that man who seemed to have emerged from an age-old thicket and, to top it off, whose "feet just weren't made to wear the white man's shoes"—as Bilong declared with a laugh the day they each received a pair. Everything about that Aloga seemed a real mishmash. Their friendship was based on the adolescent jokes they shared. Bilong was the one who told the jokes, and for him, Aloga was a never-ending source of material. The fact that they were all there together in the French army was what had sealed his authority over Philothée, who had really only joined Free France to copy his friend.

The day Bilong had been torn away from Nguet's perfume by the women of Edéa, instead of heading back home, he had rushed out along the streets of the village. Following a signal from Pouka, Philothée had headed after him. Together the two members of the little poetry circle had gone up and down paths, crisscrossing the market, with Philothée always at Bilong's heels. The strange pair had soon found themselves in front of the French military camp, and that's where Bilong confided his extraordinary plan: "I want to be a soldier."

They had arrived right when the machetes were being distributed to the tirailleurs. At first the sight of those weapons piled up in the courtyard at Captain Dio's feet had given him pause. But then the mountain of metal, and most of all the way the soldiers had all looked at them—running their eyes over the boys' cheeks as if they were women—had roused in him something he didn't know his body was capable of: a blind rage. Colonel Leclerc signaled to Dio, who stopped what he was doing to hand Bilong an improvised enlistment form; Bilong's hand trembled as he wrote down his name. That made him the first literate soldier from the region to volunteer. Leclerc decided it wasn't important to ask his age.

"What about your friend?" Captain Dio asked.

"My friend?"

I'd say that was the moment when Bilong started to feel responsible for Philothée. When Philothée hadn't answered, Captain Dio—who had a gift for discovering hidden soldiers where they were least expected—put the question right to Bilong. Leclerc, for his part, recalled the young man who had launched into "La Marseillaise" and led the whole crowd in song—something the colonists in Douala hadn't been able to do when the city had come under his command.

"His name is Philothée," Bilong replied.

Philothée hadn't stopped Captain Dio from inscribing his name next to his friend's. He had signed where he was told to, awed perhaps by the white men and their things, just as he had been when he decided to join the poetry circle. That's how, on the day when the women of Edéa had joined forces in front of Mininga's Bar to liberate Bilong, two adolescents entered into the Second World War. Love, like friendship, is a castle full of surprises. Of course, Bilong and Philothée didn't yet know just what they had gotten themselves into. On their way, they discovered all the advantages of signing up. They discovered parts of Cameroon they never would have dreamed of, met tribes they'd never before known of, and heard strange languages. Out of Edéa for the first time in his life, Philothée thanked Bilong every day for having helped him to discover the world.

If that was all a soldier's life was . . . but, alas! Who could have told him what that life really was? If only the Second World War had just let them explore Cameroon! Ah! Who could have told him what war really was? Living in a colony had limited his horizon; and given his young age, Philothée was always afraid of being roped into forced labor. Leaving was a tantalizing solution that Pouka had held up before him; the French army made it possible. The disappointment visible in his eyes was that of a starving man who realizes that yet another feast is escaping his grasp. Until that point, he and Bilong had shared their feelings and impressions, their sense of wonderment. Now, for the first time, "the lucky one" would have something different to tell him. That's certainly why he cursed, "Shit!"

"Step forward," said Lieutenant Colonel d'Ornano. "March! One-two, one-two!"

A soldier doesn't look back. Bilong didn't turn around. He didn't see the envy in his friend's eyes. He had never put his feet to the ground with such pride, such precision, never held his head high with such elegance, or swung his arms with such fervor. And the tirailleurs' song that he knew so well, never had he sung it with such conviction. He thought of his father, so impatient to see him act like a man; of his mother, who had cried the day he'd done so; and mostly of Nguet, who had revealed the man within him. She who, on the first day of their love, had held his testicles and declared, as his penis grew longer: "Here is a man." If only she could have seen him singled out from among all those thousands of soldiers come from all parts of Africa, singled out for the perfection of his bearing and the care with which he aimed his weapon. Ah, if only she had seen him that day when he was transformed by his soldier's uniform! He sang the tirailleurs' song—"Le Chant des Africains"—but really what Bilong chanted out were the psalms of the *Book of Love*, the *Lerewa Nuu Nguet*, written by the Sultan Njoya and that he reconstructed word by word in his head as he remembered his lover's body, his lover whose demands and suggestions he had written down in rhyming couplets: in alexandrines, as he had learned to do.

8

The Dunes of Nguet

Yet, oh . . . how sweet it is to hear your mother tongue as you prepare to depart! How sweet it is to listen to a lullaby from home when
your soul is facing the unknown. It was Aloga who woke Bilong up
that morning, with a serious, fatherly look in his eyes. The other
Bassas stood around him. As the false Hilun put it, they wanted to
say "one or two prayers." This was the second time since they had
found themselves in the emptiness defined by the hundreds of
incomprehensible languages that set each group apart from one another that they had gathered together to speak in the one language
that took them back to Edéa. If truth be told, Aloga was the only one
to speak, even if he gave each of them a chance to say something.

"You've said it all," was what each replied.

Hebga added, "Big brother."

And truly, Aloga had said it all. Later, his words will compete
with the image of Nguet's body in a battle for Bilong's heart, when
he sits in the truck headed for Murzuk, crossing dunes and sometimes feeling as if he's been swallowed up whole by the land rising
around him in gigantic waves of sand. On both sides of the convoy
the meharists, led by Captain Dio, advanced on their camels. At the
start of the procession was a truck carrying the company's officers:
d'Ornano, Leclerc, and several white soldiers. All Bilong could see
around him were the great expanses of sand and the rays of the sun
that stretched out ahead or behind them in turn. Sand, sand, sand,

nothing but sand. He closed his eyes, for his tears had long since dried up. When he opened them, he was again struck by the sand stretching out before him.

The sand-filled eyes of his four fellow tirailleurs reflected his own fear back at him. Lost in the belly of the earth, they hadn't even had the chance to tell each other their respective stories. But maybe they did—I'm sure they did. On the tenth day of their trek, Bilong opened his eyes and the desert before him had the shape of a breast. Yes, a woman's breast, gigantic, with the nipple pointing toward the sun. Then the sand turned into a flat belly, which disappeared into the depths of a vulva, and opened up again into two expansive legs. He elbowed his neighbor several times, but the brave fellow, a Nigerian, wasn't impressed, nor were the three others, who were from Chad; they seemed to have come down with desert sickness and weren't hiding it.

"Let us sleep?" railed the Nigerian.

It was the Chadians, however, who soon turned Bilong's visions into a joke, for what else could they do there in the back of a truck, lost in the endless monotony of the dunes?

"Cameroonian always thinking screw," said one of the Chadians with a laugh.

The others joined in.

"Him see woman everywhere."

"*Gnoxer* desert, even."

That was pretty much true. Bilong got an erection each time he thought about his girlfriend. And now she had taken on the shape of the desert just to entrance him. What would the tirailleurs have said had they seen him plunge his hand into his pants pocket to calm his *bangala*? But that's what his relationship with Nguet had become. She took on unforeseen shapes. Sometimes his girlfriend appeared as a tree, sometimes as a bird's song, or the sound of a stream; at times she was a taste, the heady taste of a mango, ah! He saw her everywhere he looked, and each time his tongue, his fingers, and his penis answered her call. That, Bilong couldn't explain—not to his mother or his sister, neither of whom would have understood. And let's not even talk about the other tirailleurs!

Twenty times a day Bilong made love to his girlfriend, and it just wasn't enough. He had her up against the wall, on the table, on the chair, in every part of the house. He lifted up her right leg, then her left, then both, to penetrate her more deeply. He took her from behind, lying on the side, and still it wasn't enough. A hundred and sixteen—no, seventeen—positions, and still there were more. Sometimes he put his penis between her breasts and moved back and forth, sometimes she held him in her closed fist, or sucked on him—a quickie between two tasks at work. Oh! What didn't they do?

If for Bilong paradise had the shape of Nguet's orifices, his comrades were imagining the one that awaited them at the end of the war: an oasis. And right then, it was an oasis that appeared before Bilong's eyes, at the end of a shallow valley. That oasis—he imagined it as succulent as Nguet's sex. He closed his eyes and ears and saw Nguet's vagina with as much precision as he saw the oasis ahead of them. He could make out the lips over here, the clitoris there, and on one side the rise of a small bushy tuft. He bathed in her evanescent perfume, felt his heart beating and his mouth go dry; then he opened his eyes and tried to catch up with the conversations of his companions, who hadn't realized that he had cum.

Those men would have burst out laughing if they had seen what he saw. But who could blame him for being afraid—afraid to death, in prey to that kind of fear that makes both heroes and those condemned piss or even shit in their pants? Oh! How many days did they spend crossing that burning desert? How many days did they walk through that endless expanse of gold? In his own mind, Bilong was making that trek across the very body of his girlfriend, who had become the Sahara. His misty gaze could barely make out the lingering lights marking the path ahead, a promise writ in scarlet. Then he jumped: the meharists who were leading the trucks waved their arms, and the convoy came to a halt.

"Kayouge," they said. "Kayouge!"

It was just a brief respite, even if their numbers were increased by the troops—English and others—who met them at Kayouge: a hundred men with heavier trucks, some of which had metal tracks instead of wheels. Lost there in the immensity of this distant place that he had always dreamed of exploring but that, now that he was here, terrified him, Bilong couldn't make out the dunes that lay before him, no more than he could foresee what he would find in the Fezzan. At that point the date was already January 6, 1941; the troops that joined his company were those of Major Pat Clayton, the very ones who had brought a smile to d'Ornano's lips the morning after that sleepless night.

Bilong didn't need to know all the details, and neither do you, really, my dear reader. As for me, the narrator of this book, I know that before him opened up one last triangle—and its hypotenuse was formed not by the truth of our Nguet, but rather by the Italian forces that our troops met in Murzuk, and especially by one certain Sicilian I'll tell you about when the time is right.

9

Homework in History and Geography

Here's a quick summary of what has happened thus far: an adolescent left his home, attracted by the succulent smell of fried fish, or by the gentle song of a turtledove, or by a woman's luscious, sweet ass, what does it matter? For this boy would suddenly find himself in the middle of a battle in the Sahara, a battle memorialized in history books, even if they have forgotten his name. Yet everything began that day, yes, it did, when Bilong joined the little poetry circle. Exhausted by counting syllables—an exercise Pouka had insisted they do repeatedly ("a poem is comprised of a sum of syllables, or feet, as we say")—he had waited for the break like a man dying of thirst. And it was then that he had found himself standing in front of Mininga's serving girls, who were eyeing the poetic fraternity from a discreet distance.

"Don't you have a glass of water for me?"

He had spoken to the girl in the lacy dress, the one with big earrings, who usually worked the bar.

"What are you doing over there?" she asked after she brought him the water, curious about what they were up to.

It was Nguet.

"Writing," Bilong told her. He drank deeply from the goblet she had given him, his legs splayed so that the drips would soak into the ground.

"Writing what?" our Nguet continued.

"Rhymes."

Hearing that, the other women chimed in.

"What's that?"

"Can you eat it?"

Bilong lost all interest in trying to explain rhymes to them.

"So," Nguet began, "instead of going to the fields with every-one else, you come here, to the bar, to write rhymes."

"Instead of chattering on like this, you should be happy that we come here to work in your bar," Bilong countered.

Mininga would have agreed with him, except she hadn't been there when the exchange took place.

"Thank you for the water."

He handed the empty goblet back to the woman who'd spoken and started to turn away.

"Don't talk too much, now," she snapped back. "But how long have you been doing that?"

"How long?" Bilong exclaimed. "You want me to get to work on you?"

"Just where is the man?" she retorted.

The other women burst out laughing. With his back to the wall, Bilong tried to give a cocky answer: "Me, I'm gonna work you over, every part of your body, until you are in tears, wah, wah, wah."

"Ah, do you hear that?"

"The kid is really something, huh?"

Bilong started to leave, still thinking that he'd had the last word, when another reply made him stop in his tracks.

"Does Mr. Poet do anything besides talk?"

The boy had frozen in place. He turned around suddenly, an in-sult ready on his lips, but the sly whispering of the women made it clear they'd figured out he was a virgin.

"Let the little kid grow up," one of them advised—a suggestion that only made him less steady on his feet.

"He has to get back to his rhymes," said another.

"I'll be waiting right here for you," replied Nguet. "You can show me how you work a woman over till she cries."

The women burst out laughing again. Bilong waded through their sarcasm, back to the table where Pouka was again explaining the importance of syllables. The maestro glared at him, but didn't say anything. The next morning, Bilong was the first to arrive in the bar. He went straight to Nguet's door and knocked.

"Here I am."

Then it was the woman who was surprised. Her hair was still loose and she had only a pagne tied around her hips. Bilong jumped right on her.

"Hey, hey, hey," she said, backing away. "Do you think that's how you go about working a woman over?"

Bilong kept moving forward, and his momentum sent them both tumbling back on the bed. The boy tore off the woman's pagne.

"Are you trying to *rape* me?" she asked.

She said "rape" in French, staring him down with the fiercest of glares. Only then did Bilong pause.

"You see, I thought you knew how to *make love* to a woman . . ."

Bilong, of course, didn't admit how simple his problem was: he had never seen a naked woman before. Still, oh! Good Lord, Nguet figured it out, all right. Instead of getting dressed, she gestured for him to sit down next to her.

"Sit right here," she ordered.

Bilong felt a wave of shame flood over him. She took his hand and, step by step, moved it over her body.

"This is a breast, you see?"

Bilong started to protest, acting out the part of an experienced lady's man ("Me, I see breasts like that every morning with breakfast, what do you think?"), but she put her hand to his lips (and thankfully she didn't say, "I know, your mother's breasts that you still suck on each morning").

"Shhh," she said. "Do you want me to yell? The whole bar doesn't need to hear us, do they? Look, see, a breast is delicate."

She showed him her nipple.

"Very sensitive."

She took one of his fingers and placed it gently on her nipple.

"You touch it gently."

Gulp!

"Now, I know you want to go straight here," she said, showing him her vulva. The boy smiled.

"Only you have to start here," she said, pointing to her head, "if you really want to work me over until I cry. Then move on to here . . ."

That's how she introduced him to the whole surface of her body, like a desert he had to cross, one part after the other, one limb after the other, even if he was dying of thirst. And that's how he discovered that his girlfriend was a whole territory for him to explore, day after day. The dunes of Nguet were revealed to him in a dark bedroom in Edéa. Like an experienced traveler, he hurried to dive into his studies of French poetry, arriving early each morning to knock at Nguet's door: he who wants to go far gets an early start, as we say. So each morning when Bilong woke up, there before his eyes he could clearly see, unclothed, another part of Nguet's body, the part of the day, shall we say—the knee, perhaps.

That's how Bilong became a regular traveler in his girlfriend's territory. He arrived before the other members of the little poetry circle, his mind fixed on Nguet's knee. He knew that to get to the knee, he'd go from the forehead to the nape, from the nape to the front of her neck, from neck to breasts, from chest to shoulder, arm, hand, fingers, and then belly; across her belly to the belly button, before heading to her curvaceous buttocks, and then on to her thigh, and finally, her knee. He soon discovered that it was Nguet's clitoris that he loved to hold between his lips, sucking on it gently, and that to get there, he needed patience and a delicate touch. Little by little, working over his girlfriend distorted his sense of time, because if he didn't want to arrive late to the poetry sessions, he needed to come earlier and earlier to the lovemaking sessions. Day by day they grew longer and soon took up whole nights. Finally, he just moved in to Mininga's Bar.

The women of La Seigneuriale weren't surprised to see him there every night. They smiled, and one suggested that he was learning how to work, after all. Bilong realized that working over a woman is like homework in history and geography. But let's move on past the twists and turns of his endlessly repeated travels, yes, let's move on, for the hero of this chapter has at least one historic role to play in this Second World War, which is where his explorations of Nguet's geography had finally led him. Let's move on past these pages in the history books that, instead of explaining the laborious efforts of a

Senegalese tirailleur named Bilong, as I have just done, focus rather on praising the efforts of the officers. If you want to read them, you can open the book *Le Général Leclerc vu par ses compagnons de combat* (Paris: Editions Alsatia, 1948), pages 34, 47, and 61.

And as for Bilong, history doesn't even mention how he discovered the cane—the one the man who was still Colonel Leclerc used as an alibi to stay away from the front, on the peaceful side of the dunes, while he sent others, Senegalese tirailleurs in particular, into the no-man's-land of the battle, even as he expected that history would soon forget those trivial details and, instead, build statues in his honor, like the one that graces an intersection in Douala. "I have a bit of a limp," he would say. "So, Tirailleur First-Class Bilong, if you want to become an officer one day, take this grenade and go throw it at the Italian plane you see over there, because the Italians are all fascists."

In any event, that's how Bilong came to find what he'd been looking for when he'd cozied up to the women.

10

The Courage of Tirailleur Bilong

And how! Leclerc knew that only a child will run to catch fire with his bare hands. So he knew, Colonel Leclerc did, that the best tirailleur is a child, the ideal soldier an adolescent. That's certainly why he hadn't asked Bilong's age when he signed up, why he wanted the boy to be chosen for this mission. The cruelty of a general is on scale with his victories, or so it seems, and Leclerc knew that his army's mission was to liberate France. If his first priority had been to get shoes for all of his soldiers, my dear reader, then Paris would be German today!

The Battle of Murzuk took place on January 11, 1941, right in the middle of the day. So the sun was high above when Bilong, Ngo Bikaï's little brother, Nguet's *ndoss papa*, Edéa's child, lifted his head from behind the dune's protective shelter to peer over the sand while his commander, d'Ornano, ordered him, with a thousand frantic gestures, to get back down.

"Are you crazy?"

Bilong stood up, Leclerc's promise burning his back.

"Take cover!" d'Ornano hissed. "Cover!"

But Bilong wasn't listening anymore. He charged forward. His feet sank into the sand, making him struggle for each step ahead. The Free French forces began shooting to give him some cover, the umbrella he didn't have. Bullets whistled overhead, too close. He ran. He wasn't wearing shoes, the sand burned his feet. It didn't matter.

The plane was the only thing on his mind, that plane in which he certainly would have loved to fly off to visit the most wondrous parts of the world, the most distant continents—that plane he'd been ordered to destroy, like an adolescent setting fire to his own dreams. As he faced the plane of his dreams, he heard Leclerc's promise—the "colonel's" promise—to make him an officer. He imagined himself in a uniform, covered with stripes, screwing Nguet to the squeaky music of those medals of bronze—no, of silver, no, gold!

Now he no longer heard the bullets splitting the air above his head, only the screech of the medals, the meowing of his stripes, the cries of his lover, because he—an officer of Free France—was working her over. At the finish line of his race—of his lovemaking—he approached the plane as one does truth, with a whisper; as one discovers the infinite, step by step. He moved closer to reach that mutual orgasm that made him push into his girlfriend again and again. The plane was a star there at the finish line, a spark at the end of his dream, Nguet's clitoris, the candy he so loved to suck on. Ah! The only thing on his mind was the nose of that plane! That's why he didn't feel the bullet shoot through his right shoulder. He shifted the grenade to his left hand and kept on running. Nor did he feel the bullet that shot through his thigh. He hopped on one leg. Another bullet went through his chest; he didn't feel it, either, even as he fell. He lay there for a moment, stunned, dumbstruck. But soon, motivated by the vision of the clitoris that was so close, by the nose of the plane—of his Nguet—he got back up, limped for a few steps, and then started running again. He forgot his own body, he was pure force of will. He was surrounded by silence when, for the second time, he was felled by another bullet, but again he got back up and took off, holding the grenade between his own teeth. Maybe the Italians, surprised by his endurance—*forza nero!*—petrified by the impossibility of cutting down this lover, this soldier, just stopped shooting?

For it was absolutely silent when Bilong threw himself on the plane—the plane that could have let him realize his adolescent dreams; the grenade sent him flying, high and away, in a gigantic explosion, unlike any he had known with Nguet. Amid the debris, he collapsed in a burst of light that tore open the sky, fell into the belly of the sand that reached up with open arms to welcome him. Silence blanketed his spirit and his body, leaving only the earth to bear witness to the beating of his heart, which kept on, thump, thump, thump. The sand freed his hand, which was still moving, animated by the force of will that had thrown him into death's arms. Ah! The Battle of Murzuk lasted all day, a long terrible day that ended with the Italian retreat. Without their planes, yes, without their planes, which had all been reduced to charred carcasses by the tirailleurs Colonel Leclerc had thrown at them, one by one, like the most succulent tidbits—each holding a grenade. If the Italians hadn't known before what a handful of tirailleurs in a column of Allied soldiers could do, well, they learned it that day.

There was only one survivor: Bilong, "Charles," Aloga would say, "the lucky little guy."

Bilong, yes, Bilong! How did he do it? Aloga, like his companions, kept reciting incantations, ritual phrases, and wiping the tears from his cheeks, for his prayers had been granted.

"Twenty bullets in his body," Leclerc will say when visiting the wounded in the clinic, "and he is still alive!"

The colonel appreciated the courage of a tirailleur, the black force, though not according to the terms laid out in Charles Mangin's book. Still, the secret of this specific tirailleur escaped him. Bilong was convinced it was his girlfriend, Nguet, who had saved him. Don't ask me how he came to that conclusion. All I know is that in his delirium, he barked out sounds in which only one name was recognizable.

"Nguet!" he cried.

And in the darkest part of the night, his voice awoke the tents with his one obsessively repeated cry: "Nguet!"

The cry of a man drunk with love, overwhelmed by the essence of his lover.

"Nguet!"

A man's cry.

Period.

Lieutenant Colonel d'Ornano didn't make it out alive from that battle in the desert. It seems he threw himself after Bilong's shadow when the young soldier fell for the first time into the hollow of the sand and lay there twitching, still holding the grenade. After giving the order to provide cover for the soldier with a spray of bullets, D'Ornano tried to protect the wounded man himself. His head was shot through by an Italian bullet that dug down into the sand, still burning hot, shot from the rifle of a Sicilian marksman. He took aim and shut one eye before he pulled the trigger, then cursed, *"Figlio di puttana!"* D'Ornano didn't have a chance to open his eyes, didn't see Bilong, that true son of his mother, Nguet's lover, his sister's brother, in short, that lady's man, lift up his foot, his knee, his whole body, and set off running at the plane Colonel Leclerc had given him the order to destroy if he wanted to become an officer in the Free French forces. The same Sicilian who killed d'Ornano also took Major Clayton prisoner—an exploit that earned him the highest honors awarded by the fascist regime. A small consolation, and insignificant, really, because that's not the end of this story.

In fact, this is how Leclerc took command of the battalion from Chad, comprised of black and white soldiers. The note from General de Gaulle didn't waste time going over something that was already a fait accompli, because among the officers who returned unharmed from Murzuk, he was now the highest ranked.

Really, history marches on.

11

German Shoes

Obviously, history marches on, in its own way. For neither Bilong's mother nor Ngo Bikaï knew that their boy was lying in the military clinic in Faya-Largeau, nor that he kept crying out the name Nguet, minute after minute. What would they have said had they known, huh? I can only imagine, because at that very moment Edéa, unlike Murzuk, was experiencing a rare burst of excitement. The town was learning the cost it had to bear so that General de Gaulle could brag to Churchill about a French victory off in a corner of the Sahara that neither man had heard of before. The cost of this prize, Edéa could have calculated it well before the battle of Murzuk, if only the Anglophone woman who sold plantains and plums in front of Mininga's Bar hadn't already shut up shop. Just seeing the rise in the price of plums would have shown the impact of the Second World War on the cost of filling a cooking pot back on the home front. But, frightened by the appetite of the recruits who looked at her like she was just another succulent plum, the woman had stopped coming. She had gone back to her native Bamenda.

"*Na akwarar make a run from Edéa-o*": these words, saying she'd been chased out by a whore, were all she left behind after ten years in business.

"*Akwarar?*" people asked.

"She's exaggerating!"

Useless to say that this didn't make Mininga happy—she thought the woman was talking about her! Between you and me, what was threatening Edéa had nothing to do with prostitution. War was the real problem. Everyone kept talking about the "war effort," about "contributions" and "participation," about "support" and "aid to the country in her time of need," about "collecting funds." Conversations only turn to money when cash is short, Fritz said. Those who are bankrupt dream of piles of cash, and Edéa was learning what happens to a small African village when the bankrupt in question is Free France.

First there was a sermon by Father Jean that everyone remembered as the one about "German shoes." The priest had announced the mass well ahead of time, and for once—perhaps for the only time in the history of the Catholic Church—it was the tirailleurs who spread the word for him. That the French army encouraged people to go to Sunday mass, that alone should have alarmed everyone, but surprising things just didn't surprise anyone anymore. No one except for Fritz, that is. But let's forget about him, since he was in Douala on business.

Ngo Bikaï had gathered all her women, but really, everyone was trying to round up everyone else. Even the employees of La Seigneuriale were there. Mininga walked through the church dressed in an outfit so scandalously blue that everyone wondered why she was decked out so beautifully if she was in mourning. Her head was invisible, lost inside a big red hat adorned with a white flower. She went and took a seat right in front of the priest's pulpit. Her serving girls filed in behind and took their places around her, treating her like the queen she certainly thought she was, except that she had to fan herself with a flyswatter she pulled out of her bag—well, at least that's what people said. M'bangue was the only one in town who refused to leave his courtyard, convinced that de Gaulle's efforts were useless, since Hitler had already committed suicide.

The pro-German voices that had kept the flames of debate burning before the French soldiers arrived in town had finally quieted down, mostly because the youths who spent their days chatting away and who had bet on Germany had woken up to find themselves signed up for the French army, since it was the French who had come knocking on their doors. What I mean is that the time of endless chattering had come to an end. As for the old men who had lived through the era of German colonization, for the most part they had now rallied to the French cause and hoped that de Gaulle would take revenge for how badly that mustachioed Kaiser had kicked them in the balls.

Edéa in 1941—it was a different day, a different era, a different war. Maybe that's why, when Father Jean announced he was going to talk about German shoes, no one understood why he was reopening a closed question. As far as Edéa was concerned, in just a few months Germany had for the second time lost the Great War—a war some still remembered all too well.

"Have you seen the feet of the Free French soldiers?" the priest asked, his clear voice echoing through the church.

Obviously, everyone had seen the tirailleurs' feet, even if we hadn't paid too much attention, because who does look carefully at soldiers' feet? But whatever, that was one of those rhetorical devices used by priests to capture the attention of the congregation.

"They go barefoot," he went on, "because even in its misery, Free France retains her humanity!"

The bare humanity of the feet of the Free French soldiers would have passed unnoticed here, because, truth be told, whether they were serving Free France or not, they weren't the only ones to go barefoot—even in the church there were a lot of people not wearing shoes. Even Ngo Bikaï, who was fairly well off, and the Mother of the Market to boot, often went barefoot, as had her mother before her. The people kept listening, curious as anyone would be to see just where the priest's logic would lead, when instead of quoting the Bible, as he usually did, Father Jean opened the pages of a book he termed infamous and read several passages out loud to prove just how awful the situation was.

"There you go," he said, "it's all written right there."

And he waved around the book that laid out all the misfortunes of the human race, especially of the black people.

"It's written by Hitler himself."

And that wasn't all he said.

"He wrote it with his own hand."

Everyone believed him.

"In German."

The infamy was palpable, visible. No one asked to read the book in question because everyone knew it was the devil's work. The priest came back to the tirailleurs' bare feet.

"Free France," he said, his eyes lighting up as he scanned the crowd before him, "worthy France"—there he paused—"our eternal France refuses to manufacture shoes out of the skins of her black people!"

He spread his hands out before him, one holding the Bible, the other the infamous book that he hadn't yet named, and never would.

"No," he said, "just no!"

The whole church agreed with him. Father Jean, acting as the referee in this match between two books with opposing ideas, looked at the two books, looked at his congregation, and then put down the horrible book and wiped his brow.

"Rather than manufacturing boots with the skin of black people, as Nazi Germany does"—here he paused significantly—"Free France has decided to have her soldiers march barefoot."

Why didn't everyone there applaud for Free France? Probably because the father—more a priest than a politician—kept going full throttle.

"Unless *you* decide that you will provide shoes for our tirailleurs!"

Very few people applaud when they are asked for money. The people of Edéa are no exception. Before anyone else would get up out of their seats, Mininga herself had to dig down into her purse and show everyone there the five-hundred-franc bill she pulled out—a huge sum of money for the time—before placing it in the collection basket in front of the priest's pulpit. Father Jean needed to do something to prod people to action; again, it was Mininga who, with a wave of her hand, challenged everyone else to follow her lead: Can anyone top that? Then she made her exit, her heels clicking loudly, trailed by her serving girls, Nguet first among them. In my narrator's notebook, those women deserve some leeway, despite all the stares that were fixed on them. They couldn't know, of course, the sorry state Bilong was in right then in Faya-Largeau.

But it wasn't Mininga's *coss coss* that everyone remembered from that day, but rather the German shoes Father Jean had talked about. Since then, the villagers exchange smiles whenever they talk about shoes; and given Edéa's history, it's no surprise that a lot of folks still preferred to walk barefoot after the war. There are those who stare intently at the feet of our soldiers, trying to see if they are wearing boots or galoshes, and our soldiers, for their part, stare back, trying to see which civilians are wearing boots. You never know, no, you never do. It's a strange habit, though, one that brought a joke to Ngo Bikaï's lips. One day three tirailleurs came knocking at her door. She gestured to the children, sending them to play out behind the house. The face of one of the soldiers seemed familiar, so she spoke to him first; in fact, he was one of the men who used to sweep the market-place for her.

"I didn't recognize you," she said apologetically.

The man smiled. Wearing that uniform, he no longer looked like a beggar.

"Your shoes suit you well," she added.

Those words relaxed the atmosphere.

12

The Neighbor Full of Surprises

The story of that man, whose name she couldn't recall, came back to Ngo Bikaï. At first he had worked in the women's shadows, and then for Fritz. She was happy he had found a place in the army. He seemed to be the leader of the group that showed up in her courtyard.

"Please excuse us," he began, his eyes scanning all around, without ever making contact with Ngo Bikaï's. "Please excuse us."

"I understand," she interrupted. "You need contributions."

"For the war effort."

"Yes."

He seemed to be searching for the words he needed.

"No, it's that . . ."

"But I've already contributed," Ngo Bikaï said, "at church."

"We heard," he began, "that the women are . . ."

He took a deep breath, looking at his companions, as if imploring them to come to his aid. Ngo Bikaï never would have believed that being a leader could weigh so heavily on someone's shoulders.

"The women?"

". . . are angry."

Ngo Bikaï would have burst out laughing if the tirailleur standing before her wasn't sweating with each word he said.

"My women?" she asked.

The evening before, several women had come to see her with a complaint they needed to get off their chests. Their request was so urgent that Ngo Bikaï had to ask Nguet to leave. Nguet had stopped by to pay Ngo Bikaï a "friendly visit," mumbling some story about Bilong she couldn't make heads or tails of. "What are you trying to say? Your hot lover left with the white men!" the Mother of the Market had snapped in exasperation. "He is gone," she repeated, clapping her hands as she spoke, to emphasize that this was old news, there was nothing else to say about it. Then her women had come to ask for her help, because life was getting so expensive, with the endless rounds of contributions. The wartime economy was making their lives more and more impossible. She barely had time to close the door behind Nguet before the women laid out what they wanted to know: how, in what ways, could they work together, either by catching catfish again, as they used to do to earn a bit of extra money on top of what their harvests brought them, or by getting the military authorities to intervene, since, as one of them said, "We just can't keep on harvesting if we don't plant the fields."

It was an exchange of opinions, a brainstorming session, like our Sita used to organize regularly in her courtyard. Nothing had been decided, Ngo Bikaï just said she would think about it. But all too quickly, word of this deferred conversation had reached the military authorities, and they had sent the tirailleurs to sort it out straightaway.

"Ah," she said, "my women aren't doing anything."

What Ngo Bikaï hoped, at any rate, was that her women were working to turn Edéa into a sanctuary of morality, in line with her own Catholic faith, but many of them were still attached to "traditional practices," as she liked to say with a smile. "Our mamas, especially."

Still, she recognized that wasn't really the case. For it was the older women who were busily organizing the *tontine* that served as their community health insurance! Yet the Mother of the Market's sense of humor didn't blind her to the fact that something was clearly wrong if a simple gathering of women led to a group of tirailleurs storming into her courtyard. She said nothing about that, however, and just tried to reassure the three men. Besides, from the backyard her kids' voices were clamoring for her attention. She started to get anxious and her eyes clouded over with concern. She was caught between her worries—which one of the women was it who had reported what had been said in her living room to the military authorities?—and her responsibilities as a mother who could only imagine what antics her children had gotten up to during this unexpected and long-wished-for moment: a celebration of their own Liberation.

"I need to be going," she said, turning back toward the house.

Was it because of the tone of her voice? The voice of an irritated mother; the voice of the Mother of the Market asserting her authority; the voice of a wealthy woman there in the misery of Edéa; the voice of a woman brazen enough to live decently in times of war; the preemptory voice of a woman who sees her former employee as a perpetual slave; the haughty voice of domination? Ngo Bikaï always wondered just what she had done *wrong*.

"Woman, stay right there," the leader of the tirailleurs ordered.

His words resonated with an age-old hatred lodged deep in his belly.

"Don't you hear the kids in back?" Ngo Bikaï began, trying to find the tone with which she had first greeted them.

Did the man even have ears? The children's voices filled the backyard, and any mother—yes, any mother on earth—would have rushed out to check on whatever they'd gotten into, especially since the children she'd left to their own devices were still quite young.

"*Take off your panties.*"

At first Ngo Bikaï thought she had misheard, because he said it in French. But an order like that, even when given in the language of demons, everyone understands. And what happened next, there in the living room of that home filled with love, has no need to be translated, because her cries, her deep cries, took over her whole body. Later, when she tries to find the words to explain to her husband—who for his part wished he understood no language that had words to express the cry she told him about—when she searches for the words to describe the tirailleur she had recognized, but whose name escaped her, good Lord, she will remember the one moment when she really fell apart, when the back door of the house suddenly opened and she saw her small three-year-old come in the living room crying, "Mama!"

"Go back outside!" she shouted. "Back outside!"

The child didn't move.

"Back outside," the tirailleur ordered.

That's when her husband fell apart. And she did, too. At that point of the story, she would always fall apart, for Ngo Bikaï will never know for sure if it was her child's eyes or the member of the tirailleur she recognized but couldn't name, that sent her soul spinning out of control. He was a neighbor—why couldn't she remember his name? She'd wander through the neighborhood, looking for his house, but each time she knocked on a door, the person who answered knew nothing about him. No one could say who he was, that nameless man, *that animal* she couldn't describe without her eyes burning in anger, in pain, in suffering, no—in a rage that strangled her and kept her from speaking, from telling all the sordid details of just what he had done to her. She will go to the military camp and talk about the attack, but there's the rub, a contingent of tirailleurs had just left for Yaoundé. "And then what?" the white commander asked. "The Free French soldiers are not brutes; are you sure, madam, that it wasn't thieves? For, you see, we are not the colonial police, oh no! You say they were wearing new shoes, is that it? And what did you say their names were?"

To think that this happened the very day that Fritz came back from his trip to Douala. Ngo Bikaï was convinced that the three tirailleurs knew her husband wasn't home, and that her little brother Bilong wasn't there, either, because, like them, he was a tirailleur.

"It could only be someone from the neighborhood," she repeated.

Fritz gazed at her in silence.

13

The Poignant Hymn of the False Hilun

At that very moment, in far-off Tibesti—although the Mother of the Market couldn't know this—a second drama that involved her was playing out. You'll agree with me that it was a good thing, in the end, that Ngo Bikaï wasn't aware of it. Yes, each place has more than enough suffering of its own. It was Philothée who announced Bilong's death. His three companions had taken turns watching over him in the clinic. They intentionally ignored military orders and organized shifts so that the boy was never alone. They were more diligent than they had ever been before. Each had his own way of helping the wounded soldier, but they all agreed that there was one prayer that made them clench their fists during the day and grind their teeth at night. Aloga was shaken. Of the five tirailleurs selected for the mission, only Bilong had come back alive from the battlefield, while of the white men who had taken part in the battle, only Lieutenant Colonel d'Ornano had died. Aloga assumed that most of those who died in war were black—contradict him if you will. Colonel Leclerc had made a big announcement about the victory of Free France over the fascists, but the false Hilun just couldn't get over the racist reality of it all. And that's what determined what he said in his repeated prayers to the Bassa ancestor, whom he asked to save "our victory."

While Philothée was on guard, Bilong opened his eyes wide, took a deep breath, and then froze, as if he were struggling to find some bit of strength left in his body, his mouth open on a silent scream, a scream he never released. Was it the ever-stammering Philothée who screamed in his stead?

"Bi . . . Bi . . ."

"What?"

". . . Ng . . ."

"What?"

". . . Ng . . ."

"What?"

"Ah!"

When the false Hilun finally understood what his eyes refused to believe, he started to sing. He wanted Charles—not Bilong, although that was one of his many names—to dribble past death as he had done in that battle he'd heard about. Because, he asked, just what is this war that refuses to let a hero die gloriously on the battlefield, only to lay him out on a clinic cot? What kind of a death is that, Aloga asked in his song, and Hebga replied as the Bassa chorus would have—for he knew that song too—asking, what kind of a death is it that tears a child from life and leaves the adults to carry on with their wretched existence? What kind of life, Aloga asked in his song, remains for the living, now that he who in his heart had wanted nothing but love had been torn from it? What kind of a death is this, Hebga asked, that takes a child, a son, from his mother and upends his whole life? What kind of a life is this, all the Bassa tirailleurs asked, that tears them from the forest and throws them away in the desert? Just what kind of death will they find so far from home?

Such were the questions Aloga asked in his song, his verses echoing off the tents in the camp at Faya-Largeau, filtering in through the windows of men who had given up everything for the liberation of a France that they didn't even know, men who had abandoned their lovers, wives, mothers, and sisters, leaving them at the mercy of vultures, only to lose their own lives as they followed paths they had never even imagined. His verses lodged deep within these men frozen by fear, who pissed in their pants and ejaculated in the depths of the dunes as sandstorms spun all around, and who trembled as they thought of the women they'd left back home, of the women they hoped to find in paradise. His poignant verses were lost along the endless trail of these hundreds, no, thousands of men—what am I saying, there were forty thousand of them—who had suddenly left the courtyards of their family homes to answer the call of a black man from the Caribbean, Félix Éboué, and had become something they'd never thought they would: cannon fodder. Aloga's song retraced the path of these men traveling to their deaths, from the dunes to the steppes, from the steppes to the forest, and maybe even brought some comfort to Nguet, that beauty whose name was on Bilong's lips at the moment of his death, or to his ever-silent mother, or that woman, that strong woman Ngo Bikaï, the formidable Mother of the Market of Edéa, who, in the silence of the home she shared with her partner, had been raped.

Aloga was singing the man who'd died too soon.

14

History's Alexandrines

Pouka was a maestro of alexandrine verses. It wasn't just the type of poetry he wrote, no, he believed that its pattern of syllables, two times six, was the very essence of poetry—which for him came down to mathematics. His thoughts on the perfect verse should not, however, be set apart from his ideal of perfection. And his thoughts on poetry in general are, of course, an extension of his political cogitations. For him, poetry was the pedestal of life itself, its placenta, if you will. It was an irrefutable formal exploration of the phenomenological principles expressed so prosaically in daily life. The poem was meant to be spoken, recited, unlike those debates where opinions emerged from the disorganized, even chaotic, utterances of multiple voices. Yet the recitation of a poem—he might even say the poem's dictation, for let's not forget he had read the Latin classics—the dictation of a poem, then, had meaning only insofar as it was the instantaneous revelation of conclusions best expressed in alexandrines.

He had at one point established a relationship between poetry and the rifles distributed to the recruits—although since 1915, people in Cameroon had been making do with those muskets used for funerals, and that didn't require a permit from the administration—because what mattered to him was the principle. This principle was as transparent as a mathematical equation predicting the shape of the country's future, and therefore it had the poetic flow of an alexandrine. Because you had to admit that there was no precedent for arming the Cameroonian populace. The poet wasn't thinking just about rifles. He was also thinking about the *coupe-coupe*, the machetes the Free French had distributed. In short, he thought about weaponry: all the instruments of death that were for him numbers, and for Free France a means to an end. Numbers that figured on de Gaulle's vast chessboard—he was convinced of it—like points marked out on a writer's blank page to form words and poems. Like poems, the Gaullist numbers could be used to calculate the limitless combinations of possibilities—among which there was most certainly one that reflected the interests of the Cameroonian people.

Pouka was used to thinking with words, rather than concepts. That's why the poem was the perfect place for him to work out his ideas, and French was his language. You see, for him, poetry refused contradictions—they were really the stuff of politics. Rhetoric was for the former what the Socratic method was for the latter, even if each fed off the other, politics sometimes making use of rhetoric—using it to fluster its adversary and not, as does a poet or a Cameroonian soldier fighting for Free France, to celebrate truth. Pouka remembered Um Nyobè and his friends, and a smile spread across his face. What they didn't really get, he told himself, were history's alexandrines, in short, the mathematics of politics. How so? Didn't the masters of rhetoric—take M'bangue, for example—didn't they compose alexandrines? For what else are proverbs? And geomancy—wasn't it based on the permutation of signs, like the writing of verse? Pouka called himself a maestro, but that was just the poetic equivalent of his father the seer; as far as he was concerned, versification, like geomancy, was no more than the manipulation of signs.

As these thoughts ran through his mind, he returned to the poem he was writing, a long poem with twenty-four stanzas, dedicated to those who had died at Murzuk, the title of which, "The Graveyard by the Desert," was a nod to his own old maestro, Valéry. He started counting syllables again and realized with horror that the third verse of his seventeenth stanza had one too many.

"Shit!" he said.

He started again, carefully placing a finger on each syllable to avoid making any mistakes and counting out loud.

"One two three four five six, pause, one two three four five six."

News of the French victory had spread through Yaoundé like a firecracker. Radio Cameroon, the station Leclerc had set up before his departure, went on about it at length. That one story had made up its entire broadcast for more than a week. Between announcements calling on men to "enlist, to reenlist in the colonial forces," each introduced with the same little melody, the station had analyzed the story, taking it apart bit by bit, amplifying and elaborating on it, at times slowing down and at others racing through, forward and back, and—this is a historic first—discussing it in native languages, in Ewondo, Bulu, Eton, and Bassa, citing the analyses of English newspapers and promising to give later those from the American press, and maybe even more. In short, everyone was talking about it in their offices; the city was puffed up with pride because it had lent its dust to Leclerc's shoes, and Ongola Palace its offices to his grandeur. Pouka himself was caught up in the fevered excitement. He showed his poem to his new boss, who suggested it be retitled "Poem in Honor of the Heroes of Murzuk." It seems that when this poem was read—or, as Pouka said, dictated—on the radio, many listeners were moved. Especially since it was read between two military marches, and followed by the famous communiqué on the need for recruits. Alas, in those years Radio Cameroon wasn't working for posterity, but for propaganda. No copies of Pouka's poem survived, but obviously that's not the end of this story.

15

News from Edéa

Reading a poem on Radio Cameroon holds many surprises, as Pouka would learn all too soon. The story of this particular reading lived on for quite some time in Yaoundé's poor neighborhoods. Two days after the broadcast, a midday message came over the radio summoning him to appear "as soon as possible" at the station's security post "for a matter of personal concern." He hurried there right away, and everyone in Madagascar who knew him and had heard the message urged him along, as they should.

"Boss," said a pushcart man, "they're looking for you on the radio."

And a day laborer, "Chief, the radio's calling you."

"*Tara*," said a tense voice, "my friend, what did you do to make the French look for you?"

Others simply said, "The radio is looking for you, *mola.*"

"Dearie, the radio, did you hear?"

The whole neighborhood was set into motion, and for what? There in front of the gate of the radio station were Augustus and Xavier, two members of the little poetry circle he had set up in Edéa, sitting on their travel bags. It was soon apparent that they were hard up, and the poet learned that they also needed a place to stay for the night, maybe longer. Pouka wasn't really surprised; several times cousins and uncles of his had appeared at his door, sometimes arriving late at night, and once even planning to stay for three months.

Right then, he was mostly just flattered to hear these two fellows call him "maestro."

"Maestro," said Augustus, giving him a bag full of plums, plums from the village, "we are so happy to see you, maestro!"

"What luck, maestro."

"Thank you, maestro."

"You found plums in this season?"

"Aaaah, maestro," Augustus cut in. Taking advantage of the warm feelings conjured by their unannounced arrival, he continued in French, using the familiar *tu*: "*You* have forgotten!"

The overly familiar form of address did not pass unnoticed by Pouka, but he blamed it on the peasant's lack of education.

"It's plum season all year long in Edéa!"

The promise of a feast of plums softened his heart, but as they walked away together, Pouka couldn't keep from asking for news from Edéa.

"Nothing new, really," said Xavier, "just France."

"France?"

The poet was stunned. The two explained that they had decided to make their way to Yaoundé without becoming tirailleurs.

"We've come to find ourselves."

"Instead of killing people."

That wasn't what Pouka had expected to hear. Clearly, he wasn't naïve about what was required of tirailleurs—he had dedicated two poems to them already, hadn't he? But the expression "killing people"—the mission for which they had in fact been recruited by Free France—had never actually been thrown in his face like that.

"And," he began, "so just what is it you've come to Yaoundé to find?"

Augustus was the one to answer.

"Our lives."

Xavier nodded.

"I see. In the end, you're counting on Maestro Pouka to help you find your way in life here in the capital, is that right?"

Pouka spoke politely, squelching the sarcasm bubbling up on his lips. He was already beginning to regret having accepted the plums they'd given him, and even more so that he had been flattered when

Augustus and Xavier called him "maestro." That honorific title had serious consequences. For, although Augustus and Xavier were still standing in the street, there was no way out of having them be his guests, unless Pouka was willing to accept the shame of "leaving his brothers outside." But as I was saying, his two guests really didn't give a shit about poetry. You could tell from the hungry way they looked at any- and everything that could be eaten in the city; saliva must have been washing down their throats. But the bean fritters that Pouka bought for them tasted too much like those they'd eat at Mininga's in Edéa, and it only took a few minutes for Pouka to read in their grateful eyes that they would really have preferred to spend a few minutes in the café-bar La Baguette de Paris.

The trio walked on, talking about this and that, expressing surprise at one thing or another. But honestly, if Augustus and Xavier had known what was simmering there in Pouka's head, they would have told him the truth: he'd planted the idea of their coming to the capital when he created his little poetry circle there in Mininga's Bar, well before Free France arrived in Edéa. He needed to take responsibility for it. At the moment, they were following him peacefully through the different quarters of the city—its well-to-do and its poor neighborhoods—silencing their surprise at seeing the man who had always worn a jacket and tie back in the village now walk barefoot like any other native. With each step, our friends were discovering the duplicity of the city's inhabitants. Ah, if they could have heard what their maestro would say to his friend Um Nyobè, three days after they'd moved in with him, when he stopped by his friend's on the way home from work just to complain about his "guests from the village" and ask "desperately for advice."

"What should I do?" That was the question he couldn't get away from; he asked it in French.

"You can't just put them out on the street," Um Nyobè declared with a stony grimace. "That's for sure."

Martha agreed. But she didn't stay around for the rest of the conversation: the kitchen and their child both called for her attention.

"Who knows?" Pouka said when she had disappeared into the back of the house. "Maybe they're just thieves?"

"Thieves?"

Back in Edéa he had sworn they were poets. Hearing that, Um Nyobè burst out laughing. Pouka agreed he was exaggerating; but speaking of crime, he was lucky he hadn't been robbed there in the Mokolo market after his last visit, when he'd left for home so late. Then it was Um Nyobè who changed the subject, suddenly seeming pressed for time. Talking about visits, he had been meaning for a few days to stop by Pouka's house—he had something important to tell him.

"Go on, I'm listening."

Um Nyobè lowered his voice.

"Your *thieves* there, did they even tell you what happened in Edéa?"

He said "thieves" in French.

Pouka hadn't heard anything, Um Nyobè soon realized. Unable to silence the truth, he gave him the details of what had happened to Ngo Bikaï, even sharing this confession from the Mother of the Market: "He penetrated her from behind, anally." The more he said, the narrower the focus of his listener's eyes. "But he didn't have time to ejaculate."

The poet blew up.

"She was sodomized?"

What could he say? Suddenly Pouka's eyes went blank. He didn't shout, "Woyo-o!" Nor did he put his hands on his head, but it was as if he had, for he clapped his right hand firmly over his mouth. He shuddered. It was no longer Ngo Bikaï he was worried about, but the two fellows he had let into his own living room. Or maybe how the story about Ngo Bikaï fit with that of the two fellows? He grabbed hold of his friend's hands. One word echoed in his mind, "sodomized."

"Why did you tell me that?"

"To ask you what *we* can do."

Pouka slowly gathered his wits, as if the word "we" had torn away the stupor that had blanketed him. He was terribly afraid.

"What does Martha say?"

Um Nyobè hadn't yet told his wife. The two men sighed. The storm that had rocked their boat suddenly passed. From the back of the house, the noises of dishes being washed suggested cooking, and the sounds of a child's voice the image of a mother juggling her thousand responsibilities. Pouka was trying to figure out how to pick up the conversation. He wanted to ask his friend how he had heard about it, how Fritz was reacting, but he fell silent. Clearly Fritz was the only one who could have shared the details of the attack. His friend was just as stunned as he was. Their silence was only broken when Martha returned to the living room, chasing their rambunctious child. She was surprised to see the two men sitting in silence.

"Did someone die?" she asked.

That was about it.

"Don't ask Pouka anything," the maestro said abruptly.

Then he got up to leave.

16

The Equations of the Good Cameroonian

To understand just why Pouka had gone to complain to his "brother from the village," you have to understand what it means to be a "good Cameroonian." It's really just another version of "the good Frenchman." When a Frenchman tucks his baguette under his arm early in the morning, who else besides another Frenchman would understand what he is doing? Because: Under his arm? And why, too, in the morning? And yet it's simple: the good Cameroonian brushes his teeth each morning, wearing a towel wrapped around his hips and those cheap plastic sandals we call *sans confiance*. No need to add that he brushes his teeth out in his courtyard: that's just another part of the code that I'll try and explain to you. He brushes them standing in his courtyard because his washroom—toilet and sink—is outside. If outside toilets are the usual thing, both in the city and in the village, the one thing that you see only in the city is the towel around the hips, a reminder of the pagne that men wear in the village. It's really simple, see? When the good Cameroonian gets up, he feels around under his bed to find his *sans confiance* and quickly puts them on; then he takes the towel he hung on the chair the night before, ties it around his hips, and heads out into the courtyard. Sometimes that really means into the street, but he doesn't give a damn, since the towel is protecting his privates. That towel is really quite practical. If he wants to urinate, he just has to lift up the corner, using his right hand if he's right-handed, grasp his *bangala* with his left, and empty his bladder into the drain, with his right hand pressed on his buttocks. He doesn't even need to give his thing a shake after, for the towel is there to dry it off. If he wants to scratch his balls, same thing. If he wants to take a shit, he just needs to lift up the back of the towel, again using his right hand if he's right-handed, and then poop. In short, the towel knotted on his left hip never leaves his body until he's ready to wash up.

At that point, the good Cameroonian spreads his towel over the opening in his wall that leads to the washroom—now it serves as a curtain. A tool with a thousand uses, it covers up the doorway or, if there is a swinging door, it covers the window, because there is no way the washroom of a good Cameroonian has both a door and shutters on the window. So you see, it is just as important for the body as it is for the setup of the washroom itself. Of course, towels aren't really made to be used as a curtain or a door, but rather to dry off the body of the one who purchased them. That's what they're for. And it's clear that this whole time, the towel itself is still dry. It's logical, right? In the worst case—say, for example, the good Cameroonian urinated down the drain and then used the towel—there are at most just a few drops of liquid on it. Of course, after he's washed up, when the towel has fulfilled the only real function it has here on earth, it is necessarily damp. At that point, according to tradition, the man whose body is now dry walks back across the courtyard, the towel again tied around his hips, goes through the living room to his bedroom, and gets dressed. He doesn't even need to take off his towel first, because he can just slip on his underwear—if he wants to wear any—or his trousers, pulling them up under the towel. He puts on his shirt with the towel still there. Once dressed and doused in eau de cologne, the good Cameroonian goes back out from his bedroom through the living room to the courtyard; only then does the towel leave his body, when he hangs it on one of the many clotheslines that run across the courtyard, as they are supposed to do. He spreads his towel out, if he can, near the door to the living room, the real entrance to the house, because he doesn't want to forget it when he comes home in the evening. That's when he'll carry the towel back into the house, now that it's been dried by the sun, which means, according to the laws of mathematics, that it will be dry in the morning when he will reach out to pick it up from the chair where he placed it the night before, then tie it around his hips, and repeat the morning routine. The same is true for his *sans confiance*, the same mathematical principles applying to both towel and sandals.

So it's no surprise that Pouka jumped when, as he tied his towel around his hips, he felt it wasn't dry. His surprise was that of any good Cameroonian, because his towel was there, where it hung every morning, without fault, but this time it was *damp*. I'm stressing the "damp" to emphasize his silent stupefaction. He mumbled an insult in French—"What an idiot!"—and thought about two equations, each with constants that he knew quite well. The first was, given that he didn't live with a woman, he had a routine and quickly lost his temper if it wasn't followed to the letter. If he wanted his guests— how long were they going to stay anyway?—to keep up the respectful attitude they'd shown by calling him "maestro," he needed to regain the upper hand and keep calm. The second equation was that—good God!—it was just seven o'clock in the morning, too early to start an argument. But what our dear Pouka had forgotten was that his citified habits were at odds with the village ways of his two guests. Sure, he was sharing his bed with them, as any good Cameroonian would do, but they had gotten up before him. He called them the "attackers" because they had explained that they got up early to take the city by storm. Take life by storm, what an idea! The poet, the maestro of alexandrine verse, would admit with a smile that he had fallen into a soft way of life. The day of the damp towel— that is to say, the day after Augustus and Xavier had come into his life, ready to take the city by storm—he had seen the two attackers there in his courtyard, sitting on cement blocks, biting their fingernails. Because he didn't want to start off the day with an argument, and mostly because he preferred to keep the peace, he spoke as if to himself, as any good Cameroonian would do in this situation.

"Whoever used Maestro Pouka's towel should take care not to do so again!" he said.

Since these words weren't addressed to anyone in particular, no one could take offense. The next day, however, it was his *sans confiance* that were damp, while his guests sat silently in the courtyard.

"Whoever used Maestro Pouka's *sans confiance* this morning should not do so again!" he said before leaving for work.

The third day, he reached around in the darkness of his bedroom, trying to find his *sans confiance*, but no luck. He looked for his towel on his bedside chair and couldn't find it, either. Wearing just underwear and barefoot, he went outside and found Xavier not only with his towel tied around his hips, but his sandals on his feet, too. Pouka did not jump for joy. No, he wasn't happy to catch his thief red-handed—with the towel around his hips and the sandals on his feet—no. Because this was an outright affront. Still, he didn't tear into that Xavier and leave him with a bare bottom as well as bare feet, for what good Cameroonian would do that to a guest? Yet all that day, while he was at work, he couldn't stop thinking about what would happen the next morning when he reached around under his bed for his *sans confiance* and then moved on to his chair, where his dry towel usually hung. Xavier had crossed the line so egregiously that his maestro was really upset. It was in hopes of putting an end to his torment that he had gone to see his brother from the village, Um Nyobè. His mouth exploded with the question that had obsessed him all day: "What should I do?" His torment was so justified, so understandable, and yet so hard to fix that he didn't really listen to the horrible story Um Nyobè told him. Because what had happened to Ngo Bikaï defied all reason.

"She was actually sodomized?"

That question, which emerged from the mists that clouded his thoughts, was the perfect illustration of the logic of a good Cameroonian.

"What Cameroonian would do that?"

That was his question.

17

In Praise of the Sahara

Sodomy or not, damp towel or not, the liberation of France, or, to use the shorthand formulation found in books, complete with a capital *L*, the Liberation, was not going to slow its pace. On January 26, 1941, right when Yaoundé and Edéa were both scandalized by the same story, the column of tirailleurs and Allied soldiers began their march toward Kufra. They had to move on because, after taking a beating in Murzuk, the Italians were aware of their presence. Even the desert has ears. And, of course, no army could shrug off the loss of its aerial support. When soldiers march, it is always epic. And this was no exception. If you wanted to make a film about it, you'd silence the soldiers' voice track and focus on them marching, because the tirailleurs went by foot. But then again, if Hollywood ever thought about telling their story, there'd be no speaking parts for the tirailleurs. They'd be filmed with orchestral music in the background, an air suggesting windblown sand, their story told by a narrator off-screen—someone like me. You'd only see the determined but exhausted faces of the soldiers, their silhouettes whipped by the sun and the sand, their bare feet sinking into the dunes, their columns snaking their way across endless expanses. And the trucks struggling to advance, their tracks mired in the sinking terrain of the *fesh-fesh*. At the head of the column of four hundred soldiers, Massu and his meharist scouts on camelback. Yet it wasn't because of the foot soldiers or the meharists that the Leclerc Column, as it has come to be known, fought a nineteenth-century-style battle—one might even call it biblical. It was their outdated weaponry. Colonel Leclerc had at his disposal no more than thirty-five trucks; four all-terrain transports, model Laffly S15; two radio transmitters; and two archaic mountain cannons, 75mm Schneiders from 1928. The Italians, for their part, were armed to the teeth. We all know they were fascists—so this is no surprise.

Let's just note that they were stationed there in Kufra's impenetrable fort. As you well know, dear reader, the pen that writes legends is always on its last drop of ink when the real story begins. And that day, a legend was born. The weapons the colonel's soldiers dragged along with them were, as we know, the stuff of myth, or of disaster. Most of the tirailleurs had nothing more than their machetes. Obviously, the military statistics do not account for Hebga, who carried his ax over his shoulder. The woodcutter was used to taking on impossible tasks and invisible adversaries. The sandy wind that rose up before his eyes, at times like a mist, at others an opaque wall, was no different from the rain that used to block his vision back in the forest, or from the forest itself where the *Man who had done that* to our Sita had hidden. He still nursed the same rage in his belly and didn't give a damn about what anyone might say about the battle later: that the tirailleurs, who were nothing more than cannon fodder, would face the Italians bare-handed. Hebga would have taken on anyone, anytime, with his bare hands, for all he needed was to invoke our Sita's name and the rage took hold of his heart once more. He was assigned to the artillery, because his ax had been classified as a heavy weapon. There was a reason for that: the ax was gigantic. Hebga marched alongside the cannons. Philothée and Aloga were somewhere ahead, with the infantry. The three Bassas had been separated, but Aloga had found powerful words to reassure them before their departure: the sand united their steps. The false Hilun had described the country that opened up before them and swore that he saw in the unbroken blue of the sky overhead the protecting hand of Bilong, their guardian angel.

Ah! Philothée should have told him that he had been praying since the start of the march for Bilong to save him, because he couldn't even pee anymore. When he tried, his dried-up kidneys only let out three or four drops, which were immediately sucked up by the thirsty desert. The poor guy thought that he had "the soldier's disease"—even though he hadn't been laid since Yaoundé! But, like Philothée's urine, drop by drop, one man after the other, the Sahara swallowed up the tirailleurs' stories. A huge hole in the heart of the continent, its gusts of sand would have blown away the chronicle of their acts if it weren't for me—me, the narrator of their glory, the writer of their tale, the poet of their bliss. There were tirailleurs who, in the middle of the desert, cursed de Gaulle's own mama's ass. There were those who tried to escape. Free France didn't even pretend to hold them back. Those deserters realized all on their own that the word "deserter" was nothing more than a bad joke, and that it was better to be killed by fascists than swallowed up whole by the maw of the Sahara. For the men who were proud to have crossed lagoon, forest, steppe, and plateau learned that the man who hasn't yet met the Sahara knows nothing about Africa. No one had sung the hymn of the desert to these men from the bush. With no warning the Sahara revealed to them its beardless face: that side of the Sahara that, while whistling a morbid tune, abused their bodies like a whore would abuse a virgin's *bangala*. During the day, it beat their brows, burned their eyes, dug holes in their throats, and ate up their feet; then at night it transformed into a bitter cold that froze their balls. Unable to sleep at night, the tirailleurs spent their days dreaming of the torment of their cold bed. They didn't know that the Saharan sands had a twin sister in Russia. But ask any good Cameroonian what he knows about Saharianas! Or rather, ask Aloga, because he in particular knew how to comfort his comrades by conjuring up images of impossible women; ask him and he'll tell you that the Bassa ancestors never sang about those *mamy nyanga*. You tell me, how can it be that our legends from the forest have no songs of praise for this Stalingrad, for this African Smolensk that is 526,000 years old? Ah, no song for the heart of Africa!

18

The Missing Song

"Forward, march!"

The colonel had decided to set the tempo for his troops' advance with blasts from his two cannons. He had arranged them so that the Italians would think he had twenty or so. Ruse has always been man's best weapon, and in this battle its use was as much strategic as tactical. Strategy: Leclerc divided his company into two battalions, one cannon covering the advance of each. This way he could attack the Italians on two fronts. Tactics: the cannons, each placed about three thousand meters from the fort at Kufra, delivered at regular intervals and in alternation twenty good shots each day.

To give the impression that there were multiple cannons, Leclerc relied on the echo they produced. He ordered that they be moved a few meters after each shot. This principle had the added bonus of giving them some protection, ensuring that when the Italians returned fire, their shots landed in empty sand. After a certain number of shots, Leclerc would modify the interval. A team of eight tirailleurs, under the supervision of a Zouave—a French infantryman—struggled to make this maneuver possible. Two were charged with loading the cannon, another with firing it off, and the others quickly moved it after each shot.

Because of his well-developed muscles, Hebga was assigned to the cannon unit. So he heard the charge of the infantry far in the distance as he clutched his ax, hands aching for action. War is an act of generosity toward the son of a bitch on the opposite side that you send off to hell as quickly as possible. That's what Philothée told himself, and for him, hell looked a lot like where he was, now that Bilong was gone. You see, his friend had died in his arms. And for this death, whose last cry hadn't shaken up the universe, he wanted revenge. In short, that was what dictated his advance toward the enemy, nothing more than that. And certainly not the fascist Italian fort—before the battle, Leclerc had told them that the fort was really France, the City of Lights, occupied Paris, and that they needed to liberate it even if it cost them their lives!

Go on, Philippe François Marie, comte de Hautecloque—for that is your true name, and you were born in the Somme—go on and ask a child from Edéa to die for the liberation of your village. Believe me, Philothée didn't give a shit about your dear village. What he saw before his eyes was the image he had conjured of that *assassin* who had killed his friend, and each time a man beside him fell—whether tirailleur, meharist, Zouave, or anyone else—he told himself that Bilong had given him one more chance to take on his assassin, to tell him he was born from a dog's asshole, and then to drive his bayonet deep into that very asshole. He wanted that perforated man to suffer, to suffer horribly, because what Philothée just couldn't bear was the thought that that man might die before going through some part of the hell that had left his friend suffering on a cot in the clinic in Faya-Largeau, opening his mouth from time to time to cry out a word he himself couldn't say without stuttering:

"Ng-Nguet!"

As for Aloga, he longed for a song far different from those cannon blasts that shook the sky. That guy had so many songs in his head; it drove him crazy to spend a whole day hearing nothing but cannon fire, the groans of men as they fell, and the cries of the wounded who lay at his feet, imploring him to finish them off. Oh, how he'd like to give a lesson in Bassa song to those fascists who had dared to make his head spin with that infernal music! There was one song in particular that he missed, one last song, one song among the hundreds archived in the forest's deep memory, and he knew exactly which one: the song that sings of the hunters, warriors, blacksmiths, and woodcutters. A symphony of the forest that would resonate through the desert. There in the sand he composed this missing song, step by step, word by word, couplet by couplet, verse by verse, harmony by harmony, fascist by fascist: he composed it for Hebga's ax.

Oh! Aloga will compose his song in his head, and sing it only later that evening when he is back in camp, when the soldiers—fascists and Free French alike—have called a truce for the night, and the woodcutter sitting beside him says that his itching hands were useless all day long. Then he'll ask Hebga to clap his hands, to clap harder and harder. And Hebga will clap his hands together, as Aloga asks him to. Then he'll ask Philothée to clap as well, and the stuttering soldier will clap.

And there, between his two comrades who, like him, had lived through another day of combat when they risked being eaten up by the infamous woman of the Saharan sands, Aloga sang his song of the forest, his *assiko*, like only Jean Bikoko Aladin knew how to sing. Aloga sang, marking out the beat on the ground with his foot, he sang his deathly *assiko*. Aloga sang, he sang his "Sahariana" while his friends Hebga and Philothée clapped. Soon the other tirailleurs joined in, and together, clapping and stomping, sometimes pounding out the beat with the butt of their rifles on a piece of scrap metal, on a goblet, spoon, canteen, or whatever was handy, answered Aloga's song. Then Philothée put one foot in front of the other, shimmied his shoulders, his belly, and showed the others who, whether they were from Chad, Gabon, Ubangi, or Congo, all knew something about this sort of forest dance. He showed all the tirailleurs how to dance to this one incomparable song, which wasn't recorded in the French military archives because, even though it was composed right there in the desert as Italian bullets flew overhead, it was sung in Bassa— in an African language.

19

The Black Force

Whether the opposing soldiers are committed to the cause or not, in war it's always a fatal mistake not to respect your adversary. What really set Leclerc apart, then, in this Battle of Kufra, was that he respected his adversaries. That's what too few books underscore. Yet Leclerc knew quite well the land where the fascists lived and breathed, and God knows that among his friends there were many who put themselves at the forefront of French fascism. Hadn't he been a faithful and often approving reader of that fascist paper *L'Action française*, even stashing many copies of it away among his things back in Tailly? Oh! Colonel Leclerc had no choice but to respect the fascists, for, after all, it was only due to the vagaries of history that he found himself outside the walls of Kufra while they were inside the fort.

What set him at odds with the Italians was the defeat of France, nothing more, nothing less. He didn't want to destroy them, but rather to give them an honorable way out, in accord with the laws of military chivalry. Didn't the commander of the Italian forces know where his sympathies lay? The Italian could have proposed a friendly agreement, a little something that would have satisfied the opposing parties because, he surely would have said, "We've known each other forever, right?" Yet let's leave these suppositions aside, because the Italian commander was an idealist. About twenty years old. He'd only just finished his military service, which had interrupted his

study of law, when he'd been sent to the Sahara—and, for a noncommissioned officer, that was a punishment.

Had he said, "Hold on, hold on, Colonel. Don't you remember
that editorial from *L'Action* praising Mussolini's seizure of power?"
that certainly would have changed things.

"Yes, I read it," Colonel Leclerc would have replied, the memory of all he read flooding back. At that point, Il Duce had friends
only in Spain.

"But what about you in France . . . ?"

"Ah! The present derives from the past!"

But this exchange never took place because, as I've said, the
commander of the Italian forces was unaware of Leclerc's fascist sympathies. What's more, before this battle, he'd never even heard of
him. A warning had come over the radio about the soldiers, many of
them black, that Leclerc was leading toward his fort. How could that
fascist have known that Leclerc's reputation would come at the
expense of his own? For him, the Battle of Kufra was as much ideological as military, whereas for Leclerc it was mostly military.

As the Italian gathered his wits, he suddenly realized the advantages of his position. Two military axioms stood out: first, that whoever fights a solely defensive war is condemned to lose; second, since
the French forces were outside the fort, they would need a truce
sooner than the Italians, because they'd have to gather their wounded
and their dead scattered over the desert, whereas the Italian wounded
and dead were already together there in the fort. The situation wasn't
great on a humanitarian front, as the Italian officer could no longer
count on receiving supplies, especially since his air support had been
disrupted after the fall of Murzuk. But on the military front, however, the Italian found himself in a favorable situation, even if international law tied his hands. The commander remembered what Il
Duce had said about that: "It's not even worth the paper it's written
on." Force, that was the only thing that mattered. The Italian commander understood, despite being trained as a lawyer, that he'd pay
dearly if he respected international law more than Il Duce did.

That's why, two weeks after having settled into a routine of
pauses, during which the Allied soldiers gathered their wounded and
their dead, one evening he gave the order for all his cannoneers to
gather in the courtyard of the fort and to shoot at the French forces

throughout the night. Never had a Sahelian night been lit more brightly. Bursts of fire cut across the clear sky, long, arcing blasts that ended in explosions; the whistle of each successive launch rang out like the whoosh of a heavenly saber. There was no pause in the Italians' repeated, systematic shots. From the other side came a confused hum of cries, vehement curses, half-given orders; chaos reigned, death expanded her reach. For an hour, no, two or three—what difference does it make?—the cannonballs pilloried the French positions, sending clouds of sand high into the night. And then there came a break, a long break. Maybe the Italian commander thought he'd managed to breach the enemy line? Whatever it may be, he sent out some of his soldiers who, crying *"Avanti!,"* threw themselves into the sand dunes, rushing over them like a cloud of evil shadows, like a horde of wild animals.

What happened next in the valley would be recorded in the annals of the world's wars as a return to hand-to-hand combat. For when they came out of their fort, the Italians believed that the French forces had been forced to retreat, to seek cover together because of the repeated pounding of their cannons. But that was wrong, for in fact Leclerc's two units came together each evening. That was when the colonel took stock of things and adjusted his tactical plans. So the French forces met the Italians, who no longer had cannons on their side, head-on. And that's when the Italian forces learned for themselves about the fighting force that is a Bassa woodcutter. Night is a blessing, because under its blanket, the lightest of weapons become invisible, whereas the heaviest explode with the full force of their metal. Hebga jumped over the sand that grabbed at his feet, tore his body from the darkness through the pure force of his muscles, hit left, hit right. Here there was a cry, there the explosion of a skull. He spun around and swung at a shadow glimpsed behind his back: an Italian rushing at him. Why don't the records of that truly horrific night recount the exploits of that man who came from the depths of Edéa's forests to inscribe the letters of his name on the desert? Then the Italians would remember the desert spirit that devastated their forces, decimated their army. Then they would remember the faceless spirit that was pure force, a black force: *forza nera!*

In the thick of his battle, Hebga was making up for the days, nights, and months he had spent crossing steppes and plains, crossing the whole of Cameroon, looking for the *Man who had done that*. Obviously, this fight would leave him hungering still. For in the depths of the night he couldn't see whose ribs he was breaking with his ax, and even less those whose faces he destroyed. As he bent down to look at a man he'd just flattened with a kick, a second attacked; he had to dispatch him with just one hand, since he held his ax in the other. Then Hebga fought the two men at once, for the one who'd fallen got back up and rushed at him, cursing in Italian. The woodcutter took one blow to the face, but he gave back many, hitting his adversaries in the belly, on the back and neck. For him, the war was degenerating into an unfair fight. Punches landed on his eyes, fractured his jaw. He wasn't giving his all to the fight, no, because Hebga wanted to see the face of the *Man who had done that*. He knocked down one assailant and pinned him to the ground. He wanted to look him in the eyes and spit in his face. He wanted to tell him of the pain he still felt in his belly from the brutal loss of our Sita—you know that story—and then smash his face open with his ax. But the second guy didn't give him the chance to. One blow to Hebga's neck, and the man on the ground was able to tear free from his grasp and get back up. As the woodcutter struggled back to his feet, a crack split the air. The man who had hit Hebga from behind was stopped in his tracks, as if struck by lightning; he fell to his knees, then dived face-first into the sand. Hebga turned: there was Captain Massu, still holding his rifle at the ready.

"War no boxing match," he said, speaking in a clipped French and using a derogatory epithet for the Italians. "Daniels no fun."

The second assailant raised his hands in the air.

20

War Is Not a Boxing Match

How can I contradict Massu? After all, what is one punch in the context of the Second World War? What is one beating in the context of a clash of rifles, cannons, mortars, bomber aircraft, submarines, and, to end it all, the atomic bomb? What is one uppercut in the context of trenches, concentration camps, and genocides? Ah! If only Hebga, that child of the forest, had known that Bassa savagery was nothing, really nothing, when compared with the kind of savagery that authorized a well-read man, with a good haircut, nice shoes, beard neatly trimmed, and mustache waxed, a civil servant—hence methodical—to write down the name of his compatriot, who was white like him, well read like him, a music lover, and a passionate reader of French poetry, on an alphabetized list that would send that neighbor to the gas chambers! For Hebga, the forced labor, the *njok-massi*, was truly the most awful thing the whites had brought to Edéa. He had always thanked the spirits that he'd never been caught, shaved, and made to sit in the mud, like so many others he'd seen treated that way. I must say that he had always followed his mother's advice: "Pay your taxes!" She knew something about this, our Sita did. She was in charge of the market and had seen too often that when the colonial police were called because people hadn't paid for their stands or their beers, things quickly got much more complicated. What did he know, yes, just what did Hebga know about this Second World War when the staunchest supporters of the Free

French general's theories about the professional military class were found in Nazi Germany? Ah! Did Hebga—who had only signed up for the war because he wanted to avenge his mother's death—did he even know what those Germans and Frenchmen had been doing to each other for the past hundred, no, two hundred years, all in the name of revenge?

Did he have any idea what men are capable of when they've been caught up in a century-old dance of hatred? He who until then had used the pebbles he loaded into his slingshot, his *ndomo ndomo*, to kill only birds, who had sharpened his machete with dexterity and determination but with innocence, not savagery, in his heart—wasn't it time he learned how to use a miraculous weapon? Or else how would he understand this hatred, yes, this hatred that suddenly appeared disguised as love? He couldn't see the Italian on the other side holding a round metal cylinder—so smooth, with a bit of a point at one end—holding it like a woman, giving it a kiss. Strange thing to do, the woodcutter would have thought, although he, too, often held his ax like a lover. But an ax isn't a shell. On the other side, among the French troops, who would be chosen for this dance with death? Night stretched over the desert, the night sky so clear and smooth it seemed like a holiday. A crescent moon traced a smile—what else could it do after seeing that man kiss a shell? Then the desert was beset by the sounds of chaos, by the apocalypse; the staccato of machine gun fire split the air, rifle blasts exploded all around. Here and there a man wheezed, cried out, and cursed under death's caress; then his body turned to rubber and fell. Men ran left and right. They peeked out from their shelters in the sand, from behind a dune's protective cover, just as an Italian gently, silently, placed a shell in the muzzle of his mortar.

Then the Italian plugged his ears. Immediately a dull blast shook the desert, leaving silence in its wake, making the moon jump; while the area around the man with the shell disappeared in an exuberant cloud of sand, a bolt of light took off from the very heart of his hideaway. The light flew higher and higher across the sky, straight as a flaming arrow, straight as a line traced by the geometric spirit of the night. It crossed the sky trying to reach the distant, smiling moon, there in the depths of the heavenly vault, aiming for its heart. As it passed, the friction of the wind created an inimitable whistle, like the sound of scissors on silk. In the distance the light curved, no longer seeking the moon. The line of light came back toward the ground, toward a distant dune, where the panicked Free French troops were hidden. Is there any soldier who doesn't know the sound of an incoming shell? Who hasn't seen the line of light traced across the sky? Its false promise to kiss the moon, its dangerous beauty— is there anyone who hasn't watched its approach? Now the shell landed on the dune, falling right into Aloga's wide-open mouth, as he stood watching it come, mesmerized by the perfect trajectory of that light through the darkness. The explosion sent the tirailleur flying up to the sky, torn limb from limb, scattered across a giant wave of sand, vaporized in a burst of flesh, liquefied in a bloodbath. His limbs, his appendages flew up: his head shooting to the left, one toe straight ahead, one foot behind, a leg to the front, his left hand to the right, and his trunk—well, it's best I not say. There was a thud of metal splitting open, of bones shattering, flesh expanding, a gigantic din that created such chaos that the universe itself fell silent . . . and stayed silent for a long while. A calm so great that it was only the next day that they realized the extent of the destruction, for the false Hilun hadn't even made a sound.

21

The Battlefield at Daybreak

Then in the morning, the mist rose gently over the desert. Like a white blanket gently pulled back, it lifted, revealing the debris of the battle scattered all around. The Italian forces had retreated with the night, Philothée noted. In fact, they'd been routed. The survivors had pulled back to the fort whence they'd come. His eyes filled with tears as he took stock of the disaster. The young man didn't know where to turn his attention; the dunes were covered with the wounded and the dead. Several dozen, at least. Here one man whose face had been ripped open, there another who had lost an arm, or a foot, and next to him yet another half buried in the sand. A guy over there had been caught by surprise and burned to death in his truck. There were bits of metal everywhere. The blowing wind was covering up a foot over here, a face over there. The Sahara was quick to swallow up the secrets of the violence that had played out on its stage.

One fear alone had taken hold of Philothée's mind: he hadn't yet seen either Aloga or Hebga. His eyes ran over the cadavers, a sinking feeling in his gut. He couldn't wrap his mind around the idea that his comrades might be feeling the same thing. To think that now he couldn't just set out across the battlefield and turn over each body, searching for his friends. The French officers' orders were clear: separate the wounded from the dead, the whites from the blacks, the Italian soldiers from the Allied. Struggling not to vomit, he uncovered a face he recognized: a good fellow, one from his company, whose face had been shattered. Another of the bodies he examined was that of a man from Ubangi-Shari, someone he used to trade jokes with. A wave of nausea flooded over him. They were all fighting to liberate the desert, but he just couldn't see beyond all the bodies.

He was struck by how many blacks had been killed. Clearly this war had turned into Africans killing Africans. He hadn't given it much thought before. The red of the chechias worn by the Italian askaris troubled him: it was almost the same as those worn by the tirailleurs. What's more, over the course of all the desert battles, their white uniforms had turned beige, just like the uniform he was wearing. His discomfort grew when he turned over a body buried in the sand that he thought belonged to a tirailleur, only to find that it was an askari. With dark skin and scarred cheeks, he might have been from Sudan or Chad. The thick mist added to the confusion of the scene. And it didn't help—no, it really didn't help—that amid the bodies and the burned-out shells of trucks Philothée found a tirailleur who had clearly lost his mind. The man sat there as if in mourning, rocking back and forth and repeating the same phrase over and over: "War not good!"

His words ricocheted across the chaotic expanse, then returned, echoing in Philothée's mind. He had no idea what to say to the man. Philothée would have liked to ask him a question, to ask whether he had seen the Tirailleurs First-Class Hebga and Aloga, his two companions he'd lost in the battle.

"War not good," said the soldier, "war not good."

The strangest thing—Philothée jumped when he realized it—was that the tirailleur was holding the body of an askari in his arms. Like a brother. He was comforting him, caressing his hair, his forehead, his body. He spoke to him in his own native language and cried, then buried him in the sand, only stopping to take back up his refrain in French. Why treat an askari like a brother? Such fraternizing with the enemy went against all orders! Yet a thought he had heard Aloga voice several times echoed in his head: "The white man's victory means the defeat of the blacks." The black soldiers who had spent the night killing each other in the dark were in fact brothers. That reminded him that he still hadn't found his two companions. Right then he recognized a muscular silhouette coming toward him through the mist, tripping over debris and bodies: it could only be Hebga.

Never had the two men hugged each other so tightly. In the chaos of the Second World War, among the hundred or so victims of this final Battle of Kufra, Philothée held his lost brother in his arms. For a long while they stood there, clinging to each other, silent in the bloody morning. His nails dug into Hebga's flesh and he felt the woodcutter's heart beat deep inside his own chest. In that moment, nothing else existed for the two silent men.

"Alo . . . Alo . . ." Philothée began.

Hebga didn't let him finish.

"Dead."

Philothée had one, two, three questions. For example: What? and When? and How? They were all meaningless, really, because there's only one way that soldiers die on the front: violently. Behind them voices grew louder, the voices of French officers giving orders, telling them to hurry up and finish the job, "unless you want to be caught out here in the sun." By that they meant: when the battle resumed. Because the battle had only paused because of the mist. Yet Philothée couldn't give up looking for Aloga's body. His stammered question and his tears ricocheted off Hebga's gaze. They were surrounded by bodies, each seeming to say: "Here I am! Come here!"

"He's over there," Hebga answered.

"You . . . you . . . saw . . ."

"Yes, I saw him."

Philothée leaped over the bodies, followed by Hebga, who tried to hold him back. He ran to where his friend pointed.

"No," Hebga said. "He's over there!"

Shit! Just where exactly? That's what the young tirailleur would have said had his tongue allowed him to speak the words needed to express his shock, his pain, his suffering, his anger when he realized Hebga didn't know either—that he knew nothing. He forgot that the war wasn't over, that it was still going on all around them, that a break in the hostilities had already once proved a trap. Philothée forgot, yes, he did, that the whole world was at war! The French officers were in a rush because they didn't want to leave their dead for the scavengers. They had discovered at their own expense just how vile the fascist brutes were. Yet Philothée wanted to see for himself that Hebga had really buried Aloga. Ah! How could Hebga tell him that a missile had at once dug their friend's tomb and buried him in it?

The desert was a vast, silent cemetery where an army, pushed there by humanity's violent battles, could disappear without a trace, swallowed up by nature's great silent maw; where, no doubt, whole peoples and civilizations had been sucked down over the thousands of years of man's history in Africa, with no one the wiser. Hebga struggled to find the words, suddenly he was the stutterer. As for Philothée, he burst into tears, realizing that Aloga, who'd previously been the butt of so many of his jokes, had shown him nothing but kindness. He realized that there was no one to sing a Bassa mourning song for Aloga, even though he'd sung such a poignant hymn as Bilong lay dying. Hebga had the bulging muscles of a boxer but, like Philothée, he lacked a silver tongue.

Philothée opened his mouth wide, trying to sing a song he wrote right there, trying to improvise a lullaby amid all those piles of bodies, at once so indistinct and so familiar. But his furious stutter wouldn't let him get through the first verse, not even the first word. Unlike the distant forest, the desert did not recognize his hymn.

Hebga dragged him away.

22

A Domestic Squabble One Afternoon

Meanwhile, life in Yaoundé continued on its parallel track: Pouka must have been convinced that Um Nyobè would greet him with a good joke, because this was his third visit to his friend in a week. Ah! His guests from Edéa, those "thieves," they were getting on his nerves. What had they done this time? Martha didn't give him a chance to tell all the details of their "attacks" on his way of life, even though they were spilling out of his mouth. She had barely opened the door when he found himself thrust in the middle of a domestic squabble unlike anything he'd ever seen at his friend's home.

"Come in, come in," she said, "I'm sure he already told you."

"Told me what, mama?"

He called Martha "mama" out of respect for her position as mother of a family. Pouka, caught off guard by her sharp comment, first smiled and then stuck out his cheek for the first of the four kisses usually offered as a greeting. On this occasion, Martha didn't follow custom. She's sulking, he thought. That's women for you!

"What's going on?"

"You tell me, you and your friend," she snapped back at him. "I'm the one who doesn't know what's going on."

These words left Pouka totally confused. His eyes scanned the living room, looking for Um Nyobè, but Martha kept on the attack.

"Yes, you tell me, Pouka, because you're *his accomplice.*"

His accomplice? Pouka spied Um Nyobè and breathed a sigh of relief. His friend was sitting at the table, looking quite the father as he fed their little one, gently sliding small spoonfuls into his mouth. The child was struggling, refusing to eat, taking all his father's attention. Martha paced back and forth in the living room.

"What's wrong?" Pouka asked, sitting down next to his friend.

That was the question he'd been hoping his friend would ask him.

"Don't ask me," his friend whispered. "*It's about Ngo Bikaï.*"

He spoke in French and also referred to his wife's friend by her maiden name. Ah! Pouka had already forgotten the details of that story about Ngo Bikaï. Like any true poet, he thought the whole world revolved around him alone. Um Nyobè glanced away from the recalcitrant child for a moment and met the maestro's confused gaze.

"So," the tired poet replied, "now Pouka is your accomplice."

Oh, women!

"Just what kind of men are you?" Martha demanded, staring at one and then the other. "I really don't know, I just don't know."

Pouka was realizing that she tended to repeat each phrase twice when she was angry. But also that he had never really had a long conversation with her. Martha was his friend's wife, that was all. If you think about it, he came by so rarely! Once Um Nyobè had pointed that out to him. "Women keep us apart, right?" he had said. Pouka would have said it was more about politics. In fact, each time he visited, Pouka found his friend in the middle of a group of friends. If it wasn't the group from the chorus, it was those who played soccer, or those who were interested only in politics. When Um Nyobè and Pouka did get together, they barely had a chance to speak.

This time, however, a woman was making them allies, putting them on the same side of a fight. More specifically, this one woman, Martha, was angry at both of them, and it seemed she kept repeating why just to make herself even angrier. Still, her rage left the men perplexed.

"Someone told you that some tirailleurs *raped* my sister," she said bluntly, "and you don't even bother to tell me."

Um Nyobè shuddered when he heard the word "rape" in French.

"No," he protested, "I told you."

"No. You didn't tell me *everything*."

"What more did you want me to tell you?"

He stared at Pouka as if he were the only person who might understand.

"The truth."

What could be simpler?

"But I told you the truth," Um Nyobè shouted.

"No. It was *my neighbor at the market* who told me. Do you even understand? My neighbor at the market!"

It wasn't the French words she used, but her eyes that expressed the depth of her outrage.

"My God!" she exclaimed. "If that had happened to *me*, what would you have done?"

Pouka suggested that she wasn't being fair, so she took aim at him.

"And you, I'm sure you're convinced that people recognize you now because of that poem you read on the radio. That's why you came here today, right? Go on, tell me how Mr. Pouka became a star. Has Mr. Pouka already met the governor? The governor must have awarded him a Colonial Medal, I'm sure of that. Yes, I'm sure."

With that she grabbed the child from Um Nyobè's arms.

"Just give me back my child if feeding him is too much for you."

Pouka had never seen Martha angry. Now there was nothing left untouched by her anger. Each face, each object, each bag of fruit, each story, even her own child just added more fuel to her fire.

"Martha, you're exaggerating," her husband interrupted.

When a woman gets angry—and this Pouka knew from personal experience—no one gets off scot-free. The child was eating hungrily. The anger that his mother would have liked to throw in the faces of all the tirailleurs in Cameroon, she now threw at those two men who stood in their place, as far as she was concerned.

"Really? Now I'm exaggerating? The tirailleurs *rape* my sister, your friend there goes on the radio to tell us that they're all heroes, and I'm the one exaggerating."

Now it was Pouka's turn to step up, because Martha wasn't just exaggerating, she had gone too far.

"Leave Pouka out of this," he said.

"Ah, right, you didn't know anything about it, is that it?" she retorted sarcastically.

"Pouka didn't know, oh no," he insisted.

His friend was ashamed by his lack of solidarity.

"What difference does it make?" he interrupted. "She was raped, period and done."

"The difference it makes," Martha announced, "is that now I'm leaving for Edéa."

The two men stared at each other in surprise.

"I can't just sit here after hearing that tirailleurs raped my sister."

Pointing the child's spoon at them, she put the blame squarely on the two men sitting there across from each other.

"Ah!" said Um Nyobè. "So, when are you going to leave?"

"Tomorrow morning."

Once again, the men could only stare at each other.

23

Love's Living Room

And that's what happened. Let me fill you in. Fritz came to meet the Um Nyobès at the train station. He took the crying child from Martha's hands, so she could get off the train more easily. Her husband followed behind her and waited for the porters to hand him their luggage. Some of the travelers jostling each other on the platform recognized him and greeted him warmly. He pointed at Martha, standing next to Fritz, and their faces lit up at the sight of the child. "How big the baby's gotten!" Only when they were on their way could the friends really greet each other.

"We'll talk back at the house," Fritz said.

The trip was made in silence. Once in the courtyard, they were greeted by the happy shouts of children and by Ngo Bikaï, who came out to hug them. She certainly didn't seem as distraught as Martha made her out to be. According to Martha, Ngo Bikaï would be in pieces, shut away in the house, imprisoned by her physical and mental distress, tearing at the skin on her face, beating her breast, and cursing heaven and earth.

"And I wasn't even there to help her. Me, her sister!"

Um Nyobè had asked for time off from work, because he didn't want his wife traveling alone to Edéa. And she would have done it, too. The writer had had to lie to his boss.

"Again?" his boss had said.

Um Nyobè invoked a death in the family, an "uncle," forgetting that he'd used the same excuse the last time he'd gone back to the village.

"It was your uncle the last time, wasn't it?" the white man asked.

"This time it's on my mother's side," Um Nyobè explained apologetically.

"Your uncles are dying pretty quickly," his boss noted.

It was the sort of reproach that was duly noted in his work file and that left his boss with the troubling impression that he was "up to something." Um Nyobè hadn't said anything else. Was his boss going to check with Martha? But once they arrived in Edéa and were greeted by Ngo Bikaï's placid face, Um Nyobè almost thought that it was nothing, that nothing at all had happened to her. She was still taking care of her children, as usual, talking with them like the same energetic mother she had always been. What had Um Nyobè expected, after all? To find her in tears, still tearing her hair out several weeks later?

"I have to put the children to bed," she said.

"Already?"

"It's eight o'clock."

She called the kids, who grumbled as they followed her. Martha headed to the bedroom after them. The door to the living room slammed shut and soon the women's voices, like those of the children, faded off in the back of the house, leaving behind the silence that Um Nyobè so wanted to avoid.

Fritz also fell silent.

Just what was Um Nyobè after? Did he want his friend to go over all the details again when he'd already told him everything on the telephone the day after it had happened? He realized that this living room that he knew so well, where he had spent hours, this living room filled with love, had changed. Framed photographs of the couple, of their children—they had three—and their parents still hung on the walls. Fritz's framed diplomas were displayed too, alongside a hanging that proclaimed "Christ is the Master of this Home." He read it several times. It was probably a reflection of Ngo Bikaï's faith, since Fritz, like Um Nyobè, described himself as "religiously lazy."

Um Nyobè stifled the question that was burning on his lips: Did *it* happen here, in the living room? A stupid, meaningless question. For what would it have changed if it had happened somewhere else in the house or even outside? Yet he couldn't get it out of his mind that somehow the living room was different now. Nothing had changed, no: the furniture was arranged as it had been, the walls were still the same color. In short, there was nothing that stood out. The living room was no different, really, from his own back in the city. Yet still Um Nyobè couldn't shake the feeling—the feeling that he was standing on a field where a battle had taken place.

He was roused from his reflections by Fritz's voice.

"They wanted to break our spirit . . . to break our spirit."

Um Nyobè looked closely at his friend. Never had he seen him so miserable; his sincerity moved him to tears. If he asked "What can we do?" he would be admitting that they had surrendered. But in Fritz's eyes he saw something quite different than capitulation. He didn't really want to talk to Fritz but to Ngo Bikaï herself. But what did he want to say? To apologize for taking so long to come? For having dragged his feet? To offer condolences? Just what does one say to a woman who's been raped? *Assia*? Did he want to talk to her just to avoid the philosophical and theoretical questions raised by his friend, questions he knew all too well, really? Was that it? Did he want to talk to Ngo Bikaï in order to escape from Fritz, who was there beside him saying the very things he himself would have said if their situations were reversed, even though what he had imagined was something totally different, precisely because he'd never been in that situation before? Um Nyobè thought that by putting the children to bed the two women had cut the men off from the conversation he would have wanted to have, from the only story he would have wanted to hear: Ngo Bikaï's.

"So, how is she?" he asked his friend.

"It's okay."

"Okay?" he insisted.

"More or less."

Except Fritz said those words in French: *"Comme ci, comme ça."*

24

The Belly of Anger

Meanwhile, the women were planning their next move. One thing still bothered Ngo Bikaï: Who had told the French that her women weren't happy? Suspicion is a dangerously sharp saw, and she couldn't rid herself of mistrust and doubt. When she crossed paths with a mother wearing a tightly wrapped *kaba ngondo*, a woman who sold *macabo* in the market, she couldn't help but wonder: What if it was her? Then she'd look at another, a *bayamsallam* lazily nibbling on the slender stick of wood women use to clean their teeth, and the same question would flash across her mind: Why not her? Even that pregnant woman over there caught her attention: Maybe her pregnancy helped cover up her acts of espionage?

Continually assailed by doubt, Ngo Bikaï knew she needed someone she could trust. So she was glad Martha had come from Yaoundé. She didn't need the sort of friend she could chat with when times were good, but rather a woman she could count on as she prepared to fight. She didn't mince her words, because as she saw it, this was really about war. When she said "war," her eyes gleamed with the anger Martha had been looking for since her arrival. Ngo Bikaï shuddered, then held her head up boldly and said:

"I know it was her."

"Who?"

"Mininga."

The facts spoke for themselves: the new opulence of La

Seigneuriale; her collusion with the Free French soldiers; and most of all, her own treachery. Still, there was one thing that bothered Ngo Bikaï: there was a missing link, a *transmission chain*, she said in French, that brought the women's words to "that hyena's" ears.

"So, one of your women?"

That was precisely the question that was bothering her so.

"I just can't imagine who could have done it."

Ngo Bikaï confided in Martha that, since "the events," she hadn't stopped running through the list of her women, but none of them seemed guilty. Besides, they had all shown her such care and compassion, coming by to visit all the time. The importance of the women's sympathy was clear to Martha the very next day: Ngo Bikaï didn't have to seek out her friends to remind them that she was there. They came to see her on their own, sometimes several times in one day.

"How can I accuse any of them?" Ngo Bikaï asked. "How?"

Martha shook her head.

"Even the hyena came to see me one day, let me tell you."

"What?"

Um Nyobè's wife just couldn't get over that. And yet, Ngo Bikaï told her, Mininga had shown up one day, *kougna, kougna, kougna*, shaking her hips with each step, *coss, coss, coss*, scuffling her feet on the ground as she always did, and then, *toc, toc, toc*, Ngo Bikaï heard her knock on the door of her own house.

"Oh, my dear," she implored, "please tell me it's not true."

How had Ngo Bikaï been able to control herself and not throw her right out into the courtyard? Just thinking about it, even now, made her blood boil. Because, she went on, Martha didn't know just what Mininga had become since her last visit. Then Ngo Bikaï described how the bar had changed; no longer the simple, nameless place where you could buy this or that, where porters were able to rest and catch their breath, it had become a veritable "hub of Franco-African relations," and was now called "La Seigneuriale"—as Martha could see for herself. Ngo Bikaï burst out laughing.

"La Françafrique, that's what that bar should be called!"

A scandal, really, she went on. Martha would never believe it, but even Leclerc, yes, Colonel Leclerc had been there. De Gaulle himself, who according to Fritz was spending a lot of time in Cameroon, had almost come to see it. Was there anything that didn't happen in La Seigneuriale? Even the "Putsch in Ongola"—as Fritz called Leclerc's entry into Yaoundé—had been planned right there! Yes, they were making plans there for the liberation of Paris, yes, in fact, for winning the Second World War!

"The Second World War?"

"Well, at least the French side of it."

Ngo Bikaï mentioned how soldiers were being recruited for the Free French forces, citing her own brother as a case in point: "Bilong, my own little brother," who'd become a tirailleur after having been dragged into that bar, and who'd even taken on a new name, Charles.

"Charles?"

"Let me tell you. I told him that I'd keep calling him Bilong until the day I died," said Ngo Bikaï with a snort. "It was Fritz's friend, you know, the one who's there with you in Yaoundé, who took him to that place."

"Pouka?"

"Yes, Pouka. He was teaching French poetry there in Mininga's Bar."

And just like that, with no warning, her brother had become the lover of some woman named Nguet, as if that had anything to do with French poetry. And then, because of that Nguet, he stopped sleeping at home, which broke his mother's heart, and all he ever talked about, twenty-four hours a day, was Nguet: Nguet, morning, noon, and night.

"Nguet?" exclaimed Martha. "But she was my friend from school!"

The two women fell silent, thinking about Nguet's career: she had gone to school to learn how to keep a home and had ended up in La Seigneuriale . . . That she had become a whore, a *wolowolos*, in Edéa was rather surprising. They didn't pause to think about the twists and turns of her story, not about how someone like them had fallen or who had orchestrated it. Martha in particular couldn't hold back.

"How can it be!"

Anger—yes, anger! It's not just something that ties your belly up in knots. It takes hold of your mind, too, twists your sense of right and wrong. Martha began to realize just how anger had tied her sister's belly into knots, twisting her mind and her sense of right and wrong. But as the words spilled out of Ngo Bikaï, in bursts of anger that turned her eyes red, Martha's thoughts returned to the Nguet she used to know. She imagined her wearing the new outfit Ngo Bikaï had described and pressed her hand to her lips, unable to believe it: A whore?

But I can tell you, after just a few evenings, a few whispered conversations as they put the children to bed, Ngo Bikaï and Martha were able to trace the transmission chain that linked La Seigneuriale to the market women and their Mother. Because Ngo Bikaï suddenly remembered that Nguet had stopped by on the very day that some of the women had come to her to complain about the French. What had they wanted? She couldn't really remember. In any event, Nguet had crossed paths with the angry women there at her door! That was the only possible answer: "It was her!"

Finally, the traitor had a name: Nguet. Martha decided it was time to pay her a visit.

"Just to say hello."

25

Preparing for Battle

The women wasted little time on greetings. They were clear about what had brought them together, and their meeting only confirmed it: they needed to approach this with cool heads, and systematically. Most important, they must not chase after catfish when there were whales swimming free. And Nguet, one older woman said, was only a catfish. Besides, that story about her and Ngo Bikaï's brother was old news! All the women agreed that they needed to focus on the big fish, the whale. Then one very skinny woman (multiple pregnancies had clearly taken a toll on her body but hadn't slowed down her mouth!) stressed that as far as she was concerned, the real whale was France.

"Why France?"

The woman pointed toward the military camp that had emptied all the men from Edéa's courtyards and turned the village's brave young men into their sisters' rapists, or even their mother's murderers. Ngo Bikaï said not to exaggerate, since after all, her little brother was a tirailleur, too. And besides, she added, it wasn't France that had invaded her home that evening, "so let's not exaggerate."

"Let's be careful," added another frightened woman, "they have rifles in that camp."

She paid no mind to the baby in her arms, sucking greedily at her breast.

"And cannons."

"And tanks."

"And planes. Don't you remember that plane?"

"How could we forget?"

In short, they'd surely provoke a massacre if they dared to follow through with what they had in mind! Declaring war on France! No, they needed to choose their battles carefully. Shifting their attention from France brought them logically back to a decidedly smaller fish, La Seigneuriale, and to Mininga in particular. However, each of the punishments they imagined inflicting on the guilty party was quickly dismissed, one after the other, because, as one woman cut in, "Between us, she's not really the one who did it."

"And besides," added another woman with rather short legs, "she's a woman, like us."

"Me? I'm not a whore!" protested one *bayamsallam*, her head tightly wrapped in a red scarf.

"So you're saying you have a pebble between your legs?"

"A pebble?"

The market was bubbling with the women's lively banter. They had decided to meet there because they didn't want to put the woman they considered their Mother in any more danger. And really, sometimes it's best to hide in plain sight. In their anonymous stands, they could speak more freely than if they had gathered in Ngo Bikaï's home, where everyone would have noticed them.

"My sisters," added the fearful woman, "we're acting like cowards, no? I mean, blaming another woman instead of . . ."

"Of what?"

"Of attacking France."

"Don't you see?" snapped a pregnant woman. "Mininga has become the long arm of France here."

"We just need to tell her that we're not happy," the woman next to her chimed in. "That's all."

"That's all."

"We won't do anything to her."

"Just tell her."

"One or two things."

"Like what?"

The women congratulated Martha, who had come "from so far

away," all the way from Yaoundé, and who had already done them such a service. You see, the day before, she had gone to Mininga's Bar, where none of them set foot anymore. In the past they'd have been able to count on the Anglophone woman who sold plantains and plums to be their spy, but she had left the place a while back. "She would have warned us!" one woman added.

Thanks to the information provided by Martha, the women were able to trace out the floor plan of La Seigneuriale, to sketch out all the entrances and exits, to get a clear idea of what the walls were made of, where the serving girls slept, and all the other details a general would need before a battle. Her visit to Nguet, "after all these years," had borne fruit. To be sure, the women of Edéa wanted to give their regards to Nguet, but mostly they had a message for her boss. Not to do any real damage, just to give her a little lesson in civility, you know.

26

The Final Assault

Here's what happened: Early in the morning a woman knocked on the door of La Seigneuriale. When Nguet opened it, she was surprised to see so many women in the courtyard. They were all wearing *kaba ngondos* cinched around their waist with a pagne. Some were wearing trousers underneath. The serving girl didn't immediately call for her boss, because she assumed that the women were heading off to catch catfish. There'd been a lot of talk about catfish lately, because money was tight, due to the "events," and once again the women had to resort to the things that helped tide them over when the harvests were poor.

"If the woman who sold grilled plantains were still here," said Nguet, by way of an apology, "she would have something for you to eat."

Because, you see, it was still quite early! But, when one woman took de Gaulle's photograph off the wall, she quickly realized that they hadn't come that early to La Seigneuriale to buy plantains and plums from the Bamenda woman. A second woman, instead of sitting down, picked up a chair and passed it to her friend, who passed it on to another woman, and another, all along a line that went from the inside of the bar out to the back of a pickup truck in the courtyard, where the chair found its place. Nguet thought she recognized Martha behind the wheel, or something like that. Her mind was spinning so fast she couldn't even ask what was going on. She called out for her boss.

When Mininga appeared, followed by her girls, she was greeted by an elderly woman with a mischievous sparkle in her eyes.

"We're helping you move, *ma chérie*," she told her. The French word emphasized her sarcasm.

"You asked for our help, don't you remember?"

Obviously, our Mininga did not remember, but could she even recall anything at that point? She waved her flyswatter left and right.

"Move? Where?"

"You need to tell us that, *ma chérie*."

The women burst out laughing, and kept passing things down the line without missing a beat.

"We're just here to do our job, as you can see."

The woman who said that was carrying a table, which she handed off to another standing at the back of the truck.

"Who gave you the order to do this?"

"How could you forget?" said the woman at the back of the truck. "Show her."

An older woman reached down between her breasts and pulled out a purse. Waving a few bills, she added, "You're the one who gave me all this, aren't you?"

"You paid up front."

"Two hundred francs."

"*Ma chérie*, do you want me to count them for you?"

Mininga was done listening to this farce.

"I'll show you, you fools!"

The insult made the women roar. Mininga jumped up and, in a rustle of jewels and lace, cut through the crowd, calling women out as she went: "Madam, I've never verbally assaulted you, have I? And as for you, madam, I suggest you watch your behavior, huh!" Her anger stood in stark contrast to the good humor of all the ladies who seemed so eager to get to work, even at this early hour of the morning: they'd come to have fun, at long last, to have some fun! Greetings and salutations!

"You'll see," Mininga kept repeating. "I'll go to the military camp."

Poor Mininga! She would soon learn two basic rules of war. First, you can only count on allies who have a real stake in the outcome of your battle. When Mininga arrived at the gate of the camp, it was still shut tight. It was barely seven in the morning. The soldiers on guard recognized her, of course, but they still wouldn't let her in. Had she been a potential recruit, they would certainly have opened the gate, and even offered her breakfast as a bonus for signing up as a tirailleur. But when a woman of her age came knocking at the camp—even if she had kept her looks, even excessively perfumed and decked out in jewels like no one else around—well, she was nothing more than an old woman, and France had no need to enlist African women as *tirailleuses*!

The second rule that Mininga learned was that if a general fails to carry through on an ultimatum, he loses the upper hand. When she returned to her courtyard without the promised squadron of tirailleurs, she was greeted with smiles and even some chuckles.

"Ah," said a woman carrying a hot plate, "we thought your tirailleurs were coming to help us."

"So just where are your tirailleurs?" another added.

The crowd roared with laughter.

"Aren't they men, after all?" another asked.

"Is their *bangala* all they have?"

"Ah! They're afraid to use a hammer?"

"Cowards!"

"Rude boys!"

"Are they afraid of women now?"

"They only know how to rape women, huh?"

"They're hiding back in the French camp, right?"

"Why don't they come here to look for their mamas?"

"Or their sisters?"

"Are they tirailleurs or manioc roots?"

"Tirailleurs or potatoes?"

Mininga looked on as her business was taken apart, watching as women climbed onto the roof of La Seigneuriale, screwdrivers in hand.

"Hey!" she shouted. "What are you doing?"

"We're taking down the roof of your bar. Do you want to give us a hand, *chérie coco*?"

"Here, take a hammer."

One sheet of metal after the other, the roofing of La Seigneuriale came down, followed by the doors and the windows. There were protests when the women started in on the serving girls' rooms, but Nguet was able to convince them that the battle was lost and it was better to surrender.

"If you don't want anyone to get hurt."

The women of Edéa were holding hammers, shovels, and machetes, while the serving girls had only pots, spoons, table knives, and plates. The morning was too beautiful to end in a brawl, and so some of the serving girls finally just emptied out their own rooms. They grumbled as they worked, but they did it nonetheless. Everyone watched as they disappeared into the forest, their meager belongings piled on their heads. None listened to Mininga begging them not to give up, ordering them to stay and stand up to the women of Edéa. The mutiny of La Seigeuriale's women almost turned into a family fight when Mininga refused to pay the departing serving girls their last wages.

"If you stay," Mininga told them, "I'll pay you later."

"No." Nguet was categorical. "Pay me now if you want me to stay."

Mininga paid her on the spot.

"Pay us, too," the others said. "Then we'll leave."

"Too much is too much."

Things almost erupted into an all-out brawl because the serving girls threatened to tear off Mininga's underwear right there in front of everyone. Knowing she wouldn't be defended by the local women who were taking her bar apart piece by piece, Mininga realized her reign of glory had come to an end. Soon all that remained of La Seigneuriale were four wall posts and one woman whose anger had turned into tears.

"You don't know who you're dealing with!" she cried, standing alone in the middle of her courtyard and brandishing a fist.

The women of Edéa didn't even answer her anymore. Everything was quiet, except for the sounds of the village waking up. Then the women who had demolished her bar suddenly turned back into simple market women; they walked back across her courtyard, greeting her politely and expressing surprise that her bar had disappeared.

"Oh my!" one woman exclaimed, her hand on her mouth. "Where did your bar go?"

"Leave me alone!" Mininga cried.

A bit farther off, an animated group exchanged gossip.

"You don't know who I am!" Mininga snarled. "*Minalmi!*"

She shook her fist at the women who whispered as they headed off. There was no way to explain to her that it wasn't personal—they just hated how she did business!

Later, when the first French soldiers came into La Seigneuriale's courtyard and found Mininga sitting on what remained of her establishment, she greeted them with the words she had been chewing all morning: "I hate you!" They quickly understood that she hated everyone, that she hated life itself, that she even hated death. In the end, a military vehicle took Mininga, her anger still glowing like an incandescent ball, to Yaoundé. Martha later swore that she'd seen her there in a bar just like the one in Edéa, a bar she opened up in Briqueterie called the Circuit, where, perhaps in the spirit of the day but also to cover her tracks, she went by the name of the Marshal.

27

The Angel of the Desert

The Battle of Kufra lasted precisely one month. On February 27, 1941, when the noonday sun burned the brightest and the desert its hottest, all of a sudden, instead of gun blasts, the clanging of cymbals was heard coming from the Italian fort. Then came the sounds of trumpets and other instruments. An orchestral rhapsody soon enchanted the desert. Baffled, the soldiers of Free France looked questioningly at each other. Their enemy had surprised them many a time, but this was more than they could believe.

"They're playing around," whispered Colonel Leclerc.

Soon the doors of the fort opened, and a form emerged.

"Don't shoot!" snapped the French commander.

It was hard to tell just what was going on. The extreme heat played tricks on your eyes, turned everything into a mirage, the whole universe into an unfathomable dance. The music coming from the fort added to the confusion. It was impossible to say just what was moving slowly toward them: an animal, a man, or a spirit? It was dressed in white, and in the shadow behind it floated something like a flag or wings.

"The Angel of the Desert," Massu said.

The French burst out laughing and were soon joined by the tirailleurs. They were all nervous and kept their rifles aimed at the advancing figure. It certainly was in no hurry! Finally, after a long moment that seemed to stretch out into an hour, but that was probably only about fifteen minutes, the silhouette of a child emerged.

"Don't shoot!" Leclerc repeated.

Nine or maybe ten years old, the child was dressed in a loose robe of white cotton that floated in the breeze. He was holding two flags. His legs were swathed in billowing trousers and his feet were bare. His face, of an exceptional beauty, was a mixture of black and white features, for he had black skin, but smooth hair and a delicately pointed nose. A broad grin could be seen on his plump lips, which contrasted with the look of fear in his eyes and the perfect naïveté of his demeanor.

"My God," Dio whispered, "my God!"

He thought he'd already seen everything in this war! No one could tell if he was captivated by the beauty of this apparition or by the scandal of this child's presence on the battlefront.

"*Non sparate!*" said the kid.

Everyone understood.

"No shoot!" he repeated, this time in French.

Shooting a bullet into his head would have been an insult to his beauty. There were hundreds of rifles with bayonets pointing at him, so many promises to interrupt his fragile existence.

"Don't shoot!" Leclerc ordered, holding his cane aloft.

He, too, seemed mesmerized by this ghostly vision emerging from the desert.

"Me, Eritrean," said the child, again speaking in French.

"An Italian colony," Dio explained.

The kid's cap made it clear he belonged to the Italian army.

"It's a little askari," Massu added.

"Don't shoot!" the kid begged. "*Non sparate!*"

A child soldier? The two white flags framed him, turned him into the Angel of the Desert every man dreamed of. He was walking softly across the sand, carefully stepping down on one bare foot and then quickly lifting the other.

"Message from the commander," he said.

"Stop!" ordered Leclerc.

The kid froze. He must have been used to obeying military rules, since he stood bolt upright, his hands forming a triangle over his head, crowned now by the fluttering white flags. Two tirailleurs went to search his clothes, fearing another Italian trick. One of them came back to the French commander carrying the letter the kid had tucked into the folds of his robe, while the other dragged the little soldier along by his ears, quickly turning him back into the kid he'd been all along.

"The Italians are offering to surrender," Leclerc announced after reading the message.

"It's high time," said Massu.

"They're done for," added Dio.

The soldiers surrounded the little askari, curious about his presence there on the battlefield. Swathed in the commentaries of the soldiers—who were unwilling to believe that his slender hands might have held the rifle that had killed one of their comrades, or that they were now bearing news of their own delivery from hell— he still looked divine.

28

Endgame

The next day, the commander of the Italian forces sent one of his askaris, a young man this time, to deliver a letter in which he repeated his offer to surrender, adding that he had only one request: that he not be turned over to the tirailleurs. Colonel Leclerc's reply was straight and to the point: his goal was not some desert outpost, but Strasbourg. And for his officers, it was Paris. Regardless, now wasn't the time to debate larger goals. The Italian noncommissioned officer in charge of Kufra wasn't surprised by this, for he, too, detested the fort that ought to have been a source of protection—as he'd been promised—but had become his battalion's tomb.

He would have given anything to be anywhere else than shut up in that shithole of a fort. One by one, starting with the child soldiers, he had his men come out into the desert, their hands in the air. Defeat is always ugly. There were several incidents—some tirailleurs tried to slap some of the surrendering men or to spit in their faces—but relatively few, since Leclerc had given specific orders on how to treat the prisoners. Two hundred seventy-three askaris threw down their weapons at Colonel Leclerc's feet and lined up in front of his tirailleurs. The dozen or so Italian soldiers commanding them sat down with the French officers to negotiate the terms. It took only a few hours.

Abandoning the bulk of their material—all except one truck for the commanding officers of the defeated army—the Italians disappeared into the endless expanse of the Sahara. Their weapons were immediately distributed to the tirailleurs who still had none. That's how Hebga and so many others, who had been armed only with machetes, were given rifles. The woodcutter no longer clasped on to his ax. The nighttime battle had shown him its limitations, and he swore to himself that he'd learn how to shoot properly. It is certainly fair to say that the Battle of Kufra had transformed the tirailleurs who had survived, for the joy that spread out over the dunes that day was that of men who, for the first time, felt themselves to be soldiers.

Now, for them, the war could finally begin.

And the war was also beginning for de Gaulle, who announced this victory to Churchill in person. Churchill set his cigar down on the table and shook his hand. Nothing else was needed; the news spread out across French Equatorial Africa. Radio Cameroon dedicated several special broadcasts to it, featuring French officials as guests. The governor spoke of Kufra as if he had been there himself and stressed that Free French victories like this one shortened the distance between Yaoundé and Paris. He organized a reception at the palace. Pouka wasn't invited. But what did that matter? The word "Kufra" entered the writer's world through another doorway. In fact, it was Martha who told him, after the French army made an announcement in Edéa, of the death of "Ngo Bikaï's little brother."

"Charles?" Pouka asked.

"That's what you call him, too?"

"What does it matter now," said the poet, "since he's dead?"

"Yes, in Kufra."

Truly, the details hardly matter at all.

THE DUNES
OF THE FEZZAN, 1942

ㅐㄴ 1

1

What Fritz Had Understood

"Listen carefully to what I'm saying. We will pay dearly for being the first in Africa to volunteer for the liberation of France. In fact, the recolonization of Cameroon began back in 1940 with de Gaulle. I know you saw him in Yaoundé. But me, I saw him speak in Douala. Are you listening? De Gaulle isn't a colonist like those we've seen here before—not like the Portuguese, the Germans, or even the English, because I've dealt with the English, too. You know, I've gone to Nigeria to sell my goods. You don't believe me? Ah, it was back when I was still trying to build up my name, and I thought I could buy merchandise there and sell it here cheaply. It was before my father died. But, where was I? Yes, the recolonization of our country that began with de Gaulle is different from what happened before. Do you hear what I'm saying? Good, it didn't start with explorers armed with contracts, like with Livingston. Forget about them, they belonged to colonization's Precambrian era, back when it was about moving into a country, starting a war, killing off the inhabitants, taking over the land, organizing raids, forced labor, *njokmassi*. De Gaulle hasn't killed any Cameroonians, no. He has asked them to contribute tirailleurs to go kill other whites. To go kill whites. Do you hear me? And those tirailleurs are all volunteers. Members of the Resistance. That's a new model right there, and it means we have to totally shift our perspective. The first thing de Gaulle did was colonize our vocabulary. Colonization by means of the French language, you see, that's really important. First, the war that France lost becomes just a battle. The collaborators, like that Douala chief, you know who I mean, what was his name? Ah, I've forgotten his name. Help me out here. You know, I heard him speak last year. Recent events have me all mixed up, I'm sorry. I know, we can't let this break our spirit. What was I saying? Yes, the French language. Very important. Look. Collaboration becomes resistance. Even the vocabulary shifts, you see? The Douala chiefs who are collaborating with de Gaulle, now they're part of the Resistance, what an idea! In Africa, de Gaulle needs men he can count on, allies. And the man he can count on is a black man. Where have you seen that before? Éboué, the governor of Chad, now he's the hero of the black world! It's a whole scheme, that's what I'm telling you. You think I'm exaggerating? Just let that idea sit for a while and you'll see. I only hope you remember what I'm telling you today, for the very first time, here in Edéa, in your brother's house. The role of his allies is very simple. They have to put French Africa behind de Gaulle, provide him with soldiers, riches. Not in the service of France. No, there is still a whole lot of France that isn't behind de Gaulle. People talk about Pétain, but what about Giraud? Yet for de Gaulle, whoever's not with him is against him. I was talking about his allies? Let me tell you. Before long, de Gaulle will start looking at Africans to figure out who will represent him in Africa. I think he'll prefer military men. Or civilians who will obey orders as if they were in the military. Straw men, you know. He'll give them responsibilities and then he'll be able to say he's giving responsibilities to Africans. The tirailleurs he recruits, they're the greenhouse where he grows his allies. I understand him. He is, above all, a military man. A tactician. He needs soldiers, generals. For the war and for peacetime, too. For peacetime, his main ally in Africa is Éboué. For war, it's Leclerc. The previous waves of colonization were strategic; his is tactical. He doesn't give a shit about skin color. But tactics, that's different. De Gaulle is a cancer in our history. As far as he's concerned, the tirailleurs are just pawns, ways to spread cancer. Don't ever forget it. For de Gaulle, the tirailleurs can never be criminals because they're members of the Resistance. For example, say you, Um Nyobè, if you stood up against him, then you wouldn't be part of the Resistance. *You would be a criminal.* It's just a question of perspective. His colonization is built on the Resistance. With networks, military bases. Like the camp in Edéa. With *circuits*. Ah! The *circuits*—whorehouses, really! You don't believe me? Listen carefully: They're all points in a network. Intersections of infamy. De Gaulle doesn't even talk about Cameroon anymore but about the FEA—French Equatorial Africa. The FEA, it's just a zone, a zone that is part of a field, a field that is bigger than any one country. The field, it's a space in the battle that de Gaulle is waging against England. I'm telling you. De Gaulle's real adversary, it's not Hitler, no. It's Churchill. If you want to understand de Gaulle, you need to know that England is no more than a tactical ally for him. Germany and France are strategic allies in Europe's broad continental network, even if for the moment they're on opposites sides of a circumstantial war. De Gaulle knows that England is nothing more than a collection of islands, while France is the gateway to a continent. England will need France more in peacetime than France needs her in times of war. No war goes on forever. France has lost the war, but de Gaulle wants her to win the peace. Peace, that's the war he's really waging. He knows that when peace comes, Churchill will have his eyes set on France. Because France will be in charge of the European network if Germany is defeated. For de Gaulle, the real threat is the English. For him, war is an opportunity, but peace is about trade. Africa is a zone on his new global chessboard. There's no more Cameroon. Except as a point in the French zone. The liberation of France can only be bought at the cost of African enslavement. But this enslavement has to be sold to the Africans as their liberation. Those who support this enslavement call themselves "liberators." "Members of the Resistance." Peace, war, battle, resistance, zone, field, networks—as you can see, everything starts with vocabulary. But it's all a scheme. It's de Gaulle who turned the commissioner of the mandate into a governor, you remember? He was the one who named Leclerc, a military officer, Cameroon's first governor, and step by step, he's setting up the most virulent sort of colonization, because it's the most hypocritical. He's giving us chains that we attach to our own feet, all by ourselves. But what he's forgetting is that Cameroon is nobody's colony. Nobody's."

Um Nyobè let Fritz speak without interrupting. They were sitting on the porch of Fritz's house, and his friend seemed possessed by a virulent fever, like he was arguing before a tribunal of spirits. Edéa stretched out before them, calm and somber.

2

Hebga's Parisian Dream

Peaceful and somber, Edéa stretched out before them. Peaceful and somber. Elsewhere, a young man was also sharing confidences; he told his dream to Philothée without interruption. Philothée was an ear, nothing more. Sometimes he made small grunts like an animal, too lazy, I'm sure, to make the effort to form a complete syllable. At first Hebga told himself it was because he was stupid, because he really didn't know the boy who, after the deaths of their two friends, was linked to him by nothing more than the memory of Edéa. He quickly realized that, stupid or not, there were advantages to his grunting silence. And besides, Philothée could understand the dream that pursued him, because he, too, had lived through the twists and turns of their march north from Yaoundé. That's how the woodcutter came to tell him the dream that was invading his nights. It was a Parisian dream. Sometimes he dreamed half of it one night and the rest the following. A very stubborn dream, really, that followed him night after night, especially when his day had been challenging, whether because of the long march through the sand or the endless training sessions he was put through.

The sun was gleaming. It was the most beautiful day, more beautiful than the fantasies of luxury that had captivated him when he leafed through the pages of *La Gazette du Cameroun* and calculated his odds of winning the grand prize in the lottery. Oh! It wasn't just the prize of a million francs and a trip to Paris that always drove him wild. Hebga imagined driving down the Champs-Élysées, a victor in full glory: a Senegalese tirailleur in his uniform. No signs of war, Paris ecstatic. The walls covered with thousands of French flags and banners. It was just like what he'd experienced in Yaoundé, but bigger, more festive, more thrilling. Most of all, there was no more Leclerc, but rather General de Gaulle himself leading the parade. A very orderly parade of tirailleurs, the first ones who had answered his call. On his shoulder Hebga held the long rifle Captain Dio had given him, with an equally long bayonet on its end. It was a compromise. He had needed something that combined a rifle and a machete to allay his feeling of being stripped bare when they took away his ax; it was the only thing that had convinced the virtuoso to give up his weapon of choice. He marched in step like the perfect soldier he was: head held high, eyes fixed on the future he knew he had given back to this city that now celebrated him, to this country that thanked him. Hebga was proud. There were faces peering out of every window of every house and in each shop door. All of France had come out to welcome the tirailleurs she had wrested from the distant forests of Africa, who had crossed the Sahara to fulfill a promise they had made silently to themselves when they were still far away and dreaming of this Paris that they had never seen, but that had become their obsession. The inhabitants of such a beautiful city had no right to be unhappy!

Paris, Hebga thought, we liberated you!

Gratitude is a virtue, and it finds expression in love. The liberation of Paris had filled the city with women who blew kisses at him from a distance. They brought their hands to their lips and then held their palms open, smiles lighting up their faces. The men were ecstatic too. They threw their hats in the air. The whole street shouted words of joy that transformed into garlands as they fell at the soldiers' feet. What am I saying, garlands? Roses, stars that spun through the air and covered their shoulders.

"Hurrah!"

"Hurrah!"

Hebga didn't turn to look, certain that behind him spread out the column of Senegalese tirailleurs with whom he had crossed through the antechamber of hell and who, therefore, deserved to be welcomed into this paradise. He knew how each man had struggled, the fear that had taken hold of all these brave fellows, whose every action was a heroic feat. Most of them had known nothing but the forest, but now, what stories they could tell of the twists and turns of their travels through unbelievable lands. They had never left their villages before and now they could talk about countries, about continents! Africa! Europe! They had known only people of their own ethnic group, and now they had discovered a new sense of continental solidarity, a new racial solidarity, a new human solidarity! Hebga didn't need to look at his comrades because the eyes of the happy city reflected the humanity for which each of them had put their life on the line. He discovered that the goal of the most bloody of wars was to make a city smile again. Sometimes a woman rushed from the crowd to give him a real kiss. She held tight to his chest. She opened her mouth to tell him about the hours, days, weeks, and years of the Occupation. But the column kept marching on, dragging him along with it. Still, she managed to utter one phrase that he caught midair: Thank you!

"Thank you, O Children of Africa! Thank you!"

Soldiers do not cry. But if Hebga had lifted his hand, he'd have wiped away a tear. Alas! But Paris didn't let him. A woman threw herself into his arms and marched along with him, keeping pace with his steps.

"Don't you recognize me?" she asked.

He looked at her.

She didn't give him a chance to find her face among all the adventures that had filled his life, where admittedly women's faces were less common than those of his fallen comrades.

"I'm the Marshal. Don't you remember?"

And Hebga relived the fervor of that night, back in Yaoundé. He revisited all the details of the room in Briqueterie, of the love that had shown him a very clear definition of ecstasy.

"Marshal," he shouted as he gave her a kiss. "What are you doing here?"

He learned that happiness has the same face in every liberated city.

"I was looking for you."

"For me?"

"Come with me!"

She didn't give him a moment to think. She pulled him from the ranks and dragged him off into the crowd. Hebga did not regret it for a moment. He knew that Paris, now liberated, would forgive him this escapade after all the dangers he'd come through. The thought of what the Marshal promised him was enchanting. He thrust his hand in his pocket to bring his impatient *bangala* back in line.

"Wait for me," he cried in the chaos of the cheering crowd.

The Marshal didn't wait. Out of breath, he stopped and watched her swim away through the crowd. She looked back at him and her smile translated her words, though they were drowned out by the crowd's cheers.

"Don't you want to screw?"

Hebga stood up straight, then hurried after her as she made her way through the growing crowd. Sometimes he could only make out her head, which bobbed up as if from the depths of the sea, only to disappear and then reappear farther off. He zigzagged between the people who offered him a kiss, a wave, or a phrase that touched his heart and soul: "Thank you!" His memory of the things she had done to him back in Briqueterie was clear enough that he pushed his way through the shoulders, freed himself from the arms seeking his embrace, the hands expressing their gratitude. He thought about her specialty, the whirlwind: she'd take his testicles in her mouth and spin them around and around until his eyes glazed over. He remembered many other things, too, surrounded by the joyful crowd, the crowd that went on and on endlessly, that grew into a thousand, no, a million forms of ecstasy. He saw exactly how he was going to ball the Marshal, how he would *gnoxe* her, how he'd fuck her, and it was as if he were back there in the middle of the Sahara: marching over dunes, his feet sinking into the sand—*nyaka, nyaka, nyaka*—his soul open to the whole long path ahead, to the expanses they would cross. His mouth was dry and his eyes were fixed on the tantalizing oasis that remained ever out of reach.

"Marshal!" he begged.

"*Vive de Gaulle!*" came the shouts from all around. "De Gaulle!"

He'd wake up trembling, surrounded by laughing tirailleurs.

"We look for that Marshal!"

"This time, you no cry 'Mama'!"

His dream of our Sita—that he didn't share with Philothée. It was far too personal.

3

The Whitening of the Black Force

If defeat is an orphan, victory has many sets of parents. In fact, the tirailleurs had quite a rude awakening after their victory. For the victory at Kufra had repercussions that soon became evident to the soldiers who had fought there. Suddenly contingents of young men began to arrive across the desert, vagabonds of the impossible, determined to take part in the battle for the liberation of France. They were for the most part young Frenchmen who, now that they had left the country to join Leclerc's forces, were ready to make the tirailleurs forget that they had been the first ones to put their lives on the line. Others came from neighboring countries: Belgians, Spaniards, and even Germans; there were Poles, too. A cosmopolitan band, but all white, although they were joined by a scattering of Libyan goumiers. They were united by their shared hatred of Hitler, by the goal of breaking his last ball, and also by how poorly equipped they were. Like castaways in the desert, they explained how they'd been moved by the news of the victory at Kufra broadcast on English radio. The youth of a continent ground down under Hitler's boots seemed to find its lost pride, and those who joined up with Leclerc were drooling at the idea of soon dying for France. Soon, but with dignity.

Defeating the Italians, that meant they'd beat the odds in death's lottery. The results were clear: now there weren't just machetes to distribute, but rifles, grenades, machine guns. From the United States and from England, Free France soon received many all-terrain

vehicles, and even bomber aircraft. Since they wanted to die with
dignity, as some of them put it, the only thing they still needed were
uniforms. But really, the uniforms didn't mean that much because,
unlike the tirailleurs—some of whom had received their first pair
of underwear as a gift from Free France—these mercenaries for freedom arrived fully dressed. Integrating them into the ranks added a
surprisingly multicolored hue to Leclerc's troops. Soon the growing
waves of men who sought a dignified death swamped the tirailleurs,
who were now in the minority. I'm sure you recall that when Leclerc
left Douala, his troops were comprised mainly of the twenty or so
tirailleurs Dio had placed at his orders, to which were then added
the hundreds of Cameroonian recruits picked up along the way, as
well as the Senegalese tirailleurs they'd found at the base at Faya-
Largeau. That gives you some sense of how his column, and its
firepower, had grown. Now add up the number of those who died
along the way, most of whom were black. From his five thousand
men, he had chosen two hundred for the Battle of Kufra, where
many tirailleurs fell, just as they had at Murzuk, where Bilong had
been wounded and later died. I have already mentioned the consequences of several of Leclerc's decisions, whether practical or just
misguided, which resulted in a high proportion of deaths among the
black troops.

Do the math and you'll see that, if the total number of tirailleurs
was falling—because the colonel wasn't getting any more reinforcements from Félix Éboué—the number of white volunteers was rising. I won't trace out the two curves here, because the math is quite
obvious and easily understood. The whitening of Leclerc's troops
modified the composition of the battalions and, consequently, de-
layed the new recruits' face-to-face with death. Why was it the tirailleurs who complained about this? Listen: The time when white
soldiers would automatically outrank the tirailleurs had passed. The
new white recruits needed to start out at the beginning, at the bottom of the ladder. But that wasn't how it always happened. And the
tirailleurs who had proven themselves on the battlefield had often
been promoted. For example, after the feats of courage witnessed
by Captain Massu, Hebga had become a tirailleur second-class. Even
if rank meant nothing to him—a sentiment common among the black

soldiers—many tirailleurs found it unacceptable that the new recruits be treated, or even promoted, as if they had fought at Kufra.

In fact, the majority of the tirailleurs had been assigned to the
infantry, while the new white recruits were more likely to be placed
in the artillery. The color differential was so obvious that the Nazi
press expressed its indignation, as we well know: the front lines of
the French army were dusky, while the rearguard was rather white.
Schwarze Schande! Rather than facing whites, Nazi soldiers were bat-
tling against blacks. In his "psychological training" speeches, as he
called them, which he gave each morning, pounding on the ground
with his cane, Colonel Leclerc insisted on the courage of the tirailleurs who braved the enemy cannons. None of those whom he called
"valorous warriors" would have raised even one little finger to say,
"Pardon me, Colonel, sir, valorous warrior means shit, I prefer artillery." The capacity to handle military equipment, the glaring tech-
nological advantage of Europe over Africa: those arguments would
have quickly silenced the complainer. What's more, while a breach of
military authority might have been dealt with diplomatically at the
start of the desert campaign, there was no room for debate about it at
this point. "Court-martial!" Some tirailleurs, confident because they
were the ones who had taken control of the desert, gave vent to their
surprise, and even grumbled about it to each other. "Oh, get a look at
the whiteys there!" But still they believed the new recruits were
ready to die for their homeland—and quickly! Yet a simple survey
would have revealed that some of those white men who had come out
of nowhere had been assigned as mechanics, even if they, too, had
never seen a truck motor. As for the few Africans who were assigned
to the artillery, they were relegated to such menial tasks as brushing
away the tracks left across the desert by the motorized troops—and
for that they were called *tirailleurs-balayeurs*—sweep-shooters. And
then there were those tirailleurs like Hebga who just didn't give a
damn about any of this and who always volunteered to be on the
front lines: for there was nothing that made the woodcutter—the
Ax!—happier than the idea of cutting down Germans one after
the other. Even if they chose to attack him barehanded—like the
Italian Daniels he'd fought before—that would be no problem for him.

But Hebga, he was in the minority.

That's when the German word *Kanonenfutter* made its way into the tirailleurs' vocabulary. I won't say that they actually used the word itself, because no one, whether they're a tirailleur or not, can describe themselves that way: cannon fodder.

Time passed. There was a vague cloud still hanging over the camp, a mood difficult to describe, something that no one could pin down. In any case, the tirailleurs felt their lives were being sold short, in terms of the cost of Rommel's bullets. No, they weren't blind to segregation or racism. But to them, this was just more of the same: life in the colonies had made them expect and put up with the worst whenever they had to deal with whites. The more I think about it, the more I tell myself that the toxic atmosphere created by the progressive whitening of the troops, and by the concentration of all the black soldiers in the infantry, produced a tension that put all the tirailleurs on edge. In short, the cohesion that had characterized the Leclerc Column up till then disappeared. I'm sure you'll say that the desert and geography imposed their own logic on the way history is understood. After all, the tirailleurs in question were used to Africa and the heat. Okay. You'll ask me if I've forgotten to account for the anxiety produced by waiting for the Germans to attack. And you're surely right. But let's not forget that, much later, when de Gaulle himself makes the decision to keep the soldiers—the very ones who had crossed the Sahara to liberate Paris—from marching under the Arc de Triomphe, he will cite geography, except in that case he'll take the cold as a pretext. The cold! "Since the winter weather in the Vosges presented risks for the health of our black troops," he wrote in his memoirs, *Mémoires de guerre*, volume 3, page 33, "we sent 20,000 soldiers from Central and Western Africa who had served in the first DFL and in the 9th Colonial Division to the South of France. They were replaced by an equal number of maquisards who we were then able to arm."

Those tirailleurs, it was understood, would soon be sent back from the South of France to their home villages. Heat here, cold there, the results are the same: doubts about the tirailleurs. Because, of course, it wasn't just the action of one stupid new recruit—one wearing eyeglasses—who refused to drink from the canteen Philothée handed him, preferring that of the white soldier beside him—it wasn't his stupidity that was the cause of what happened one day.

4

The Stutterer Speaks

Okay, here's what happened: Philothée threw the contents of his canteen in the fellow's face, clearly that was going too far. It's difficult for me not to take sides in the brawl that ensued, black soldiers on one side, white on the other. I am Cameroonian, after all. Except that I maintain Philothée did it for reasons other than skin color. For you are my witness, dear reader: I have carried this boy through this book all the way from Edéa, when he was just another member of Pouka's little poetry circle. The fellow with the eyeglasses with whom he was fighting, well, I don't even know his name. He's just made his way into my story now. And besides, why did he start with that racist move?

I can assure you of this: Philothée was shocked—with that shock a child feels on hearing a racist insult for the first time. In Edéa he didn't often run into whites . . . I can also clarify that if he threw the contents of his canteen in the face of the fellow with the eyeglasses, it was less because of the whiteness of that white man than because he was unable to pronounce the insult. That insult, it was a word in Bassa. Don't ask me which one, because what matters is the battle that followed.

Everyone came running as soon as they heard the first blows. The soldiers made a ring around the fighters and placed bets. Some bet their mess kit. Others their shoes. Or their caps. No one bet their rifle—that would have been too much. It was only a fight, after all: *un chaud blo.*

"Give it to him good!" said Hebga.

For the first time he was playing the cheerleading role that Pouka had always filled for him in the past: he was the *ambianceur*.

"An uppercut!"

All the tirailleurs were rooting for Philothée.

"Cut balls worthless shit!"

"Smash face him!"

"Mamy nyanga!"

"You see that?"

"Kid's strong, huh?"

"Cameroon!"

"Cameroon!"

"You givin' up? Givin' up?"

"I bet underpants!"

"No joke!"

"One!"

"Again!"

"Destroy potato!"

"Come on," said the young soldier. "Come on, destroy me, then!"

And Philothée kept coming. Hebga's voice rang in his ears. It rang everywhere, really: in his balls, in his hands, in his neck. Don't ever make the mistake of doing your warm-ups next to an old athlete! Hebga kept telling him, in very clear terms, that there was no Bassa—and the tirailleurs added, no-o, no Cameroonian, the Senegalese said no way, no African, and then all the tirailleurs said as one, there was no, no, no, and no, not one black man—who had ever been beaten by a white man in a boxing match. And Hebga knew something about that—he was the champion of Cameroon!

"Show him you're a Bassa!"

"You're a black, ain't you?"

"Show whitey there that black man no potato!"

And Philothée showed him. Well, no, he was actually taking hits from the French soldier. One right in the face. Blood flowed from his nose, but he had blackened his adversary's left eye. It seems there's pleasure to be found in making the son of a bitch in front of you suffer.

"Is that all?" said the soldier.

So Philothée gave him some more.

And more.

Philothée was only making sounds. Little sounds. Animal sounds. Each of his blows emerged from a double stutter. A triple stutter. It grew louder, starting down in his belly, where unpronounceable trisyllabic phrases were jammed up, phrases like: "worthless shit" and "dumb jackass," along with the tetrasyllabic, like "dirty racist," or even more complex phrases, like *you mamy pima!*"

Ah! This wasn't a battle, but a fight between the word and someone who wanted to see his adversary dead. Because if it was a battle—here this is Hebga talking—of course Philothée would have won! Don't ask him what he based his analysis on, because you haven't forgotten who he was: the Ax! But in any event, he didn't have time to elaborate a Bassa metaphysics of muscle, or to recite the thirty-one lessons a boxer needs in a critical situation. Loud as a thunderclap, Philothée hammered home one powerful phrase: "*You mamy pima!*"

"Stop this nonsense now!"

That was the voice of Captain Dio. He was responsible for training, for whipping all the recruits—wherever they came from—into shape. A passage opened up in the ring of excited spectators and there was Dio, in full uniform, cap on head.

"Stop that now!"

Of course, in that far-off corner of the desert, it wouldn't have cost him anything to hold back his orders, to join the soldiers and enjoy a free boxing match. It wouldn't have cost him anything to organize this sort of contest among his recruits, either, a black boxer against a white boxer. The soldiers of the company, white and black alike, surely would have loved it. Everyone was truly crestfallen when Captain Dio put an end to the group's entertainment.

"Ah!" they sighed together, whites and blacks.

But they were divided when the score was tallied, because there was a score to settle after all. Captain Dio declared in fact that Philothée was in the wrong.

"And now," he added, speaking to Philothée, "Tirailleur Second-Class Philothée, apologize."

It would have been easier to get a nice, polite apology from a meharist's camel. This was cheating, a swindle, and all the blacks rebelled.

"Whitey there started it."

Except that Philothée's porridge was still dripping from the face of the fellow with the eyeglasses. No joke, it was porridge Philothée had in his canteen!

And it was hot, too.

"Philothée, apologize!"

Philothée tried one syllable but was interrupted by the tirailleurs' loud chorus of protests.

"I . . ."

Expecting an apology, his adversary puffed out his chest and, with a smile on his lips, cleaned his glasses.

"I . . ."

"Tirailleur second-class Philothée, we won't wait all day for your apology!"

"I . . ."

Was he giving in to the tirailleurs who were pressing him not to apologize to that ruffian?

"Tie him to the post," declared Captain Dio, "one week."

An uproar among the tirailleurs.

5

Sporting Friendships

Oh, yes. It's a classic part of boxing matches. The spectators are always surprised that the boxers who bloody each other's faces are actually buddies. Tirailleurs and white recruits alike were therefore shocked when, a few days after the battle, they saw Philothée and the bespectacled soldier walking side by side. They figured that Captain Dio had gotten the apology he demanded. But it was the young French recruit who had retracted his complaint, since his "eyeglasses weren't broken." In all his time in Africa, Louis Dio had never met anyone like him. Anyway, the volunteers who made their way to Leclerc's camp from the homeland, so eager to die in order to liberate France, all behaved quite strangely, at least that was what Dio and the others like him who "really knew Africans" thought. These new arrivals spoke with the blacks as if the era of colonization were over!

Bah!

The fellow with the glasses, Alexandre Fouret, was a young Parisian who dreamed of being a writer—with several manuscripts in his bag and, I'm sure, several rejection letters from editors. A fan of the Russian Revolution, as he soon revealed. He had always said he'd been born too late for Spain, and then the Second World War had knocked on the door of his little studio, at #3 rue Saint Jacques, in the fifth arrondissement. He kept a journal of his adventures in which one could read of his disappointment that the black man with whom he'd struck up a friendship stuttered. Yet he will come to recognize the many advantages of Philothée's silence. And, by the way, just where did you get that strange name, Philothée? It's a rare one, even in France. Fouret was the only one who recognized the name from the poetry circle: "Philothée O'Neddy?"

The guy from Edéa couldn't remember anymore. What interested him was the discovery that you could say something to a Frenchman besides the usual, "Yes, boss," "Yes, Colonel," "Yes, Captain." That really changed things, even if he still preferred to listen. Every Marxist adores an audience. Fouret didn't complain about having Philothée's ear. He explained that his own first name was rather reactionary, but oh well, there was nothing to be done about it. His parents were Catholics, fanatics, really. Had his tirailleur friend ever heard about Lenin? Fouret stressed that he had joined up not to rebel against his Catholic parents who had named him, but to prove that Lenin's theories needed to be adapted to the historic moment.

"Capitalism's final stage," he said, "is Nazism."

He fell silent for a moment, just to make sure Philothée had really understood.

"This war is necessary," he continued, "even if it's not the solution."

He didn't wait for an answer, having understood how to keep the conversation going. "Why? Because it fails to get to the root of things."

"Roo . . . roo . . ."

"Yes, the root, that's capitalism. Our real war is against capitalism. This war is a distraction, but we don't have any choice: Hitler forced it on us!"

Obviously, they only had such conversations during their breaks; the rest of the time they were busy doing drills, checking their equipment, marching across the desert, standing guard, being alert. In short, being a soldier in the Second World War that didn't address the root of the problem and that, moreover, according to Fouret, was financed by capitalists. Philothée discovered that he and his friend had something in common: they despised the war for which they had volunteered. The Cameroonian remembered the soldier who kept repeating on the battlefield: "War not good." What had happened to him? Oh! War's true self was revealed in little, veiled signs floating in the timelessness of memory. He called them "the Truth," according to the general theory of life and death that he was patiently elaborating, in the silent puzzle of his wordless mind and its confrontation with the brutal reality of things.

Philothée couldn't know it, but the relationship between capitalism and war had been examined back in Yaoundé only a few days earlier by another Frenchman: Jacques Delarue, whom Um Nyobè had met at the neighborhood soccer field. He went there each weekend to train with his friends and referee games. Marc had introduced him to Delarue as his "colleague," and Um Nyobè hadn't failed to pick up on the irony when his friend, that ardent defender of Cameroon's interests, suddenly adopted a deferential attitude toward a Frenchman. Delarue was a rather well-built guy—he looked like a policeman, but with an engaging smile, and he was a good defender. To everyone's surprise, he opted to train with the blacks—usually the colonists played among themselves—explaining that he didn't live far from the native quarter, "so why cross the whole city just to play soccer with your boss, huh . . . ?" Everyone thought it was a reasonable decision. Still, he was something of a curiosity, especially for the children who cried out, "*Nta'ngan! Nta'ngan! Nta'ngan!*" as soon as he got the ball—not to mention when he scored a goal. They gave him a month, "no longer," before he'd adapt to the reality of this country where playing soccer had made him the butt of the children's jokes.

Sporting friendships quickly overcome barriers of race, nation, and even war: Um Nyobè's fellow soccer players soon learned this simple truth, the same one Philothée's comrades had learned on the battlefields of the Sahara. One Sunday after a game, Um Nyobè invited Delarue to come back to his house, as his friends Marc, Ouandié, and Etoundi usually did after practice. He was the first white man to cross the threshold of the house in Messa. To tell the truth, he made a very different impression on Martha than he had on her husband.

"He's a spy for the governor," she said after he'd left.

"Very well," said Um Nyobè, "he can tell the governor how one of his subaltern employees lives."

"I don't like his face."

"Well, since you at least like his hands and feet, that's enough to make me, your husband, happy."

"Did you see his eyes?"

"Oh! I was looking at his mouth instead."

"And that goatee?"

Both of them agreed, however, "He talks a lot."

Delarue had Marxist tendancies, too, as he put it. He preferred to call himself a "union man," even if that really didn't mean anything in Cameroon in 1942, when there weren't yet any unions.

"There aren't any in France, either," he clarified, "they're *illegal* over there, too."

Illegal? There he made a mistake, one that Marc—ah! Marc!—was quick to correct.

"Here," the man who always knew better than anyone else added, "there've never been any unions."

"Well, then," Delarue replied, "you need to start some."

That's how the friends discovered the Frenchman's practical side, always coming up with the most rational solution to life's problems. For example, why cross the whole of Yaoundé to play soccer with whites when there's a team in your own neighborhood?

And why let some imbecile rap you on the knuckles with a ruler when you can organize and show him what's what?

And why head off to war when you can get transferred to a colony and live the good life?

"Pacifism's rational, right?"

Conclusion: Delarue was a pacifist.

"There's no more room in France for bastards like me," he admitted one day.

"You're exaggerating."

Thus, another side of his personality was revealed. Beneath his apparently easygoing demeanor, he liked to be the center of attention. Martha was waiting for the day when her husband would clash with "that Delarue," since the two men's personalities were so similar. Yet they became very good friends. Another of life's surprises. Since his visits were attracting too much attention, especially from the children who celebrated each time he came by, and no doubt the

colonial administration would soon notice as well, Delarue suggested a practical solution to Um Nyobè. He'd no longer come to
the friendly gatherings, or to Um Nyobè's house at all, for that
matter; they'd only see each other at the soccer games, after which,
under the guise of talking about sports, he'd offer advice on the
matters that were troubling them and about which Delarue knew a
thing or two. If there was something urgent, Marc could pass along
the message. They learned that he'd been trained as a lawyer, but
had never practiced in France: to his mind, defending criminals was
useless because it was society that produced the crime. And the
foundation of that society was capitalism, which found its definitive
expression in colonialism. He had come to Cameroon as an observer,
to gather research for the book he was writing on the political economy of colonialism. "And, it goes without saying, because of the
war"—he preferred to stay out of that altogether. To cut short a story
that would be much longer and more detailed than what I've said
here—for Delarue also believed that he was being tailed by "the
dogs"—he became the shadow adviser of our Sunday soccer-playing
politicians.

6

Friendship Above All Else

But Delarue didn't really know that colony known as Cameroon! On January 3, 1942, Um Nyobè's boss wrote the following explanation of why he'd given him a rating of 18/20 in his last performance review: "An agent who knows his job well, but who is inconsistent in his service; a good agent; a little too pretentious; not promotable." Since until this point the writer had only received high praise, in this lower-than-expected evaluation one can discern the consequences of his nighttime meetings with his soccer friends Ouandié, Marc, Jérémie, and Etoundi. One can even recognize the enactment of Leclerc's directives, given when he was still governor, and that no-good Cameroonian could ever forget: "*I have seen others already more aware of their rights than of their duty; they must be firmly put back in their place. We are not afraid of them.*" In any event, Nyobè was learning the cost of his growing political responsibilities. Could it be that his boss was afraid of him—the agent?

The fact is that our man was paying for a friendship far older than the one that linked him to the soccer-loving French lawyer: Fritz had told him that he was going to have a Christian wedding to make his marriage with Ngo Bikaï official and that Father Jean said he needed someone to stand up for him.

"So," Fritz concluded, "I thought of you."

Obviously, Um Nyobè couldn't give his boss that reason: the marriage of a childhood friend, especially since it was a second wedding to the same woman—even if it was a Christian ceremony this time. That just didn't sound serious, because what does the French administration care about a childhood friend? Is he a relative? Even taking into account the broader sense of family in Africa, there were limits! Of course, Um Nyobè and Fritz had known each other since their first years on schoolroom benches. But if that was his argument, his boss would certainly have replied that if he needed to go to the weddings of every one of his friends from grade school, as well as take part in the funerals of uncles and aunts, he'd have no more time for work. And Um Nyobè had already run through his list of dead uncles—the one every good Cameroonian keeps on hand for such situations.

When he was standing in front of his boss, with words of his "father's serious illness" on his lips—a bad excuse if ever there was one—his boss went into such a rage that he pounded on the table.

"No, no, no, no, and no!" he cried. "Mr. Ruben Um Nyobè, would you kindly do your work before you bury your whole family?"

What could he say?

"There is no excuse," his boss went on, "for such unprofessionalism!"

There the writer made the mistake of arguing.

"My father isn't dead," he clarified. "I'm just asking for leave so I can take him to the hospital."

Between you and me, you can't let anyone mention the death of their father like that without reacting. That's the sort of thing that brings bad luck. I can assure you that any good Cameroonian would have done what Um Nyobè did. But do we need to say that the French colonial administration really didn't give a damn about good Cameroonians? It preferred those who didn't ask for leave—even just a few days—in the middle of a war. As for Um Nyobè's boss, as far as he was concerned he preferred employees who didn't talk back, even if he would have done the same thing in similar circumstances. The last straw was that despite this, the writer went back to the village for his friend's wedding! Ah! Um Nyobè, you, too! Later you'll try and talk to us about man's exploitation of his fellow man! As if you didn't already know enough about white men!

Um Nyobè had his reasons. He knew that his boss couldn't do

without his best writer in the middle of the war. Who was there in the pension office who could have done his job as well as he did? Certainly not that boss of his! Um Nyobè could take off work because he was a workaholic. In short, his father's illness did the trick, and Um Nyobè had no regrets about it because the wedding of Fritz and Ngo Bikaï really stood out in the annals of Edéa. People often say that you should wait a good while before getting married. Those two, it seems, had taken that advice to heart. The marriage coincided with the start of the rainy season, and on that day a fine mist of rain fell from the sky. It was taken as a sign of the spirits' blessing. The first rain of the season.

The wedding couple wore their finest clothes. Never before had anyone seen Ngo Bikaï wearing a dress with a low-cut neckline. Fritz had bought her what the women were wearing in Douala, that is to say, fashion from Paris. He himself wore a tie and a three-piece suit, made to order at the boutique Paris Comes to You; the shop's tailor, newly arrived, was the talk of the town. The couple were stationed behind a long table decorated with flowers and lined with bottles of all sorts of liqueurs. Their living room was aglow with their obvious happiness. The guests formed a line, first offering them words of blessing and then moving down the gigantic table, where a whole array of dishes were displayed, crowned by a succulent African threadfish—a real captain—and an assortment of condiments.

Let's skip over the church service, because no one really paid any attention to Father Jean's sermon. No one—not even Ngo Bikaï— saw his benediction as anything other than a social formality. He read the text from his Bible. He might just as well have read from the Book of Nature itself, because the sky showed more inspiration than he. He stressed the couple's happiness, the warmth of their home, the lifelong love they would share. Yet these three things were nothing new for the couple that stood before him. The walls of their home were like a museum dedicated to their life together; their three children, also dressed in European-style clothes, sat beside them; and their happiness was there for all Edéa to see. Father Jean had come into their lives rather late with all his benedictions. But good manners require that you listen to a priest until he decides to stop talking.

"God is great," he concluded.

"Amen!"

His benediction signaled the start of the meal. At Nguet's signal—yes, you are reading that right, Nguet—several people rose to serve themselves from the dishes. They sat right back down, however, when M'bangue indicated that he wanted to speak. He cleared his throat. There are things that are best not to hear with your mouth full. People started to whisper, worried that he was going to start talking about Hitler. Yes, there are some topics that will spoil your appetite. But no one was going to interrupt the Old Man, especially not Nguet. M'bangue looked around, as if surprised to be given such leeway.

"It is good that you've gotten married," he said to the happy couple. "*At last.*"

That eased the tension.

"Especially as you're getting to your older days," he added.

That's just how M'bangue spoke, always making reference to "older days." In Edéa the devastating force of his pronouncements was well known, as was his sense of humor, so everyone there was hanging on each of the words he delivered so sparingly. The married couple most of all. But a smile could be seen on M'bangue's face. The beam of light from the sky that fell on him drew all the guests close together in the living room, even as curious onlookers gathered to peek in through the windows. More than anyone else, Fritz and Ngo Bikaï were pleased that M'bangue seemed uplifted by a touch of grace.

"The sky has opened up," said the old man, "the future is yours."

His esoteric words surprised no one. But people exchanged glances when he lifted up a bottle of whiskey that he was drinking all by himself.

"For the French are going to leave this country."

This was in 1942! No prediction could have been more poorly received. Ngo Bikaï's women, who were trying to keep things organized around the table, turned into real police officers. Even Um Nyobè stood up in exasperation. It's so easy to spoil a mood with talk of politics! Who knew that better than he? M'bangue's speech had sent a wave through the crowd, turning all eyes toward Father Jean. The only Frenchman present was smiling politely.

"Papa, we've heard you," Martha said.

Called from the back of the house by Nguet, she knew she had to do something.

"I'm not done yet," M'bangue insisted. "I'm not done."

"We know," Martha cut in, "we know!"

"France has lost Africa's future. Cameroon will be independent," he said, his voice rising above the chaos his revelation had provoked. "Independent."

Shaking in spasms, he seemed in the grips of a larger vision. He brandished the whiskey bottle threateningly, his eyes ablaze. The hungry crowd was growing impatient. Fritz started to stand up. Discreetly, his wife held him back: M'bangue was in good hands, that was clear.

"Papa," Martha interrupted. "Keep your visions for tomorrow."

Another woman added, "For now, just sit down like everyone else."

"And eat."

"Drink."

The authority of those women was all it took; M'bangue lowered his eyes, just as one might close the Book of the Future. Never before had women given him an order, and he couldn't get over it. He cursed these new times that showed no respect to old age, and especially the women who clearly didn't give a damn about the future of the country and the world. The visionary's silence gave way to the devil's vitriol. Didn't he know that, whether true or not, there are only a few select visions that can be shared at a wedding table?

"You can't change the future," he grumbled.

"We know," Martha kept repeating. "Papa, we know."

"Cameroon will be independent."

She politely made him take a seat.

"We know."

7

A Surprising Catch

Yes, it was Ngo Bikaï's women who had taken charge of the wedding. Not only the party, but also dressing the bride; they bought all the things needed for the dinner and cooked the food, too. A few days before, they had gone to catch catfish. They wanted both to get something to eat, since most everything was in short supply, and to work on a project together. The Mother of the Market organized it. Since Martha had arrived in Edéa a week before Um Nyobè, who had stayed behind for work, she was acting as the Mother of the Market's right hand. Ngo Bikaï had insisted on it.

Um Nyobè's wife had been her true confidante for some time. Especially since the whole to-do with Mininga—that's what Ngo Bikaï called the incident that had brought the two women closer together despite the distance. Fishing for catfish, she hoped, would be another step on the path of their friendship's renewal. In fact, more than friendship, it was working together that allowed the women to define their social structure. It reinforced the authority of the Mother of the Market, showing the women who had put their stands under her control that she could take care of them when times were tough. Public opinion—by that I mean men's—didn't recognize her importance, and it was wrong. The collective power of the women was rooted in her.

It was up to the Mother of the Market to choose the activity for the women. They could, for example, work together in someone's field, say our Sita's. The project's success confirmed the woman's authority. For our Sita, death had signaled both the end of her reign and, really, her failure. Ngo Bikaï had decided to go for fishing because her father was a fisherman. The Sanaga River was her domain and, having grown up in the fishing trade, she convinced herself that the river would help her to show everyone the strength of her hand. The women didn't use pirogues—those were reserved for men. But the smaller branches of the river were just what they needed to catch catfish.

They set out early in the morning, paying no heed to the rain that followed them along. At sunrise they were already singing as they pulled gourds full of water from the stream: joyous apparitions covered in mud. Their faces were dripping with both sweat and water. They'd wipe their faces off with one hand and dive back into the water, into the mud. They told each other stories to lift their spirits, traded jokes to keep up their courage, wisecracks to make the work go faster. Rarely did the women express as much joie de vivre as when they were working together. Martha, who'd been cut off from these moments since she'd moved to the city, realized how much she'd missed them, and also how hard she had to work to keep up.

"You're doing just fine," one older woman said encouragingly.

Whether they had a *kaba ngondo* tied tightly around their hips, a pair of trousers, or just a simple loincloth, the women wore nothing on top, leaving their tattooed chests and backs exposed to the sky and its water, while their feet massaged the mud in an endless dance. Martha's clothes made it clear she had really come home to the village. Everyone still recalled with a smile how she had led the campaign to kick Mininga out of town. What am I saying, "recalled"? It was still the news of the day, the basis of their lively banter. It made all the women laugh to see how Martha had changed—no longer the city woman she'd seemed at first.

"You should have seen her," said one woman, imitating how Mininga walked. "You should have seen her heading off to see her tirailleurs."

"*Kougna, kougna, kougna.*"

"It seems she walked right out of town."

"Don't say it."

"In those high heels of hers?"

Suddenly the rain came pouring down, but that didn't dampen the women's spirits. Sitting under a tree on the stream's bank, Ngo Bikaï watched them work. From time to time she'd start singing a song and the women would join in. Although she sat a ways off, protected from the weather, she was in charge of the work. When she gave the signal, the women stopped chattering and, with nimble hands, began rhythmically tossing basins full of water over the little dam they'd built in the stream, a dam of twigs, stones, and whatever else they'd found. Women work with a focus like none other! Conversing all the while, they built their own little dam there on the stream's muddy bottom. Soon a catfish splashed in a woman's hands, the first catch met with joyous shouts. That catfish was cause for celebration; as the women sang, it was lifted up to the sky, offered to the universe that blessed it with a light drizzle of rain, encouraging other fish to make the same decisive leap.

"Look there," said one of the fisherwomen.

In the distance, a silhouette was cautiously approaching.

The women froze, speechless. Slowly, each step seeming like a provocation, Nguet came into the silence her appearance had created. She was dressed in mourning clothes: a white robe. Flustered when she hadn't found Ngo Bikaï at the market, she had come to look for her at the river, dressed as she was. Nguet had clearly walked through the rain, for she arrived under the shelter of a multicolored umbrella. Her ghostly appearance, the water falling from the sky, everything made her seem quite lost—and in fact she was unsure of where she was headed. Still, she was beautiful, projecting a calm that pierced through her grief. It was only when a gust of wind tore the umbrella from her hands and tossed it upside down on the water that the women woke from their trance. Martha took several steps toward her.

"Do you want to join us?" she asked.

Nguet was hoping for nothing more.

"First you have to speak with our Mother," Martha added, gesturing with her gourd toward the spot were Ngo Bikaï sat.

Silently, Nguet moved toward Ngo Bikaï, still carefully weighing each step. The women paused in their work, trying to follow the conversation unfolding between the two who had been joined by life's tragedies, but they couldn't make out a single word. They could only guess at the depths of their whispered exchange, and all breathed a collective sigh of relief when the two women hugged each other long and hard. Some women applauded, and joyful laughter erupted when Nguet asked Martha if she had an extra gourd. Um Nyobè's wife replied with a bright smile.

"*Wandafoot*," she exclaimed. "You want to catch catfish and you don't even have a gourd!"

The joke did the trick. Everyone burst out laughing.

"And dressed like that!"

They welcomed Bilong's girlfriend into their ranks with raucous good humor. Nguet lifted up the hem of her robe before wading into the water, a reflex or habit from her past life of gallantry. The women laughed again, and even harder, when they saw her stylish shoes. She hesitated, as if unwilling to get her clothes wet, although she was already soaked through, or to dirty her muddy feet.

"*Mamy nyanga*," said one woman, "you want to fish wearing those *coss coss*?"

"You'll ruin them!"

The beautiful girl didn't reply, but just stepped into the mud, and so brought this long story, this reminiscence of a painful war, to a close. Later, Martha will tell her husband that those belated condolences were the best catch of that rainy day when the women went looking for catfish; and that she had emerged from her mud bath with a clean conscience.

8

The Universe in Ecstasy

The real news of the day was that Martha caught a threadfish—a "captain," as we call it. Oh yes! No one believed her at first when she said her basket had captured the chief of all fish, a captain. She didn't even believe it herself.

"A captain!" she cried. "A captain!"

She lifted her basket into the air, displaying the big dancing fish, the biggest catch of the day.

"A captain!"

The women dropped their basins and came running. The captain was a surprising catch in this stream. The men were lucky if they hauled one out of the Sanaga River with their big nets. But here in this stream?

"A captain!"

Martha was so happy that she dropped the fish. It jumped out of her basket and fell in the mud at her feet. The women pounced on it, managing to grab it with their hands. Everyone was thrilled with this lucky catch. The fish was now struggling in the more confident arms of an old woman who ran from the water and threw it up on the shore, where it kept flopping. The women's many voices filled the space with shouts of joy, and ululations that wrapped the rain and the very universe itself in an incomparable brilliance—really beyond compare.

"This is for our Mama," declared an older woman.

"*Woudidididididi!*"

There was Ngo Bikaï.

"Take this."

The older woman handed her a machete, and Ngo Bikaï gently rapped the fish on the head, methodically, like she was counting out a beat. Caught up in the moment, the women responded to each rap with a joyous shout. The fish kept struggling for a while longer, writhing.

"Do you need help?" a happy voice called out.

It was a joke. A formality.

"Ah! Ngo Bikaï, you are our captain!"

The fish stopped struggling.

"Captain!" a woman shouted.

"*Woudidididi!*"

"Our captain!"

"*Woudidididididi!*"

The fishing expedition reached its high point in this expression of universal ecstasy; the women crowned the one they had chosen to lead them. Martha began to sing and the others joined in. They danced around the fish that one woman held up over their heads, they danced around Ngo Bikaï who had joined in the dance, they danced and shouted. Holding gourds or fishing baskets, they were the color of the mud from which they'd emerged, and they were dripping with the water that had given them their treasure. Together they jumped, joined by a transformative joy.

"*Woudidi!*"

It was as if these women had been turned into spirits, water spirits whose faces and bodies were camouflaged by the brown earth, turning them into an indistinct magma that sang instead of speaking, that wove sounds instead of shaping syllables.

The chorus turned to celebrate Ngo Bikaï.

"*Woudidididididididi!*"

Having rested in the tree's protective embrace, Ngo Bikaï was the only one who wasn't the color of the earth, whose body wasn't wet and muddy. She stood out among her women; she was their captain, like that fish one woman held up over her head. But water from the sky would link Ngo Bikaï to the mud of the river that had crowned her, because she, too, was earth, nothing but earth; because she was also water, and nothing but water; because she was a woman, and nothing but a woman. The thunder's clashes could do nothing about it, nor could the gusts of wind that had the trees swaying left and right. And so, dancing and ululating, she was led back to the village, a woman among women, surrounded by her muddy pack.

Ngo Bikaï walked at the front of the group of women, as they, with arms outstretched, held the biggest catch of the day over her head. The group followed her, their gourds filled with the catfish they'd caught. Their song brought everyone out of their homes, the children especially. The whole village came to greet them, joining in a spontaneous parade that foreshadowed the long-delayed wedding celebration.

Several days later the group of women—now dressed in European fashion, perfumed, coiffed, and accompanied by several men in jacket and tie—went from Fritz's home to Father Jean's church, extending the ecstasy of the Mamy Watas who had emerged from the depths of the forest, from the depths of the river, and crowned their captain: Ngo Bikaï. Then a man called Fritz stood in front of the priest and took her as his wife.

Only a handful of the fisherwomen were there to witness the blessings at Father Jean's church. The others, under Martha's leadership, had taken charge first of Ngo Bikaï's rear courtyard and then, in the following days, of her kitchen. They scaled the captain's back, pulled out its innards, cut off its fins, poked out its eyes, and slashed its skin with eight straight cuts. Using onions, bouillon cubes, lemons, olive oil, and spices—*bongo*, *pèpè*, and *djansan*—they made a marinade in which the fish swam for hours, twenty-four hours, yes, before it was cooked for thirty minutes and then given pride of place on the living room table, covered with onions and diced celery, surrounded by all the necessary accompaniments. It was a feast for the eyes of the many guests who invaded the married couple's living room, just waiting for the first among them to dig a fork into its exquisite flesh and taste the *mbongo tchobi*—the Bassa black stew.

As we know, all of this happened before M'bangue gave his

predictions for Cameroon's future. He was interrupted. Because after the women had recognized Ngo Bikaï as their captain, after the tragic death of our Sita, there was nothing, really nothing that interested that happy crowd less than knowing what the French wanted.

9

That *Schouain* Rommel

Since we're talking about the French and their wants, if it hadn't been for Captain Dio, Hebga would have given up on shooting practice and gone back to his ax. Things had been happening on the war front. Hebga, he would have said "Come what may," and "Rommel, so what?"—even though that name sent the camp into an unparalleled uproar. Leclerc had a personal grudge against him, they said, because before coming to the Sahara he had occupied a part of France, including the colonel's own village, and the one where de Gaulle had been born, too. Rommel was Free France's bête noire. They even dubbed the cardboard cutouts that were placed on the sand hills as shooting targets "Rommels."

He was called the Desert Fox. Who cares about that fox? Hebga said to himself. You have to obey orders, put your gun to your shoulder, and aim.

"Take a good look at him," Dio said.

Hebga stared at the silhouette spread out on the sand.

"Do you see him?"

"Yes, Captain."

"Fire!"

Hebga cocked his finger.

"No, you're too slow," Dio snapped.

Then they did it again.

"Imagine you're looking at your enemy's face."

But that was where things went wrong. For whatever Hebga tried—and he tried everything—he just couldn't imagine the face of the *Man who had done that*. Dio knew nothing about that old story—that very long, old story.

"Okay, tell yourself that he's a very bad guy."

Hebga didn't need to convince himself of that. He had lived through that evil, the evil committed by the *Man who had done that*. The image of our Sita's severed arm came back to him. He spit onto the sand. Dio thought he hadn't understood the point of the exercise, and struggled to find another way around the communication problem with the simplified French he and Massu used to speak to the tirailleurs.

"Enemy bad bad," he said.

"*Schouain*," Hebga replied.

"Yes, him *schouain*."

"Him Nazi."

"Nazi."

"Nazi *schouain*."

"Nazi *schouain*."

The captain pointed again at the silhouette there on the sand.

"Yes, Captain."

They'd go through it all again the next day, and the day after that. Because Captain Dio was the one charged with training the tirailleurs. Ah! He would have made things easier for himself if he had just used a picture or sketch of Rommel as a target. The problem was that for a Senegalese tirailleur, there was no difference between Rommel and Leclerc, or Dio himself, for that matter. Captain Dio realized it was just as hard to imagine an enemy there on the sand as a friend in the forest. Yet the tirailleurs needed to understand that de Gaulle was different from Rommel, because General Charles de Gaulle was not a Nazi.

It was so hot that everyone always felt dizzy, like the sun was making your brain swell. Off in the distance, the wind sang its morbid song. It kicked up the sand, which got in your eyes and blinded you; got into your mouth and left you thirsty. The noises from afar were all jumbled together, cries and tirades, orders and groans. Dio couldn't pay as much attention to each of the soldiers, but he knew that any lapse in shooting practice would be fatal. His soldiers would become cannon fodder for Rommel. Dio got himself back under control and focused again on Hebga, the man with the ax. Were the tirailleurs responsible for their own tragic fate? Ah! Dio, all too accustomed to blaming the army of Vichy France, could lay no blame on Free France! But there were all these new soldiers to train, the same lesson to go over again and again, each time slightly differently. The increase in the numbers of troops was posing unimaginable problems, especially with the assignment of black soldiers to the infantry. Free France was counting on them and at the same time needed to protect them, at the risk of having to bury them all in a mass grave! Captain Dio got himself back under control.

"Let's do it again."

"Him Nazi *schouain*."

"Very good. Now you shut left eye."

"Left eye."

Each time, Hebga closed his right eye. Dio was getting angry. What a shitty job this was!

"You look enemy."

"Nazi *schouain*."

"Very good. Now, fire."

Hebga fired.

"Very good, very good for today."

"Thank you, Captain."

The sun ate away at your brain, made your eyes bleary. There in the sand, an enemy's silhouette looked like a mirage. The exercise was done without bullets. They had such limited supplies that, until England delivered what they needed, they couldn't waste a single bullet. The balance of power had shifted since the United States had joined the war. But would those American soldiers be landing in Africa anytime soon? When? Dio imagined Free France's meeting with soldiers of the Afrikakorps, which would include woodcutters who had no idea how to shoot a rifle. Cannon fodder. And Captain Dio imagined just what would happen when his soldiers needed to use machine guns. They'd have to start the training all over again. Bah!

Hebga, if only he could have spoken to Dio in Bassa, he would have said that he wasn't afraid of that *schouain* Rommel, and if needed, he'd take him on in hand-to-hand combat, like he'd done with those Italians. That *schouain* Rommel could ask who he was and anyone would tell him about Hebga. That *schouain* Rommel had a lot of machine guns, supersonic planes, all-terrain tanks, no doubt, but they only did one thing—the same thing as when our Sita had been torn limb from limb. And no one dies twice. The woodcutter grew all the more certain that the *Man who had done that* could be none other than that *schouain* Rommel himself. Captain Dio's shooting practice was helping him to understand it all clearly. In his heart, Hebga thanked the French captain, because he had crossed whole countries—forest, plateau, steppe, and desert—looking for the *Man who had done that*, and now that his silhouette was slowly coming into focus there on the sand, all he had to do was wait, trembling, for the moment when he'd see the face of that Nazi *schouain* Rommel!

10

Getting Caught Up

Life hadn't stopped back in Yaoundé, things kept going, same as always. For example, Martha hated it when people traipsed into her living room on muddy feet. That was "the least of her flaws," said Pouka, teasing her. This time, however, as he again came to visit his friend, he didn't even have a chance to think that phrase to himself because, just as he caught the enticing smell of *mbongo tchobi*, Martha's voice greeted him sharply from the living room: "Take off your shoes!"

Um Nyobè had opened the door. It was raining as it rains only in Yaoundé. Despite his umbrella, Pouka was soaked. He took off his dripping wet socks and tossed them on a basket of avocados— the produce Martha sold and that she had lined up, as usual, along the wall. The wind buffeted the windows and doors in surprisingly violent gusts, as if the sky were taking revenge.

"You're here to get caught up again, huh?" said Um Nyobè.

He was amused by his friend's rather frequent visits, and whispered to him that he should put a damper on his appetite, even if the house held out the promise of a delicious meal: Martha wasn't happy he had skipped her sister's wedding in Edéa.

"Tell her that I couldn't get leave. Working for the white man isn't like selling in the market, is it?"

Pouka was stopped short by the reply:

"Go tell her that yourself."

Thinking twice, the maestro decided it would be impolite to tell Martha that he hadn't been there for Ngo Bikaï because of the French, especially after the "events."

"Ah, I'll leave it alone," he said. He went to sit down in the living room. "She can't understand."

Pouka knew Martha. He understood her moods, her bad temper—which, according to him, came from being a *bayamsallam*—but also her angelic sweetness. He promised himself that he'd figure out what to say to her. He went over to the kitchen for a quick hello and then came back to talk with Um Nyobè about what had him so busy at work.

"I never should have taken this job."

"Then you'd be unemployed?"

"That's true."

Um Nyobè described in detail the wedding ceremony and, most of all, his discussions with Fritz. His face grew serious.

"Fritz says he wants to move to Douala."

"Douala?"

Even Pouka was surprised.

"His brother who works for the trains is down there, you know."

It was true. Yet this decision seemed to both men like running away. And then, why did he agree to get married if he was just going to leave town? Pouka and Um Nyobè knew Fritz well. His decision to move to Douala didn't fit their image of him and they couldn't figure out how to answer the thousands of questions that popped into their heads.

"What does Ngo Bikaï say about it?"

"I don't know."

Ngo Bikaï had been so busy organizing the wedding that Um Nyobè hadn't found the time to talk to her openly. He would have asked her, of course, if she liked Douala so much that she was willing to abandon her women. Pouka was sorry that Martha wasn't part of the conversation. She was so close to Ngo Bikaï that she was sure to have an opinion about it.

"With women," Um Nyobè began philosophically, "you never know."

The falling rain muffled the sounds of their conversation, or else

Martha would have heard them from the kitchen, where she was preparing the evening meal.

"You should know," Pouka observed.

A delicate topic. How many times had Pouka changed the topic as soon as it turned to marriage? Suddenly, from the roof above came a clattering din. The two men looked at the ceiling. The rain falls violently in Yaoundé; sometimes it tears off roofs and leaves couples caught making love lying soaked in their bed. That's the story people tell, at any rate.

"Sometimes I think about moving," Um Nyobè announced, "but maybe it's not worth the trouble."

He wasn't really talking about the roof. Pouka tried another topic. Um Nyobè then said he was thinking about asking for a transfer to Edéa.

"Because of Fritz?"

Um Nyobè had expected him to ask instead if it was because of Martha. There were times when Pouka's obvious lack of interest in others really surprised him.

"No," he replied, "my boss is just driving me nuts."

"At least he let you go to Edéa."

"If you only knew . . ." Um Nyobè began.

"Martha will be happy. Pouka is sure of that."

"If it were only up to her, we'd have left Yaoundé a long time ago."

"About that," Pouka said, again changing the topic. "Do you know someone named Delarue? Jacques Delarue?"

"I've met him a few times, at soccer games."

Um Nyobè didn't go into detail about his relationship with Delarue. Not because he didn't trust Pouka. He just wanted to know where the mention of his name would take their conversation. He still remembered Delarue's words of caution, how he saw himself as the target of persecution, and how the stories he told always revolved around him. He also remembered why he'd come to Cameroon, the book he was writing, and the question Um Nyobè had asked himself when Delarue had talked about his activities: I'd like to know what the other Frenchmen think about him.

"He was repatriated."

Those few simple words made the two men fall into a deep silence, broken only by the wind rattling the shutters on the window.

"Um Nyobè," Martha shouted, "will you shut the window? The rain is coming in, can't you hear it?"

"Ah! The rain!" he cursed.

He was talking just to fill the space, because he was really thinking about what his wife had said about Delarue: "He's a spy for the governor." And now, not long after that, Delarue had been repatriated by that very governor. He smiled; it didn't really surprise him at all. His friends would be disappointed, he thought. Especially Ouandié, who had been kept from meeting the French "defender of the black man" by his school examinations. The state of war made it easy to miss meetings. Outside, the rain was tapering off.

The rain in Yaoundé is like that: violent and short-lived.

11

Identity Theft

Pouka went back home without ever telling his friend what had been going on at his place. The mention of Delarue's name had sent his conversation with Um Nyobè off on a tangent, and then the question of Fritz's decision to move to Douala had left him speechless. He had left with a full belly, but without having told Um Nyobè that he had ended up kicking out his two guests, Xavier and Augustus.

The two boys had just gone too far. They had started by using his name to buy things on credit at the neighborhood grocer's. It had taken Pouka a while to realize what was going on because everyone in Madagascar respected him, since he was the only writer in the neighborhood, and then the reading of his poem on Radio Cameroon had made him a bit of a local star. Because he helped people out here and there, writing letters or other documents that can destroy the chances of anyone who is illiterate in their dealings with the colonial government, there were lots of people who owed him.

The neighborhood residents readily agreed to give Xavier and Augustus credit when they claimed they were buying food or other things for the "maestro." But everything has its limits, and you can't just live your whole life on credit. Little by little, people noticed that the "big man" of the neighborhood was getting too much on credit. People wondered if he was in trouble at work. Or, rather, were the white men paying him enough?

Everyone blamed the war for forcing them to tighten their belts, and of course Xavier and Augustus repeated, "The war, yes, the war!" When Pouka realized, he let the neighborhood know that Mr. Pouka always paid cash for his purchases and that he had no intention of changing his ways. But he didn't blame his guests in public. He understood them: they were hungry and were looking for work.

"Why didn't you tell me?" was all he asked.

"Maestro," Xavier replied, "we were ashamed."

"We were hungry," added Augustus.

"Shame doesn't feed a man," Pouka snapped.

He started leaving them a little spending money, which he set on the table before he left for work, so as not to embarrass them.

However, when the rains began and he found his shoes soaked and slightly muddy, though carefully replaced under his bed, he was alarmed. The incident with the wet towel came back to him. Someone had worn his shoes. They'd tried to polish them, more or less, but asking a villager to polish a pair of leather shoes the right way was like asking a plum to eat itself. At least, that's what he thought.

Oh! Pouka could have complained out loud about his guests that evening, or in the morning before he left for work, as he had done when things had started to go wrong. But he preferred to lay a trap for them. So one day he came home early. It was raining. His boss understood how the rain in Yaoundé affected his employees' schedules, so he hadn't even had to come up with an excuse. Once home, he sat down in the living room and waited for his two guests, who were still out. To pass the time, he picked up *The Flowers of Evil* and began reading, even though he already knew all the poems.

He hadn't finished reading "The Sun" when he heard his guests' voices and Augustus came in.

"Sit down," he ordered.

Xavier was right behind him.

"So it's you," Pouka said, getting to his feet.

The boy tried to escape, but Pouka blocked the door.

"So it's you," he repeated.

It was Xavier, in fact. Really? Someone just glancing in would have mistaken the boy for Pouka the Maestro. Dressed in the tergal jacket Pouka only wore on special occasions, and wearing his white striped shoes, he even had on the puffy multicolored cap that Pouka reserved for those moments when he wanted to look the part. When he was a "wandering poet," as he said with no little pride. What's more, the trousers he was wearing were wet from the calves down, as were the shoes, and they were muddy, too. Pouka was furious beyond words. Back when he was setting up the little poetry circle in Edéa, he had chosen for himself the role of Gérard de Nerval. His friends, Um Nyobè in particular, had warned him several times: he was losing his mind. In his vanity, he felt he had multiple personalities. Now, for the first time, in his own house, in his own living room, he really thought he was seeing the alter ego that amused his friends. He thought he was face-to-face with his double. Wasn't it Pouka himself who was trying to escape?

"Why?" he asked simply.

He was asking himself, really.

Believe me, Pouka breathed a sigh of relief when Xavier answered and he heard a voice that wasn't his own.

"There's a girl in Briqueterie," he began.

"Nonsense! Nonsense!" Pouka was expecting to hear a whole romantic story, something fantastical, surprising, and Xavier was just stammering out some anecdote about a poor neighborhood, it made no sense, something about a whore he wanted to impress with his European finery, a tale about a piece of ass he was trying to scam, just another of those urban tales that circulate by the thousands in Yaoundé. Ah! Pouka couldn't have been more disappointed, but he was also just as furious because he felt he'd been ripped off several times: by the villagers, by Yaoundé itself, which hadn't been able to come up with a better, more fabulous story for them, and by literature, which hadn't ever surprised him, not even once.

"Get undressed," he said curtly.

Trembling, Xavier did as he was told. Piece by piece, he set his host's jacket, shoes, pants, shirt, tie, and socks on the living room table, until he was standing there totally naked. He wasn't wearing any underpants.

"Now get the hell out," Pouka said calmly.

Xavier ran out, bumping into the table as he went. Some of the clothes fell. Pouka noticed that he didn't even try to hide his genitals. Augustus hadn't moved, as if he had nothing to do with it.

"You, too," said the master.

Augustus jumped.

"Me?"

"Yes, you."

"What about my bags?"

"Get the hell out."

Pouka had finally raised his voice, as if it had taken that last question about the bags to make him lose his cool. He went into the bedroom, gathered up the boys' belongings, and threw them out the window, into the courtyard. Then he sat down in his living room and picked up his Baudelaire again. His hands were trembling with anger. Literature was how he calmed himself down when he was feeling crazy. The next day, right at the same time as he had kicked his guests out, he knocked on his friend Um Nyobè's door. It was still raining, even more violently.

Typical for Yaoundé.

We already know what happened next.

12

I Am Not an Other

A few days later, it was Um Nyobè who stopped by to visit Pouka—at his office. Did location figure into their equation of who was visiting whom? Honestly, Um Nyobè didn't give it a second thought. He was out of breath, and the wind that rattled through the city brought him no relief. His friend appeared at the end of a corridor.

"Looking for Pouka? Here he is," he said, "come on, office number fifteen."

Um Nyobè couldn't believe his eyes.

"Why are you looking at me like that?" Pouka asked, then quipped, "I'm not a woman, am I?"

"Did you hear what was on the radio?"

Pouka hadn't heard anything on the radio. Just then, a white employee, one of Pouka's colleagues, stopped in front of them, and gave them the news in a breezy way that Um Nyobè couldn't have matched.

"Hey," said the white man, "I thought you were dead."

"Dead?"

Stunned, Pouka stared at the two men who were staring at him.

"Weren't you listening to the radio?" Um Nyobè asked.

"Clearly not," the Frenchman confirmed.

He took them to the radio station headquarters straightaway, without waiting for the announcement of the poet's death to be rebroadcast. The journalist who had made the announcement was a young Frenchman with childlike round cheeks; he was wearing a colonial cap even inside his office. The man who'd driven them there in his car then took them all to the police station, where the officer was clearly just as thrilled to see that the poet was still alive and well.

What had happened? A man carrying papers that identified him as Pouka, *écrivain-interprète*, had been found cut into pieces in a back alleyway in Briqueterie, "lying in a ditch." The violence of the crime was unlike anything they'd ever seen before in Yaoundé. The machete had done its job. The commissioner, quite scandalized, couldn't hide his indignation: never in his whole career in the colonies had he ever seen anything like it. The dead man's genitals had been cut off.

"They were the only pieces missing."

With his hand in his pocket, Pouka gave a quick squeeze to his testicles.

"So, you maintain that you are Louis-Marie Pouka?"

"Pouka, the son of M'bangue."

He searched his pockets for his identification, but no luck.

"I don't understand. I always carry my identification with me."

"In these times of war . . ." the police commissioner observed.

Really, it wasn't prudent to go out without your identification, especially when you were black. With the war, Yaoundé had suddenly become more violent and more suspicious; there were patrols circulating continually throughout the city, demanding that the black population show their papers. Pouka was lucky he hadn't been stopped.

"I must have left them at home."

"Are you sure?" the commissioner asked. "My men went to the place where this Pouka was employed. No one there knew him."

"I changed jobs," Pouka replied, "because of the war."

He kept patting himself all over, checking his pockets, even his pants pockets, over and over again. Never had he been made so happy by such a turn of events: if it had been him . . . ? He turned to Um Nyobè.

"Yes, I can corroborate that," he said. "He changed jobs."

The testimony of the French employee was written down first in the dossier. An old colonial habit that made no exceptions for the blacks who served in the French administration.

It was a very long day for the two friends, because the commissioner wanted their statements for the report. The police officer who took care of it looked terrified. He kept on shaking his head as he typed, looking at Pouka and shaking his head. He stared at Um Nyobè's identification with an intensity that surprised the two friends. He asked Pouka repeatedly why he didn't have "his papers"?

"Lost? Stolen?"

"Lost," Pouka said, for what else could have happened? The commissioner interrupted to give the officer a communiqué to type, another announcement he wanted broadcast on Radio Cameroon. Since his writing was chicken-scratch, the officer couldn't decipher it, so the commissioner told him out loud what he wanted announced to the capital.

"It's simple," he said. "The dead man found in Briqueterie was *not* an employee of the French administration."

He was smiling broadly. As for Pouka, despite the announcement that cleared up "a most unfortunate rumor in these troubled times," he was aching to know the truth. Ah! Pouka, wasn't this just the sort of announcement that has become all too common on Radio Cameroon since then? One of those announcements that seek to spread propaganda rather than to lay out the truth about Cameroon? He later learned that the French administration was less interested in spreading information than in dissipating the rumors about the "traitor working for France," who had been liquidated.

By whom?

Pouka's colleague questioned the commissioner on how the case would be handled. Visibly surprised, the commissioner looked at him kindly, then turned toward Pouka and smiled.

"You are alive, my dear Mr. Pouka. Take joy in that and please accept my greetings on behalf of the French administration."

Later Pouka and Um Nyobè ran as they made their way into Madagascar. They hid their faces behind their briefcases.

13

After the Rain, the Moment of Doubt

The day after a rainstorm the sky is always clear, as if the capital's demons, once chased from the streets they had overrun, revealed the city's true beauty. Clean streets, houses with newly washed walls, and fresh air signal the return of Yaoundé's youth. When the rain falls hard enough, it doesn't even leave mud behind. The people themselves feel lighter, because the rain doesn't only wash the city, but bodies and souls as well. Yet when Pouka left his neighborhood, he noted the shifting gazes of the people around him, and wasn't surprised. The rain that brightens the city also frees its monsters. At least that's what people say.

"Hello!" he said, although he normally only responded after others greeted him.

"You slept well?"

Some of his neighbors sped up.

"Hello, my brother!" Pouka called after them, his words bouncing off their backs.

"What are we going to do, hey?"

He forced himself to be polite. Would he have to go from door to door, knocking at every home in the neighborhood, to assure everyone that he, Mr. Pouka, was alive and well? Would he have to let them pat him all over? Ah! He'd figure out a way to make them realize that he was the same old Pouka that they knew. The evening before, he had found Augustus shivering outside his door, distraught by what had happened. Still, Augustus was able to fill him in, tell him just what had happened to Xavier.

"Did you go to the police?" Pouka asked him.

"No."

Here's what had happened. Xavier hadn't stopped passing himself off as Pouka. Like a starving man who is hooked after his very first bite of a bean fritter, once Pouka had stripped him bare and chased him out of his house, he had come back disguised as the man who had allowed him to live the good life in the city. But why did he need to take on Pouka's identity? Quite simply, because he hadn't told the truth to the woman he'd fallen for in Briqueterie, the same woman he'd tried to tell Pouka about the other day. He knew—and it made Xavier miserable—that if he told her the truth, it would be the end of their affair. He was sure Pouka would understand. Because what woman, especially what whore in Briqueterie, yes, what whore anywhere in the capital, would take a villager between her legs as she did with him, if she had known he was just a native from the sticks?

"She was feeding him and everything," Augustus added.

"On credit?"

"He said he'd pay her at the end of the month."

Now, what whore from Briqueterie would have refused credit to a writer? But it happened that this *wolowolos* had a husband, or a lover, or a pimp—either Xavier didn't know or he didn't care, because what man employed as a writer by the French administration is afraid of a tirailleur? Xavier had asked her, the whore/married woman, to give him a quickie, *vite-vite*. Whore and married woman— those two things just don't go together, Pouka had to admit. And to top it off, the woman's name was a flourish that made the poetic maestro roar because, as Augustus announced, "she was called the Marshal."

"The Marshal?"

What a story! But okay, he'd just let that poor neighborhood story play out in meaningless verses because, he told himself, it was just the woman going on, and most likely when things between them were getting hot and heavy. Or maybe it was Xavier going on. But he didn't take into account the jealousy of that tirailleur—"a

Chadian," Augustus added, as if that mattered when it came to the question of masculine jealousy, "who went by the name of de Gaulle."

"De Gaulle?"

Whatever the case, the night before, the famous de Gaulle had caught his girl with her head between Xavier's legs, and in the Marshal's mouth a member that was not his own. He had reacted like the tirailleur he was when confronting a bad-bad enemy. He had grabbed his machete and—chop-chop!—decapitated Xavier, who didn't even have the chance to cry "Help!" or to put his *bangala* back in his pants.

"And how does my identity card fit into all of this?" Pouka interrupted, feeling quite nauseated by this whole affair that, frankly, was making his alexandrine verses explode.

It had been in Xavier's back pocket at that fateful moment.

"He wasn't even using it anymore," Augustus added.

"And what about the woman," Um Nyobè asked, "where is she?"

"I don't know," Augustus had to admit.

His hands were trembling, his mind was blank, and he really just didn't know—nor could he say how she had escaped. He really wished he knew nothing about it at all, although he'd been watching Xavier's exploits through a hole in the Marshal's wall.

Briqueterie could hide the worst of criminals, so don't think you can just go there and find our Marshal in the mob of *wolowolos* in the neighborhood who all called themselves the Marshal. Not only did Augustus have no idea what her name really was, he couldn't even remember her face clearly. Why would he have gone to the police? As for the criminal tirailleur de Gaulle, only France could say where he was hiding.

"They're gonna arrest me, aren't they?" Augustus sobbed, sitting between the two French civil servants. "They're gonna arrest me, right?"

Um Nyobè imagined how the commissioner would react if Augustus came to his office. To the standard police question, "Your papers?" he'd reply that he had none. When asked "Who killed Xavier?" he'd say: "De Gaulle." Going to the police station without proper identification would give the commissioner the right to hold the poor fellow in jail for forty-eight hours. And what would happen if he accused de Gaulle of murder?

"The French will accuse me of killing him, right?"

Pouka and Um Nyobè exchanged glances. The murder wouldn't earn him a life sentence, but the death penalty.

"What proof do they have?"

"Proof?"

In his own village logic, Augustus had understood how the police in the capital worked: What difference was there if the commissioner arrested Augustus or Xavier or Peter or Paul? This would be an open-and-shut case—a good thing, since the war was heating up on the home front. His desk was piled high with files about men who beat their wives, some of whom were pregnant, beat them so badly they broke their ribs; men who were drunk in public and insulted the French administration; thieves who committed crimes in broad daylight. One murder case closed meant one fewer on his desk. After all, the war was actually being fought elsewhere.

"They're gonna arrest me?"

"You're not going to run off now and hide in the maquis," Pouka said.

The poet didn't know what else to say.

"What do you think?"

Yes, what did Um Nyobè think? He took stock of the disaster that was his friend's home: there were books on the armchairs, clothes on the table, and in front of the door, a towel soaking wet from the rain was swinging back and forth with the wind. All clear signs of the absence of a woman's touch, Martha would have said. He really liked Pouka, but suddenly he wondered just why he had come to pay him a visit, because now he had stepped right into the middle of some business with a Marshal that really had nothing to do with him.

"This little guy needs a good lawyer," he said.

14

The Insurrection of Soldier Fouret

Alexandre Fouret was one of the rare white soldiers who could be found in the courtyard with the Senegalese tirailleurs. Exchanges among the soldiers fighting for Free France were not always smooth. The Africans sometimes made fun of him, as did the white soldiers, for that matter: everyone wondered what he was doing there. Had anyone paid more attention, they'd have realized that this intellectual—a student from the Sorbonne—had nothing at all to say to the legionnaires who had come there, as they put it, "to break some Fritz." The book that sat by the bespectacled soldier's bedside was, in fact, something written by Germans: *The Manifesto*. And he was reading it in the original, to boot.

Philothée thought the Frenchman was Marxism personified. For Fouret, let's be clear, the Senegalese soldier (only much later would Fouret learn that his friend was in fact from Cameroon) was something like a therapist. The war leads to all sorts of compromises. Chief among them: that you have to accept whatever ears she provides, especially if you intend to lead ideological training sessions.

Philothée didn't know that these sessions, where Fouret spoke and he listened, were courses on ideology. They sort of reminded him of Pouka's little poetry circle, although only a little, since Pouka wasn't white.

"It is inconceivable," Fouret said. "France asks black men to die for her, but she can't even be bothered to treat them like men."

Believe me, those weren't Philothée's words—as you know, he had a stutter.

"I have to write this down in my journal," Fouret remarked, whenever he came up with a quoteworthy sentence. You see, he wasn't just talking for nothing. His audience was at once his friend's silent conscience and his own journal, in which he wrote about the future revolution. Because for him, war was a laboratory where he could try things out in advance of the real war, which would have to encompass the whole world.

"A class war."

Yet Fouret had a moment of doubt there, when faced with Philothée's eyes, eyes as silent as a goat's. He wondered what mattered most, really: "class war or racial war." War—and this camp in particular—had shown him a side of his analysis that he hadn't thought about till then.

"It can't just keep on going like this," he said.

"*Ngou . . . ngou . . .*" stammered Philothée.

"Impossible."

Philothée thought about the library that contained all this wisdom; now it was under German occupation. His heart ached at the thought that the books that had taught him about freedom were now held captive. As for Fouret, sometimes he was unsure about which path to follow, *The Manifesto* or *The Insurrectionist*, Vallès's novel about the Paris Commune. For him, the insurrection needed to keep going, but can an insurrection be perpetual?

"What am I even doing here in Africa?"

He asked himself that question.

"Idealism must be defended," he replied, "because France is idealism's homeland, and Paris its capital.

"*Ngou . . .*" said Philothée again.

"And then," he whispered, "learning how to use weapons. You never know . . ."

There was no school where one could take a course called "An Introduction to Revolutionary Action." At the Sorbonne, his philosophy professors taught none of the authors that interested him, like Bakunin and other nineteenth-century thinkers. It was essential, he said, to adapt their ideas to the present day, to the burning questions of our times. Stalin's USSR was no model, "because, unlike Lenin, that guy's no idealist."

"You see what Stalin did with Hitler?" Fouret asked.

He answered himself:

"A real dirty trick! Now he's paying the price. It was inevitable, wasn't it?"

"*Ngou* . . ." said Philothée.

"It was after the fall of Smolensk," he confided, "that I joined Free France. They flattened that city, just like this desert here."

He gestured toward the desert of the Fezzan that spread out all around them. They stared out over its blanket of sand, where the wind spun around like a huge, angry monster. Sometimes their eyes fell on rocks, sometimes on palm trees, and sometimes, only rarely, on stone-paved roads. It didn't matter whether he was hunkered down in a foxhole with walls of dancing sand—the only shelter the desert offered the soldiers—or if he spent the night marching, Fouret could always indulge in his revolutionary reveries.

Suddenly a distant noise brought them to attention. The camp exploded in confusion as the warning rang out: "The Jerrys!"

"It's Fritz!"

"The Germans!"

In one leap the tirailleurs took their positions.

Fouret ran back to his division.

"Tirailleurs, take your positions!"

War gives no advance warning. As for the revolution, it would have to wait until tomorrow.

15

In Jerry's Shadow

Fouret raced across the camp, cutting through the wind and the groups of soldiers on his left and his right who were getting into position, cutting through the shouts of the commanders whose deliberate words made order out of chaos. His mind heard nothing but the call to war, the drumbeat of his heart. "I am a soldier of Free France," he repeated, "I am a soldier of Free France." A piercing call made him run faster and faster, his feet sinking into the sand, breaking free only to plunge back down and, again, break free. He struggled over the little dunes whose stubborn sand kept dragging him back down. Finally, he threw himself behind a wrinkle of sand, and took his position in the ranks of the white column, behind the motorized cannon.

It was a false alarm. A Heinkel adorned with an iron cross and flying at low altitude had revealed to these soldiers for the very first time, after three long years spent crossing forest, plain, and desert, the face of their enemy. Colonel Leclerc's cane rose up, pointing straight at the sky.

"Don't shoot," it ordered.

The order was passed back, echoing through the ranks.

"Don't shoot!"

"Don't shoot!"

The desert itself found its voice in the wavering echo of those words. But could anything erase the anxiety visible there on those death-worn faces? Who could stop those sand men, their rifles glued to their cheeks, who kept their eyes peeled, as much out of curiosity as out of fear, on the lookout for any sign of the silhouette of those who had brought them there? Philothée recalled how the sight of that first airplane had caused such excitement back in Edéa. A machine scattering leaflets signed by de Gaulle.

Then the Heinkel disappeared into the sandy mist. It was just flying reconnaissance, but what was there to find?

The *tirailleurs-balayeurs* had swept their traces off the desert, leaving nothing behind but the barren sky's own furtive shadow that slid across the night like a zombie, and that hid away during the day in the valley's recesses. But was it that easy to erase one's past? Today it was a German plane flying recon. The next day something else would interrupt the two friends' conversation. Fouret's entrance into Philothée's orbit had pushed Hebga back into the shadows. Yet Hebga saw how Philothée had been taken under wing by the white man; he smiled and shrugged his shoulders. He thought about his relationship with his cousin Pouka, who grew up admiring Hebga's feats and hard work, and then had become a man on his own terms. Of course, he would have preferred their friendship not fade away in the silence that grew between them, but life is made up of infinite possibilities, no? Once he asked Philothée to introduce him to his new friend, and the boy happily did so right away. But Fouret, usually so loquacious, had nothing to say to Hebga. It seemed the wood-cutter's presence plunged him into the deepest of silences.

"You what company?" Hebga asked.

A banal question.

"I'm in the motorized company number five."

"Me, Cameroon mounted company."

Hebga noted that Fouret was the only one who didn't speak to him in simplified French. But they spoke about nothing more than the weather and their respective units. Later the woodcutter happened upon Fouret lost in a deep conversation with Philothée, and the mystery of their relationship was suddenly quite clear to him.

You try to figure out what's behind a friendship. Me, I think—and these are just my personal thoughts on the matter—that given a choice between heavy-muscled morality and a deep, speechless silence, Fouret preferred the promises inferred by things. Rather than clear-cut facts, he preferred infinite possibilities. I understand Fouret's doubts, and have the distance to explain the reasons for his choice.

The soldiers had a long path ahead of them! A long and unchanging path—which meant they soon fell into a routine. The conversations between the two friends were a routine. Were it not for the war and the ever-present threat of an attack, the routine would have been their day-to-day. If death hadn't been nipping at their heels, that day-to-day would have been life itself.

Until then, for Leclerc's troops, life was no more than the path ahead.

16

Night March

While the column advanced through the night, Leclerc had finally been given seven planes, and had borrowed one more, a Blenheim. Yes, the English had made good on their promise to provide support. There were five hundred vehicles in total, including all-terrain trucks. The numbers of men kept growing, too; there were now five thousand tirailleurs, including many Libyan goumiers who had joined Massu's company of meharists, as well as nomads, mostly from Tibesti, whose camels served as scouts for the column's advance.

During the day, the planes scouted the path ahead. They took off before the morning mists rose, and you could hear their violent roar in the distance. They had taken the war on their wings and shifted the battlefield to the clouds. Sometimes an enemy plane seeking revenge veered away from the battle and dived down toward the company. Everyone needed to take cover, and fast. The plane scanned the desert, but the *tirailleurs-balayeurs* always did their job perfectly. The enemy would disappear in the distance, its bombs and bullets still safely in its belly. The soldiers shouted with joy!

"Daniels!" the tirailleurs cried. "Daniels lost!"

Once an Italian plane attacked the fort that Leclerc's company had already abandoned. At a safe distance and sheltered by the dunes, the soldiers watched this spectacle of war with the satisfaction of knowing that all the living had left the fort. The Italians pounded it for an hour, then disappeared in the distance, happy, no doubt,

thinking they had forced the French to retreat; soon they'd be surprised to see the threatening shadow of those very troops advancing
toward them. Even Colonel Leclerc couldn't keep from laughing.
Right there in front of him was proof of his own military genius.

At nightfall, his column fell into formation, a straight line across
the desert. Comprised of men from all nations, indistinct in their
common humanity, they advanced in an orderly way, a line of un-
certain shadows, different silhouettes, stretched out over kilometers.
The desert opened up its belly to them. The sky didn't reveal the
men's faces; the desert loaned them the chill of its winds, the damp
of its sand.

Sometimes, to keep their spirits high, they sang silently to
themselves—they couldn't risk awakening the Sahara. All along the
convoy's trail, the detritus of war piled up, remains of the battles
waged from above: burned-out carcasses of trucks, twisted bits of
metal, abandoned remains of encampments, and soldiers transformed
into fugitives. The Italian army was in retreat. It employed a scorched-
earth strategy when it could, but most of the time it was no match
for the force of Leclerc's rage falling from the sky.

When the sun rose, the desert showed it could also be the cemetery of ambition, burying under a blanket of sand and silence the
most expansive of dreams. Its endless back revealed spaces where
battles no longer needed to be waged. Night turned men into shadows who, with the rising of the sun, discovered the diverse faces of
their own companies. Although separated—with Hebga at the back
with the Cameroon mounted company and Philothée in the first infantry batallion—they each discovered the ever-growing solitude of
a tested army marching on toward victory.

Leclerc spoke to the gathered troops of the dream that was
emerging at the end of the days and nights of their march across
the desert.

"Before us," he said, "lies the sea!"

He struck the sand with his cane and stared into the soldiers'
eyes.

"Just as blue as in Marseille! Before us lies Tunisia!"

He paused.

"But our goal," he continued, "is Strasbourg! Remember that!

Our column will not stop until the whole of France is free! From Brittany to Alsace! From Paris to Lille!"

The soldiers applauded and cheered, "*Vive de Gaulle!*" and "*Vive la France!*" The refrain of "La Marseillaise" rose up. But more than the far-off image of life in Paris—for what did Strasbourg or Paris really mean to Philothée?—what roused Philothée were cries coming from behind a rock.

First the soldiers raced down the dune, rifles pointed. The sand filled in their steps. Then they slowed down, walking carefully, nervously. Philothée made his way around the rock and found an Italian soldier sitting there, his face lifted up to the moon. One of his arms was missing, he was covered in blood. His amputated hand was lying in front of him, amid the detritus. A missile had disfigured his body, but his eyes told of a different battle. He lifted his remaining arm, imploring death, asking for the merciful release of a bullet. Tears flowed down his sand-covered cheeks. He'd been abandoned by his comrades, for all around him were the footprints of many camels.

"Commander Branchietti," he said, "Branchietti!"

His voice was drowned out by the chaos all around him. Some wanted to run him through with their bayonet, others to cut off his head. When Philothée began to vomit, his comrades' violent urges were suspended.

"Stop!" shouted a voice.

It was Captain Dio.

"Stop, you can't kill him!"

The company of tirailleurs moved back, holding in their frustrated rage but still shouting out their rancor.

"He's a war prisoner!" Captain Dio continued. "Don't touch him!"

So Leclerc's column just left him there in the desert. The Sahara's evil song drowned out the insult—"*Figlio di puttana*"—that he spat out at the back of the hero of Free France as he raised up to the sky the one arm he had left.

17

Kinderlieder

In Edéa, Fritz was packing his bags. It was night. It was raining. The only sounds heard in his bedroom were of water hitting metal rooftops and the wind's song whistling through the trees. Determined to get everyone to Douala, he didn't want his family to miss the morning bus. This was a challenging moment, because he really didn't know what to leave behind. There are objects that you have dragged along with you all through life and that, when the time has come to move, suddenly seem to be of no real significance. Then there are others that you suddenly discover among your old things. There in open boxes, overturned crates, or outdated bags, buried treasures surface suddenly from memory's depths. Mostly it was his father's things that troubled him, relics from his life as an askari in the German colonial army, the traces of his life as a veteran.

"Old memories," said Fritz.

That era was before his time; his father had rarely talked about it even with his friends, and never directly with Fritz. He wanted to forget all about it: he had been forced to repress it by the French administration, which had kept making problems for him because it suspected he harbored pro-German sentiments. Becoming a farmer and starting to grow *macabo* had sheltered him from the suspicion that his military know-how had earned him. As his father's heir, Fritz had taken possession of bags of his belongings, old papers and a few books, some utensils—in short, the ordinary things that make up the story of a life, a life Fritz hadn't known much about.

In the middle of all this bric-a-brac, he found a little book with colored pictures. The title *Unser Liederbuch—Our Songbook*—was written on the cover in strange letters, along with pictures of three children, one who must have been the same age as his eldest son. He first thought of calling Ngo Bikaï to show her his find—the two didn't share a bedroom—or maybe his children, but he thought better of it. He opened the book's dusty pages.

"*Kinderlieder*," he read, although with a French accent, placing the stress on the second syllable, *der*, then he clicked his tongue in surprise, "1902!"

He carefully leafed through the book, pausing on a familiar song, "O Tannenbaum," page 46. He started to whistle and then softly, almost silently, began to sing:

O Tannenbaum! O Tannenbaum!
Wie treu sind deine Blätter!
Du grünst nicht nur
Zur Sommerzeit!

It was in fact December, he thought. There were two piles at his feet. On one side he'd put everything he wanted to throw out, mostly a lot of his father's things, and then on the other, things, primarily his, that he wanted to take to Douala. That book was added to the Douala pile; he smiled for a moment and picked it back up. He went to church so rarely!

"This will surprise Ngo Bikaï," he said out loud.

Or maybe the children. He called the older one. The kid didn't reply. He went toward his wife's room, because that was where the children slept. He opened the door and came into the darkness.

"Shhhh," he heard from the shadows.

He paused for a moment and then went back out.

"She's always putting the kids to bed," he grumbled, pulling the door closed behind him.

He stopped in the living room, because the rain coming in had left a serpentine path across the floor.

18

The Separation of a Loving Couple

It rained all night long. The next day, Fritz came into his wife's room, happy and eager to share his news.

"Do you know what I found yesterday?"

Then, suddenly, he fell silent, lost his voice. Her room was just as it had been the day before. Ngo Bikaï hadn't packed anything, hadn't filled any of the empty boxes he'd put together for her. Even her purse was still hanging on the wall, in its usual spot.

"I . . . I don't understand," he mumbled.

She didn't answer.

"Do you want me to help?"

"No," she said calmly. "You'll be going to Douala alone."

Ngo Bikaï's voice invited no debate. He knew her determination, even if there were times when he had been able to get her to change her mind. But doing so always took a lot of time.

"Okay," he began diplomatically, "we'll take the next bus."

If they were going to pack Ngo Bikaï's things, they'd miss the bus on which he'd reserved space for the family. Before long the driver was going to come into their yard, beeping his horn. He'd ask him to come back later and give him a little something to convince him. What he didn't understand was why his wife was just sitting there on the bed she hadn't made—or taken apart, yes, apart—with their younger child still dozing in her arms, and staring at him as if he were speaking some unknown language.

"Let's calm down," he said.

"Precisely, you calm down," she said. "The baby is still sleeping."

The baby! he thought. It's always the baby! He wanted to say something, one word, two or three, but then he stumbled, and went back out of the room. He wanted to slam the door behind him, but merely shut it. The baby! he thought. Always the baby!

He stomped nervously around the living room for a moment, then went outside to check on the basins he'd placed under the eaves the night before. They were full. No wonder the water had run into the living room. He grabbed a towel hanging there and began to mop up the floor with his foot.

"Okay," he said, when he saw Ngo Bikaï come out of her room. "You have to explain to me what the problem is."

"I've told you already, I'm not going to Douala."

"I don't understand . . ."

"What is there to understand, Fritz? There are two possibilities: either I'm going to Douala or I'm not. There's not a third option, right?"

He couldn't believe what he was hearing.

"Well, then," she went on calmly, "I've given it some thought, as you have, no doubt, and I've decided I'll stay in Edéa."

"Because of your women?"

Ah, Fritz! There were so many things he could have said, why did he bring up Ngo Bikaï's women? He had always supported her work. I can say there had never been a husband more supportive of women's rights than he was, because he saw it as part of the broader struggle for freedom—that the woman question was in fact its most burning metaphor. He and his friends, Um Nyobè, Pouka, and the others, had discussed it time and time again, and he had always maintained that women were the very image of oppression. First, they were oppressed by men in the home, and then in public life by the colonial system. In fact, he had wanted his married life to be the living example of the importance of this freedom.

Yes, Fritz was a feminist. He had put off celebrating his marriage to Ngo Bikaï in the Catholic church, which she had joined only later in life, because he saw Catholicism as part of the French colonial system that needed to be challenged; whereas the traditional marriage that had joined them together for so long sanctified a union they had both entered into freely, and with the support of their community. He had clearly supported his wife's rise to a position of authority among the market women, and he had even done what he could to make it possible, since he'd given her the funds to set up her business. Ah! So why did he bring up his wife's women now? Did Fritz feel guilty because if he hadn't gotten her pregnant years ago, maybe she would have become the first woman to work for the colonial administration? Or a writer like Um Nyobè and Pouka?

It was Fritz who had built his wife's stand in the market, wasn't it? That he now turned against the women he had encouraged Ngo Bikaï to join, "with his own hands" (he could still see himself wielding the hammer, holding nails between his lips, as he built the shed for her); yes, that Fritz now turned against Ngo Bikaï's women, after he'd been the one to take her to our Sita's house and introduce her—well, that just showed that something had gone seriously wrong. Fritz could see it still: he'd knocked on our Sita's door and, when Hebga answered, he'd asked the question. He remembered as if it had happened yesterday:

"Where's your mother?"

"She's gone out."

Ngo Bikaï had wanted to go home, but he, yes, he had insisted.

"We'll wait, then."

So Hebga had found them chairs and then they waited, Fritz and Ngo Bikaï, whom he introduced to the Mother of the Market as "my fiancée." You see, Ngo Bikaï's belly was already showing the bump that would become their first child.

"Because of my women? Why?" Ngo Bikaï echoed his words.

She knew it was over. Over. In her mind she kept hearing the song the women sang when they'd put the captain as a crown on her head, marking her as the Mother of the Market, and signaling the ecstasy of the universe. She clearly remembered her sister Martha pulling the fish out of the river, the captain that had given its blessing to her ascension and reinscribed on her body her strength as a woman. She had given birth to their first child in the market, and the women had carried her in their arms; they'd supported her, cut the umbilical cord, and then placed back in her arms the son that they hadn't named, because she knew that was Fritz's prerogative.

Fritz!

"The children will stay here," she said simply, "with me."

"You're keeping the children?"

Never had Fritz felt so powerless as on that day in the living room of his own house. Standing before a woman. Looking around him, he saw the photographs of his family, the walls of his home, the Christian motto that was hanging there, and then he paused, his eyes on a picture from his wedding day, one they'd had taken after the ceremony in Father Jean's church. What hypocrisy! Suddenly he exploded.

"What about me?"

Fritz, shut up!

"You," his wife said, "you are leaving for Douala, no?"

"I'm talking about the children."

"They are your children, Fritz," she said gently. "I have no intention of separating them from their father."

"Separating them from their father! But that's just what you are doing!"

"You're the one who's leaving, Fritz," she clarified. "No one is keeping you from staying here with us."

Then Ngo Bikaï went back to her room, where the children were still sleeping, leaving Fritz alone in the living room. The water that was still flowing made a circle around his feet.

How Many Months of Silence

In fact, that was the first conversation Fritz and Ngo Bikaï had had in that living room as a married couple. After "the events," you understand. That tempers flared is regrettable, I'd say, but, all things considered, it was better that this living room, which had been filled with love and the liveliest of political debates, find its voice again. Really, since what had happened there, silence had taken over. Fritz had never found the words to tell his wife what he felt after the rape. Ngo Bikaï had told him what had happened, and together they had scoured the town to find the criminal who, everyone said, must have been mobilized and was perhaps already in the Fezzan, out in the middle of the Sahara desert, one of the thousands of tirailleurs who'd enlisted in Colonel Leclerc's column in order to liberate Paris and France from the Nazi boots.

And sex? Fritz hadn't ever stopped making love to his wife, because Ngo Bikaï had continued coming to his room once the children were asleep. Ah, dear reader, don't ask me whether it was Fritz or Ngo Bikaï who made love more passionately, because that's asking too much of a narrator. Okay, for those who want to know all the details of the Book of Love, after "the events," it was as if Ngo Bikaï were overcome with a desire to feel her husband penetrate her. An overwhelming urge to feel "Fritz's *bangala* rubbing my vagina," adding "right in the middle of the day, sometimes I was as wet as a river." Those are her own words, yes, and she added that she wanted to make love even when she had her period. What positions didn't she propose? Fritz penetrated her on the chair, on the edge of the bed, up against the wall, "doggy-style." When he wanted to pull out, she held on to his testicles, begging him at times, and when he was wiped out, she'd take his penis in her mouth and suck, and suck. She screamed so much when she was about to climax that Fritz would slow down, and then, trembling, she'd sob and say, "Hold me."

And, then, for you who don't want to read all those sorts of details in a novel, let's just say that Fritz loved Ngo Bikaï. Fritz had always loved Ngo Bikaï. What made their separation so difficult was that they had nothing to blame on each other. Even the love they shared had not waned. It was as unchanged as the furniture of their home.

But it wasn't in their living room that Fritz had asked her to marry him; it was in his bedroom.

"We're already married, you fool," she'd replied.

They had just made love. He had watched her get up and wipe between her legs with a towel. She was about to go back to join the children when he grasped her hand.

He had laughed, because she had, too, and then swatted him with the towel.

"Let's get married again," he insisted earnestly.

She stopped laughing.

"In the church," he added.

Yes, it was Fritz's idea that they get married in Father Jean's church! She hadn't said yes. No, Ngo Bikaï had left him there in his bed that still smelled of her. The next day she said, "If you still want to marry me, know that Father Jean insists there be a sponsor."

"A sponsor?"

He had expected her to say a witness, but what was the difference? They had thought about it together, lying in each other's arms, going through the names of their friends one by one, those from Edéa at first, and then those living elsewhere. They thought of Pouka and then Um Nyobè. "Yes, Um Nyobè." Because of his "calm strength." That's how Fritz put it. And it really did sum him up. They had kept Pouka in mind as a backup in case Um Nyobè couldn't escape from his "job for the white men." That's why they'd burst out laughing when Pouka had sent his regrets for not being able to be there. Yes, they had made the right choice.

"I told you so," Fritz declared.

Ngo Bikaï wished her brother Bilong could be there, but obviously, there was nothing she could do about it. The war! That awful thing! But she had hesitated over having Um Nyobè as sponsor, because of Martha.

"She's my sister," she explained.

"And so?" Fritz asked.

"It's like we don't have any friends in Edéa."

Yet Um Nyobè and Fritz had a lot of friends, as we all know. Choosing someone from Edéa as sponsor would have certainly ruffled the feathers of more than one person, but grown-ups always find a way to smooth out those sorts of things. Their friends were grown-ups, capable of understanding the most complicated issues, the most political of negotiations, the most unexpected decisions. That's really what makes up most of an adult's life and conversations. Fritz had debated the pros and cons of a religious ceremony with his friends, laughed when they teased him, discussed the possibility of holding the ceremony somewhere else, and sighed because La Seigneuriale was no longer there.

But, since "the events," Fritz felt that something inside him had died. He couldn't put his finger on it, and didn't really want to know, because it wasn't to him, but to his wife that the tirailleur had done that. Because he didn't really want to know, he had gotten caught up in philosophical questions when he confided in Um Nyobè the next day on the phone.

"They wanted to break our spirit . . . to break our spirit."

"I don't see any other explanation," Um Nyobè admitted, as I'm sure you recall, my dear reader. In case you've forgotten, it's in the chapter "Love's Living Room" of this very book.

From the "we" implied by "break our spirit"—a "we" that meant Fritz and Um Nyobè—Fritz had moved on to talk about a second one, the "we" of his marriage with Ngo Bikaï. That's the "we" at the forefront of this chapter. He used the first when he spoke in the living room, the second, he said it in his bedroom, love's bedroom. Don't lose patience, because in the dizzying confusion between those two "we's," you'll find yourself caught up in what I call the drunkard's psychology. Fritz's decision to move to Douala had been made when he was blind drunk, and Ngo Bikaï knew it was her own body that he was running away from, a body that was in some sense dead to him. Although he didn't have the courage to tell her, Ngo Bikaï realized it quite quickly on her own. She knew you can't save a marriage that has grown cancerous by running away, and that's why she had decided not to go to Douala. She wouldn't find happiness there. And she knew it.

20

A Problem for a Lawyer

So there in Edéa, an exemplary couple was being torn apart by the circumstances. At the same time, in Yaoundé, Pouka and Um Nyobè were facing a different problem. A problem for a lawyer. They were worried about the poor peasant who'd lost his way in the city and gotten caught up in a story involving a Marshal and a de Gaulle—one of those poor-neighborhood stories. Both of them saw him as the perfect victim.

"Ah! If only Delarue were here!" Um Nyobè cried.

"Delarue?" Pouka asked in surprise.

That's when Um Noybè told him the true story of his connection to "that famous Jacques Delarue you asked me about, you remember?" He listed all the political advantages that connection would have meant if Delarue hadn't been "chased out of the country."

He remembered how Marc had served as an intermediary: maybe if he dug through the archives of his dealings with his now-expatriated colleague, he'd know whom to contact.

"We could all go to his house," Augustus suggested.

Yes, that was the victim speaking. Even Um Nyobè was shocked. So he changed the topic.

That's just how Um Nyobè was: more straightforward than secretive, more practical than theoretical, or, as Pouka might have said, "more prosaic than poetic." In any event, here his common sense came through. They really did need to get in touch with his friend.

"Okay, then," he said, "I'll take care of it."

"How so?"

"I'll go to his house."

Pouka, aware of the irony of the situation, looked at Augustus.

"What about him?" he asked. "Will he just stay here?"

"Where do you think he should go?" Um Nyobè replied. "Besides, it's raining, don't you see?"

And so once again Pouka found the offender, whose bags he'd tossed out into the courtyard, back in his living room. He didn't pause to think what would have happened had he not thrown the two fellows out of his house.

As for Um Nyobè, when he got to Marc's house his friend wasn't there, so he waited a few minutes, at the suggestion of Marc's wife. She was surprised, to say the least, that her husband wasn't already home, given the hour.

"It's the rain," she kept saying, "it's surely the rain."

Um Nyobè knew Marc. He knew he was too busy with politics to have a mistress, so he tried to reassure his friend's wife. Marc must be at a meeting in town, he said, that must be it. Then he suddenly realized that there was no one telling his own wife not to worry!

He decided to say goodbye to Marc's wife and rush home to reassure his own before Martha got any crazy ideas. He didn't want her to be left alone with their child for dinner that evening, especially since you just don't know what could happen in times of war. And then Martha had certainly heard the story of Pouka's supposed murder in Briqueterie. It wasn't her husband who'd been killed, of course, but still, that kind of news would make anyone nervous. So Um Nyobè ran home rather than back to Pouka's as he'd promised. He planned on giving him a call the next morning as soon as he got to the office, to let him know he hadn't caught up with Marc and to revisit the question of the lawyer—in other words, to find some other solution. Yes, that's what he'd do first thing in the morning.

When Um Nyobè called Pouka, the phone rang but no one picked up. It was noon before he was able to reach his friend.

"I've been looking for you for hours," was the first thing he said.

"So now you're my boss?" Pouka snapped. Quickly changing tone, he added, "I was at the bus station."

"Why?"

"The villager, don't you remember?"

This wasn't the sort of conversation they could have on a phone belonging to the French administration. That evening, at Pouka's, Um Nyobè realized that his friend had actually kicked Augustus out again.

"Why?"

Pouka was visibly upset; his conscience was eating away at him.

"Pouka paid for his ticket."

"All that because of a problem with a lawyer?" exclaimed Um Nyobè.

"And Pouka waited for the bus to leave."

Just what had gone on in that house last night? Um Nyobè would never find out, and for good reason.

"Now he can go look for that de Gaulle of his in Edéa."

"You went too far."

"By now he's already there. Pouka isn't going to fall into the same trap twice."

Um Nyobè shook his head. How cruel Pouka could be! Who would have thought that the maestro would close the book so brutally on the failed poetic experiment he'd begun with the little poetry circle? Did anyone need to remind him of that old story? That eccentric adventure? He was still just as vain. Yet now that was all water under the bridge! History is our only mistress.

21

Three Mutually Exclusive
Mathematical Possibilities

It was 1942: there's no way Pouka could have known that another one of the rejects from his little poetry circle was continuing his Gallic peregrinations. In several cities abandoned by the Italians—by the "Daniels"—the Free French soldiers were greeted with tricolored banners that read THE FRENCH, or sometimes FRANCESCI, or even GAULLISTI. Philothée was there with them. Hebga too. Children darted around the tanks and trucks loaded with heavy machine guns and cannons. Victory is a deliciously addictive intoxicant, and the soldiers—white and black alike—who until then had only the desert as a companion, suddenly became men once more, that is to say, vulnerable to victory's cycles of ecstasy. Why didn't Leclerc warn them about the carelessness born of joy? Was he too busy reading the congratulatory telegrams pouring in from unlikely places—from General Giraud, even!—that he didn't think that the loser gave his kiss with a knife hidden behind his back?

Let's leave those two Cameroonian soldiers alone for the moment. Let's not blame the victim, though you can't say he's totally innocent, either! There are differences of degree, differences erased by euphoria, by soldiers who dance in courtyards brought under submission, by the exuberance of people who don't even understand the language spoken all around them—Arabic, in this case. Do not tell me that Leclerc was a lover of the French language! Do not tell me that it was the emotion he felt when he read General de Gaulle's name there in Italian that made his mind go blank. But it may have been the Fezzan's rapid fall that led him to believe things were going to be easy from then on.

Ah, Leclerc!

He'd not yet come face-to-face with the tanks of that *schouain* Rommel, the bête noire of Free France—and yet now he took a vacation! I can't come up with any other word to describe the fact that he took ten days away from the front on the pretext of an inspection tour with General de Gaulle, a tour that brought the two men to Yaoundé and many other places across French Equatorial Africa. You can try to tell me that he still needed more soldiers, for without soldiers, war doesn't work. But did he have to go look for them himself? What other explanation is there for this tour except that General Leclerc—he'd been promoted after Kufra—felt that the Italians didn't matter anymore, so he could gad about from one side of his fiefdom to the other? Ah! You could say he was retracing his steps— the victor who still hadn't liberated Paris, or rather Strasbourg, for that matter. He was retracing his steps because the recruiting drives in Yaoundé had been wildly successful, especially since the high chief of the Ewondo had put his weight behind them.

Leclerc was heading back to Ongola because the voice of Charles Atangana—yes, the one from *Mount Pleasant*—had succeeded in doing what neither Radio Cameroon and its endless propaganda nor the governor of Cameroon had been able to do: enroll all the young Ewondo men as tirailleurs for Free France and raise an army of twenty thousand men in Yaoundé.

And so on and so forth.

You must understand that I am angry about this, because someone has to take responsibility for how blithely the tirailleurs headed into the desert. Yes, I know, they ought to have been more careful— yes, I mean our dear Philothée; they ought to have screwed a little less in the cities they conquered—and yes, I mean our dear Hebga. And what else? Really, what else? If you must blame the victim, you also have to recognize that the fault does not lie wholly upon the subaltern's shoulders! Think about it: cheered up by the mangled bits of metal scattered along the path his company followed, under the protection of the planes that cleared the way ahead each morning, carrying a machine gun provided by England and the United States, fed meals that the war subscriptions of villages across French Equitorial Africa provided without interruption—"Send meat! Meat!" General de Gaulle had said long ago in that speech in Douala—even Philothée was head over heels about his old rifle, his Chassepot, and that says it all. Who could blame him? Who?

"Made in 1866!" Fouret had roared during one of his sessions with Philothée, indignant at the sight of the thing the Bassa man was cleaning. You try to explain why Hebga's being issued a weapon from 1866 in 1942, especially when he was about to face the *schouain* Rommel's panzer division, was a "lousy crime." Clearly those were Fouret's words. As we know, Philothée didn't answer, or at most made indistinct grunts, because he was actually speaking less and less in this desert that parched his throat and troubled his mind. Maybe fatigue was getting the best of the men, especially the tirailleurs from the forest: "Cameroon mounted company, attention! March!" The very smell of the desert had left them stunned; like dead plants, they swayed back and forth, buffeted by the wind that roared endlessly over the dunes. They lifted up clouds of sand with each of their steps and then buried their feet again, as if they were moving statues.

Still, when the Italian land mine sent him flying up into the sky with a spray of sand, Philothée was open to considering all possible explanations. What am I saying, "was open to"? He was scattered in a thousand pieces over a huge swath of the desert. A hand here, a foot there, his trunk lying on the sand, covered with clumps of red, black, and yellow. Curiously, his mouth, still attached to the charred trunk, opened to scream through the layers of sand, to scream and scream.

"*You mamy pima!*" he said.

Buried deep in the sand, he caught his breath and cried out.

"*You mamy pima!*"

He had stopped stuttering.

Then suddenly he called out "Hebga!"

There were tears running down his body, or over the sand, because sand he had become: crying sand.

"Hebga! *You mamy pima!*"

At once Fouret and the other soldiers began to shoot, and shoot.

He had the advantage of sitting behind a piece of heavy machinery, and he kept shooting like never before, the machine spitting out a constant barrage of fire. He shot and spat curses, shot and spat curses. But if he was shooting and cursing that much, it was because after Philothée's shattering explosion, Hebga had heard his name over the whistling din of the bullets and broken ranks. Ah! Fouret was shooting, not to kill Italians but to protect that "son of a bitch," that "shithead," with his weapon from 1866 held out in front of him, who was jumping through the sand, zigzagging around the bullets: Philothée was still calling for Hebga.

What would you have done in his place? Hebga ran to where his friend was buried in the sand, where he found his brother chopped to bits, where he found the essential parts of Philothée, his trunk, or what remained of it, and the bellowing mouth. That's where the versions of his death diverge, depending on whether you were a real true Senegalese tirailleur, meaning a black man, or a so-called Senegalese tirailleur who was actually Camaroonian, and also a black man, or a white man, which means not a tirailleur at all: three distinct mathematical possibilities, each mutually exclusive.

Two Sorts of Tirailleurs, Plus One

In the first version of events, told to me by a real true Senegalese tirailleur—you see, Senegal had until the end of 1942 sent its soldiers to back Pétain, and had only just shifted to the Gaullist camp—anyway, according to that real true Senegalese tirailleur, he swore he'd never seen anything like it—"Cameroonian, they strong, huh." He said Philothée suddenly began to talk, to talk, just as he'd been screaming and screaming before. Then, grabbing on to Hebga's neck with the stump of a hand he had wrenched out of the sand, he started to tell him, in a jumbled rush of parched words, what had just happened, and then summarized all he had learned about this Second World War, starting with his introduction to poetry, then on to French philosophy, and his introduction to Gaullist ideology.

He first spoke about the little poetry circle in Edéa, where he read poems about love, and also about war, those of Apollinaire, for example. He moved on to the *ndolo*, the love found in Briqueterie, where, in the bed of his first *wolowolos*, he swore that the Second World War was the best thing that had ever happened to him. This led him to what he had seen when crossing the desert, including the tirailleur whose head had been torn open, lying there in the middle of all the bodies and repeating, "War not good! War not good!" He told the story of the Italian cut in two by a French shell, and noted the irony of the story, since hadn't he just been cut down by an Italian shell?

"Except in your case it was a mine," Hebga noted.

For the woodcutter had learned to distinguish among the instruments of death Free France made him face.

In a rush of words, he explained his recent conversion to Marxism-Leninism, thanks to Fouret the revolutionary—or was he more of an idealist? Then he said that Leclerc, he wasn't worth the trouble. And Philothée spoke on and on, trying to catch up on all the years when he hadn't been able to express the thoughts churning in his belly before inevitable death caught up with him. He spoke and he spoke, his torrent of words giving the Italians time to reload their rifles, using up the cover the French forces provided Hebga, who, now unprotected, took a bullet right in the back because he'd crouched down to listen to Philothée's long tirade. Hebga spread out his hands, as soldiers do as they fall. Another bullet hit him in the neck, propelling him forward; he landed on Philothée, shutting his mouth for good.

As I've said, this is one version of events. According to the second, the one told by a soldier idiomatically labeled a Senegalese tirailleur, but actually from Cameroon, everything that happened there that day was just another Bassa story—pure witchcraft, you know! And you can understand that that Cameroonian tirailleur—referred to as Senegalese—wasn't himself Bassa, because he said that Philothée began to talk—both versions are in agreement there—but added: the Italians had retreated and left their treacherous mines behind in the sand in hopes of slowing the advance of the Free French. The soldier who told me this version added that Philothée had grabbed Hebga by the neck and pulled him in close to whisper in his ear, laughing as only someone whose body has just been cut in two and who knows they're about to die can do, "It was me, the *Man who had done that*!"

Hebga's eyes grew wide. It made no sense. Philothée couldn't have managed to cut his own body in two with an Italian mine—even if Hebga thought the *Man who had done that* deserved nothing less.

"I'm the one who screwed your mother!" Philothée went on.

And he burst out laughing. At that point I asked the tirailleur who was telling me his version of things: "What man could swallow such a lack of respect?"

"Cameroonians are strong," the tirailleur telling me his version of things noted succinctly.

"I'm Cameroonian, and I'm not that strong."

"Bassas are strong."

All that remained of Philothée was his trunk, stuck there, with his face peering out from beneath the sand—all, that is, if you don't count the stump of a hand with which he held on to Hebga's neck, so that he could whisper right in his ear and tell him how back in the woods he had taken his mother in so many ways that she'd been torn to pieces.

"I'm the *Man who had done that*," Philothée kept repeating.

Hebga couldn't believe his ears.

Philothée explained that the best place he'd found to hide had been right next to Hebga—becoming his shadow, invisible in the bush, and stuck to his side everywhere else. After he'd done that to our Sita, to avenge the humiliation her son had inflicted on him in that boxing match long ago, Philothée had come out of the forest and taken a seat at the bar in La Seigneuriale, certain that Hebga would show up there for a beer once he'd given up on his futile quest. That's what happened. Being part of Pouka's little poetry circle made his hiding place all the better. By putting himself in Hebga's shadow, he forced the woodcutter to look everywhere but right behind him.

Oh! He certainly paid a price for sticking that close, because Philothée had to enter into the Second World War, still trying to avoid Hebga's ax. He'd lived through everything we've seen till now just to stay hidden, because it was really him who had done that to our Sita: he was the Panther. Hebga was determined to look the Panther in the eyes before slitting his throat. Philothée knew that, so he kept hidden. As an added layer of camouflage, he decided he'd no longer speak, only stutter, so he could keep control of his story, keep it from spilling out like a bad bout of diarrhea. Hebga couldn't believe his ears.

"I'm the one who did it," he repeated. "Hebga, it was me. Charles is my witness."

"Bilong?"

"Even the old man M'bangue is my witness."

"Pouka's father?"

"Close by, but invisible. You remember?"

"And I thought you were my brother."

"I am the Panther."

"Your own brother is the one who kills you."

"There, we can agree."

"*Schouain!*"

Hebga drove his bayonet into Philothée's mouth and the blade cut right through his head, which only then fell silent.

"*Schouain!*"

Then Hebga raised his rifle, suddenly useless there in the middle of the Second World War, and then turned it back on himself—him, a Cameroonian-Senegalese tirailleur—and sent a bullet right into his head, stunning everyone around—especially the other Cameroonian tirailleur, aka the Senegalese tirailleur who told me the story, who swore he'd never seen anything like it.

"An assassination and a suicide right on the battlefield!"

"Believe me, Cameroonians never miss a chance to tear each other apart."

"Tell me about it."

"It's *ndoutou.*"

"No, only a Bassa could do that."

Clearly he wasn't a Bassa—my guess is he was Bamiléké. Don't ask me why I thought that, my dear reader, it would take too long to explain and, really, it's beside the point.

Now let's move on to the third version—that of a Free French soldier, but not a tirailleur—Fouret's, to be clear. Obviously, he stressed what the French were doing—and to bring them into focus, he needed the Italians, who were on the other side of the scene. "So," he said, "we provided perfect cover for Tirailleur Second-Class Hebga, who, overcome with emotion, had rushed into the barrage of enemy bullets to reach Philothée, his very close friend, and mine, too, who'd been killed by an enemy mine. That sort of thing happens because war, it's not just a hunting party, you know. It's war. Sometimes soldiers crack. In short, that's what happened, he cracked. His comrades did everything they could—so did I, I want to make clear—to provide him with cover. Alas, the only fault to be found lies with this damned war, because had Hebga ever even learned to use his rifle?" The Free French soldier recalled that for a long time Hebga had used an ax that belonged in the Middle Ages, and what's more, that he called it de Gaulle.

"Strange, isn't it?"

So, positioned there in front of the enemy with a rifle he didn't know how to use, the soldier—people called him a woodcutter, but that was an insult, wasn't it?—was really executed. Looking carefully, it was clear the poor guy hadn't even cocked his weapon!

"Really?"

"No joke! France uses black soldiers for cannon fodder."

"But they're the ones who liberated . . . France."

"What a joke! With their machetes? No, really, the only thing that could have saved that soldier," Fouret went on, "was speed. Speed."

"Explain that, sir."

"You need to conjure a clear mental image of the enemy, find him, take aim, and pull the trigger. Boom."

"But the enemy there was invisible, no?"

"Sir, the enemy is always invisible."

Obviously, after the war, Fouret stopped believing in the revolution of his youth. Tired of waiting for Stalin to become a socialist, and the USSR truly Communist, he had replaced his library of Parisian idealism—which he hadn't found after the war, since the Nazis had destroyed it in his absence—with the little anthology of Gaullist principles, and the image of France it put forth. In other words, the war had unintended consequences for everyone. As for me, the narrator, I wasn't impressed by all the details of his tale, and even less so by the fact that he'd had the good fortune of surviving to write the whole story. I hope you won't be, either, my dear reader. But let's move on.

23

Truth's Infinite Probabilities

You see, if we take our set, Ω, of the primary events that took place in the desert, which correspond to the three tales told by soldiers from Leclerc's column who witnessed the deaths of Philothée and Hebga, but were unable to intervene (x_1 = the real true Senegalese tirailleur; x_2 = the actually Cameroonian Senegalese tirailleur; and x_3 = the white soldier), we can associate a number x to one of the values— x_1, x_2, x_3—to describe how the central event took place. The number x is called the random variable, and for us, it is the equivalent of the truth—truth being contingent upon one's perspective, as we all know.

A random variable is defined once you know the probabilities— $p(x_1)$, $p(x_2)$, and $p(x_3)$—that correspond to the different possible values of x, such as we have defined them in chapter 22. These probabilities are evidently the following:

$$p(x_1) + p(x_i) + \ldots + p(x_n) = 1$$
$$x = 1$$

Therefore, x is the variable of truth, but this can only be random, because it depends on the individuals that I've chosen from among all those in Leclerc's column to tell me their version of the facts, and on the probability of their surviving the Second World War, and the probability of their actually witnessing the events firsthand, when they were part of an army of more than five thousand men, both black and white, including real true Senegalese tirailleurs, Cameroonian-Senegalese tirailleurs, Chadian-Senegalese, Gabonese-Senegalese, etc. So we agree that establishing the truth of what happened to the Senegalese tirailleurs must perforce be complicated, with the version that is told of their participation in the Second World War and in the liberation of France contingent primarily on the nationality of the narrator of the tale. And I am, after all, Cameroonian.

Let's get back to Pouka. After calculating all these probabilities, the next step for him would have been to write the first draft of a poem. The draft would be written hastily, with no real sense of form: the formless forms of a feeling, with structure coming only later. He wrote a poem, of course, to tell of the drama that had just taken place in the middle of the desert, but in the end what he had wasn't the stuff of pure alexandrines. This manner of dying, far too strange, had unhinged his poetical-mathematic reasoning. His poem was addressed to "those who died in the Sahara." It's well suited to that moment, which, when I think about it, is really beyond explanation.

Sahara, Sahara, O arid and somber plain
Where brave soldiers
Seeking honor now sleep, stoic, in great numbers
After battles so punishing.

You saw them die, submerged by great numbers
Of Attila's warriors;
Now they sleep among those vile ruins
Left by bombs exploding.

I won't try to establish the correspondence between the alexandrines of some of this poem's verses and the formula for calculating probabilities that I laid out above, even if I know that the theory of the correspondence between mathematics and poetry is precisely the Germanic theory of poetry, and the reason why Pouka defined himself as the maestro. I'll concede it is so, but let's move on.

24

The Desert Campaign

Or rather, let's get back to the matter at hand, yes, to war. It had consequences for everyone. Except, of course, for our four Cameroonian tirailleurs, because they have died, and death awaits us all, regardless of the Second World War. The Sahara swallowed up their lives and, more than their lives, their stories. In that way the desert is like memory itself. A story exists only when it is told. Do with that what you will: if no one talks about you, you're nothing, as we say in Yaoundé. Do not ask the dunes to remember the battles that have taken place there; do not ask the sun that endlessly scorches the earth to recall the dead, even if it has turned its gaze away from them for no more than a few nights; and most of all, do not ask French history books to recall just who inscribed Liberation, with a capital *L*, on their streets and pages from 1940 to 1943! Ah! The Sahara is more brutal than the most forgetful of men, for Leclerc's troops pushed on to Tripoli, on to Paris, on to Strasbourg. There are still those who can prove that the four Cameroonian soldiers did in fact parade under the Arc de Triomphe in August of 1944, and not only in their dreams, although Leclerc's historians celebrate the fact that he raised the French flag in Strasbourg as he had promised several of his men back in the stifling heat of Kufra.

History is a whore that everyone screws in their own fashion. What is certain is that the desert campaign was decided on the battlefield as much as in offices in London and Brazzaville, and soon thereafter in Algiers and, later, Paris. At least twice, the outcome of that African campaign was decided in the place where de Gaulle had relocated the French government—so, in what was then the French capital. It's enough to remember his tirailleurs' entrance into Yaoundé to know what happened in Paris in August 1944. In the City of the Seven Hills, the plums are ripe. That month of August is described with delectation, not because of Parisian joy, which soldiers entering the city, including Leclerc himself, had already encountered several times before and, therefore, no longer held any particular historic significance for them. But because of the succulence of those fruits that you squeeze in your hand to loosen the pit, those plums that taxi drivers eat while driving, tossing the pits out the car window as they go.

If you visit Yaoundé, ask any taxi driver—like Fritz way back when, they are all defrocked intellectuals, unemployed college graduates, sometimes even university professors trying to round out their salary—and he'll remind you that France's African war, far from being over, still rages on as a cold war. And the tirailleurs who disappeared in the Sahara on that day in 1942 still make their voices heard in the hubbub of the roundabout in front of the Central Post Office, which is still awaiting a statue of its hero; in the depths of the former gubernatorial palace that winks at it from the neighboring hilltop; and all across this city of Yaoundé, which has since then known only defeats. Yet, in those moving universities, those moving lecture halls that are the taxis of Cameroon's capital, just ask any of those town-criers who are the intellectual taxi drivers of my hometown, and who, as they talk to one passenger after the other, deconstruct the universe; who, as they drive along the streets and through the poor neighborhoods, explain to you the reasons for France's massive, ongoing military presence in Chad, in Gabon, in Senegal, "although, for England, colonization has long ended"; who list off the reasons for the eighty coups that have taken place across Africa since 1960, most of them in the French sphere; who trace out for you the Parisian ramifications of the crisis in Côte d'Ivoire; the Elysian sources of the war in Congo-Brazzaville, of the dictatorship in Burkina Faso, of the military coups in Togo, in Niger, in the Central African Republic, of the war in Chad; who reveal to you how the French were implicated in the genocide in Rwanda, as well as in those of the Bamiléké and the Bassa; who can explain to you why France holds the mineral rights in Francophone Africa, even though the International Organisation of La Francophonie includes Africa's poorest nations; who tell you plainly and without metaphor the reasons for Paris's unflagging support for the likes of Senghor, Bokassa, Eyadéma, "all former tirailleurs," and for men like Biya who really don't give a damn; who know everything without ever actually telling you how they do; in short, just ask any Cameroonian, and they'll tell you that de Gaulle would have been nothing without Cameroon, and most of all, yes, most of all that:

"France is nothing without Africa."

"Is that so? Well," I say, "just look at the Central Post Office! Since 1939, it hasn't changed at all, isn't that so? If anything, it's even uglier today, am I right?"

How I love to debate with my compatriots!

"Is France going to rebuild it for us?"

"France owes its lifeblood to Cameroon," they insist. "My dear friend, Paris was liberated by us!"

"*Bèbèla!*"

"Go tell that to the French." That's what I tell them.

"Do you believe," they snap back, "that de Gaulle would have been taken seriously by Churchill *for even one minute* without the victory in Yaoundé?"

I love how they are so precise: "for even one minute"!

More Cameroonian nonsense! I want to shout. Just more Cameroonian nonsense!

Listen, they tell me: First, Churchill began to pay attention to de Gaulle's theories only after Yaoundé. He also needed to convince Roosevelt. After 1940, especially after 1942, things moved quickly once the United States joined the war, furious because of the attack on its navy the year before in Pearl Harbor. De Gaulle had no choice but to offer up the African coast, African cities—like Algiers and Casablanca!—to the growing Allied forces. The landing at the beaches in Normandy was modeled on that of Algiers, itself based on the experience gleaned in the failed landing at Dakar, on September 23–25, 1940. Really, it all goes back to Leclerc's landing on the shore at Douala, in a little pirogue, the night of August 26, 1940. The people of Yaoundé—just ask any intellectual taxi driver, he'll say the same thing—they all know that plum season signals the ripeness of those fruits in a very particular way; those plums, which de Gaulle ate in Yaoundé's courtyards, mark the start of a joyful harvest season, even if he threw the pit out the window of French history. "He will bring together France's last putsch and Africa's first," Fritz predicted, and along with him the good Cameroonian thinks that the putsch in Ongola paved the way for the ones in Algiers and then Paris, where de Gaulle finally took power in August 1944. The people of Yaoundé sometimes regret that Paris lived through such calm times after 1944, while their hometown was besieged by the fear of possible coups, like those that actually took place in the other African capitals. Obviously, I'm not trying to say that people would complain about a coup d'état against Paul Biya, who, like his predecessors, lives to follow Paris's orders. The intellectual taxi drivers will tell you straight out: "*Mola*, Yaoundé is not another neighborhood in Paris, huh! If there's a coup d'état here, *bèbèla*, Biya will shit his pants!"

History is written by the victors. It's really too bad that the books that show us pictures of the victors of the Second World War don't take our taxi drivers into account. Ah! Does that mean that the tirailleurs didn't, in fact, offer up to newly liberated Paris that black force that she wanted to take in her arms? Was it a waste of time that Free France whitened the French army, especially Leclerc's forces? Or does it mean that the discussions between de Gaulle and Churchill didn't transform France's destiny, as they were supposed to do, or turn her back into the great power of de Gaulle's dreams? On all of these questions, the Sahara remains strangely quiet. But that's not really a problem, because while the desert gave everything to Leclerc, what did it learn that it didn't already know? When Pouka met Fouret in 1947, he saw a man comfortably settled down. His words mentioned the war only rarely, and then just to express his surprise at how badly things had turned out. He spoke to Pouka as if he came from a far-off continent, a continent that knocked on his door, "as it had knocked on France's," bringing more questions than answers. He had become a Gaullist because, as he said, de Gaulle was luckier than Louis Napoléon had been "with his African generals."

"Like Napoléon?" Pouka asked quizzically.

"Let's not exaggerate," Fouret chastised.

He paused, reflecting for a moment.

"It's the dialectic," he went on. "It's the dialectical process of Africa coming to save France."

An ironic smile lit up his face. Several times he used the phrase "Third World" to refer to Africa, a place he now knew quite well. The war had given him a newfound power, the power to travel extensively, in Africa primarily, "in our dueling field," he added with a laugh. The memory of the desert campaign was still fresh in his mind. He was by that time teaching philosophy at the University of Bordeaux, where he'd become the butt of the leftist students' jokes—by that I mean, most of the students'—since he'd added the writings of Marx and Hegel to his courses.

"Revolution," he said to Pouka, "it's up to the Third World to lead it."

"Why?" the maestro asked.

"Europe is tired of change."

Pouka noted the weary features of this man who had abandoned his dreams. So it was Professor Fouret who one evening introduced him to Jacques Delarue, who taught law at the Sorbonne, the famous professor the poet had first heard about back in the homeland, and who'd come to Bordeaux to give a lecture. In his hotel, Delarue immediately asked Pouka what had become of Um Nyobè. Pouka couldn't tell him much, only that his friend was involved in union activities, that he still liked talking politics and playing soccer—he was captain of a team, in fact. He thought he saw a glimmer of doubt in Fouret's eyes, but also the conviction that Cameroon's future was still in play. What Pouka didn't tell him was that he had actually gone to Paris because of Delarue, because he wanted to continue the legal studies he'd begun in Bordeaux. Instead of giving Pouka advice on the study of law, however, Delarue had encouraged him to enroll at the School of Oriental Languages in Paris to study anthropology. He gave him the addresses of several people he said he knew, including

one man from Senegal by the name of Léopold, who, he added, had
been a tirailleur and also wrote poems. Pouka confessed that he had
a manuscript in his bag, *The Tumultuous Reveries*, that he hoped to
have published.

"That will make Léopold happy," Fouret said with a nod. "He's
working now on an anthology of poems by black writers, I think."

That caught Pouka's attention.

"I'm more of a man of action, myself," Fouret added.

He revealed that his stay in Cameroon hadn't made his life easy
since he had come back to France.

"Ah! Gaullism! I should have realized."

And that brought the conversation back to Cameroon, to the desert campaign, and the year 1942.

"Everything was decided in 1942."

"In 1940," Pouka insisted. "With the events in Ongola."

How could Fouret have known? One thing is certain, however: the maestro was not one of the poets chosen for Senghor's
anthology.

25

Between Us Women

History kept marching on. After Fritz's departure for Douala, Ngo Bikaï asked Nguet to come live with her. Let's not dwell on Fritz's decision, because it was painful, oh so very painful, for each of the parties concerned. The children. Ngo Bikaï. Fritz. Ask anyone who has gone through a divorce and you'll hear all about it. Choices are easier to make when they're theoretical, Fritz realized. He couldn't blame Ngo Bikaï for anything, because if there was a victim in this, it was her. And what about him? When you can no longer blame the living, you blame the dead. Rummaging through his father's belongings, he found something that brought him some peace. Discovering that an askari is the equivalent of a tirailleur, and a tirailleur an askari by another name, was a revelation that freed his conscience, freed his hands. He could walk away from everything his father had bequeathed to him, no regrets; and so he set off on the road to Douala, his pockets empty, leaving behind a pile of bags full of his own belongings in his room.

"Keep it," he said to his wife when the two met one last time in the bedroom, their love's bedroom. He pointed at the two piles he'd made. "That's for the kids."

Obviously, he was lying.

Ngo Bikaï sought to heal the wound of their separation by moving Nguet into the room just a few days after Fritz had liberated the space. A father can never be replaced, of course, but something needed to be done so that the children would stop asking over and over, "When is Papa coming home?" Luckily, Nguet had her own way of talking to them. She became Ngo Bikaï's right-hand woman, not out of a sense of obligation, but rather by default, because, as you may recall, that had been her sister Martha's job before. But Martha was in Yaoundé.

There was something else, too. Nguet was pregnant. By whom? More than mourning Bilong, it was that bit of news, the impending birth of a child, that brought the two women back together. It didn't matter who the father was! Ngo Bikaï sympathized, she understood. The soldiers of Free France had left behind them many round bellies.

At first Nguet had hesitated.

"But you'll be better off at my house," Ngo Bikaï pleaded.

"But I have a room of my own!"

"If you move in with me, you'll have the run of a whole house!"

"I'm going to give birth soon."

"Precisely," and that's the argument that finally won the day. "I'll help you deliver the baby."

Nguet, who had been living on her own, explained to Ngo Bikaï that although her name sounded like a Bassa one, she wasn't really from Edéa. Ngo Bikaï let her know that there was no question of her returning to her native Foumban so late in her pregnancy. With Ngo Bikaï, she wouldn't have to rely on neighbors to help when the baby's time came. She'd have a sister right there with her: *a sister-in-law*. That was an easy argument for her to understand. And that's how it happened.

One night, Nguet opened the door to the room where Ngo Bikaï was sleeping with her children.

"My sister," she whispered.

"What is it?" Ngo Bikaï asked as she came out of the room, holding a lamp and rubbing her eyes.

"I think," said Nguet, "I've become a child again."

She sounded like she was talking to her own mother.

"Why?"

"I've wet my bed."

That's how it all began. An inauspicious night for the birth, because it was raining. Ngo Bikaï could have run through the night, calling her women together, but could she leave a woman in labor alone with the children? No, she could never do that.

"Let's go to the living room."

And there, together, they waited for the first contractions.

"Get undressed," Ngo Bikaï said, once the contractions had started, "and put this on."

In that living room that had been the scene of such a long story, she helped Nguet put on the *kaba ngondo* she herself often wore to the market.

"Walk around the table."

Where had she learned the art of midwifery? Having gone through three pregnancies, she knew she needed to wrap her arms around Nguet and hold her up, because Nguet was tired.

"You have to keep walking," she insisted.

The two women made their way around the table, which on the day they celebrated a now-failed marriage had held one of the biggest captains ever; under the watchful eyes of photographs depicting the ghostly remains of a family, they walked all through the night that swallowed up their words as the rain fell, harder and harder, in big drops on the roof and ground. They retraced the path of those who had shared in the joyful meal. Step by step, one contraction after another, Nguet reinscribed in that living room the love it had lost, the love of a brother, Bilong, the love of a husband whose photos still hung on the walls, the love of Ngo Bikaï who had learned to see her as a woman like any other, the love of a child who commanded her every move.

"Walk," said Ngo Bikaï.

"I can't take it anymore."

"You must keep walking," the Mother of the Market insisted, "until the contractions are much closer together."

Ngo Bikaï recalled the mathematics of a pregnant body. She kept track of Nguet's contractions systematically, as if they were in her own body. Then, when they reached the right number, she held the exhausted woman gently around the hips and guided her toward Fritz's room, helping Nguet to lie down on the bed where she had so often sought and found love, love that had now departed.

"Spread your legs wide," she said.

And Nguet did as she was told, bracing her feet against both sides of the bed.

Ngo Bikaï massaged her belly, using an oil she'd prepared just for this. Gently, but firmly. With great patience she spread open her sister's legs, the lips of her vagina, her whole body. The details of her own pregnancies ran through her mind. But a first pregnancy is not like a second one, or a third. This was Nguet's first.

"The first birth always takes a long time."

"Does it hurt?"

"That depends."

Ngo Bikaï knew that there was no use lying.

"Tell me a story," Nguet asked.

So Ngo Bikaï told her own story.

"Another."

Ngo Bikaï told the story of her love with Fritz, how they'd met, her own first pregnancy, the birth of her first child, the start of her business, in short, her whole life. At the same time, she was massaging Nguet's vagina. She spoke gently as she rubbed. Tears flooded her eyes. Using more of the oil, she rubbed first with two fingers, then with four, then six, finally all ten fingers. Soon Nguet no longer heard the voice that had been talking her through the birth. All of a sudden the child in her belly began to move, timidly at first, and then with determination. It was as if, alerted by the story he heard, he first strained his ear to listen more closely, then moved his body to listen even better, then poked out his head to see who was talking.

"I see the head," Ngo Bikaï said. "Push!"

And Nguet pushed.

"You're doing great," said Ngo Bikaï, holding Nguet's feet wide apart, "you are brave, you are courageous. Now, count one, two, three, and push."

And Nguet pushed. A flood burst out from her vagina, soaking the bed. The head appeared. Nguet cried. Ngo Bikaï started counting again.

"One more time! Push!"

The strength of her voice carried Nguet along. And Nguet

pushed, carried away by the child who wanted to know the happy ending of the story of which he'd heard only a few painful chapters, chapters that weren't about him. Nguet pushed and excrement poured out of her rectum. Nguet pushed once more and the child leaped from her belly, falling into Ngo Bikaï's hands. Lifting the baby by his feet, she gave him a little swat on the behind. The baby gave his first cry. Ngo Bikaï cut the umbilical cord.

"Here is your child," she announced to the exhausted mother. "It's a boy."

Nguet was crying and laughing. In her love, she found the strength to hold to her breast the little one who had just been torn from her womb, from her body, from her heart. She didn't even feel the placenta coming out of her belly. Ngo Bikaï, who had spent the whole night between her sister's legs, finally stood up and covered Nguet with a towel. She rushed to bring water to clean up the blood and fluid that had spilled over everything, that still flowed from the happy mother. Suddenly she realized that her three children were in the doorway, where they'd been watching the whole scene in silence. She jumped but didn't miss a beat.

"Bring me some water," she asked the oldest, then said to the others, "Come say hello to your new cousin."

The new mother was whispering a song into the babe's ear, a rosary comprised of thanks and praise names. She sang and cried. She spoke to her child of the men who had left. Of far-off countries. She called her newborn son Bilong, and also Hebga. Bilong Hebga. The children repeated the names, amazed by the nursing babe.

"Bilong," said the eldest.

"Bilong Hebga," Ngo Bikaï corrected with a smile, happy at the thought that on this child's birth certificate her little brother's name would be inscribed, instead of "*father unknown.*"

It was as if, in the room where the birth had taken place, a new family was emerging.

"Doesn't he have a first name?"

"Bilong, that's his first name, his father's name," Nguet replied.

"And Hebga?"

The two women suddenly exchanged a knowing glance.

"That's an extra name, a given name."

"Given to whom?"

"That's a whole other story," said the new mother.

A really long story.

The story of all the women on the home front.

26

That's How Friendships Are, Too

Um Nyobè and Pouka learned only later that Ngo Bikaï and Fritz had separated. It doesn't matter which of them took it worse. The maestro simply asked why even get married if you're just going to divorce the next day? Let's leave it up to Um Nyobè to put him in his place.

His plans foiled again by the rain—because at the start of the season, the rain in Yaoundé just doesn't stop falling—Pouka was only able to meet up with his friend after work, when the weather died down. The two writers agreed that, for a man, life without a woman is a hard bed to lie in.

"Don't you have anything to eat in this house?" Um Nyobè asked.

Food wasn't the only problem on his mind. He knew Pouka never cooked anything anyway. Except for a table and chairs, and two armchairs, his house was empty. Um Nyobè peered out at the courtyard that had become a lake, where the falling rain left big circular drops like so many water lilies.

"I have some of Martha's *mintumbas*," Pouka said, disappearing into the back to get out the manioc cakes.

To come all this way, only to eat his own wife's cooking! Um Nyobè burst out laughing. "Don't you think you'd better get married, huh?"

Pouka sensed that his friend was on edge because of their unfinished conversation.

"I just don't understand," Um Nyobè continued, "I don't understand why you made Augustus go back to Edéa."

"He'll wait for you there, ready to be your houseboy," Pouka snapped.

"Oh please," Um Nyobè cut in, really irritated by that insinuation, "leave me and Edéa out of it. You know that my boss is giving me hell. Why are you always trying to change the topic?"

A good question, because Um Nyobè and Pouka had never really talked through their differences one-on-one.

"Pouka will never run away from an argument," the maestro protested, sitting down at the table next to his friend. "It's just, Um Nyobè, I'm not a *speechifier* like you."

He gently freed a *mintumba* from its wrapping of leaves, revealing its yellow heart; the room was filled with its juicy smell. He then cut it up into several even-sized pieces.

"A *speechifier*?" Um Nyobè repeated, echoing his friend in French. Laughing, he took the piece Pouka offered him. "You should hear yourself speak. 'Speechifier,' really!"

"How about politician? Is that any better?"

"And you? What does that make you, then? And, Pouka, don't just say you're a poet, like always, because this time that's not going to work, my dear friend. What kind of a person is it who opens his home up to a poor young man, struggling to make his way in life, and then throws him out? What do you call that?"

"Ah! Because you were there to take care of him, is that what you say now?"

"The lawyer, don't you remember?"

"Um Nyobè, that's the problem with you. You believe in the justice of men. You want to establish a republic built on justice, you want to be the Saint Just of that republic. You always try to get to the root of things, but you know full well that that republic only recognizes one regime, the regime of terror."

"What do you mean, *terror*?"

Um Nyobè said the word in French.

A gust of wind drove the rain into the room. Pouka went to shut the door. The room fell into darkness.

"Revolutionary terror, my dear friend. Robespierre. Stalin," he said as he sat back down. "You read the newspapers. So don't play stupid."

"When one forgets the physical reality of the victim, everything is lost," Um Nyobè declared sententiously. "Even heaven disappears. *A world without sacrifice has no heaven.*"

"So who is it who needs the victim?"

". . . And a world without heaven," Um Nyobè went on, as if Pouka hadn't said a thing, "that's the definition of terror, *my dear friend.*"

As shadows filled the room, their discussion continued on like that, moving between Bassa and French, with no rhyme or reason, and from philosophy to politics, without transition.

Pouka got up to turn on the lights. Not surprised that the electricity had gone out—"It's the rain"—he went nonchalantly to get a hurricane lamp from the back of the house. He returned and placed the lit lamp on the table. In the light's glow, he saw Um Nyobè in a pensive pose, staring off in the distance. He looked, as he often did, like a man who battles with ideas: forehead lifted, eyes bright, a clenched fist held in front of his face, as if his palm held the fleeting butterfly of one final idea. Pouka hated that pose and quickly broke his friend out of it.

"What terror?" he repeated. "French history gives us one example." Standing in front of Um Nyobè, he waved his arms. "Would you prefer German history? Or that of the USSR? For the moment, you are in a weak position, no doubt. The victim, yes, that's an easy out, but it doesn't last. You can say that because we were colonized, we are victims. But what you're forgetting is that the colonized subject is also defined by the system. Like any other victim. The victim is a parasite, despite himself. You can't get around it, Um Nyobè. You have to start by accepting that."

"Accepting what?"

"Accepting that France is in us."

"Ah! And France, then, just what does she accept? Nothing?" Um Nyobè rose and whispered in Pouka's ear: "My brother, France is a hen that eats her own eggs."

A childlike smile lit up his face. He thought he'd scored a point.

"And the eggs you're talking about, that's us, right?"

"Do you think we're plums?"

"Um," said Pouka, somewhat rattled, "you dream of tossing a few slippery plums under the feet of the French who are here in this country, don't you?"

Schadenfreude!

"Don't tell me you don't think about it."

"And you, why don't you tell me what you think?" Um Nyobè retorted. "You hide behind poetry, but never say what you really think. Don't tell me that it's because of the French language, because your father, and you know what a thinker he is, he has only ever spoken Bassa. So, in your opinion, Pouka, why doesn't France accept us? Look at what she's doing here! France thinks she can come and take away our brothers, just like that, without taking any responsibility, and turn them into tirailleurs; that she can ignore the laws she wrote herself—don't you remember? *Liberty, Equality, and Fraternity*—and break the balls of whomever she wants? That's why she's at war, isn't it? To defend her values? So why doesn't she respect those universal values here, too? Why does she act like such a savage in her own backyard?"

The rain was coming down so hard the windows were rattling. The roof was shaking with exceptional violence. Um Nyobè had taken the precaution of warning his wife beforehand: he had something serious to settle, but of course he hadn't given her all the details. He'd find the time to tell her the whole story later, he told himself. The lawyer recommended by Marc had shown him new sides to Augustus's story, new chapters, new perspectives. He was a union supporter, French—Gaston Donnat was his name—a pacifist who had, like others, chosen life in the colonies to avoid war. Um Nyobè hadn't yet broached the topic with Pouka, but he was realizing that the war opened up a new field of possibilities for them. He had started to look more closely at the colonists, noting that, especially in these somber times, there were some rabble-rousers hidden among them. Yet Pouka had already spoken to him about Delarue with a certain disdain, as if patting himself on the back because the colonial administration had sent him away.

"Do you know what your problem is?" Um Nyobè asked.

"You'll tell me."

"Drop the sarcasm, Pouka. Your problem is that you don't know which side you're on."

"I don't think there are sides here, Um Nyobè; the situation is really quite clear. You are talking about liberty, right? Equality, and just like that, you think that it's France that has best expressed those ideals."

"Your inability to imagine yourself without France is surprising. What would *Mr. Pouka* be without France?"

"Um," Pouka replied, visibly shocked by the *Mr. Pouka*, "you can get married more than once, but none of us will ever be a virgin again."

Um Nyobè picked up a piece of *mintumba* and chewed it slowly.

"Once colonized," Pouka went on, "there's no way to rid yourself of the West. That's our dilemma. Simply put, the West has occupied our future. As a result, it becomes our heaven. Yet, of all Western countries, France is the one that still represents ideals that matter. You, my friend, are just keeping the illusion going. You and I, we work for France. I won't say that we're assimilated, but almost. We are writers. But me, I'm a realist. *A poet of reality*, if you will. I see the world as it is and sing of it. That's what I do, nothing more. It's what I've always done.

"*A poet of reality?*" Um Nyobè echoed. His intonation transformed the descriptor into an insult! "Are you so naïve, my brother? Your reality there, isn't it reinvented each day? That de Gaulle who is always there, what do you think he is doing with the soldiers he recruits among us? Don't you see that he's reinventing reality in Paris? Just consider France. Doesn't she offer up two versions of her reality? On the one hand, a German version, on the other, I don't know, maybe French? Or English? Doesn't she represent what we ourselves are: on the one hand, a former German colony, and on the other, a joint French and English mandate? How many realities do we Cameroonians add up to in the end? Just who are we *in reality?*"

"There," Pouka interrupted, "you sound just like Fritz talking."

"Oh, and about Fritz . . ."

"Have you heard from him?"

The two friends fell silent. Um Nyobè suddenly went and opened the door, staring out into the city's dusk.

Outside, it had stopped raining.

Only later did Pouka understand that, on that day, he had forced his friend to reveal himself as the leader he would become for us all.

For Cameroon.

Ruben Um Nyobè.

THE DOMESTIC FRONT HAS ITS OWN CALENDAR, AND THEREFORE ITS OWN STORIES, 1943

此上 亇

The Poet of Reality

History is our only witness. But who is history's witness? What's more important is being its agent. Our children and grandchildren will judge our turpitude. Stop being indifferent, that's already one in the win column. Our conscience is as vast as the world, and we know what we are capable of. We are wise to allow those who are turning the world into a fiery pit to dance a little longer on the edge of the volcano they have created, for patience is the virtue of the blessed. We are blessed. Those are the thoughts that ran through Pouka's mind: "I am a poet of reality." He proclaimed it proudly; by observing things, he said, he could account for the myriad probabilities of their actualization. That's what made him the maestro. He was his father's son, no doubt, M'bangue the geomancer, who had taught him the rules for reading the world and predicting the future. He knew that alexandrine verse is the product of combinations similar to those which, when drawn in the sand, allowed M'bangue to foresee so much without being surprised. That, he believed, was what Um Nyobè didn't understand, even if his father was a geomancer as well. Pouka knew that divination elaborates every symbol in its system, that each of the signs is a piece in the pandemonium of the future, which is composed of precisely 256 verses. Those, multiplied by the four initial symbols, allow for 65,536 possible verses. Go ask Um Nyobè, or his philosophical mentor Fritz, if in their calculations of Cameroon's future they were as mathematically precise as M'bangue when he predicted Hitler's suicide in 1940, and our country's independence in 1942, or in the alexandrines of Pouka's collection *Hitler; or, the Hydra's Fall*!

For many Cameroonians, Fritz is a legend, as is Um Nyobè, for that matter—may the spirits protect them both! Yet, with or without geomancy, the maestro was surprised to learn of Fritz and Ngo Bikaï's divorce, even if he wasn't surprised by the way their story played out.

When he arrived in Douala, Fritz first stayed with his brother. He, who'd grown accustomed to a certain opulence, had to adapt to the life of his brother (Fritz had never really respected his brother who worked for the railroad, and who more or less represented for him all the ill born of misguided dreams). Yet there is none hungrier than the man who has once eaten his fill. Fritz's stay in Douala was soon upended when the train workers rose up in September 1945, pounding on their employers' doors to ask for better wages. They went so far as to organize a widespread strike, the first in Cameroonian history. Fritz was on the front lines when a colonist's bullet hit his left eye. His assassins were spared because, so argued their defense, they had only responded to the provocation of "rioters" brandishing banners where Cameroon was spelled German-style, with a *K*, and in bright red, or that proclaimed CAMEROON IS NO ONE'S COLONY! Fritz, of course, was one of those carrying the banners. He fell along with dozens of other strikers whose lives were all cut short. The Free French administration filed the case away in the ever-thicker dossier it kept on what was left of the pro-German supporters—those who didn't want to accept defeat—and then promptly forgot about it.

Ngo Bikaï, for her part, also garnered some attention: one day, she asked the women to come out of their kitchens and bang on their pots and pans at the stroke of noon. They did this for a full month to let Free France know the costs of the war effort she was forcing everyone to bear. The tirailleurs refused to go into homes to put a stop to the loud spectacle. Did the daily concert of empty pots, there in the deepest reaches of the forest, have any effect on Paris? Certainly not. Did de Gaulle hear the din they made? Not likely. Still, all of Edéa burst out chattering as never before when the next order came down: a sexual boycott. The Mother of the Market asked the women to abstain for a week, just one week, to give their men what they wanted only if they committed to the *real* battle. There again, Free France could do nothing about it. The sex strike got everyone talking. Some men thought it was a joke: in their minds, Ngo Bikaï wanted to pull all the other women into her own situation because she was frustrated. Others talked about turning to the *wolowolos* or doing things together that women don't know about. The women threatened to extend the strike for another week, maybe a whole month. Some threatened to strip themselves bare in public, to cast a curse by showing their bare bottoms in the street. Did they go that far? You tell me! It remains that no one was unaffected by this. The bars spread news of the sex strike, and the *circuits* made sure it went everywhere. That's how the news reached Yaoundé and its poor neighborhoods in particular. In Briqueterie, notably, it exploded like a pack of matches in a powder keg. Maybe even Martha got caught up in the frenzy that swept through the women in the capital? Regardless, Um Nyobè soon got the transfer he wanted to Edéa. A few months later he was joined by Ouandié, who had finally finished his studies and was teaching somewhere in the country. Was it because Ngo Bikaï's operation relied on what one might call a tactical deployment of intimacy that it's not mentioned in any of the history books? Yet it was the start of the Cameroonian Revolution, the one that has not yet borne fruit.

A Few Words of Thanks
and About My Sources

Nothing grows all by itself. The composition of a book has a story all its own. This novel never could have been written without the existence of a certain number of books and of people—whose fates and dates have been altered. Let me thank them here and ask that those whose lives and words have been changed forgive me. I am thinking, first of all, of the books *Louis Marie Pouka: Pionnier de la poésie camerounaise*, by Patrice Kayo; and *Félix Éboué: Grand commis et loyal serviteur, 1884–1944*, by René Maran, one passage of which I have reproduced here. Other significant works include *Colonial Conscripts: The* Tirailleurs Sénégalais *in French West Africa, 1857–1960*, by Myron Echenberg; the book of photography *Returning Memories: Pier Luigi Remaggi in Axum, 1935–36*, edited by Paolo Bertella Farnetti; and the analysis of geomancy in *African Fractals: Modern Computing and Indigenous Design*, by Ron Eglash. I will never forget the web pages that also inspired me, nor, of course, the *Lerewa Nuu Nguet*, the Sultan Njoya's *Book of Love*, which was completed on June 5, 1921, in Foumban, one of the first African *ars erotica* that we know.

My thanks, too, to Laure Pécher—the one and only!—to Pierre Astier, Konrad Tuchscherer, and Kassahun Checole, who gave me access to documentary archives that allowed me to build my historical vision of Cameroon's present, and also to the brave women of Togo who inspired the novel's conclusion. May Joseph Fumtim find here the expression of my eternal gratitude to him and to Éditions Ifrikya, which published Patrice Kayo's book. It helped me understand what it meant in French colonial Africa to be a writer, a civil servant, and, most of all, part of that class of writers in Yaoundé who had the privilege of seeing the most significant episodes of world history play out there in their own courtyards—because they were aware of it and, especially, because they had the tools to make sense of it. These are the writers: Rémy Gilbert Medou Mvomo; Pierre Eloundou; Ladislas Eloundou; Alima Ouandié; Tchoungui-Ngono; Thomas Ngandjon, aka Job Nganthojeff, who on January 23, 1960, in the neighborhood of Nlongkak, formed a little poetry circle, led by Louis-Marie Pouka and René Philombe, and made Yaoundé into the world literary capital that it is our duty—we the Cameroonian writers of today—to say is still being crushed by the tyranny established in our city in 1940.

Princeton, 2010–2012

Translator's Note

When the Plums Are Ripe brings alive the buried stories of Cameroon's participation in World War II, but it is also, perhaps primarily, a novel about language: how the places of contact and friction between languages complicate—at times enriching, at others impeding—communication. From *Dog Days* to *Empreintes de crabe*, via *elobi*, *La Chanson du joggeur*, and *Mount Pleasant*, Patrice Nganang's writing consistently attends to the interplay of speech and script; finding ways to suggest what language obscures was a primary challenge of this project. I hope I have done justice to the many voices, to the many registers of speech, writing, and extra-verbal communication in this novel, and I apologize for any places where my translation stammers.

This translation came to fruition thanks to the support of many people and institutions. First, my thanks to Patrice, who again entrusted his novel to me, and to Pierre Astier, his agent, who arranged for Farrar, Straus and Giroux to publish it. My thanks, too, to the editorial team at FSG, notably Laird Gallagher, for their support and guidance. My work benefited from the financial support I received from the National Endowment for the Arts, which awarded me a Translation Grant in 2017; the French Voices program of the French Cultural Services, which supports the publication of translations in the United States; and the New College Faculty Development Fund. My colleagues at New College provided support at critical junctures;

a special *merci* to Jocelyn Van Tuyl, for her advice about World War II terminology, and to Elzie McCord, for his help with mathematical formulas. To my friends and siblings and mother, who have always been there when I needed you most: words are not enough, so I'm sending hugs. I am, as always, especially grateful for the voices of my children, Jacob, Miriam, and Ben, who help me to hear the present.

A NOTE ABOUT THE AUTHOR

Patrice Nganang was born in Cameroon and is a novelist, a poet, and an essayist. His novel *Dog Days* received the Prix Marguerite Yourcenar and the Grand Prix littéraire d'Afrique noire. He is also the author of *Mount Pleasant* (FSG, 2016). He teaches comparative literature at Stony Brook University.

A NOTE ABOUT THE TRANSLATOR

Amy B. Reid is an award-winning translator who has worked with Patrice Nganang on multiple projects since 2001. In addition to *When the Plums Are Ripe*, she translated Nganang's novels *Dog Days: An Animal Chronicle* (2006) and *Mount Pleasant* (2016); she is currently working on *Empreintes de crabe* (2018), the final volume in Nganang's trilogy about Cameroonian independence. In 2016 she received a Literature Translation Fellowship from the National Endowment for the Arts for *When the Plums Are Ripe*. Her other translations include *Queen Pokou: Concerto for a Sacrifice* (2009) and *Far from My Father* (2014), both by Véronique Tadjo. She is a professor of French and Gender Studies at New College of Florida.